CAMP JEFF

a novel

TOVA REICH

SEVEN STORIES PRESS
New York • Oakland • London

Seven Stories Press
140 Watts Street
New York, NY 10013
www.sevenstories.com

Library of Congress Cataloging-in-Publication Data

Names: Reich, Tova, author.
Title: Camp Jeff : a novel / Tova Reich.
Description: New York : Seven Stories Press, 2024.
Identifiers: LCCN 2024032873 | ISBN 9781644214213 (hardcover) | ISBN 9781644214220 (ebook)
Subjects: LCGFT: Novels.
Classification: LCC PS3568.E4763 C36 2024 | DDC 813/.54--dc23/eng/20240719
LC record available at https://lccn.loc.gov/2024032873

College professors and high school and middle school teachers may order free examination copies of Seven Stories Press titles. Visit https://www.sevenstories.com/pg/resources-academics or email academic@sevenstories.com.

Printed in the United States of America

9 8 7 6 5 4 3 2 1

To Walter

1.

They called it Camp Jeff, short for Jeffrey Epstein, named in honor of the benefactor who had endowed the famous center in the Catskills for the reeducation of #MeToo offenders caught in the hashtag. At first there was serious resistance to the project, not so much to the idea, which, in general, was deemed salutary, redemptive, but rather to calling it by the donor's name, thrumming as it did with so much negative resonance. That, however, was the only condition on which this visionary Jeffrey Epstein— the good Jeffrey Epstein—would not budge. He had made his fortune in potions and creams drawn from original recipes passed down through the matrilineal line, into which he had poured every drop of his male energy. With such a background, when it came to women, strong and powerful was his personal preference—he wanted only to be knocked out with awe. Maybe a day would come when the name would become permanently soiled and unusable—like the name Adolf Hitler, for example— but in the meantime, statistically speaking, it was likely that there was more than one man still at large called Jeffrey Epstein. Why should he let himself be robbed of his good name, why should he collude in its defilement due to one rotten carrier? No, he would put the name—his name!—right out there to grab the attention span of the public. It would flash like a beacon cautioning all comers that they, too, could end up like the bad Jeffrey Epstein, swinging from a noose in a jail cell, a suicide or murder victim, take your pick, but at the same time, it would also send the message that not every Jeffrey Epstein has to be a pervert and a deviant. The good Jeffrey Epstein would cleanse the name, he would purify it as with one of his Hungarian bubby's magic Magyar lotions that kept you forever unblemished. The renewal of the name would be reflected in the renewal, the rehabilitation, of the sinners. He envisioned a network of camps stretching well beyond New York State, beyond the borders of the USA, internationally: Jeffrey Epstein Worldwide—yes, JEW, unfortunately. Because, though nobody dared to utter this out loud as part of the conversation, a disproportionate number of the hashtagged were, as it happened, Jews, like the recipients of the Nobel Prize.

The camps would be situated in the rural outskirts of the great coastal cities bookending the American heartland, and it was anticipated that they would be populated largely by representatives of the fallen leading lights endemic to the particular shining metropolis in the latitude. In the flagship New York Camp Jeff, for example, you already had your respectable concentration of literary and media types, your intellectuals, your finance guys; in the prospective Boston offshoot, you could count on servicing your academics and scientists; in San Francisco, your tech boys; in Los Angeles, titans in The Industry, and so on. But as it turned out, thanks to the mordant humor of the gods, Camp Jeffrey Epstein, the branch in the heart of the Catskill Mountains, remained alone of its kind, one and unique, and consequently, with nothing to rival it, the most prestigious and sought after. The elite of the fallen, in particular its proud intelligentsia—that is, those who were not out-and-out rapists and pimps and traffickers, and who had not actually landed in jail and indeed had not even been fined but instead simply had been publicly shamed while muttering abjectly sorry-sorry-sorry, then instantly removed from whatever lofty position they had occupied, and from polite society in general, as if pincered like a louse between the tips of long steel tweezers, extracted and shunned—every one of these outcasts singled out for reprogramming wanted desperately to get into Camp Jeffrey Epstein New York. Even if it meant enduring the insult of reeducation, especially the demeaning group sessions and other moronic communal requirements, nothing but lowbrow brainwashing, bottom line, refereed by pathetically inferior nobodies no less, it remained their top choice. Competition for acceptance to Camp Jeff, the New York branch, was brutal.

It was located in the swath of the Catskills that in its heyday had been known as the Borscht Belt, in the once-gilded old Lokshin Hotel and Country Club that the good Jeffrey Epstein, patron and philanthropist, a man who prided himself on being endowed with normal domesticated sexual appetites unlike his namesake, had rescued from collapse and abandonment, and set about renovating and refurbishing to meet the highest standards suitable to a rehabilitation center. The fabled attraction of the old hotel, now on the way to a full remodeling, top of the line, was what had been called in the old days the Murray Lokshin Casino and Lounge, honoring the establishment's visionary founder, where once, in those golden years, the best talent, singers, dancers, and especially comedians, brilliant rising jokers, had been showcased. The former Murray Lokshin Casino and Lounge, now known as the Jeffrey Epstein Social Hall, had been totally reconfigured, thanks to the generosity of the good Jeffrey Epstein, provided with all of the prescribed larger and smaller public and private spaces for the performance of serious therapeutic group dynamics as well as individual self-examination, reflection, healing. Yet in a gracious, truly a nostalgic, nod to the golden days of Jewish immigrant striving and hopefulness, the honorable Jeffrey Epstein had also arranged for a section of the Murray Lokshin Casino and Lounge to be carved out for a cutting-edge theater space called the Zuzi Epstein Playhouse, a tribute to his lost daughter, named for her formidable great-grandmother—the girl who had exited too soon, exercising her right to choose. Upon its stage, inmates, or "campers" as they were called, from the world of entertainment could get up, and as one of them, that wise guy Gershon Gordon, the world-famous literary powerhouse and public intellectual, put it, expose themselves.

Indeed, a good number of the campers were true celebrities whose sojourn at Camp Jeffrey Epstein New York was one of the primary features that made it such a desirable destination for those hashtag degenerates self-channeled to the reeducation track. The acclaimed comedian Arnie Glick, for example, a camper there, was known to venture up onto the Zuzi Epstein Playhouse stage as often as would be tolerated to unload himself of some Glick-shtick to keep in shape for his desperately fantasized comeback. The finale, which every insider breathlessly anticipated, occurred when his co-inmate Gordon would roll up in his wheelchair to the foot of the stage, dressed in his trademark blacks—black sports jacket, black turtleneck, black jeans, the entire ensemble topped by a black velvet yarmulke setting off his signature white bouffant, his hair having gone prematurely, or, better, precociously, white—as the master (who would have found Gordon's particular head covering most disagreeable) once nailed an ambitious, albeit fictional, Bostonian, also a self-styled writer and intellectual. Thus decked out, Gershon Gordon would boom out, "Shut up already, Arnie Prick," the entire audience of inmates chanting along in jubilant chorus.

"Oh, Arnie Sick, Arnie Very, Very Sick," Glick would wail so desolately, so penitently, a living testament to the success of the indoctrination by the mental-health storm troopers to which he had been subjected as an element of the Camp Jeff deprogramming, and he'd go limp and deflate into a puddle right there on the floor of the stage, as if resigning himself to be wiped up and flushed into the sewers, dragged off ignominiously from the wings by a cane hooked into his collar as in the legendary Lokshin days. It was a smashing routine, classic, Gordon and Glick, Vladimir and Estragon. What were they waiting for? With full faith they awaited the day when the nightmare that had ensnared them in the hashtag would come to its inevitable end like every other fad, like every other perverse fanatical craze that had gripped society over the millennia, and real life would resume. On that day they would make their reentry into the newly enlightened world as if emerging from a leper colony, climbing out of a pit crawling with scorpions and snakes, they would go forth together, born again, welcomed and hailed as honored survivors.

At Camp Jeffrey Epstein New York, Gershon Gordon, so gifted, so charming and erudite, trapped by the legend of his own precocity and ambition into a career as eternal prodigy and potential, was acknowledged intellectual royalty; gratefully, Arnie Glick accepted the supporting role of Gordon's personal fool. The duo were joined by the news anchor Bob Bloom and the talk show host, Bob Blatt, the Two Bobs, fallen media giants dragged out of the tube, their names and faces instantly recognizable in every household across the fruited plains, far surpassing in primetime fame whatever nod had ever been allotted to Gordon or Glick. Together, the four of them made up what Arnie Glick, scarred forever by his high school years, from which he still extracted most of his material, called the Popular Group, the coolest clique on the premises having the most fun right in your face, everyone longed to crash their party. They were the Gang of Four, as the more evolved Gordon dubbed them, the

Four Amigos, the leading nutcases in the cuckoo's nest. Brandishing the power of their quartet, they took sad satisfaction during this dark intermission in their once radiant trajectory on earth in sabotaging the staff of inferiors—the mental-health mafia, therapists of every school, all of them women by birth or choice, including the administrators and the nurses of course, sculpted and toned for those emergencies when fitness and force would be required. All four of them, Gordon and Glick, Bloom and Blatt, were enviably good talkers, that was their trade, it was how they had once earned their living, seduced their benefactors, supported their habits, but here at Camp Jeff, they all deferred to Gershon Gordon, by unspoken consensus Gershon Gordon was their voice. This was because, as Arnie Glick explained, Gershon Gordon got into Camp Jeffrey Epstein due primarily, though not exclusively, to sins he had committed with the so-called harassments that came out of his unzipped Jewish mouth, whereas they, the Two Bobs and Arnie himself, had sinned without foreplay, with the clipped Jewish weapon that suddenly, startlingly, they yanked out of their pants.

With regard to Gershon Gordon's apparent so-called disability, no one could say when exactly he had retired full time to a wheelchair, but there was little doubt that it had taken place not long after his name had appeared on the list of carnal offenders nailed to the wall in the public square—nor could anyone confirm what injury or illness he had suffered, or what chronic condition he endured, it was all a sacred mystery. Following his hashtagging, first came his shapely apology to any woman he might unwittingly have harassed, it had been a case of an action committed b'shogeg, he had explained—even in those circumstances of public mortification he could not restrain himself from flaunting his exotic erudition—but the fact that it was unwitting was no excuse of course, he went on, he should have understood the subtext, he should have gotten it, he should have known better, he had not been sensitive enough, he took full responsibility, God Herself did not have the power to pardon him for whatever affront he might have committed against a fellow woman (and he had known many stunning women fellows, as a serial member of the elite societies), only the injured party herself could exonerate him. He therefore begged the forgiveness of any woman living or dead whom he might inadvertently have offended, he would bring a sin offering of a fat female lamb or a fat female goat to sacrifice on the altar of the Temple when it is rebuilt, speedily and in our lifetime, he prayed.

The spiteful dissemination of his statement on so-called social media was instantly followed by further public shaming larded with mockery, and his permanent removal from prime civilized society. Not long after his banishment it was reported that he had been spotted shuffling around his house arrest hunched over a walker, and then came word that he had landed full-time in a wheelchair, but even that news did not soften the hard hearts of his enemies. Even two years later, around the time that he was warehoused at Camp Jeff, a not overly friendly website reported that the outcast and pariah Gershon Gordon had been heard to assert that the reason he had been sentenced for life to a wheelchair was that he no longer could walk because he no longer had anywhere to go—and moreover, he had revealed, due to the puritanical epidemic that had swept the land, the lower portion of his body, from the waist down, had atrophied from lack of use and been rendered completely vestigial. Among the hundreds of comments that had metastasized on the site, one stood out for its venom, from a woman who identified herself only as Yet Another Gershon Victim. She noted that since most of Gershon Gordon's offenses originated in his tumescent brain and manifested themselves in what spurted out of his meaty mouth and in the poke of his pudgy paws, all upper body appendages and apertures exposed and known before God's seat of honor, these obviously were the parts of his anatomy that should now have withered and become vestigial from lack of use rather than his lower portion as he claims, and therefore he should be positioned in his wheelchair upside down, with his old man's spindly legs sticking up and his giant flat feet flapping toward the ozone like the dried-up leaves of a potted plant that the house maids had forgotten to water, the contrapasso to fit the crime, as in the visions of hell of those creative Christian geniuses Dante Alighieri and Hieronymus Bosch.

"So classy—but for God's sake, lose the alliterations!" was Gershon Gordon's response when apprised of this victim's still-smoldering vengefulness. "Love that catalogue of body parts though," he went on, "but do I detect a hint of stereotyping there, even, God forbid, a whiff of antisemitism coming from that direction, or is it all just in my tumescent brain?"

He was aiming this question at his visitor to Camp Jeff, his old buddy from way back in kindergarten at yeshiva and now his lawyer, Shepsie Fink, who had, after some hesitation, taken the risk and informed him of the existence in the ether of this hateful blurb. For, of course, Gershon Gordon had not seen the commentary himself. He was a well-known critic of the seductive web, also known as the net, both terms fittingly evocative of a trap, not only within the perimeters of Camp Jeff, where it might have operated as a distraction from focusing on the hard work of repairing oneself that urgently needed to be attended to, but also in his past life, where, as he had so often argued, it held the brain captive, flattened thought, leveled the public forum, coarsened the ambience, and so on. Thus, he had only found out about this latest bit of nastiness during one of the rare, strictly controlled visits from the outside world, limited almost exclusively to a camper's closest family members, which almost never included a wife but always, you could count on it, a mother, living or dead, and also on occasion, by necessity, a lawyer—in Gershon's case, Fink, a guy he could trust without reservation, thanks to the muck of a deep past they had crawled out of together. In any event, it had been a key element of Gershon Gordon's meticulously honed image, until he had lost control of it, that he was something of a venerable Luddite fossil who guarded his intellectual property against all electronic intrusions coming in or going out, draining his creative juices. Proudly he relied exclusively on his raw brain cells, he let it be known, no personal devices whatsoever, no computer, no email, not even a cell phone—I go clean, empty, he liked to boast, displaying his pudgy hands, open, with nothing in them, tugging on the flaccid lobes of his ears, unplugged. But on account of this noble abstention, in the days when he had still been a major player on the scene, days now forever behind him, urgent matters related to business, communications from important contacts, and so forth, had to be conveyed to his attention by his fully wired assistant in the outer office of his suite, with her promising writing style, which he had so attentively mentored, and the beguiling packaging of her exquisitely tight skirts and sweaters, her official uniform, he joked, which he always took such pains to appreciate down to the most minute stitch, to explicate and parse with all the brilliance of the critical faculties he applied to the latest literary masterpiece. Could she possibly have been the author of this pitiful spitefulness? Of course not, she was so pathetically fond of him, her face opened like a bud powered by his solar rays whenever he appeared in her zone. Anyway, this was not her prose style at all, he had tutored her on his knee himself, he would have recognized her voice insofar as she had a voice, and this was not it.

Gershon delivered a friendly slap to each of Fink's acne-scarred cheeks in mock chastisement for having taken on the role of messenger of unpleasant tidings. Then he let himself go, reminiscing about the little outings he and Shepsie used to treat themselves to as kids, to the ladies'-intimate-wear sections of department stores, two yeshiva boys in yarmulkes, a public desecration of God's name and very bad for the Jews, stroking the silky nighties and panties and bras as they walked by the display racks, running their hands along them, like rippling the leaves of the bushes and hedges while strolling down Avenue P in Brooklyn, New York, making celestial music. "And do you remember our favorite porn whenever we got so lucky, Fink? What were our sexual preferences after all? Normal, Wholesome—Appropriate!" Gershon declared. "Girls not boys, adults not children, humans not animals, alive not dead!" Did Fink happen to remember that dirty movie they had watched together on TV in a motel room late one night during some kind of class trip, maybe a tour of the New Jersey and Long Island cemeteries to visit the graves of holy men and rabbis, may their memory be for a blessing? Two self-styled intellectuals sitting completely naked side by side on a bed facing the camera, he a man, she a woman, so indecently out of shape, so soft and lumpy, yet still so vain—she fussing with her stringy hair, he lovingly bunching his pubic beard—blabbing the whole time about existentialism or something, which naturally triggered arousal, then flopping on top of each other, groping, fumbling wildly, panting, such klutzes, such schlumps, such a sorry sight, faking it, but not like your divine actors and actresses on the big screen fake it, gods and goddesses dancing the choreographed dance of sex without even breaking wind to the envy of the rest of humankind who never could perform at such ecstatic heights—then up they come for air and right away it's back to the discourse—"I do believe the topic was Lacan, Jacques Lacan," Gershon said. "Ever hear of the guy, Fink? I think they were talking French, they had a Brooklyn accent as thick as Shapiro's kosher wine, those two sad naked specimens, Jewish for sure, yeah, they definitely looked

Jewish." This Yet Another Gershon Victim, by her own account, who had carved her immortal thoughts about his personal body type into the universal record? Yet Another Miserable Specimen, that's what she is, physically and mentally, like our lady of the Lacan in that dirty movie. Maybe he had given her a compliment once to brighten her day, tried to make her feel a little better about her sorry little self, made a real effort to take her seriously, but tukhes on the table, bottom line, she was completely forgettable, definitely not his type, that's for sure, he was just doing her a favor, Fink, a hessed—and this was his reward? "Whatever happened to flirting?" Gershon Gordon suddenly cried out to his childhood friend, the lawyer Shepsie Fink. "It's the end of the human species. How can we expect procreation to proceed without the lubricant of flirtation? How can a person fulfill the first positive mitzvah of the Torah incumbent upon every male, to be fruitful and multiply in this day and age, when good old innocent wholesome flirting can destroy your life forever?"

Shepsie Fink gave a shrug. He had no idea how courtships were carried out in this day and age without the K-Y jelly of flirtation, he agreed, stealing his friend's bright idea and ruining it, as usual. Maybe online, he ventured, like every other shopping experience? Arranged marriages, maybe? Rape? He looked at Gershon sitting in his wheelchair opposite him at the table in the Camp Jeff dining room eating his kosher lunch in its aluminum-foil packaging after having poured water over his hands and recited the prescribed blessing, his black velvet yarmulke clipped to the strands of his hair that burst out behind in a grizzled white bush streaked with rust. Shepsie remembered how the two of them had tasted their first bacon together, how together they had picked up their first hookers on the path to enlightenment—and now this, the trappings of religion—who knows, maybe God was even in the picture? It could only have come from terrible suffering and humiliation, Shepsie concluded, that was the only explanation, a solace, a refuge, an opiate, a sign of weakness, need, surrender that he had never expected from such a formidable personage as Gershon Gordon—or George Gordon, as he had once confided to Shepsie, the official name on his birth certificate, bestowed upon him by his parents, the survivors, out of an abundance of caution, as they say, assimilating his documentation in the event of another inevitable antisemitic flareup, another Holocaust, God forbid. Not like George Gordon, Lord Byron, the poet, whom Gershon's parents had never heard of anyway, Gershon had explained to Shepsie. No, to Gershon's way of thinking, it had always been like the other Lord George Gordon, the one his parents also never heard of, that maverick who led the Protestant riots against the Catholics in England, the charismatic leader of the King Mob as immortalized by no less than that best-selling author Charles Dickens—ever hear of Dickens, Shepsie?—and then this unstoppable free spirit Lord George Gordon goes and gets himself a bris, turns himself into a super glatt kosher Jew, and ends up dying in a jail cell with a mezuzah on the door.

Shepsie's eyes took in the Camp Jeff mess hall, then came back to rest upon the inmate George Gordon, and he shook his head. Two George Gordons, like two Jeffrey Epsteins. And now this one is talking p'ru ur'vu—the first mitzvah of the Torah? Shepsie was thinking. Already in his early sixties, Gershon had definitely given this injunction his best shot, but in the final analysis, all he had to show for it was his rebel daughter, Yalta, who was now out of his life along with her mother, Marilyn, his third and definitely his last wife, the only one of the three to have actually converted to Judaism, renamed Yiska by Gershon himself, he for whom names possessed such power and import. It happened at the private celebration following her immersion in the ritual bath—Yiska, according to the commentators, an alternate name for Mother Sarah, also a convert, the first Jewess, the far-sighted prophetess with a bitter sense of humor that got her into a lot of trouble, Gershon elucidated hermeneutically, raising a glass of arak to Yiska, wife number three. His first wife, almost half a century older than Gershon and the most powerful agent in the book business, fell off her chair at an award dinner one night and never recovered, for all Fink knew she might still be alive at the facility in which Gershon had deposited her. His second wife, a black nightclub singer only twenty years older than Gershon, made a final commitment to the lesbian side of her nature not long after marrying him, went off the next night to her permanent gig at the Carlyle Hotel and never came home, didn't even bother to call. Yiska, age-wise of Gershon's generation, only nine years his senior, was a social worker at a shelter for battered women. After standing faithfully at his side smiling through the entire miserable unfolding of Gershon's public disgrace, when the day arrived that he parked himself in the wheelchair for the foreseeable future, which, accustomed as she was to medical paraphernalia, should not have been such a big deal for her, Yiska announced, "No way I'm pushing you around in that chair for the rest of my life." And she dragged Yalta off her beanbag and walked out the door.

It was then that Gershon was struck by the full realization of how low he had fallen in the world—even Yiska, reliably blessed with a traditional spousal loyalty ethos, had spurned him. Until that moment, when the door had slammed behind his wife and daughter and he found himself alone in his wheelchair in the empty apartment, he had managed to sustain an elevated sense of himself. He was a martyr sacrificed to the suffocating prudery and narrow self-righteousness that had gripped the human race like a pestilence and was threatening to end it, he was the victim of the unquestioning acceptance, without a trace of skepticism or irony, of any accusation brought by a woman and no due process whatsoever for the accused, it was a matter of dogma that the woman was always to be believed. Even in his state of shame and isolation, he had still at first found ways to justify himself, to distinguish himself from the other sinners, he had kept his faith in his exceptionalism, he still believed that in the fullness of time, when humankind came back to its senses, he would emerge a hero, a prophet even, he would be celebrated for his complex understanding of the dynamics between men and women, he would be honored for his noble resistance to the tyranny of all the mindless simplifications that had so contorted the sexual transaction, he would be hailed for his protest against the unfairness, the one-sided allocation of responsibility, of blame and punishment. When Yiska took Yalta and abandoned him so heartlessly, the air grew heavy with his solitariness. She left him utterly alone, struggling to keep his faith in his chosenness, in his future redemption and resurrection.

For a brief period after he lost his family, he attempted to hold on to his dignity and personal sense of worthiness by getting back to work on his proposed manuscript, tentatively titled "Let Us Now Praise Famous Men (and Women)," for which his first wife, the literary agent, had succeeded in obtaining so unprecedented an advance for him at the time that it had been trumpeted not only in trade publications but also in the general press and media. Though the manuscript was now overdue by almost three decades, he allowed himself to believe he could resuscitate it. Still, despite this resolve, he could hardly bear at first to take it up again. Excavating it at last, he submitted himself to the torture of leafing through its pages. It consisted of the elegant eulogies he had composed for the fabled writers, intellectuals, artists, statesmen, and so on, in whose orbit he had circulated, in whose aura he had luxuriated, and who by implication had, in turn, basked in his own luminous presence. It would have been so easy to collect these pieces from the five-star publications in which they had first appeared. What had stopped him from finishing the job? It wasn't simple laziness, he sensed, it was something else, something deeper and more telling, something touching on the scope of his powers, fear of what full-frontal exposure might reveal about his limits, he did not want to go there. And now he was faced with an almost thirty-year gap to fill in, the project was so hopelessly dated, the dead men and one woman he had so far eulogized were forgotten, their name recognition, like their flesh, turned to dust and ashes, and worse, when for a few unguarded seconds he looked at the pile with the same cold eye he would routinely cast on the work of others, it seemed such a toadying display on the one hand, and such naked grandiose self-presentation by association on the other.

"Crap, crap," Gershon muttered, the first words he had spoken all day, breaking the silence. He hurled the pages to the floor, where they scattered and settled in among the heaps of cardboard containers and plastic utensils and other decaying waste matter left from the food he had taken to ordering in several times a day and stuffing himself with now that no wife and daughter were present to civilize him, the empty beer cans and the wine bottles and coffee cups and other accumulated detritus, and all the mounting signs of despair. Clad in the stained pajama bottoms with the strings at the waist dangling loose, and the soiled T-shirt he hadn't peeled off in days, his trademark triangular white beard now ragged on his face, transforming him into his grandfather Getzel, for whom he had been named, the ritual slaughterer and circumcizer from the Polish shtetl of Oświęcim, gassed in the neighborhood death camp, Auschwitz. He launched himself out of his wheelchair onto the sofa, curled up with his nose wedged into a cushion, and went back to sleep.

This is how his childhood friend and now his lawyer, Shepsie Fink, had found him on that evening when he finally stopped by after weeks of guilty procrastination and avoidance. He stood outside the door of Gershon's apartment, still hesitating, then tentatively rested a fist upon it as if collecting the courage to knock. Miraculously, it opened of itself, no one had ever bothered to lock it or even to seal the door properly shut, he wondered how long it had been in that forsaken state. Fink trudged through the rooms, cutting a path through the devastation, bringing the back of his hand up to his nose to smother the smell, until he arrived in the living room and took note of the bloated heap planted on the sofa and sorrowfully absorbed the reality of what had become of his old friend Gershon Gordon, that golden boy so full of promise—eating too much, sleeping too much, bathing too little. I'm looking at a textbook case of depression, was Shepsie Fink's profound thought just as the great prehistoric creature lodged in front of him stirred, then rolled over, the front slit of its pajama bottoms parting to reveal his poor maligned manhood. A voice rose up, muffled as if from underground, testing its powers to travel from the abyss up along the airwaves and make contact with another living being. "And you know what else, Fink?" it spoke. "I also haven't jerked off in weeks. So yeah, that's depression." He had not lost his gift of insight bordering on the prophetic, Shepsie saw. Alas, he would always be the wunderkind.

Taking care not to insult the friend of his childhood by questioning his right to occupy a wheelchair, Shepsie helped Gershon off the couch—he was so uncharacteristically submissive and defeated—and pushed him into the filthy bathroom, a black skin of mold sheathing its walls. In an act of exemplary tenderness, he washed his friend's soft, unloved body and dressed it in some clean clothing that lay abandoned at the bottom of a wardrobe. Then he filled more than a dozen black garbage bags with the wreckage from all the rooms, including the discarded unfinished pages of the manuscript of collected eulogies—eulogies to himself as it turned out—and hauled it all down to the communal bins. He threw out a sack of potatoes that had decomposed into a black soup reeking of mortality along with all the other decaying food in the kitchen, passed a rag over all the surfaces, took some eggs out of the fridge, cracked them open, relieved that they gave off no sulfurous underworld smell, and fried them in some leftover oil, since the butter had gone rancid. He pushed Gershon's wheelchair up to the table, set out two plates after wiping them clean on his shirt sleeve, and sat down on a chair opposite his friend. They ate their eggs with ketchup, just as they had done when they were boys, it had always been one of their favorite meals, fried eggs and ketchup, luckily some blackened dregs remained in the plastic Heinz bottle stuck to a shelf on the refrigerator door. Shepsie boiled some water and poured it into two glasses, plopped the lone shriveled scrotum of an Ahmad teabag that he had found in a drawer first into one glass and then into the other. He brought the two glasses of tea to the table and gave the darker and richer one to his friend.

As they were blowing on their tea and slurping it, just as their fathers had done before them, Shepsie very casually asked Gershon if he remembered Hymie Fallick from their class at yeshiva. Of course Gershon remembered Fallick—Fallick was the second smartest kid in the class, Gershon reminisced, and besides, he's now world famous, the most notorious alumnus of our yeshiva—our worst nightmare, the rabbi who stuck cameras all over the mikvah to video the naked ladies dunking in the pools purifying themselves from their periods so they could go home and have sex with their husbands after more than half a month of nothing, gornisht. It was all over the news, a shonda for the goyim. Pretty screwed up guy, right Fink?

"Fallick happens to be one of my clients also," Shepsie advised Gershon. He was bound by the rules of lawyer-client confidentiality for everyone's sake.

"Also?"

Gershon pushed the heels of his palms against the table as if he were setting out to roll off and away forever into the sunset. "Let's just say that I hope you're not comparing me to Fallick, okay, Fink? The guy's a weirdo, a fucking peeping tom, a pervert, a convicted criminal rotting in jail. It looks like you couldn't get him off, Fink, you didn't do such a good job in court for him after all even with your Brooklyn Law night school degree. . . . Whereas whatever I did that landed me in this situation is exactly what men have been doing for millennia, and until now nobody complained—or if they complained, nobody listened. Maybe I'm just living in the wrong century."

Shepsie stretched out his hand and placed it on Gershon's, as if to calm him. He wasn't making any comparisons, God forbid, Shepsie assured Gershon. "It's just that I feel sorry for the guy—for Fallick," Shepsie clarified instantly. "He's sitting there all day in his jail cell learning the tractate Niddah, it's the only thing he reads, the only Talmud he studies, it's his favorite tractate, about periods and menstrual cycles and blood and impurity and ritual baths and all that stuff, he knows it all by heart, and all he wants is a havrusa, he just wants some guy to sit and learn a little Gemara with him, a study partner—is that too much to ask? He's so alone, like in solitary confinement, loneliness is such a terrible thing—you know what I mean? So it just occurred to me that you're also alone—of course it's a very different situation, no comparisons intended, but anyways, I thought you might be interested," Shepsie said, "a page a day, like daf yomi, fifty minutes tops, like a therapy session, the only difference being that you just do Niddah, it's the only tractate you learn, like you skip straight to the dirty parts, you don't also have to do all the other sixty-something masekhtas that take more than seven years to finish at that rate. And also, you never have to actually see the guy in person, you can do it all by remote control, by telephone, for example, since you don't have Skype or a computer or anything, kind of like old-fashioned pen pals, like when we were kids and we used to play chess with some serial killer or rapist on death row by sending a postcard with our next move—remember? It's not like I'm telling you to go visit him in jail or anything like that, God forbid. And bottom line, you can quit anytime you feel like it. It would be such a big mitzvah—to reach out to the poor guy, he's lost everything, you know, his wife also left him after the scandal broke—I'm not comparing, I'm only saying. And by the way, Gersh, another big bonus if you become Fallick's havrusa is that you'd get to know Niddah inside out, one hundred percent, everything you ever wanted to know about Niddah but were afraid to ask, you'd be like a specialist, like a kind of gynecologist, OB-GYN, a real doctor, not like that PhD or whatever you were once going for. I thought maybe we could work something out between you and Fallick that would be good for both of you."

"No way I'm doing Niddah with Fallick," Gershon enunciated with bitter finality after a long silence. Then shifting tone, he added, "Besides, I'm reading Proust. In French. A page a day. Proust's my daf yomi. Ever hear of the guy, Fink? Jewish, in case you were wondering."

Was it possible that Shepsie Fink did not know, or had forgotten, that Hymie Fallick had been the rabbi who had overseen the conversion of his ex-wife Marilyn, a.k.a. Yiska—the hottest rabbi for the job at that time, most highly recommended, five stars, with a waiting list ten miles long? The only reason Fallick took Marilyn on, jumping her to the top of the conversion candidate list, was because Gershon was a celebrity. And could it also be the case that Fink did not recall that major profile on Fallick in the *New York Times*, when the scandal broke for which he, Gershon Gordon, had been a primary source, in which he had been quoted as saying, among other things, that Fallick had the coldest legal

Talmudic mind he had ever encountered, he was like an antisemite's dream caricature of the Pharisees accused of murdering Jesus, that of all the rabbis he, Gershon Gordon, had ever known, and he had known plenty in every shape and form, Fallick stood out as the one possessed of the least amount of spirituality, not even the size of a lentil, and with a dirty mind on the level of a teenager with suppurating pimples? It must have been a moment of delicious schadenfreude for Fallick when he, Gershon Gordon, had been netted in the hashtag, so unjustly scooped up along with all those certified harassers and abusers and masturbators and rapists, those genuine misogynists, whereas he, Gershon Gordon, truly loved women, he loved them with all his heart and with all his soul and with all his might. Not long after Gershon had been fingered by the hashtag harpies, Fallick, from his jail cell, had taken the trouble to send him his idea of a sympathy note, handwritten: "In case you were wondering whether I videoed your wife dunking naked in the mikvah for her conversion, I just wanted to reassure you—she's not my type, too fat." What could Fink have been thinking, pairing him with Fallick as a study partner, and to learn Niddah of all things? Unbelievable. Talk about impurity. The guy was a leper.

Even so, a few days later, Gershon Gordon found himself taking down from his bookshelf one of the great maroon tomes of the Talmud from the full classic set of the Vilna edition that his father had given him when he had set forth to college, a punishing reminder of where he came from that he could never bring himself to unload after the old man, a survivor of the death camps, was shot in the heart by some hooded kid pointing a weapon at him from the other side of the counter of his dry-cleaning store—For God's sake, Pop, you should have just handed over the twenty bucks so that I could have gotten rid of these damn books once and for all. Now, having gone through his own personal holocaust, as he allowed himself to characterize it when privately reflecting on his calamitous fall, he cracked open one of the volumes for the first time, the one containing Niddah, releasing into the atmosphere a stale dust cloud of regret and disappointment. He had studied Talmud in yeshiva until the age of eighteen, its baroque pages and labyrinthine discourse instantly launching him in those days through his inner escape hatch to even more intricate fantasies and daydreams of girls and glory. During all those endless, wasted hours of Talmud, Gershon had essentially not been there, he had not been present, though in later years that did not stop him from sprinkling remembered references, mostly to stories and personalities animating the text, into his writings and talks and social patter, in seminars, meetings, panels, at dinners, at parties and other opportune public occasions throughout his brilliant career. His daughter's name, Yalta, was one of those nuggets, an allusion to the cameo appearance in the pages of the Talmud of a singularly rare feminist who refused to take it lying down, true royalty, the daughter of the exilarch, the king of the exiled—in retrospect, how ironic. In choosing this name for his daughter, as he had explained in a little toast at a celebration in lieu of circumcision marking her birth, lifting a bright flue of champagne, he was blessing her with Yalta's liberated spirit, the courage to raise her voice and insist on her due in every encounter—like the women who had raised their voices and destroyed his life, no doubt similarly blessed at birth by their loving fathers, it would later ruefully strike him.

His idea now was to apply himself to studying Niddah on his own, without a partner, moving along at his own pace, a page a day, just as Shepsie Fink had proposed, but alone, not under the influence of that voyeur, that psycho, Hymie Fallick, who was no doubt far more adept than he at slogging through Talmudic folios in the traditional manner of a harnessed believer. But Gershon, it should be remembered, had been celebrated as one of the most articulate public intellectuals and interpreters of classic and contemporary literary texts, and that's how he intended to approach the material, aesthetically, from a secular, universalist angle—the Talmud as Literature. He would keep a journal, filling it with the dazzling original insights that popped into his head, connections, associations, elaborations, digressions, references, streaming his consciousness along with the sages across the centuries as he took his daily dose of Talmud with a cup of Ahmad tea beside him on the table, a brand he patronized for what he fancied to be its linkage to oppressed Palestinians, never mind that the tea was certified kosher. What could ever render a cup of tea unkosher short of dropping a pig knuckle into it? Gershon wondered. Maybe the answer was buried in the Talmud.

His goal was to plow through the tractate in order to get to the bottom of how the sages of the Mishna and Gemara perceived the nature and value of women, their place and uses in the scheme of things, especially urgent in the light of the zeitgeist that had brought about his, Gershon's, tragic fall. He would put it all into context, he would offer new insights, he would riff on the rabbis, he would be reborn as a latter-day commentator, the new and improved Rashi, and perhaps by the time he came to the end of his Niddah study, he would also have amassed, as a byproduct, a sweet pile of papers with words inscribed upon them, maybe even a monograph, maybe even a book that some brave and daring publisher would be willing to bring out despite the author's public shaming, his ravaged name, his noxious reputation as an abuser and harasser, so manifestly undeserved.

2.

Through dogged perseverance, by slamming himself against the wall of his own resistance day after day, Gershon Gordon arrived, by the time he set out to Camp Jeff, at what was for him a satisfactory way to maneuver through the text of tractate Niddah, which, though he never quite acknowledged this truth in his solitary hours of study, he found at first, and in many ways continued to find, excruciating, a tangled thicket threatening to provoke unaccustomed doubts about the size of his personal mental equipment—doubts that called for their immediate quashing to save his life. Cloistered by choice in his apartment with no English translation of the text at hand, no Google, no trot, no pony, no rebbe, no teacher, no study partner, the Hebrew he had mastered in his early years, which had always been such an affirming source of pride for him and which he had trusted would get him through the Aramaic, did not deliver, it did not decode, especially when it came to unlocking the peculiarities of rabbinic thought patterns over half a millennium, their idiosyncratic maze of digressions. Things got easier, though, once he succeeded in formulating what for him was a workable conception of the sages' agenda in Niddah with regard to women and their deadly anatomies—hotbeds of impurity, while unfortunately, at the same time, necessary and indispensable instruments for the fulfillment of the mitzvah of procreation incumbent upon every God-fearing Jewish male. The rabbis were seriously hung up on matters of purity and impurity, ritual and otherwise, Gershon concluded, the pestilential transmission and contagion of impurity to every susceptible human or object—first-degree impurity, second-degree impurity, third-degree impurity, father of impurity, father of all the fathers of impurity, and so on. Above all, it seemed to Gershon, they were obsessed with what came out of women—the blood that spilled regularly or irregularly out of "that place," from the unclean opening leading to the womb/tomb, the kever, unique to every female body, even in some cases from a baby girl's body at the moment of birth, a newborn with a period, and as for a dead old lady, she was doubly impure, by virtue of gender branded a niddah to add to her woes, a corpse with a period, the mother of all mothers of impurity.

But it is also noteworthy that not a single day passed in his study of the tractate Niddah that some morsel ripe for plucking did not come drifting onto the page to spark a host of original ideas that he could snag for his journal and elaborate upon in so many brilliant and novel ways that the sages themselves could never have foreseen or imagined. A case in point was the day on which the letter arrived inviting him to join the first cohort of the newly endowed Camp Jeffrey Epstein New York branch. It was a thick letter of acceptance, and he had not even applied, he had not even known until then that such a place existed. On that very day he was studying the fifth chapter of the tractate Niddah. He had just reached the discussion of what is considered to be the permissible age for a girl to be initiated into sexual intercourse, which turned out to be, according to the sages, three years old and one day. Anything prior to that was unacceptable, he was relieved to learn, it was equivalent to sticking a finger in a person's eye. He had just written down in his notebook that a jab in the eye could really be extremely traumatic, it could have lifelong consequences, he had begun to spin out the word *bloodshot*, his mind segueing from shot with blood to the blood of a burst vessel in the eye, to the blood of the penetrated hymen, to Hymie Fallick, when he lifted his own mournful eyes shot through with swollen red veins to the window and noticed the mail carrier exiting the building. He rolled out the door, into the elevator, then down to the lobby where he found the letter with the return address, Jeffrey Epstein. Could someone have actually started a charitable foundation in honor of the late pedophile and sex trafficker? Were they asking for a donation? He tore open the envelope immediately, right there on the spot, in full view of the ranks of mailboxes and the tower of Amazon packages on the desk behind which the doorman officiated, and he instantly marveled at the uncanny connection between what he had just learned in the tractate Niddah regarding the age at which it was acceptable for a girl to be introduced to sexual intercourse and the arrival of this letter. For the late Jeffrey Epstein, as was common knowledge, had a thing for very young girls, though as far as Gershon could recall, he personally had never seen one as young as three years old and one day among the lithe beauties gliding through the rooms of Epstein's mansion on East Seventy-First Street off Fifth Avenue in New York City, or for that matter, on any of his other properties.

Obviously, this was an invitation that he had no choice but to turn down, Gershon bowed to that reality. Had the foundation been aware that Gershon Gordon had on more than one occasion partaken of the grotesquely extravagant hospitality of the certified criminal Jeffrey Epstein, the bad Jeffrey Epstein, there is no doubt that they never would have invited him into their program. On top of that, were Gershon to risk accepting, he would not have put it past Yiska to leak such a juicy tidbit as their divorce negotiations dragged on. The last thing he needed at this time in his life was another scandal. Besides, why would

he willingly submit himself to the forced confinement of a rehabilitation program with its inane mindset and pneumatic jargon
and all its petty restrictions? Rehab as a concept was antithetical
to his very essence—soft, parochial, bourgeois, falsely hopeful,
delusional in its faith that human beings could change or control their own urges and desires, it was an enterprise in stark
contradiction to his aesthetics and intellectual spirit. It was one
thing to have chosen, since his hashtagging, to remain self-clois-
tered within the four walls of his own apartment more or less full
time, studying Talmud and composing a new commentary in
case anyone was interested, an excellent use of his valuable time,
but it was quite something else entirely to voluntarily let himself
be institutionalized, at the mercy of the self-described trained
staff and trained professionals sinking in the brain slop of their
own clichés, he could hardly imagine a fate more horrifying.

Back in the apartment, he braked just inside the door to
examine the glossy photos of the Camp Jeffrey Epstein venue
and facilities in the brochure that had accompanied the invitation and had now slipped out of the envelope onto his lap.
Something about the place drew him, he realized, it was as if he
had already dwelt there in another life or, as was more likely, had
once been an invited speaker or guest of honor there at some
conference or retreat. He was experiencing what was for him,
nowadays, a rare throbbing in the region of the groin. Maybe
he had had a quick fling there with one of the attendees, the
name on her identity badge now blurred forever, the spasm he
was experiencing in his loins was an involuntary physical reflex,
out of his control, not his fault. It was only when he read in the
small print of the glossy foldout the electrifying fact that Camp
Jeffrey Epstein was located on the site of the former Lokshin
Hotel and Country Club, now remodeled and refurbished to the
highest standards of contemporary luxury, comfort, and func-
tionality, that Gershon realized why the place felt so intimately

familiar—its main building, the Jeffrey Epstein Social Hall, formerly known as the Murray Lokshin Casino and Lounge, the lobby, the dining room, the tearoom, all of it so piercingly evocative and haunting.

He had spent the summer between high school and college there, at Lokshin's, first as a busboy in the dining room and then taking over as a waiter from a Yeshiva University premed who was forced to return home after contracting from a Barnard sophomore what everyone hilariously called the kissing sickness, mononucleosis, but which he, Gershon Gordon, happened to know on good authority was the clap, gonorrhea. It was Dr. Zoya Rubinchuk, the on-site Lokshin Hotel and Country Club physician, who had revealed to him the true diagnosis. As a Russian, she had only contempt for the ridiculous Western conceit of doctor-patient confidentiality. Also, as a Russian, she was experiencing an intense attraction to him, Dr. Rubinchuk announced in her cigarette voice, she recognized his true soul from the books he lugged around the hotel grounds, Saltykov-Shchedrin, Goncharov, Gogol. For her part, she considered herself a doctor in the tradition of Chekhov and Bulgakov; her medical license, lost with the rest of her baggage when she escaped from the Soviet gulag, was secondary to her art. This was Gershon's summer of nineteenth-century Russian masters, he had meant to attract certain types of susceptible girls with his books, girls with dark wet hair like the beard of a goat trailing out of the crotch of their one-piece black bathing suits, plastered to the silken inner sides of their thighs. That was as high as he had aspired then, but, to his great good fortune, a real woman, Dr. Zoya Rubinchuk, had been irresistibly drawn to him, she declared—for his high literary tastes, for the way he so correctly kept himself apart from the others, from those American materialists, passionless, middle class, bourgeois, naive, ignorant of real suffering, completely unserious. She recognized him as a true fellow member of the intelligentsia, like herself, she whispered to him one afternoon in bed in her cabin behind her infirmary, as outside on the lawn the children of hotel guests lay on their bellies with their naked buttocks turned up to the sun, which, as she explained, was the only effective treatment for impetigo, "dirt sores," as Dr. Rubinchuk's mother had called them, in Russian of course—direct contact with the sun was her mother's surefire folk remedy, it worked every time, never mind your antiseptic, soulless American medical science.

What if one of those kids had taken it into her or his head to pull up his or her drawers and come looking for the lady doctor in the bedroom? For Gershon Gordon, not quite eighteen years old, this was thrilling. She was in her late thirties, Dr. Zoya Rubinchuk, her glossy black hair parted in the middle, usually gathered in a low bun at the nape of her neck but now flowing loose, she looked like Anna Akhmatova, he whispered with lips pressed on her ear, or maybe Mrs. Virginia Woolf, though far more passionate, physical. His words made her crazy with desire. She was old enough to be his mother, the smell of her cigarette smoke from afar was enough to crush his pelvis, he could barely swallow coming up the hill to her infirmary—first love, like in Turgenev, and it had all happened at the Lokshin dacha.

He gazed down at his lap where the brochure lay, alive with a rush of longing for the place. How good it would be to return, even in an abject therapeutic mode. He could handle it, it would be for him a sanitarium, a true magic mountain. He would climb the hill to the old infirmary and look for a sign of what had once transpired there on that lawn among the trees where the naked boys and girls had lain so idyllically, their smooth behinds like flowers soaking up the healthful rays of the sun. He would speak to the mighty spirit of the goddess Dr. Zoya Rubinchuk, which surely lingered somewhere in that place, he would thank her for teaching him how to cherish older women, he would tell her that she was the influence that had opened him up and made him responsive to all the women he had married, starting with his first wife, Beryl Brook, surely Dr. Rubinchuk had heard of Beryl, a renowned literary agent, at least twenty years older than even you, Dr. Rubinchuk, old enough to be your mother and my grandmother, my personal Anne Hathaway, maybe I was overreaching, maybe I was overdoing it out of nostalgia, still, I have no regrets.

In the ensuing years Gershon had, of course, diversified his portfolio with women of all ages, younger women as well, though never, of course, as young as the nymphets favored by Jeffrey Epstein. For one thing, their inane patter was intolerable, it made his brain cells shudder, and besides, messing with these kids would have been against the law, he could have ended up in jail, a fate far worse than the ignominy in which he now found himself, however awful it was. In Gershon Gordon's canon, older women always retained a hallowed place. Not long before the dark hour of his ruination he had been engaged in what others might ignorantly and, he might add, spitefully, have character-ized as the "seduction" of a superrich widow who was, as Dr. Zoya Rubinchuk had been, twenty or so years older than he, which granted, at that point in Gershon Gordon's life, meant she was in her eighties. She had just agreed to bankroll a journal devoted to the intellectual and moral life that would be entirely his—his vision, his control, his baby. They were already drawing up the papers when the hashtag came crashing down upon his poor head put on this earth to suffer, and predictably she shook him off in disgust, fat-lipped Jewish vermin. Still, at the height of his celebrity, when, as happened on occasion, he was asked to offer his ideas about education, his response had always been, in its way, a homage to Dr. Zoya Rubinchuk. Two things, he would say—for the mind, fluency in a second language, for the body, lessons in love, preferably from an older woman, as essential as all the other extracurriculars provided by every conscientious middle-class parent, such as swimming lessons, tennis lessons, karate lessons, and learning how to ride a horse.

Jeffrey Epstein had seen this comment somewhere and noted it. It was what prompted him finally to extend an invitation to Gershon to take his place among the luminaries at his table. "You were always on my A-list," Epstein assured Gershon, seated not too far down from him at his left. "I always meant to have you for dinner," he added, licking his lips. Teasingly, Epstein inquired (as had others before him whenever Gershon's peda- gogic pronouncements were aired) why his program seemed so skewed toward boys. "Are you proposing a similar curriculum for the education of girls?" Epstein probed with an insinuating smile, emanating no discomfort whatsoever with regard to his own scandalous preferences, his terminally smeared reputation. Gershon began expanding, but was soon distracted by an odd little gesture performed by Epstein with his raised hand, a kind of wave of dismissal, or of beckoning, or, as it turned out, of both at once. "Never mind, I get it," Epstein said, silencing Ger- shon instantly, and at the same moment the fresh female minor he had invoked appeared, took her place behind his chair at the head of the table, her face stretched into a smile, the chain link of her orthodontia glinting off the candelabras as she gave herself over to massaging his shoulders and neck.

At all the dinner parties at the Epstein mansion that Gershon attended until the invitations stopped coming, he did not see the same girl twice, as far as he could determine, floating in, smiling at critical intervals, to administer the necessary rub down to the back of Epstein's neck and head and to his shoulders, and then disappearing under the table, crouching behind the long swag of the draped cloth to massage his feet, as Gershon elected to conclude rather than any other possibility too flagrantly contemptuous of the assembled, himself included. They were all of a type, these girls, clearly a reflection of Epstein's taste, an untutored Jewish boy's fantasy of classic beauty—blonde, narrow hipped, high breasted, long legged, perfect ivory complexion, cute little nose, gentile looking, between the ages of fourteen and seventeen, you could hardly tell them apart. And at every dinner party for as long as he lasted Gershon could count on Epstein flicking his hand in that signature gesture several times an evening to summon one of those beauties out of the stable and at the same time to clip the prolixity of one of his guests, some Nobel Prize winner, say, earnestly commentating, for example, on the feasibility of Epstein's plan to set up a facility to sink into suspended animation the bodies of certified superior males for future thawing and propagation on earth, cut off with that characteristic flip of Epstein's hand, lightened by a casual joke, such as, "Don't worry, I'm only planning to freeze my penis." It made no difference at all to Gershon whether this habit of preventing dinner table discussion from going too deeply into a subject reflected Epstein's concern with betraying the limitations of his knowledge or education, or whether it derived from simple boredom, or from having already grasped the point, or from feeling himself being too outrageously manipulated for a major cash grant to an institution or program of some sort, or from something else altogether. Whatever it was, Gershon Gordon absorbed and accepted it, and soon it transpired that whenever one of the distinguished guests was stricken with a sudden bout of expertise logorrhea, Jeffrey and Gershon would telegraph a quick insider glance of recognition to each other across the table seconds before Epstein, the host, would raise his hand to deliver the commanding signal that cut it short and produced the girl.

It was not very long before Gershon found himself being ushered past the public outer chambers of the mansion on East Seventy-First Street, into its cavernous private innards crammed with massage tables and sex toys, computers and office equipment, bookcases packed with bestsellers in hardcover, and on every surface, hundreds of framed photographs of the master of the house posing alongside princes and prime ministers and ex-presidents, titans of business and the arts and the media and the academies. "That's me with MBS," Epstein said. "That's me with Woody."

"And that's you with Adolf?" Gershon asked as they contemplated a massive painting commissioned by Epstein showing him posed in front of what looked like a Nazi death camp gridded with barbed wire, alongside a prison guard with a patented black brush mustache, a lacquered black hair dip, and gleaming black jackboots.

"It's to remind me that they can come for me again anytime, friend," Epstein said.

Gershon wagged a finger at Epstein. "That's a big no-no, Gatsby—diverting holy holocaust imagery to prop up your own private little trauma. Naughty, naughty." And he actually tsk-tsked.

Epstein gave his patented smile, which later, at the height of his notoriety, would be described as a smirk or a sneer, but which Gershon, at the time, took as an expression of shared superiority, the smile of a fellow member of a secret society. He threw an arm over Gershon's shoulder and directed his gaze up to the chandelier on the ceiling two stories high from which a human-sized sculpture of a naked woman was hanging—from below a perspective straight to the source of all life. "It evokes Bathsheba, showcased on the rooftop, holy mother of the greatest dynasty of all times," Gershon commented in the sage tones of a seasoned critic. "Because, as you no doubt know, every Epstein is a genealogically certified major descendent of King David, alive and everlasting, in the direct line of Davidic royalty, from which in the fullness of time via the necessary, albeit sinful, jumpstart union of David and Bathsheba, the Messiah will also come—with a pit stop," Gershon added, "that before he can be revealed as the long-awaited savior, the anointed holy Epstein must first immerse himself in the lowest depths of immorality and sin, in the sewers and the scum, out of which he will rise cleansed, sanctified, the radiant redeemer. It all fits together so perfectly," Gershon marveled. "Can you think of another Epstein in our time with greater name recognition, who more resembles his royal ancestor, fighter and fornicator, plucking his lyre? You're the man."

Epstein was nodding his head. These words now being spoken to him were confirmation of what he had always known in his heart about himself, his election, his exceptional destiny. His attention span did not contract in jaded disinterest, as was his wont, as Gershon moved on now to riff further on the name theme by speculating on what might be the correct Hebrew counterpart for Jeffrey. "Yiftakh, that would be the best fit," Gershon concluded, "as in Jephthah of Gilead, Yiftakh Ha'Giladi, in the Book of Judges"—Gershon was much stronger on the Testaments than the Talmud—"son of a prostitute, head of a band of outlaws, called upon by the elders to lead the battle against the Ammonites, famously vowing that if the enemy is delivered into his hands, whatever comes out of the door of his house first to greet him when he returns victorious and in peace from battle he will offer up to God as a sacrifice, a burnt offering, to be consumed entirely on the altar's fire. For God's sake, what could Yiftakh have been thinking by taking such a vow? It could have been a dog running out first to greet his master, a slobbering filthy dog, absolutely impure, one hundred percent treif. But no, thank God, it was only his daughter, his virgin daughter, his only child, he had no other, neither son nor daughter. How old do you think Jephthah's daughter was when she was the first living creature to dance out of the house, shaking her timbrels to greet her triumphant father, Yiftakh?" Gershon speculated. "A ketanah, three years and one day, perhaps? Nine years old, maybe, presenting with two pubic hairs? A na'arah, in her most marriageable prime, in her eleventh through the first half of her twelfth year, her virginity having reached its perfect stage of ripeness and tautness to reassure even the strictest connoisseur that he had gotten a good deal, that he had not been cheated? Certainly she was no older than twelve years and six months, not yet a bogeret, for sure," Gershon went on, dredging up the few nuggets he remembered, all of them sex tinged, from his more than a decade of being force-fed Talmud, showing off for Epstein with these juicy bits. "No, no way was she a bogeret, mourning her maidenhood in the hills. A bogeret would likely have already been subject to some form of carnal encounter by the age of twelve and a half, probably unnatural, to protect the prized merchandise, but even with just the normal wear and tear of life, she would already have been only half a virgin by age thirteen, her virginity by that point would already have been deteriorating, growing flaccid, by fourteen or so it would be a rag, by fourteen all she would have been good for was to be sacrificed on the altar, no one would have mourned her, no one would have remarked it. You're definitely living in the wrong century," Gershon said to Epstein, "your fourteen-year-old beauties would be considered one hundred percent over the hill, believe me."

Gershon could get away with what from others in Epstein's orbit would never have been countenanced, banning them forever from the bounty and perks of Epstein's singular world. Gershon could go rabbinic and scold Epstein for taking the Shoah's name in vain, he could go soft and literary and call him a Gatsby, Jay for Jew, wining, dining, serving up sex as the pièce de résistance, no matter, they'd never let him into the club anyway, whatever happened, in the end they would blame him for everything, he could go Old Testamental and even Talmudical and offer up daughters, his own and the daughters of other men. Epstein gave Gershon license, he trusted Gershon, Gershon was blood.

They were two intense, driven Jewish hustlers from Brooklyn aligned in age, Jeff and Gersh, with shocks of silver and ivory hair and crinkle-eyed charm, one perpetually tanned and one roseate with intellectual passion, one in signature polo shirt and khakis, the other in strategic blacks, two damaged smart kids out hustling in the jungle in casualwear, one in financial affairs and the other in cultural affairs, both with a preference for discordantly aged women, too young or too old, as personal statement with subtext. They had so much in common, spoken and unspoken, they were family. "Look, I'm a registered sex offender, friend, okay?" Epstein put it to Gershon. He would go over it once only, and then between them the topic would be closed forever. "Everyone knows that older men making it with young girls is a fact of life since time immemorial, even in our day and age it's still considered completely natural in enlightened societies throughout the world. The time will soon come, inshallah, when the entire Western world will also wake up to this human evolutionary biological reality, and then the whole business will be normalized, like homosexuality. At that glorious hour it will all become legal, the persecution will end, and I'll be hailed as a martyr and a hero, like Oscar Wilde. Hey, nobody's forcing these girls, they're already seasoned teenaged operators," Epstein said to Gershon, "there's plenty in it for them too, big bucks, affirmative action big time, they're not three-year-olds, for God's sake, I don't mess with babies, these kids are old enough to do the math. You'd think the morality cops would leave me alone—right? A rich guy like me, a mega donor, a major philanthropist dumping millions into top research projects at the fanciest universities. Thanks to my deep pockets, the woolly mammoth will soon be roaming the plains again, the human genome will get a badly needed makeover. So why are they harassing me? Do they bother the old-fart billionaire WASPs and other assorted Christian types screwing their little Lolitas and Annabel Lees? They're all just a bunch of fucking self-righteous Nazi racists and antisemites. You really ought to write about it," Epstein said to Gershon.

The last time Gershon set foot in the mansion was under the waxing new moon on the night of Epstein's annual Yom Kippur break-fast at which every New York operator, gentile, Jew, and idol worshipper, made a point to drop by to raise a glass of Dom Pérignon and pluck a piece of ethnic herring on a silver toothpick from the extreme buffet. Officially, it was a family affair, but Gershon's wife Yiska had absolutely refused to accompany him to the den of a convicted solicitor of minors for prostitution, she announced, a certified pimp and rapist, day after day she struggled to save battered and abused women from slitting their wrists, she said, she knew what these men were capable of— and of course under no circumstances would she even consider allowing their daughter, Yalta, fifteen years old, for God's sake, to attend such a gathering.

But true to the feisty Talmudic heroine whose name she bore, who would never have countenanced anyone telling her where she may go or where she may not go, Yalta materialized at Gershon's side just as he arrived at the lofty wooden doors— lofty enough to let in a helmeted knight with plumage astride an armored horse—of the Epstein mansion, Gershon's specially ordered white Yom Kippur Crocs softening from the heat of the radiant electrical system under the sidewalk that melted snow in winter. "Hey Dad," Yalta called out so sweetly, and she slipped her arm through Gershon's, pulling him along past the barrier of bouncers to make their grand entrance as a couple, old man and girl.

A few days earlier, Gershon's essay, "Program Poshlost: The Intellectual and Artistic Philistinism of America's Creative Writing Programs" had come out in the *New Yorker* magazine, placing him, in his view, squarely in the minyan of the masters, from Gogol to Turgenev to Nabokov—he could now officially be considered their rabbi and spiritual counselor. Several publishers had already approached him with proposals to turn the piece into a book, already he was in negotiations with two of them. He was feeling relaxed, fulfilled, deservedly famous—in Epstein's great hall packed with name recognition, he regarded himself as being among the more deservedly recognized. He was a personage, he was warmed by their eyes upon him, an effect enhanced by the wall of World War One prosthetic glass eyeballs from floor to ceiling of the art installation that dominated the space. As Yalta loaded and reloaded her plate from the extravagant spread, Gershon contented himself with drinking Epstein's very good and very costly wine on an empty stomach while at the same time observing the master of the house in the distance working the vast room, trailed by four statuesque and formidably competent-looking female staffers of drinking age armed with headgear and electronics. There was no rush, he could wait, he and Jeffrey had a special bond, a unique relationship, eventually Jeffrey would get to him, they would embrace, they would bless each other in Hebrew, their code, with a good new year, they would wish each other an inscribed place in the book of life, Jeffrey would take one look at Yalta enjoying her food so lustily and exclaim, Who is this ravishing beauty, where has she been all my life?—and Gershon would introduce his daughter.

"Who invited you?" were Epstein's first words addressed to Gershon's back as he was retrieving his refilled wineglass. Gershon turned sharply, inevitably spilling a few drops of the precious red wine on the elegant white kittel robe he had worn like a shroud all day at the Yom Kippur services in the synagogue, and now for effect continued to wear at the party over his blacks. "Shit, they forgot to take your name off the list," Epstein said. He beckoned to one of his aides. "Erase him from the book," he ordered.

Epstein hadn't even noticed Yalta; inexplicably, Gershon felt vaguely offended. Caught there in his wine-stained kittel and absurd white Crocs instead of his usual tight-fitting boots of the softest black leather with their kid lining cuffed just below the knees, his fleshy mortality on view and undefended, Gershon recognized that something had happened, something final, something unalterable and unfixable. Epstein had turned on him, he had closed himself off, become impenetrable, as cold and as hard as a piece of ice, whatever had once existed between them seemed now to be irretrievably blotted out, Epstein had taken himself away. Yet Gershon continued to stand there as if paralyzed, even as he was beginning to absorb the finality of his sentence. He had a right to know the reason for his banishment, it was such a stunning and radical shift, the least he deserved was an explanation.

"You're kidding me," Epstein spat out. "I can't believe you don't know. That piece of shit you wrote for that rag about writing factories, schlock art, fake feelings, fake meaning, fake whatever? You think you're some kind of genius—right? Well, pal, there's such a thing as respecting a friend's privacy, especially if you're let into his confidence, if you're invited into his inner sanctum, it's a matter of basic human loyalty. Did you really have to use as an example for this posh-shit-list art, or whatever the hell it's called, my poor stuffed poodle standing beside her stuffed turd on top of my white grand piano in my private quarters? I trusted you. I named that bitch after my mother—you knew that, she was very special to me, I confided in you. Have you no decency, sir? Such a violation—unbelievable!"

"I didn't use your name," Gershon responded feebly. "Nobody knows it's your mom."

Epstein shook his head, marveling at such dimness. Gershon's fate was sealed, as in the closing of the gate of mercy at the end of Yom Kippur day, he was cut off from the presence with no hope of appeal. It was useless to fight it, the chance that Epstein would ever revise his view was less than zero, hopeless, the romance was over. Epstein jutted his chin toward Yalta. "Your daughter?" Gershon nodded. "How old?" Gershon mumbled her age. Epstein looked her over, up and down. "Lose ten pounds, kid," he said. "Then get back to me."

It was such a shocking end, like a sudden death, Gershon was numb with disbelief. And then, even worse, on top of that, he was alarmed by the realization that he might actually have been plunged by this loss into a state of denial, the first of the official stages of grief, a theory he had once so publicly debunked in a brilliant think-piece as a reflection of our shallow culture impoverished of all organic, unpackaged feeling. To aggravate matters even more, he was appalled to find himself moving right along exactly on schedule to the next stage of grief—anger. Until that moment he had not fully realized how furious he was at Epstein for denying him a fair opportunity to defend himself properly, for discarding him in the ashcan like an old plaything that had lost its stuffing, for leaving him flat, as they used to say in Brooklyn. Added to that was his rage at having been so summarily cut out of the Jeffrey Epstein roadshow before he had a chance to fully explain and elaborate on the subtle and complex reasons for his acceptance of so sordid a bargain in the first place—the trips in the private planes, the visits to the ranch in New Mexico where Epstein was training like a champion to seed a world record of ripe young wombs, the estate in Palm

Beach, the island in the Caribbean, the royalty, the billionaires, the world leaders, the superstars, the food, the wine, the parties, and all the rest of its lethal fallout, best forgotten, best blocked, best purged. And then, in the end, just like the lady promised, along came the final stage of grief—acceptance. Gershon had been amazed at how quickly and predictably it had arrived, even for him, it was all so ordinary and common.

But now, halted in his wheelchair just inside the door of his apartment with this miraculous invitation to Camp Jeffrey Epstein in his possession, Gershon was suddenly overcome by an all-encompassing sense of light and lightness, of liberation, it seized him like a revelation. This—this!—was the last stage of grief, he realized at once. It was not acceptance, the old lady was dead wrong, it was and always would be liberation. And it had not come to him easily, so much had to be endured and traversed and processed, not least Epstein's squalid death and his own personal undeserved downfall, his entanglement in the hashtag, to finally arrive at this unshackling, this release. He now recognized that his descent into the filth of Epstein's lair, followed by his public shaming for his own far less virulent sins, was a narrow bridge suspended over a black hole of infinite depth that it had been necessary for him to cross in order to arrive at the other side purified and enlightened, ready to go forth unafraid—liberated. Now it was he who rejected Epstein, no longer Epstein who rejected him. He had been cleansed of all lingering stigma stemming from his involvement with Epstein. He could seize it and transform it. He was whole, he was deserving. He could now proudly and in good conscience, without fear of exposure or ridicule, set forth to Camp Jeffrey Epstein New York, auspiciously located in the familiar old Lokshin Hotel and Country Club, to shape the story, to transcribe it, to bring it into existence. The invitation lay cradled there in his lap, beckoning.

As for the hideous rehab component of the set-up, he would

deal with that when he got there. Let the soft-brained so-called professionals wallow in the smug self-satisfaction of believing he was coming to them for reeducation, for "therapy." He, for his part, would think of his forthcoming sojourn at Camp Jeffrey Epstein on his own terms, as a sanctuary for the creative reworking of all he had suffered. He was bursting with Epstein material. As an authorized insider of Epstein's universe nevertheless possessed of clear-sighted artistic distance, he would pull out the strands of the story one by one and weave the full picture to astonish and illuminate. What better place to do this work than at the eponymous Camp Jeffrey Epstein New York? Forget the pathetic little daf yomi musings. He would contact an agent at once to nail down a proper advance for the Epstein book before setting out. Camp Jeffrey Epstein New York would be for him a writer's retreat, a precious residency at an artist's colony free of charge, albeit acquired at such terrible personal cost, the perfect setting for the healing creative act.

3.

By the time the official orientation of the seed class of Camp Jeffrey Epstein New York took place in early February, the exclusive Gordon-Glick-Bloom-Blatt clique had already solidified, like a gefilte fish jelly, clotted into too familiar a smell. Without ever acknowledging the connection, during that opening week, as the traumatized campers stumbled in and took up residence, these four instinctively closed ranks not so much on account of the media presence they shared, to greater or lesser renown, but more for the sake of managing the fallout from having over the years encountered one another among the chosen on the deluxe properties ruled by the outcast Jeffrey Epstein, still reviled even now as he lay neutralized in his unmarked plot next to his mother and father in the Jewish cemetery of Palm Beach, Florida, what remained of his overworked organ gnawed by maggots and worms. Like Gershon himself, the other three must surely also have paused when, in the sloughs of their banishment and isolation, they first held in their hands that singular invitation to be reconstituted at a facility bearing the name and all the resonances of the certified sex degenerate. They, like Gershon, must have hesitated as they weighed whether they should recuse and disqualify themselves on the grounds of a self-compromising prior association, of having sampled the infamous Epstein's tainted largesse. Were this to become known, it would without question arm their enemies with further smug confirmation, revive the invective, the hideous hashtag scandal—an intolerable scenario. The only sane option was to turn down the invitation for the sake of not drawing further unsavory attention to their already battered spirits—but then happily, like Gershon Gordon, each one of them, in his own way, found a respectable excuse to do something nice for himself for a change, and accepted.

Among the four of them it was understood that the circumstances of their past acquaintanceship were never to be even winked at, much less detailed out loud, even among themselves. They were initiates in a secret society, though anyone with a device could easily have accessed their linkage to one another in a variety of configurations on relatively innocuous non-Epstein turf in a previous life, including the famous two-part in-depth interview that Bob Blatt once conducted with Gershon Gordon on television, in which Bob hailed Gershon as the Jewish Kitsch Killer, and Gershon, flattered to a state of terminal well-being, nevertheless saw fit to suggest, in a trademark display of provocative irreverence, that to keep with the alliteration, Bob could have replaced "Jewish" with the K-word—"And this *K*, unlike the one in *knife*, is not silent," Gershon had added emphatically. The K-word! Gershon had paused to let his comment sink in with all of its implications for every race and creed, he gave out a deep testosterone guffaw as he adjusted his lower parts in his seat, and proceeded to dazzle one and all with a mini essay, composed on the spot, on the very phenomenon and fate of forbidden words and their pathetic euphemisms, including the unutterable names for God Himself, also reduced to its letters, a hollow burden for all.

Granted it was in the interest of all four of them that during their sojourn at Camp Jeff, their former connections specifically to the loathsome namesake of their current benefactor and patron remain classified. Their confederacy was a form of insurance policy, mutual protection against their shared vulnerabilities, but even so, they still held on to some of their principles, even they had their limits. When, during that opening week leading to the formal orientation, the hedge-fund mogul Max Horn showed up and trotted immediately over to their table in the dining room to greet them, brazenly remarking on what an uncanny coincidence it was that they always bumped into each other on the real estate of one Jeffrey Epstein or another, Arnie Glick, the comedian, shot back, "So when did they let you out of the slammer, scumbag?" No way that sleazeball rapist Horn would be accepted into their fraternity—that was nonnegotiable. The four amigos, as if hearkening to a higher signal well out of the range of so coarse a specimen as Horn, dismissed his existence, they sank their heads as one into their troughs to focus on their feeding.

By then, Gershon was already eating out of a specially ordered kosher aluminum-foil bento box, with the full black bowl of his velvet yarmulke emphatically positioned forward on his head, not to be mistaken for a mere fashion statement. Horn took notice. "Nice beanie, but don't count on much of a return from *that* investment, bro." Could Horn, a certified felon, really be one of their fellow campers? He must have deployed his rancid connections with the topmost thug to engineer some sort of filthy private deal, a golden pardon. Whatever their sins, as far as the four of them knew about each other, they had mostly not been committed on any of the Epstein assets—in contrast to Horn, who was known to have particularly favored the spread in the Virgin Islands, not for the curated little blonde teeny-boppers with the glittering orthodontia, which was the house specialty, but for the glut of local black help—the maids, not the maidens. He would corner them in some stale room as they were performing their housekeeping routine, slam them down onto the super plush king-sized bed, unzip, do his business, stuff their purse with a hundred-dollar bill, rezip, then leave them to clean up the mess, which after all was why they were there in the first place. "He thought they liked it, he thought he could do anything he wanted to them because he was so rich and powerful," Bob Bloom, the news anchor, said, recalling an interview he did at the top of the hour with Horn on the eve of his conviction. "And you know what?" Bloom mused, "It's a funny thing, but those girls in the office or wherever who later #MeTooed me? I also thought they liked it. I thought I turned them on, I thought they felt honored."

Over the next few days before the official opening of the program, not a single meal in the dining room passed without Horn dropping by their table at some point to reminisce at top decibel about the good old days before the fall of the Epstein empire, entirely unfazed by their pointed disregard, their unwavering focus on their food, the steady stream of their conversation that deliberately excluded him. "Clinton, that jerkoff? He didn't come to the island for those little Lolitas either, no way. He came for the madam herself—you know, Jeff's Gal Friday, Lady CPO. No more messing with the Little Rock sluts with the big hair, forget about those upper-middle-class zaftig Jewish princesses. Can't say the same for that fat putz of a prince with the ridiculously low IQ though—arrested development, so naturally his highness heads straight for the teen angel trash sprawled at the pool in their itsy-bitsy bikini strings, bottom triangle patch only, grunting like a pig, he almost couldn't hold it in—pathetic, a royal pain in the ass." And so on, sullying meal after meal.

It was a sorry campaign of harassment that Horn conducted, though not one of the four men seated there was concerned that the rantings of this lunatic darkening their airspace could damage them or, for that matter, even be heard in the vastness of that dining room—and besides, who would ever be interested in his demented juvenile ravings anyway? It was truly an enormous space, though thanks to the tasteful remodeling by the good Jeffrey Epstein's wife, which had transformed it from a ballroom motif with gold satin draperies and crystal chandeliers into an industrial expanse of slate, glass, and steel, or maybe due to the optical contraction of advancing years, it no longer seemed as huge or as cavernous as it had that summer Gershon had worked there, first as a lowly busboy and then as a full-fledged waiter, when it had been packed to the rafters with hundreds of Jewish so-called useless eaters, endowed, thank God, with excellent appetites and a determination to get their full money's worth, rendered even more urgent by the cataclysm that had engulfed them in Hitler's evil empire, the insatiable hunger it had left inside them.

Now though, in its new emanation as the bootcamp refectory for elite pariahs, the dining hall was also safely underpopulated. Apart from the table where the four of them sat, and Horn's assigned table a good distance away, where he would deposit himself alone to refuel whenever he took a few minutes off from hounding them, there were only two or three waiters idling about and what looked like kitchen staff—in a distant corner a Chinese guy holding a bowl of soup or some other fluid up to his face, the cook, most likely, taking a break, and across from them, a couple in super Orthodox Jewish drag, a man and a woman whom Gershon naturally assumed had been hired to supervise a kosher kitchen to accommodate his reconstituted religious convictions, the legal right of every prison inmate, his dietary preferences. He directed his companions' attention to this pair, pointing out that the woman's uniform of a turban concealing every remaining strand of her hair, and her dark tent-like housecoat shrouding her heavyset figure from neck to ankle was a far more extreme fashion statement than the man's costume of a stained white button-down shirt and crumpled black trousers with half-zipped fly stretched across the girth of his short pudgy body, soiled fringes dangling limply in the general area where the waistline must once have been, a full black velvet yarmulke flecked with dandruff like Gershon's own, bushy tufts of wiry nose and ear hairs visible even from a distance, and a wooly black beard smeared with gray or maybe food droppings more and less recent. These were significant anthropological markers, Gershon insisted, you needed to recognize the signs, identify the tribe and the types in order to survive in the jungle. It might interest them to learn, Gershon went on, that the corner of the dining room this ethnic couple was now inhabiting was where his station had been located that summer he had been first a busboy and then upgraded to waiter, when this grand destination had been known worldwide as the Lokshin Hotel and Country Club. It was the summer of his first love, he confided to his companions, with a fiery Russian woman twenty years his senior, the in-house hotel practitioner and provider. She taught me everything I know, Gershon asserted. That was more than forty years ago—unbelievable, it seemed like yesterday. He was planning to treat himself to a nostalgic excursion tomorrow for old time's sake, up to her infirmary where she had instructed him in the techniques of proper lovemaking, a very useful, and, Gershon believed, essential skill for every boy to acquire. You have very good hands, she would say as she tutored him so strictly, Gershon could not hold back from inserting that detail. It was a compliment his mother and her friends applied exclusively to top surgeons who cut you open, tinkered with all your kishkes, then stuffed everything back in again and sewed you up to finish the job—good hands. The infirmary was up a pretty steep hill as he recalled, he probably could use some help with his wheelchair. Did anyone care to join him?

"What time?" Max Horn piped up. They all turned to stare

at him, stunned. He was still stationed there by their table, they had so internally erased him.

During breakfast the next morning Horn did not take his eyes off them for a second, following them out of the dining room the minute they rose, loosening their belts after having fortified themselves heartily for what promised to be an arduous trek. He narrowed his surveillance to Gershon Gordon who was, of course, the pivotal figure, the guide, without him the entire expedition could not materialize. Max Horn parked himself comfortably in one of the lounge chairs in the lobby right by the fountain shooting up plumes of iridescent water, which the interior designers had so wisely decided to retain during the remodeling, in a nod to the hotel's legendary past. From this perch he had an excellent view of the door to Gordon's room. It was situated on the main floor, thanks to the mysterious ailment that had confined him to a wheelchair. Horn was prepared to sit there and wait all day, if necessary, but only about half an hour went by before he heard the thrilling after-breakfast crescendo of toilets flushing throughout that hushed palace. Gershon Gordon soon rolled out of his quarters with a blanket spread over his knees, unseasonable for this mild winter morning, joined soon after by his trio of fellow travelers.

They set out with Gershon in the lead, Arnie Glick, scrawny and unfledged like a boy, pimples still punctuating his forehead, curled up in Gershon's warm lap with the blanket's comforting silky border against his nose, squealing, Whee! Whee!—and the Two Bobs in back of the chair, grasping the handles on either side, steering and maneuvering. Some distance behind them trudged Max Horn, unacknowledged, a nonmember, officially neither present nor accounted for. Gershon led them through the rolling estate, past the great pile of the spectacular main building, peaking in stone turrets and towers, still retaining so much of its signature Lokshin romantic glamor, past more stone and rustic structures, guiding them into territory now strictly off limits to the elite, pampered Jeffrey Epstein campers, past septic tanks and cesspools, rodent-infested garbage dumps and pits overflowing with twisted pipes, shards of leprous dishes, smashed furniture, sodden bedding, the entire exposed under-belly of the operation, rows of one-story lopsided bungalows that seemed to be sinking into the ground, clearly meant for the menials. Surely he hadn't been housed in such quarters during the summer he had arrived there, first as a mere busboy and then risen to the lofty status of waiter, surely this is not the land-scape he had passed hastening breathlessly to the infirmary of Dr. Zoya Rubinchuk for another lesson in love—surely the good and proper Lokshins would never have exposed their historically traumatized guests, who had already seen more than enough for one lifetime, to such blight on the way to the doctor's office to have their temperatures taken rectally—always rectally, the only correct method, according to Dr. Rubinchuk. Gershon felt him-self to be strangely disoriented. He remembered the landscape as steep, hilly, but this terrain was flat, pocked with stagnant pools of what looked like quicksand, filmed with a greenish scum, strange prehistoric insects with long transparent wings hovering close to the surface of murky opaque lakes of mud and slime. "Maybe it looks so ravaged because it's winter now and then it was summer," Gershon said out loud. Maybe it's because I was young then and so full of promise, and now I'm old, and so full of—promise.

The Two Bobs extended the lower portions of their bodies behind them, harnessing shoulder muscle for the effort of pushing the wheelchair, a climbing simulation meant to soften the disappointment for Gershon, though the ground beneath their feet remained level as they plodded onward for a distance far greater than anticipated. "There's no other way to go, this is definitely the right direction," Gershon Gordon was saying. "I have an excellent sense of direction, my mother, the Holocaust survivor, would tell everybody—I always follow my Gershon, my mother used to say, I would follow my Gershon to the ends of the earth, Lead the way, Gershon, I'm right here behind you." But then abruptly the contour of the landscape began to change, they found themselves on an incline, unexpectedly steep, only instead of rising, as Gershon had expected, it sloped downward—they were beginning their descent. "You see, I was right," he said. "It's basically the same concept when you think about it, down up, up down, a mere variation on a theme." Arnie Glick was now clutching the arms of the chair to keep himself from sliding off Gershon's lap into the abyss, while the Two Bobs, white-knuckled, gripped the handles behind with their combined power, arching their shoulders back to prevent the chair from dragging them to the bottom, where, before them, as in the bowl of an arena, there appeared what could only have been their final destination—a vintage split-level house like a stage set circa mid-1950s, with the shredded back seat of an old Chevy leaning against the disintegrating white shingles beside the ragged screen door in front, and a pile of old tires on its other side, on top of which some plastic red geraniums poked out of a number-ten can with almost all of its label peeled off except for the faded words *Cling Peaches*.

"It's not exactly how I remember it," Gershon was saying as he led them around the house in the unlikely hope of finding some memento from those lost times. How he remembered it was almost as a magic cottage in the woods fashioned out of marzipan and madeleines, and naked children sunning in front with edible buttocks like halvah, like Turkish delight. They passed two cars, a classic wreck ruthlessly gutted, including the recycled tires and back seat now on retro display against the façade of the building, but the other incongruously a late-model silver Mercedes, impeccably maintained. Strewn all around were twisted bicycles, beat-up buggies, rusted-out tools, shovels, rakes. Approaching the back of the house, they stumbled over ropes and wires and traps, sank into heaps of apocalyptic ash and incinerated vegetation, meant to ward off animals and aliens, foxes, raccoons, coyotes, deer, ill-fated four-legged, two-legged, wheel-legged creatures like themselves. Hauling themselves onward to the other side of the house they were almost blinded by a clothesline hung with shimmering whites—white uniforms, white skirts, white blouses, white stockings, white cotton ladies' undergarments, slips, brassieres, and other assorted unmentionables, all so depressingly practical and uninspired, Gershon reflected. From his earliest years he had been such a loving connoisseur, a true aficionado of ladies' intimate wear, creative lingerie, but not this stuff, he was thinking dejectedly, no, not these stained bloomers and shapeless granny underpants. As if to punish him for such unkind, ungenerous thoughts, his brow suddenly was whipped by what at first he imagined to be the metal fastener of one of the schmattes suspended from the clothesline. Gershon cried out, "A garter belt! Nobody wears a garter belt nowadays! It can only be Dr. Zoya Rubinchuk's! How well I remember it!" He stretched his arm up from his wheelchair to claim this artifact as his well-earned souvenir, dragging down the entire clothesline and all of its ghostly whites along with it.

The garter belt was nesting in his lap when they came back around the house to its front door flung open with its ravaged screening. A handsome black woman was now standing there with her hands on her hips, filling the entire entrance with her stately presence. She was clad in a white uniform like those they had just witnessed draped in multiples on the clothesline, now trailing behind them on the downed clothesline like a mythic serpent.

"Give it to me," she said to Gershon.

With uncharacteristic docility he deposited the garter belt in her strong, steady outstretched hand. "Yes, I know it's not Dr. Zoya Rubinchuk's garter belt," Gershon admitted mournfully. Dr. Rubinchuk's garters were attached to a heavy-duty girdle, synthetic, pink flowered, made in the USSR, they didn't dangle from shiny lace ribbons like these. Just then Max Horn darted forward, heedlessly tracking his muddy boots over the laundry. Oblivious of Gershon rapt in his garter-belt nostalgia, entirely unmoved by the aesthetic of undergarments, which in his view were just another obstacle to be overcome in the quest for the prize, he positioned himself in front of the black woman in her white uniform who towered over him, leaning too close, breathing too hard, panting. Seized by an uncontrollable, shameless urgency, he demanded to know if she would be working at the hotel that afternoon. Tomorrow? The next day? When? What time? What floor? Which rooms?

"Behave yourselves, boys!" commanded the woman in her immaculate whites. Her voice was the voice of the universal mother. "Better listen if you know what's good for you."

"There will be consequences," she said.

She pointed to a path nearby that curiously, unexpectedly, led downhill.

Not too far away they could see the turrets and watchtowers of the old Lokshin hotel, Camp Jeffrey Epstein for the correction of perpetrators of inappropriate sexual behavior.

"What you boys need is a Time Out," she said. "Go to your rooms. Now. Right this minute. You're grounded. Don't make me say it again. I'm counting to ten."

4.

Three days later there she was again, planted in front of them in her signature white uniform in the common room, the hub of the Jeffrey Epstein Social Hall, the former celebrated Murray Lokshin Casino and Lounge. It was an eerily warm Monday morning in February, the entire inaugural class of Camp Jeffrey Epstein New York—ten in all, nine men and one woman—had finally drifted onto the premises and settled into their cells, and now here they were together for the first time, clutching their handouts distributed at the door, to enact the ritual of the official orientation, a required activity, attendance mandatory, no excuses, no exemptions. They had settled themselves in loose identity groups on the three sleek leather sofas arranged in a U-shape, drawing in superfluous warmth from a great blazing fireplace, courtesy of their benefactor, the good Jeffrey Epstein, who spared no expense. Of the three women who ran the program, positioned on the stage with their backs to the hearth facing and flanked by their charges, she was the first to rise in her brilliant white uniform to introduce herself. Her name was Ms. Smiley, she claimed, smiling severely, this was how she preferred to be addressed, we need to respect each other's personal preferences. Gershon turned to enlighten Arnie Glick, who was leaning for support through this ordeal over the arm of the sofa against the wheelchair. "Like grade school," Gershon said loud enough for the relevant party to hear. "What is the teacher's first name? The eternal mystery, the key to her power."

Ms. Smiley let that pass for now. She was a nurse, she said, she was a certified first responder, she referenced her creds—caretaker, provider, though of what it was not exactly clear, it was open to interpretation, something biological, health related, loosely mental, vaguely medical, which explained why she had been assigned lodging in the old infirmary, Gershon now grasped, you didn't need a license to be put up there, as he knew from personal experience. She would be the first station of their triage, she said, their go-to, their full-time, their hands-on, their front-line worker, their main man, their camp mother. "Which means she's the low girl on the totem pole," Gershon interpreted to Arnie Glick, indicating the three women facing them. "Yeah," Arnie said, "like the Miss America pageant—third runner-up." He was fiddling with his fly, even third runner-up is dangerously stimulating. That was when they all noticed that Ms. Smiley was equipped with a silver whistle attached to a hook dangling from a silver chain, the only ornament on her crisp white uniform. She had just blown the whistle. "Inappropriate!" Ms. Smiley said when she extracted the whistle from between her teeth and let it drop back into the hollow of her cleavage, where it seemed to settle like a body part. "One blast means inappropriate," Ms. Smiley clarified, her eyes boring stigmata into Glick's hands on his zipper. "Please do not disrespect me. Remember that, boys." What might two blasts mean? They could only speculate.

"Lose that bloody whistle, Smiley," Max Horn demanded. "You're freaking the kid out."

He was pointing to the sofa opposite the one he was occupying—to Arnie Glick, shaking uncontrollably, moaning, his hands now pressed against his face, his head burrowing into

Gershon's shoulder. The Two Bobs had glided along the sofa away from Glick in his throes as from mortal contagion, leaving one shallow bowl in its fine leather, then merging again into a single entity at the opposite end. Across from them, Horn appeared poised to dart from his seat to rip the whistle off Ms. Smiley along with everything else, but his launch was arrested by the too-Jewish couple sharing the sofa with him, who almost simultaneously pulled out from somewhere inside their ethnic costumes their own personal whistles, standard plastic, hanging from a lanyard like a dog tag, and let out a blast. They had earned their whistles, they were educators, former headmasters, principals of Jewish madrasas, she of a religious academy for girls, he of a yeshiva for boys, those were their personal preferences, not to be questioned, thank you for giving us permission, Ms. Smiley. He was known in the tabloids as Rabbi Tzadik Kutsher, the wrestler, though everyone called him Dick for short, and she was none other than the notorious Rebbetzin Zlata Schick, the private lesson giver. They had read about each other in the press scandal pages, Jewish and general, their victims slouching forward to testify to their post-traumatic permanent scarring, mugged by the passing years so that it was nearly impossible to believe they could ever once have been objects of desire. Yet these two perpetrators had never met in person until they instinctively joined forces and established their own private ghetto pod in the Lokshin dining room, where they had been pointed out and parsed by Gershon Gordon.

With one arm draped over Arnie Glick's shoulder to calm him, Gershon now spoke up, addressing the assembled with supreme authority, with his old fluency and confidence, as if he were giving a lecture in a stately wood-paneled hall, chairing a seminar at a major conference, in a manner so natural to him from another life. "Ms. Smiley, I honor you as a whistleblower," Gershon said. "If not for whistleblowers like you, none of us would be here today at Camp Jeffrey Epstein, breathing in the pure clean air of these awe-inspiring Catskill Mountains. Thank you, Ms. Smiley. With your whistleblowing you are fulfilling an important mitzvah in our Torah. Rebuke—yes, rebuke and rebuke your neighbor, our Torah commands us. How long should we keep on with the rebuking?" Gershon asked no one in particular, obviously armed with the answer and intending to provide it himself. "Until your neighbor punches you in the face, says Rav. Until he curses you out, says Shmuel. Until he insults you and reams you out in turn, says Rabbi Yohanan. That's straight from our Talmud, by the way, the sages had a thing about one-upping each other," Gershon added with assumed mastery, redirecting his attention now from Ms. Smiley, the duly honored whistleblower, to her colleague, another of the three female program facilitators, Hedy Nussbaum, who had been intriguingly described in the handout distributed when they arrived at the orientation as not only the possessor of an accredited degree in social work but, on top of that, the author of a novel—and as if that were not enough, she also had a PhD in rabbinic studies, with a specialization in Talmud of all things, from YU. "Yeshiva University, right?" Gershon now inquired, casually asserting a privileged-insider track. It had always been, for him, a tender point that he had never completed his doctorate, he the golden boy so famously bursting with promise—but a PhD from an outfit like Yeshiva University, where you needed only to show proof of circumcision to get in? He could deal with that, with no collateral damage to his self-esteem.

"Yale. Yale University," Hedy said coldly.

She now stepped forward to address the group, a compact, determined woman with a riot of coiled black hair, emphatically distancing herself from Gershon taking such unwarranted liberties, assuming such proprietary intimacies, distancing herself for that matter from all seven Jews on their sofas and wheelchair, bracketing her on either side, implicitly squeezing her into their personal categories as if they owned her. She sought now to focus her attention on the three men directly facing her—the Asian American, the African (or, more to his preference, Jamaican) American, the Generic American—relaxing on their team sofa, silently relishing the predictably squalid spectacle, perfectly willing in this setting to let the Jews duke it out, let them take over even this sordid little world in their time-honored, arrogant, yet subtly cringing way. Her strategy now was to bring these three into the conversation, as they liked to say in the trade, but Dick Kutsher would not cooperate, he could not rest, he was springing from his perch on his sofa between Max Horn at one end and Zlata Schick as far away now as she could manage at the other end. Kutsher was stabbing his hand wildly into the air, crying, "Ooh, Miz Nussbaum, ooh, Miz Nussbaum," as if he were in extreme physical distress, like the kid in elementary school despised by all, who either has an urgent need for a toilet or knows the answer to the question and just has to be the one to eject it, it was a matter of life and death.

"Rabbi Kutsher!" Hedy said sharply, hoping to puncture his fit, but he instantly took the pronouncement of his name with honorific to mean that he had been called on, given permission, loosening him so completely that everything he had been holding back inside now came spilling out. "I just cannot sit here silently," he said, actually getting up from his seat and climbing on top of the sofa, no longer sitting but standing now on its leather cushions as on a synagogue bima, "and let this am-ha'aretz ignoramus boor Gordon blabber on about the glory of whistleblowers and such ridiculous schtus like that. I'm sorry to have to say this, because the poor schlemiel is a cripple in a wheelchair, but I'm the one with the whistle, so I know from whistleblowers, and no way is this about whistleblowing or liberal, left-wing garbage like that in any way, shape, or form. What this is about is being a rodef and a moser, the lowest of the low, a Jew who pursues his own people and hands them over to the goyim, a snitch, an informer, a traitor, the dregs, scum, the most dangerous kind of Jew, a malshin. For such a lowlife Jew there's no hope, it's your religious duty to kill him, or her, even in the street in broad daylight to stop him, or her, from doing his, or her, dirty work—those are the words of the great Maimonides, in case you were feeling a little perplexed, Miz Nussbaum. I'm not stuck here in the pits of the Catskill Mountains in the middle of the winter, in a brainwashing program named after a sex maniac because of some kind of so-called whistleblower. I'm here thanks to your old-fashioned moser, my fellow Jew, who squealed on me to the goyim, never mind true or false, who turned me over to the enemy, and ever since then my whole life is finished, over, kaput, flushed down the toilet."

Hedy Nussbaum, PhD, MSW, not quite five feet tall with a head of dark frizzy hair so full it looked as if she might tip over, nevertheless stood there taking it, still feeling sufficiently in control despite the inappropriate rumblings, deeming it therapeutic to give Kutsher the space to vent, to get it out of his system, letting the rant fade out organically, without any intervention from her side, before moving forward with the agenda. "Thank you, Rabbi Kutsher," she said at last when she judged the caesura to be final. "We appreciate your input, but right now I need you first of all to please get off the couch with your muddy shoes, if you don't mind, and to please sit down properly and wait your turn like every other team player. Thank you. The three gentlemen over here have not yet had a chance to contribute. You and your comrades are not the only ones in this program, I must remind you. We have ten members in all."

"Ten members? A minyan—right?" said Max Horn.

"No way," Arnie Glick, temporarily restored, spoke up. "I think one of us has no member." He smiled brightly in the direction of Zlata Schick. "Female? True, false, or none of the above?" Zlata did not react, she had compressed her bulk even deeper into the corner of the sofa opposite, seeking to dematerialize. Arnie turned to Gershon, his mentor, his guru, and posed a question. "What does the Talmud say about a woman being allowed to join a minyan if she has a full mustache?"

Gershon shook his imposing head housing his legendary brain in disapproval. "Inappropriate, Glick, we do not reference in public the physical features of those in our lines of sight. If I were the proud owner of a silver whistle, like our lovely Ms. Smiley here, I would give a blow right now and call you out." Then, moved by the doglike appeal of Arnie's countenance, Gershon added, "Minyans and mustaches—that's not my department, it's not my area of expertise. Why don't you ask Dr. Nussbaum over there, she's the licensed Talmudic authority."

But before Glick had a chance to redirect the question, Zlata herself spoke up. "Those three token gentiles sitting over there to give the program a little diversity? If they tried to join the minyan, believe me, they'd get in before me in a heartbeat, even with my mustache." Her voice was disarmingly young, light, playful even, with a rising interrogatory lilt at the end of her clauses, no doubt picked up from her legions of violated girl students and with a New York edge, her content equally unexpected, entirely at odds with the medieval message delivered by her comportment and her accessories.

"Ma'am?"

It was the all-American of the three goyim, at ease in his corner of the sofa closest to Gershon, wedged in his wheelchair between this archetypal gentile on one side and Arnie Glick, fully charged, on the other. This was a man who looked like he could flip back his blazer lapel to flash a silver badge, but he was in his former life until defenestrated a medical doctor with a specialty—Dr. Fritz Rosenberg, MD, OBGYN. Titles and degrees, for those who possessed them, had so insensitively been included in the Camp Jeffrey Epstein orientation handout, Gershon had noted, alongside names for both staff and campers. Rosenberg— an unfortunate name for such a stock character goy, Gershon reflected, it must have been a source of lifelong discomfort for him, not for its associations with the top Nazi Rosenberg executed at Nuremberg, but due to the fact that, despite appearances, more than once it must surely have caused him to suffer the indignity of being taken for a Jew.

His "Ma'am?" had elicited a stiffening thrust of full-body alertness from the social worker Hedy Nussbaum, a look on her face of tense focus, but he had meant it for Zlata Schick, though maybe Zlata was simply not accustomed to being addressed as "Ma'am" in so gallantly gentile a fashion, and in any case her turbaned head had by then receded like a turtle's into her plus-sized sack. Even so, he pushed forward to make his point as if responding to Zlata, touching on the lady's obvious allusion to affirmative action and other such abominations used to shore up diversity as the explanation for his own inclusion in the Camp Jeffrey Epstein program, as well as the inclusion of his two new colleagues, both distinguished men of color, seated here to his left on the designated Shabbes goy sofa—the venerable clergyman Father Clarence, and the world-renowned chef and restaurateur Wesley Wu (yes, a cook, Gershon was in the ballpark on that one).

"The stigma of affirmative action!" Rosenberg lamented. "The assumption is you're not as good as the guys who get accepted solely on the basis of merit, you needed that extra oomph to get in, that big booster shot. But being accepted by the Camp Jeffrey Epstein program for perverts and sex predators only with the help of affirmative action, as the good lady implies about goys like us? That means that compared to you, we're not as bad— right? So we're honored to serve as your diversity chits here at

Camp Jeffrey Epstein New York, if that's what you need us for, we could all use a little vacation in the country. You're looking at three proud affirmative-action goys who have tried in their life's work to do their best for the boys and girls and others who turned to us for help—we tried, we're human—don't we get any points for effort? If it's any consolation, whatever you guys did to get in without the help of affirmative action, it couldn't have been all that bad either, considering you're sitting here today in a recycled luxury resort instead of a prison. Our program's namesake, on the other hand, your co-religionist, the late Jeffrey Epstein now rotting in hell, he ended up in jail, hanged in his stinking cell by contract killers hired either by Israeli intelligence, directly by the Mossad, or by one or more of the seriously powerful players old Jeff had spied on, on assignment for the Zionists. Your Jeffrey knew all the dirty little preferences and secrets of these bigshots and VIPs, every inch of all his properties was wired and bugged, the beds, the johns, the sex toys, everything, the hitmen fixed it to look like suicide but only an idiot would swallow such a crock. Bad as he was, though, even your faith-based fellow Semite registered-sex-offender Epstein had the redeeming feature of not messing with girls younger than fourteen. Okay, so maybe an estrogen-pumped thirteen-year-old bombshell lied about her age and slinked in now and then, but take it from an expert, all of his technically underage girls had already passed through the stations of puberty—adrenarche, gonadarche, thelarche, pubarche, menarche—bingo! Forget the arbitrary legalisms, these gals were ripe and ready. You don't need to be a specialist like me to figure out where Epstein's fourteens-and-up were on the spectrum. These were mature specimens, fully developed, fertile, in their sexual prime, body hair and body odor, the whole bloody mess. For the real connoisseur and/or degenerate, twelve is the absolute upper limit, twelve is practically over the hill. Consider India, for example."

Who is this paranoic messenger from another world? Gershon Gordon was thinking. What could have inspired him to start winding down his demented spiel by invoking India of all the possible sexpools on the planet? Clearly, he, like Gershon, had been fatally distracted, transfixed throughout this entire orientation ordeal by the mocha-skinned goddess enthroned up front in her green silk sari trimmed with gold, a diamond stud in the cleft of her nostril, rich, oiled black hair scented with patchouli, as exquisite and refined as a Mughal painting inlaid with mother-of-pearl. Her name at the top of the program—Dr. Zoya Roy, chief psychiatrist, director—had cast Gershon into a fever, every flutter of his plumage in this room over the course of the last hour or so had been for her sake, to attract her eye, but it had taken this misogynist Nazi sadist Rosenberg to smoke her out, because now at last she stepped forward, she was now center stage, standing with her back to the fire between her two ladies-in-waiting, the stern and stately whistler Ms. Smiley on one side, the overachieving little neurotic Jewess Dr. Hedy Nussbaum to her left. She had risen to defend her native land, the rape capital of the world.

Or at least that's what Gershon assumed she was talking about, he was far too agitated to zoom in on her discourse. She was fully in his line of vision now, her entire form down to the radiant toes of her silver Nikes with feathered wings poking out from under her sari, divinely exotic, it was as much as he could take in, he would not allow the moment to be deflected by attending to what was actually coming out of her mouth. For now, he gave himself over to feeling that something in his life had truly come full circle—from Zoya to Zoya. So Zoya was also a Hindu name, it seemed, or maybe it was Muslim, whatever, it was all one subcontinent swarming in the misery of its afterlife. She had manifested herself here before him, Zoya reincarnated, transmigrated across ethnic and political and mortal boundaries, she had crossed state lines and life lines for his sake, an old soul, as they say, drawn by mystical forces back to Lokshin, once more in the guise of some variation on the doctor theme, and here he, too, had been channeled by unnamed powers, to be healed by her. It was all too auspicious to dismiss as mere coincidence. He had been brought here to be fixed and she had been brought back to fix him, it was her only hope to escape the lacerating wheel of birth and rebirth.

Until this moment, Gershon Gordon, increasingly observant in his religious practice, had openly scorned such user-friendly kabbalisms as tikkun and gilgul. These were the province of maudlin Jews and sponge-headed Hollywood types, but now he had been brought face-to-face with Zoya's gilgul come back to Lokshin to do the work of tikkun, she in the form of an Indian spirit healer and the hotel itself in the form of an ashram named for a lecher and a rapist. She had come back to repair the damage she had done to him when he was not even eighteen years old, an eager, innocent, unworldly yeshiva boy, she had shaped and defined his lifelong erotic career intellectually and in practice, leading inevitably to his downfall and disgrace. It was far from the romance of older-woman wisdom he had so pompously flogged on so many platforms. Personal divine supervision had intervened on his behalf to orchestrate events, bringing them together again, he and Zoya, at the Lokshin Hotel and Country Club, forcing him to accept the sad truth that he could not even derive some sort of perverse comfort from the subtext of virility and power implicit in the status of certified #MeToo abuser. The matter was far more degrading. In the empire of abuse, he was just another victim.

She had taken Rosenberg's India bait and come forward in full array to greet the inmates—Dr. Zoya Roy, chief shrink at Camp Jeffrey Epstein New York, in whose web he now once again found himself caught. To the extent that Gershon in his personal consternation of the moment was able to track what she was saying, he could detect no effort on her part to address the prompt of India in the context of abuse—to confront the issue of rape as India's national sport, either in team or individual configurations, the expendable targets spanning infancy to great-grandmotherhood, but with a preference for the most succulent ages of six to twelve, exactly as that creep, Rosenberg, who would know, had intimated. In fact, despite the provocation of her folk costume, and the implicit threat that she might at any moment launch into a classical temple dance with bells on fingers and toes, her accent was pure upper-middle-class *Goodbye, Columbus* New Jersey, served up with a smear of Ivy League striving, she never alluded to India directly at all, as far as Gershon could determine. India was simply inferred from her aspect among the nationalities, ethnicities, religions, races, classes, genders, disabilities, and so on that she listed, all entitled to verbal deference in enlightened civil societies, she asserted. She was reading from a document disseminated by the Department of Diversity, Equity, and Inclusion, Gershon thought he heard her say, but unfortunately he missed the name of the outfit that had generated it, maybe the All India Untouchables Psychiatric Society. She had already noted some very serious language lapses at this morning's meeting, Dr. Zoya Roy declared with utmost severity, inappropriate personal references and blatant prejudices that crossed the line, and she was hereby serving notice that such talk would not be tolerated in their community. Ah, Zoya, Gershon reflected, still so elitist, still so strict, so uncompromising, my darling ideologue, no matter the ideology—the same old girl I once knew, yes, biblically, and yes, loved.

He was so completely in thrall to the wonder of the vision of Zoya redux set there like a jewel in the bezel of her two handmaids, showing her to advantage, and above all to the staggering epiphany of how she had shaped and ultimately derailed his life, that he was capable at first only of tuning into and out of her presentation with staccato concentration. In consequence, most of the legatos were lost to him in these preliminaries. By the time he could bring himself to bestow full attention on what she was saying, she was already outlining her therapy method, known as Zoyaroyan Psychoempathy, with its defining feature, its center-piece, a one-on-one public confrontation between survivor and offender, admittedly a variation on the restorative-justice theme, the hottest item in the current legal market—though from the sound of it, Gershon thought, more like a cheap concept ripped off from reality TV, only without the rising background music. In its Zoyaroyan form at Camp Jeff, as far as Gershon could make out, it would involve a public hook-up between victim and victimizer, in which victimizer is condemned to sit in enforced silence in the center of the healing circle facing the victim full body, listening without interruption as s/he offers up a detailed recounting of what the victimizer had perpetrated upon her/him, with the ultimate goal of channeling the victim's pain via the transference of psychoempathy, the victimizer becoming, in effect, the victim.

But he was already a victim, Gershon wanted to shout, he had already been shamed and punished enough, the undeniable proof was visible, here was what was left of his battered flesh, parked right here in his wheelchair listening now with dazed attention. What had he gotten himself into by accepting that poisoned invitation to this Camp Jeff? he now was wondering. Which of his authorized alleged victims could be persuaded to let herself be schlepped up here in the cold to, let's face it, a third-rate provincial dump like Lokshin to bring him to a state of ecstatic psychoempathy? This type of intervention might not be for him after all, given, among other trademark features, his cultivated intellectual distaste for any demonstration of lowbrow sentimentality, especially in group settings, his natural skepticism and cynicism with regard to the whole genre. Participating in such a farce was liable to induce in him the side effect of a fatally insulting fit of hilarity of a hopelessly incorrect kind, it would not do the job.

Dr. Zoya Roy continued to unveil the nature of the confrontation between survivor and offender, leading to the expected healing climax. "You should not be alarmed if there is weeping on the part of your survivor," she said, "screaming, passing out, breathing difficulties, spasms, convulsions, vomiting, incontinence, and other bodily presentations on the road to a full catharsis—to a full validation of what she or he had suffered at your hands, and ultimately to full empowerment. There might even be a chance that some form of forgiveness is extended at the finale," she noted, "though that is not required, nothing is required of your survivor—my advice is, don't count on it." She slowly let her gaze pass along the semicircle flowing from her, her eyes resting probingly on each face. She was like an icon looking out at you—you thought it was you looking at her, but you were mistaken.

"As for you," she now went on addressing them collectively, "offenders, branded sinners—the goal for you is through the application of serious listening skills and sincere and genuine absorption of your survivor's narrative, to achieve the Triple-A Trifecta—to go from Acknowledgment to Accountability to Atonement, in short, to Psychoempathy, taking on the crushing weight of your survivor's personal pain and suffering and feeling it, not in a clichéd way but truly feeling it, abjectly, empathetically, making it your own, in the best-case scenario, with luck, even achieving a level of reconciliation, yes, even to the point of being inspired to dig into your savings or retirement funds and extend reparations. This is something you need to go through," Zoya said, "in order to be restored to the world of the living, the human race." Gershon observed her closely as she nattered on, dazzled by her intensity, her gravity, her conviction. It took everything in his power to suppress the urge to call out that if all else fails, there are always drugs, straitjackets, electroshock, sterilization, castration, lobotomies, and so on—if only to puncture her adorable self-assurance and lighten the mood.

Now she was going on about her own role in the process. In these encounters they were not to think of her as a physician or psychiatrist or anything high-ranking or titled at all, nor should they think of her as some sort of lesser variety of therapist or mental-health practitioner, an alternative healer or spiritual guru, she implied but did not say explicitly, and certainly, as this is a kind of camp after all, they should not lump her in with a head counselor or cheerleader, or some similar banal type. Nothing like a judge or referee or umpire either—more like a coach, maybe, but not quite, as her personal interventions would be kept to a strict minimum—definitely not an arbitrator or mediator or anything of that nature, as these would not be negotiations, there would be no give-and-take, no concessions, no dialogue. The basic operating principle is that only one party talks and the other listens, one party is guilty and the other is innocent. That is the given, the starting point and the end point. You are the guilty party. The practice of psychoempathy requires you to be positioned in stereotypical female receptive mode, regardless of gender preference, as the injured party unloads and seeks release, to assume that position for as long as it takes to penetrate, truly penetrate, until the full extent and nature of the damage you have wrought finally sinks in, until you finally, finally get it, until you personally experience the full thrust and shredding of the pain you have inflicted. As this process unfolds, it might be more correct to think of me as a kind of go-between, Zoya suggested, an enabler, though that term is also not quite right either, carrying as it does so much negative baggage.

She was foraging for the perfect word to define her role. Gershon would have liked to help her out, words were his métier after all. But maybe the word for a phenomenon like Zoya simply does not exist, it struck him suddenly—a realization that hit him just as Zoya herself also seemed to cease to exist. A fat man topped with a bronzed toupee had materialized in front of her, blocking all signs of her presence on the stage, erasing her completely. He addressed the group over her trailing voice, which faded out along with her physical being. It was nothing personal. He was intent on projecting his persona, launching himself full blast. He didn't see her, he hadn't noticed her, she wasn't there.

He happened to be on the property that morning taking care of some business, he was saying, finding no need to identify himself, so he thought he might just as well drop by to welcome them personally, introduce himself and his inner circle, his first lady, Mrs. Zoya Epstein, former model, but still as fabulous as on the day I met her, thanks to good Slavic bones and my bubby's secret formulas. Just look at her. He gestured without turning his head to the statuesque figure towering behind him a few steps to his right. "More than six feet tall, a monument to her sex—isn't she something?—taller even than my two personal IDF body guys, genuine sabras, trust me, folks, you don't want to mess with these boys, you don't want to make the mistake of thinking they're just leaning against the door over there relaxing, chewing their gum and scratching their balls at the same time, take my word for it, don't make any wrong moves, they're as alert as wolves." He indicated with a jerk of one shoulder the twin musclemen in black suits and black T-shirts, dark shades, earplugs, shaved heads, the bulge of the weapon. "Assi? Uzi? Say shalom to my good friends here."

"Call me Jeff—deal?" the good Jeffrey Epstein said. "Any suggestions, complaints? Don't be shy. We're here to serve you, that's what we're here for. So—what do you think of my girls here?" He flicked his hand backward without turning around, indicating the three invisible employees he took for granted were ranked there behind him, incidentally grazing Hedy's breast, unfortunately, as she was the shortest of the three, the closest to his height. "Top notch team, five stars—for you, nothing but the best. They'll straighten you out, don't worry, turn you around in no time, send you back out into the big wide world to go on contributing to the arts and sciences or whatever the hell. I'm telling you, you've served your time, we need you out there, you guys are the real essential workers—so, so special. Then, after we do you, we roll in the next batch who got caught, poor schmucks, you should excuse the expression, and fix them up, turn them around too, like an assembly line—and so on and so forth, a real public service. Because I want you to know, friends, that I believe you've been handed a whopping raw deal, I believe that by coming here to Camp Jeffrey Epstein you are finally facing that fact, telling the world that regardless of gender you're not going to take it anymore, enough is enough. Some chick says you touched her tukhes or some other body part maybe twenty years ago, or maybe you said something quote-unquote inappropriate to her, whatever that means, and then some more chicks chime in, even those dogs that no man ever looked at, much less ever wanted to touch any piece of—where is it written that women never lie?—suddenly, they're all coming out of the woodwork with some story or other, no girl left behind, that's their motto, and before you know it, it's unanimous, you're a pig, you're out, canceled, gone, exiled, a leper, like you have the cooties. Well, gentlemen, consider Camp Jeffrey Epstein as your personal spa, here you will take the cure, here you will be vaccinated against any future recurrence. Yeah, we're gonna fill a big fat syringe with some good Jeffrey Epstein cream and stab you deep in the nuts or wherever to protect you for life, and that's a promise. In my book, it's you poor suckers who are the real #MeToo victims. Some babe had a bad time, here was her chance to get even, tit for tat, if you get my meaning, and you got caught. You never got a chance to defend yourselves, you got kicked out of the world forever, no terms, no time limit, no bail, no parole. Excuse me, but whatever happened to due process? It's like the Salem witch trials all over again, mass hysteria, that's what it is in a nutshell, you're burned like a steak on the fire or like a fire on the stake or whatever. Well, the time has come, you're not taking it anymore, you've paid your dues, now with the good Jeffrey Epstein cure flowing through your system, you'll be able to stand up and fight the invaders, no one will ever be able to screw you again, Never Again, you will officially become Survivors—#MeToo Survivors—no one is ever allowed to say a bad word against a Survivor, you will be untouchable."

Was he done? Why didn't he gather his forces then, having expelled his wisdom and his largesse, and return to the obscene den of his vulgar castle? Instead he just stood there, as if waiting for something. Were they expected to rise now to give him a standing ovation? Lucky me, Gershon was thinking, clamped in his wheelchair, at least I have an excuse. Epstein's three female slaves, Zoya, Hedy, and Smiley, materialized from behind their boss and entered the ring, their hands raised in the exaggerated pantomime of applause, pedagogically demonstrating to their charges the proper etiquette called for by the occasion. To his left Gershon could hear Rosenberg the goynecologist muttering, "For Christ's sake, you fucking stiff-necked Yids, clap, clap—are you just too goddamned chosen to get up off your fat asses and show some gratitude for a change?" He stood up. "Bravo Jeff, we'll do you proud, you can count on us," Rosenberg shouted, clapping lustily, but all the others sat on in silence, weighed down by accumulated despondency, battered by the prospect of even more humiliation to be heaped upon them by punishing therapies in this institution before they were considered to have paid their dues and set free. Only Zlata Schick joined Rosenberg upright on her edematous feet, but she was not applauding, she was flapping her raw hands wildly and calling out, "Mr. Epstein, Mr. Epstein, don't you remember me?"

Zlata's cries obliged the good Jeffrey Epstein to pause as he was exiting with his entourage to bestow his attention out of formal courtesy on this freak, this mockery of the eternal feminine. His bubby would gag in her grave if she caught him socializing with such a grotesque. Not a single dab of revitalizing cream had ever touched that skin, she had let herself go, her body a bulbous sack of onions.

"You probably don't recognize me"—Zlata's girlish voice was now intensely shrill, her words packed tight, streaming in her urgency to get them out—"I used to be best friends with your daughter, Zuzi, in high school, at Dalton, my name was Zoe Flug in those days, before I saved my life and did t'shuvah and returned to the faith and got married and had thirteen children, they should all live and be well. Zuzi and I took math together in Mr. Epstein's class—you know, the other Jeffrey Epstein, the bad one, the very cute, very cool, very bad one, he was a high school math teacher for a little while in those days, sucking up to the millionaire Wall Street dads at Dalton and striking it rich, he was good at numbers, he never even graduated from college but he was hired anyway to teach us math by our headmaster, Mr. Barr—the Epstein-Barr Virus we used to call them, Zuzi and me, super contagious, super dangerous. I used to sleep over at your penthouse on Central Park West all the time in those days, Mr. Epstein, I guess you just don't remember me, you had a different wife then, a starter wife, Zuzi's mom, not so fancy like your upgrade. I also look very different now, Mr. Epstein, I realize that, I know I changed a lot, Zuzi and I always joked about how her dumpy little Dad and our super horny math teacher had the same name. He really, really liked massages, the evil Jeffrey Epstein—he liked other stuff too, he taught us a lot, a whole lot of stuff that wasn't on the syllabus, unmentionable stuff, he hung out with us, he came to our parties, he trashed empty apartments with us up and down Park Avenue and Fifth Avenue, we were only fifteen years old, Zuzi and me, underage, minors, I was very sorry to hear about what happened with Zuzi, Mr. Epstein, if only she had realized how slim she was, how beautiful she was, inside and out. Well, at least you named your nice playhouse after her, may you be comforted among all the other mourners of Zion."

Prodded by Dr. Zoya Roy, Hedy Nussbaum drew up to Zlata as to a roadblock, admonishing her in the Holy Tongue to sit down and be quiet, this is neither the time nor place, but Zlata would not submit.

"Just one more thing, Mr. Epstein," she raised her voice even higher in desperation, struggling to shake Hedy off like an irrelevant distraction, then frantically grasping whatever time slot might still be available to her to get out the well-known fact that a man who beats his wife and children due to his own personal lack of self-esteem was most likely abused himself when he was a kid, according to all the experts, right? "And the same is also true for every one of us here, Mr. Epstein," Zlata managed to get out, "terrible things were also done to us when we were young, to our bodies and our souls, terrible things when we were innocent and full of hope, unspeakable acts, violations, abuse, we were stricken with the Epstein-Barr Virus and we have never recovered, we have a fatal preexisting condition, we have PTSD, our self-esteem is in the garbage can, it's a vicious cycle, whatever we did later on in our lives, we couldn't help it, we were ruined, we were damaged goods and we damaged others in turn, it's not our fault, all the experts agree."

She was crying now, fat sloppy drops pouring down her face,

she looked to Gershon's eyes like a landfill dissolving, and then she began to let out otherworldly howls as the good Jeffrey Epstein fled with his retinue escorted by Dr. Zoya Roy, followed by all the freshly oriented inmates, gentile and Jew, with Gershon Gordon in his wheelchair steered by Arnie Glick, bringing up the rear like a plug. Trailing them all, as if an afterthought, was Zlata herself, conveyed in a bellhop's luggage cart conveniently abandoned in the bushes outside the Jeffrey Epstein Social Hall of this former hotel, still equipped with a few ragged bungee cords to strap her down like an overstuffed duffle bag. In this way, Zlata was expertly transported by the mighty provider Ms. Smiley, blowing her whistle in a steady march rhythm as she processed, Dr. Hedy Nussbaum, MSW, trotting alongside holding on to one of the rusted upright metal poles of the luggage cart, making a mental note to order proper stretchers and restraints for the inevitable future patient breakdowns as she and Smiley pushed Zlata deep into the Lokshin valley of the shadow of death past the mysterious lake to a faraway place from where her lamentations could no longer disturb the sleepers.

5.

The festering question that had popped open in Gershon Gordon's brain as Dr. Zoya Roy unveiled her grueling therapy scheme emerged in the ensuing days and weeks as a major stumbling block to the implementation of the program. Powered by his own wishful thinking, Gershon had anticipated with smug pleasure how difficult it would be to induce the victims to make the pilgrimage up to Camp Jeffrey Epstein, even with all the built-in incentives: free transportation there and back (first class by air, by land in a chauffeur-driven limousine with tinted windows), full accommodations, a luxury suite and gourmet dining, unrestricted spa privileges, and so on, crowned by an overflowing gift basket of skincare products, cosmetics, and fragrances courtesy of that beacon of female founder entrepreneurship Zuzi Epstein & Sons, Ltd., in short, a total pampering experience for as long as it might take to get the job done, and, at the same time, a truly generous daily stipend topped by an honorarium for valuable time spent away from your very important pursuits worthy of our highest respect, ladies. Still, the victims refused.

Added to the unexpected difficulty of luring certified survivors up to Camp Jeffrey Epstein, there was also the matter of identifying them. Hedy Nussbaum, singled out as the administrative workhorse of the leadership triumvirate, to whom the task of coordinating the Zoyaroyan Psychoempathy showdowns had been assigned, was astonished to learn that some of the campers could claim victims in head-spinning multiples—the educators in particular, the physician, the clergyman, those with easy access, opportunities too tempting for mere flawed mortals to resist. Unsurprisingly, not one of the abusers was forthcoming with "victim names," asserting, credibly in many cases, that they had forgotten, they had never bothered to find out the names of these so-called victims in the first place, assuming such bona fide victims truly existed, if they existed, most likely they had no names. Hedy was compelled to plumb the virtual universe to summon up those survivors who had gone public, and then, in vain, to try to coax them out of retirement. When even these public-domain figures refused to let themselves be hauled up to Camp Jeff to be publicly purged by Dr. Zoya Roy's mental and emotional and spiritual colonic, Hedy was obliged to humbly beg them for references, names, and, if possible, contact coordinates for survivors who had not yet come out. In most cases, again she was denied.

It was a monumental task to which, during the day, Hedy could apply herself only in snatched intervals between the group sessions, in all their thematic variations and human configurations, that it was her responsibility to lead. She would rummage in the overstuffed backpack she dragged around everywhere, it was her signature accessory, searching for her laptop, which she now routinely included in her hoard for just such unexpected breaks in the routine, exploiting any unforeseen gap to try to make a dent in her survivor-trawling mandate. Evenings often were consumed by staff meetings, planning and reviews, now and then an enrichment lecture by some self-help guru or recovered predator that all were required to attend, effectively rendering it impossible to carry on with the task of locating the survivors even after hours. And, as would be expected, there were also the inevitable crises of varying levels of urgency at unpredictable times, even while inmates were still on best behavior, starting as early as orientation day, such as the Zlata Schick meltdown, and also that same evening, at the very first full communal dinner, when Wesley Wu invited Father Clarence to accompany him into the kitchen, certainly an operation that a chef of Wu's stature would be interested in checking out.

A single glance as they entered from the dining room through the double doors, however, revealed to Chef Wu at once that this was one of those joyless, soot- and grease-smeared galley kitchens, a long, narrow wooden addition to the imposing stone Lokshin edifice, with small high windows stained with grime and the smashed remains of dead moths, yellow light bulbs hanging from wires, and an eternally wet concrete floor sloping gradually but unevenly from the rear entrance opening to the delivery road and the field beyond down to the sunken drain punctuating the grand doors leading into the dining room. In this sweltering underworld place, which the health inspectors passed over and forgot, there were no smuggled Chinese girls as delicate as blossoms ready-frozen in available positions, bending over at a ninety-degree angle to set a tray deep in the oven, or kneeling on the floor to stack the lower shelves. It was populated by sullen undocumented types bailed out of the local county jail in private deals with the town police—addicts and alcoholics, probably, murderers, rapists too, most likely—slave labor, Wesley figured. "Nothing to see here," he proclaimed, turning to Father Clarence, but the priest was already gliding from boy to boy as in a dream, stroking faces, caressing arms, shoulders, along the curve of naked, sweat-polished backs down under trouser bands to where the hips began to flare, murmuring, "Soy padre, chicos. Confesión, por favor?"—question marks snaking fore and aft, in every position. It demanded the firm intervention of Ms.

Smiley to extract his tongue from the ear of a velvety brown boy, with the assistance of her sidekick, Hedy, of course—the on-site crisis-intervention team.

The two women were already in the dining room when Father Clarence's por favors rang out from the kitchen so poignantly. It was a requirement of their jobs to be present at every meal, circulating like hostesses on a cruise ship, Ms. Smiley dispensing medications, closely monitoring the full ingestion of every capsule and pill, Hedy floating from table to table to greet the guests, as they were called in this setting, now and then sitting down to chat with strained familiarity in these early days of the program, usually on the subject of the weather.

The weather that February was far and away the headline, a freakish heat wave creeping down the entire Eastern Seaboard of the United States. On her lunch rounds almost two weeks after the orientation, Hedy referenced this intimation of global catastrophe by fanning herself menopausally with her yellow legal pad as she took a seat at the kosher table beside Zlata, who had just been released from wherever they had disappeared her to following her disruptive and highly embarrassing out-burst at the orientation, what in another, less enlightened age might have been diagnosed as a classic fit of female hysteria that would have earned her a life sentence in the attic. Across from the two women sat Rabbi Tzadik Kutsher, methodically working his way through every entrée offering on the menu—meat, poultry, fish, vegetarian, he had ordered them all. As far away from them as he could get, at the opposite end of the huge dining room, a separate kosher table had been set up for Gershon Gordon, who had refused to be conflated with those two perverts, as he labeled them—pedophiles, a blot on the Jewish people, he'd rather starve. At another table during that lunch, in a corner of that vast, nearly deserted space, the financier Max Horn was rhapsodically describing to his tablemates, Dr. Fritz Rosenberg, Father Clarence, and Chef Wu, the flight simulator he had installed in his New York brownstone, at the foot of his massive bed, an exact replica of the Northrop Grumman B-2 Stealth Bomber, the pilot's module lovingly rendered in precise detail, the instrument panel, joystick, software, hardware, the works—"My personal cockpit!"

"Porn," Rosenberg muttered. "Everybody knows they control the industry."

No one had expected such heat in this season, the replacement of the archaic Lokshin air-conditioning system had accordingly been put off until the official onset of summer. As delicately as possible, Hedy was trying to encourage Zlata to divest from some of the shawls she had come out of purdah wearing, seven shawls in all, like seven veils, on that blistering day. She had adopted the look of the extreme matrons of Jerusalem derided as the Taliban Ladies, Hedy recognized the uniform, the female enforcers shapeless in their multi shawls who posted themselves at strategic points in the women's section of the Western Wall and other holy sites to carry out the stealth operation of ripping off the long, stylish sheitels from the heads of married women, wigs deemed sinfully provocative by these modesty cops, shaming their victims by exposing their flattened, sunlight-deprived hair meant to be seen by husbands only, if at all, exposing their vain heads like the shaven heads of women who had consorted with the enemy in wartime. Either Zlata was simulating madness by taking on this uniform, burying herself under all of those schmattes, in this way seeking to escape whatever criminal charges might yet be leveled against her by the schoolgirls whose innocence she had polluted, as was alleged by some of her more spiteful fellow campers, or in her failure to engage with Hedy, she was reflecting a state of near catatonia induced by the drugs that had been pumped into her system during her isolation. The best she could do now in response to Hedy's importuning was to organize her tongue and lips to grunt out what sounded like "dik-dik-dik," which some interpreted as a reference to how repulsed she was by Rabbi Tzadik Kutsher sitting there beside her, stuffing himself in so unseemly a fashion, but which Hedy, of course, with her advanced Rabbinics degree, easily deciphered—zni'us'dik, modesty, for modesty's sake, to attain the highest level of zni'us by concealing her gross female indentations and protrusions, that was why Zlata needed all those shawls. "Like that famous Jewish mother Kimkhit who was always held up as the paragon of modesty to all of us girls—right?" Yes, Hedy had understood, she khopped, she got it. "You know, Kimkhit, the one who claimed that all seven of her sons rose to the splendor of serving as high priests in the Temple, some even at the same time, which is better even than producing seven brain surgeons—this was Kimkhit's reward for never once exposing the braids of her hair even to the beams of her house. Well, I hate to disappoint you, but lots of Jewish mothers have been equally zni'us'dik, they have taken every single modesty precaution they could think of including guarding against the prurience of the house beams, yet it didn't help them one bit with how their kids turned out, as even our sages note," Hedy tacked on subversively, casting her eye across the enormous chamber, clearly alluding not only to the diminished prospects of Zlata's brood of thirteen, the offspring of so notoriously tainted a mother, but also to the mothers of all the campers feeding at this very moment here in this mammoth temple to gluttony—those mothers, too, must also have tried their best despite their limitations and deficiencies. Nevertheless, in a gesture of outreach, Hedy now accepted the topmost shawl that Zlata was holding out to her to encourage enhanced zni'us, a glossy black synthetic, draping it over her head and shoulders, modeling it playfully.

Abruptly, this show of sisterly bonding was cut short, interrupted by a bulletin. The media stars Bob Bloom and Bob Blatt, the Two Bobs, visually signaling the heart-stopping prompt for the imminent delivery of breaking news, inevitably bad, rose as one from their seat at the table they shared with Arnie Glick, tapping both sides of the water glass they held up together, each with the spoon in his free hand. Silence was achieved throughout the great hall. The two men's sonorous TV-tuned voices knelled in chorus: "Be it known that on this twenty-first day of February, in the winter of the year of our Lord, two thousand and twenty, the temperature reached seventy-nine degrees Fahrenheit, the highest temperature ever officially recorded for this day in the State of New York. Fellow Camp Jeffers, you have been forewarned." In tandem they dropped back down into their seats, launching Arnie Glick from his like a projectile. He landed on the tabletop itself, crying, "Arnie's a-hot, Poor Arnie's a-hot"—tearing off his T-shirt, his jeans, his underpants, every covering that suffocated him in this surreal torrid zone except for his flip-flops.

"Make yourself decent, you three-inch fool," Gershon Gordon hissed at Glick as he sped by in his wheelchair across the polished floor and out the door, rewarded in passing by a full-frontal closeup of the pathetic nakedness of his sidekick, the flasher, the jerkoff artist. The double portion of apple strudel with two extra scoops of melting vanilla ice cream that Gershon had remembered to take along with him on a plate in his lap did not go unnoticed by the social worker Hedy Nussbaum.

Hedy, like Gershon, could also not help but take note of Arnie Glick's unruly clipped organ, which had brought him so much grief in proportion to its size, but there was no time now to dwell on the pity of it all, or on any of its ironies or ambiguities. She was rushing after Ms. Smiley, who had instantly swung into action at Glick's inappropriate exhibitionism, taking advantage of an exposed buttock to subdue the subject with the syringe she drew out in a flash from her holster, then swaddling him in a castoff tablecloth, hoisting him over her shoulder, he so gaunt and insubstantial, she so mighty, and racing with him through the steaming, tubelike kitchen out its rear delivery door to where her Mercedes was parked, shoving him into the back seat alongside Hedy with a peremptory command to do whatever it takes to prevent him from soiling her interior through any of his unplugged orifices during the quick ride up to the infirmary.

The next few hours were taken up triaging this new crisis, obliging Hedy to cancel all of her afternoon group sessions. By the time she was done it was nearly five o'clock on this apocalyptically torrid day, all that remained was an abbreviated slot of singed daylight, the sun would set in less than an hour. She could, as was her conscientious practice, constructively utilize this unexpected hiatus to perhaps make some progress in her survivor hunt for the psychoempathy sessions, so vital to the success of their program, to her job security and tenure within it, to the dogged ambition of her boss, Dr. Zoya Roy, but she was drained, wiped out by the accumulation of the unnatural heat and the persistence of suffering. She would go for a walk instead, she decided in a minor burst of defiance, while it was still daylight. As a staff member, she had already been up here at Camp Jeffrey Epstein for several months preparing for the arrival of the campers, yet she had never seen the lake. She did not even know where the lake was. She would find the lake.

It seemed to Hedy, as she trekked in the waning light, that anyone else would have found the lake straightaway. But she, so overeducated, so padded by all those diplomas as well as by the inner tubes of her black down coat from head to toe, even in this heat, since the calendar said February, winter, and she was tethered to words—she continued to wander on the stony pathways and through the fields of thistles and thorns and among the aging pines until, in the end, it's probably more accurate to say that it was the lake that found her. The outside world—she didn't much care for it, she was thinking as she dragged herself along. From a distance, in the dying light, she observed a large discordant object, perhaps an abandoned piece of furniture, something that, like herself, also belonged inside. It, too, was in the wrong place, lost, it seemed to be giving off a flickering light, as if pleading for help. Drawing closer, she instantly recognized Gershon Gordon's wheelchair. As she stood there taking in its emptiness and all that it might signify, warm water lapped over her boots and she realized she had finally reached the lake.

A thin crescent moon was already visible in the rapidly darkening sky. By the remains of the light, she now cast her eye over the surface of the lake, slate gray in color shading toward black, an overturned wooden rowboat protruding from the muck, abandoned to the beetles and worms, here and there in the distance, clumps of reeds spiking upward like a warning barrier in the absolute stillness, a primeval coating of scum over the face of the water. It was an artificial lake, she now recalled having been told, created by the founder, Murray Lokshin, to upgrade the attractions of the resort, and named for his wife, Ethel— Lake Ethel. What kind of creature could survive in such a fake lake? Panic constricted Hedy's throat as she stood in the shadow of the forsaken wheelchair, she knew she should pull out her cell phone at once from her swollen backpack containing all of her life's essentials and try to call for help if only she could pick up a signal. It was her duty, her responsibility, not just for herself, least of all for herself, above all for the deluded souls under her care, but she felt wasted, paralyzed. She craved oblivion, nothing less, to crawl into a dark tunnel with the chipmunks and other rodents, to curl up in the mud and gravel there on the shore of the lake and let sleep overcome her, encircled by coyotes and foxes and bobcats, shrieking and howling, a banished princess waking up in the wrong fairy tale. The awful presence of the empty wheelchair never for a moment let go of her, spiders were spinning their webs in its secret dark corners, snakes wrapped themselves around the spokes of its wheels. It would be sinful to make use of his chair, she thought, but she was so tired, and now it seemed to be calling to her, beckoning—sit, sit. She moved toward it, she let herself down on the very edge of its seat, making contact with its surface with only the most minimal private rear portion of her body, which she had never seen in person, the existence of which she was obliged to acknowledge whenever she carried out the act of sitting in public, her back arched forward to a point just short of tipping over, her elbows on her knees, her hands covering her face, sealing the darkness.

She recalled how that very morning, as the heat was rising, she and Gershon happened to arrive at the entrance to the group meeting room at the same moment, and if only to lance the clotted silence between them, in desperation, she had let drop that she had finally succeeded in making contact with one of his survivors. The survivor seemed inclined to make the trip up to Camp Jeffrey Epstein to face him one-on-one in a Zoyaroyan Psychoempathy session, she was pleased to inform Gershon. His chair screeched, braked, blocking their advance, and he stared up at her with blanched eyes, yellowing with age, like his nimbus of white hair. "What's her name?" he demanded. She didn't feel comfortable revealing that information to him at this point, Hedy responded, but it would not be too hard to find out if he made the effort. Your survivor has published an article all about how you sexually harassed and abused her but she also thanks you in the article for teaching her how to write. "You mean, so now she's blaming me for her writing too, whoever she is?" Gershon shook his head, the world had just hit a new low. "Well, just so you know," he went on, "if she's so desperate for the publicity and actually manages to drag her fat ass up here on her whirlwind pathetic booklet tour, she can talk to an empty chair. Better yet, she can talk to my lawyer, Fink."

An empty chair, he had said, such as the one she was occupying now. Hedy had expected him to go into reverse at that point, exploiting the shock of her survivor-availability disclosure as an excuse to boycott the group therapy session that morning, even in the face of the mandatory attendance rule. Instead, to her surprise, he shifted into gear and bolted into the room, threatening to raze everything in his trajectory. But the disturbing information she had just delivered to him, intensified by the unnatural heat clamping them breathless, rendered his behavior during that morning session even more troubling than usual. As far as Gershon Gordon was concerned, from the moment the treatment protocol in all of its repulsiveness had been laid out at the orientation by that reincarnated quack Dr. Zoya Roy, with all of its flagrant violations of human privacy and dignity, he had determined never to submit himself personally to such a farce masquerading as therapy and, furthermore, to do everything in his power to win over the other campers to his side and sabotage totally the implementation of the program. Already he had succeeded in dividing the group, tightening the bonds of the original Gang of Four, himself, Glick, and the two celebrity Bobs, who, in his view, all deserved a pass as nothing more threatening than unwitting normal male hunter-gatherers operating in newly charted sexual territory. But in the interest of nailing a firm majority, and, maybe unconsciously, out of a measure of tribal loyalty, he also tolerated an affiliation with the two mortifying Jewish educators Rabbi Tzadik Kutsher and Mrs. Zlata Schick, and in addition, for the sake of inclusion and diversity, he extended the privilege of a loose membership to those two simple goyish'e souls, Father Clarence and Wesley Wu, the master chef thrilled to bask in the fading name-recognition glow of the Two Bobs.

That gave Gershon eight out of ten, a solid majority, more

than enough to crush this sadistic Zoyaroyan Psychoempathy quote-unquote treatment plan forever, this public shaming, like the stocks, like the scarlet letter, this brazen assault on their constitutional rights as set out in the Eighth Amendment—cruel and unusual punishment. With this band of eight firmly in tow, he could be spared having to hold his nose and recruit to his cause that sleazeball Horn, that creeper and crawler, that public-intellectual groupie, forever sucking up to him as a fellow above-average Semite, claiming insider privileges. Ditto for that Nazi Rosenberg, Gershon didn't need him either now, that Mengele medical experimenter on unsuspecting young females with their heels in the stirrups, blind to what was happening to them behind the screen of their peaked knees draped in a flowing white sheet. Visions of his daughter, Yalta, rose before his eyes rendering intolerable any unnecessary contact with that creep Rosenberg—his luminous little girl, Yalta, now already a brilliant young woman, between driving and drinking age, turning down Harvard to attend circus school and swallow fire.

Still, it had not escaped Gershon's notice that those two loathsome rejects, Horn and Rosenberg, along with the four adjuncts he had allowed to join his campaign in subsidiary roles out of necessity, were the real thing, certified criminal abusers, their names worthy of inclusion on the official sex offender registry. Come to think of it, was not that registry a public document accessible to all even after the accused had paid his debt to society, and therefore also a form of eternal public shaming, cruel and unusual punishment, banned by the Constitution and the Bill of Rights? Never mind, he would defer such quibbles for the time being. The threat of an abuse-survivor infestation encouraged and supported by the medical bosses was far more pressing now that some of these losers were starting to poke their noses out of their holes and sniff around, including the nameless creature he had just been informed about, doubtless a specimen he would be too embarrassed to take credit for as his own personal victim. Enough already, his darkening countenance seemed to be saying that morning, Hedy recalled, he'd had it up to here, he was not going to take it anymore, he was coiled in his wheelchair as if about to spring, his body language was screaming, Bring them on, we're ready to roll, we'll riot in the cells, we'll burn down the house.

There, by the shore of Lake Ethel, Hedy sat, perched stiffly on the rim of his wheelchair, reliving the morning—the heat, the tension, swallowing up the airspace. Every morning, he delivered his body to the group meeting without fail, performing a hostile act of passive resistance as a nonparticipant in the face of his required physical presence, a gesture of open disdain that Hedy experienced as directed at herself, unbearably insulting. He never spoke, never contributed to the group discussion, the only sounds that came out of him were the voluble oral processing of the remains of his breakfast that he invariably dragged along, or his snoring, mouth agape, when he would drop off asleep, his head lolling and jerking in his wheelchair, dreaming of riding the subway. Occasionally he passed the time reading newspapers, magazines, journals, each page flip like a slap, groaning, muttering, bursting into peals of scornful laughter, but mostly he wrote as if in a frenzy of inspiration—on five-by-three index cards held together with his daughter's hairbands and scrunchies, they filled him with such tenderness. It was common knowledge that he was writing a book, it was rumored that he had a seven-figure advance, his two-finger typing on his old portable Smith Corona mangled the peace at night and sullied the dreams of his fellow campers, all of whom were convinced that the book he was banging out was about them.

But on this ominous morning, marked by the calamitous rising heat and the news of the imminent appearance of his self-described victim, he indulged in none of his usual stunts. He merely sat in his wheelchair with his chins splaying on his chest and gazed darkly at Hedy's big Jewfro, emitting such negative vibrations that the discussion, already deflated, collapsed entirely. In desperation, Hedy resorted to pulling out from her bulging backpack an artifact she referred to as her talking stick, polished willow with a knob on top, which she had picked up long ago at a souvenir shop on a Navajo Nation reservation in Arizona, or maybe it was Apache in New Mexico. She passed the stick to Arnie Glick, immediately to her right, to start the conversation. Obediently, he held it up to his mouth, intoning, "Testing, one, two. Does everybody hear me? Is this thing working?" Then suddenly grinning, as if he had just figured out the true purpose of this familiar object, his hand cupped the stick and began moving rhythmically up and down its length, eyes closed, moaning, grunting. "Feh! Feh!" Rabbi Tzadik Kutsher sputtered, "Such a dirty mind, like my distant relative by marriage, the president of the United States, but he, at least, is good for Israel." For four years already, Kutsher had been impressing everyone in his circle with the assertion of this lofty genealogical connection, relying on the notorious variations in Jewish surnames to render his miserable little boast plausible to himself and others. It followed, then, that a personage with such a distinguished yikhus as himself should definitely not be seated next to a lowlife like Glick. With his bottom still affixed to his seat, he now waddled across the room in his chair, relocating as far away as possible from this pervert with his filthy mind and filthy mouth.

"So inappropriate," Hedy declared, fixing Glick with her thoroughly disapproving gaze. Instantly, she mobilized to snatch the stick out of his smutty hand, passing it now to her left, to Dr. Fritz Rosenberg, who, shaking his head, features puckered in disgust, refused to touch it. Zlata Schick, just released from confinement that morning, in her assigned seat to Rosenberg's left, then received the stick obediently from Hedy, clamping it with a corner of one of the shawls in which she was shrouded, and immediately she began using it for its obvious purpose, to bang herself over the head, propelling Hedy to grab it from her at once and to pass it along to Father Clarence sitting on the other side of Zlata, a position between two men that, as a pious woman, she would never have countenanced had her brain waves not been reset by all those antidepressants and other assorted opiates over the past two weeks. Father Clarence accepted the stick only after wrapping it with his own handkerchief embroidered in one corner with a gothic cross. He proceeded to hold up the stick and wave it around in the air, as if sprinkling holy water or maybe incense on the lepers, and he blessed the congregation. The Lord be with you, let us pray.

Onward it traveled around the talking circle, each one in turn summoning up whatever energy remained in the abnormal heat to contribute some syllables to the noise pollution, until it reached Gershon, who examined the object with contempt, then hurled it across the room, where it crashed at Hedy's feet. It was the opening shot, obviously the thing was a weapon no matter how it was deconstructed, and for the first time at group meeting, Gershon deigned to contribute. "Face it, Hedda," he said, "as a therapist, you're just no damn good. Maybe it's time to go back to your official expertise—you know, Talmud, teach a daily session, like daf yomi or something, or just do it on the days when there's a nice juicy, dirty page. Anything is better than this."

"My name is not Hedda, it's Hedy," she had enunciated syllable by syllable, now recalling her response to his insults that morning on the lip of Gershon's wheelchair by the shore of Lake Ethel, on a black night outside the borders of civilization. She had always hated it when anyone called her Hedda. It happened often, it was a constant irritation in her life. She was not Hedda, not Hedda Nussbaum, not the archetypal victim and masochist who enabled the man to go on smashing in her nose undeterred as the child lay dying, a cautionary tale to all women. She was Hedy, Hedy Nussbaum, Hedda's first cousin on their father's side, both of them named for their grandmother, Hedyota, a woman of no consequence recycled to ash in the ovens of Auschwitz.

"Let him call me Hedda," she now whispered fervently as she continued to occupy his ghostly wheelchair. She was praying, something she had not done in years, offering herself to the cruel spirit hovering over the face of Lake Ethel. "He can call me whatever he wants, God, I don't care what he calls me," she prayed. "Just please don't let him die on my watch, God. Everyone will say it was my fault, they'll all blame me, I'll lose my license, I'll end up in jail. I'll do anything, God, I'll even do your daf yomi class if necessary. It doesn't matter. Just don't let him die on me, God, that's all I'm asking."

The response was instant, like an out-of-office email.

"Hedda! Hedda! Get your ass out of my seat, the chair you're sitting in is holy."

Could it really be He? Was she hearing voices? Who could she say was calling? Digging her cell phone out of her overstuffed backpack to check, she slipped off the seat as if it were electrified. No missed calls, no voice mails, no texts, no messages. Pressing and swiping blindly, she managed at last to hit on the right combination to switch on the flashlight. A prehistoric beast covered with mud and reeds was crawling on its belly out of the lake onto the land, as if evolving to the next stage, slouching to be born, the water lapping over its spongy bulk. Stunned, she pulled off her down coat and threw it over him lying there at her feet. "For God's sake, Hedda, get me back into my chair," he commanded. She bent her back and obeyed, it was for God's sake, he had said, she had made a bargain with Him. He called her Hedda, she would answer to Hedda.

As she arranged him in his chair, tucking him in up to his chin under the civilizing screening of her coat, the words erupted from him like water spurting from the mouth of the nearly drowned. He had gone down to the lake to immerse himself in it since it was such an end-of-time crazy hot day, he had just woken up from his siesta, he would use the lake as a mikvah, he had decided, he needed to purify himself in consequence of the nocturnal emissions he was having all night long every night and today also during his siesta, he woke up stuck to the sheet as if with super glue, due to the fact that the place is teeming with Zoya witches past and present, it was not his fault, it was spontaneous combustion, he had no control over his base animal urges—"And then I got tangled in the bullrushes, and instead of a princess saving me, I get Hedda Nussbaum, just my luck. Now get behind my chair and push me back to my room, woman, and don't open your mouth, don't talk, don't say a word, the last thing I need now is your trademark psychobabble gobbledygook."

In silence, guided by her cell phone and praying to God the entire time that the light not fail her, she steered him back to the hotel, now Camp Jeffrey Epstein for the rehabilitation of the crème de la crème of #MeToo offenders. He, too, did not speak other than to snap out terse directions when it quickly became apparent to him that she had no idea how to go, she was lost in every sense of the word. But outside the door to his room, as she was about to deposit him for the night, she girded her loins with strength and dared to open her mouth for the first time in order to pass on to him the vital information that she had prayed by the shore of Lake Ethel that if God returns him safely she would teach a daf yomi class just as he, Gershon, had so sagely proposed. She had made a neder, she had taken a vow, and as a woman with neither father nor husband to nullify it, she had no choice but to fulfill it.

As she was telling him all this now back inside the protected environs of Camp Jeffrey Epstein, she found herself regaining some of the confidence of authority. The new daf yomi seven-year-and-five-month cycle of a page a day of Talmud happened to have started less than two months earlier, on January fifth, she informed Gershon, and the good news is they were still doing the first tractate, Berakhot—Blessings. But not to worry, the Camp Jeff daf yomi would be a far more casual affair, no way would it be the daily drudgery featuring animal sacrifices in the Temple with priests wading in blood up to their knees, and levels of impurity and required priestly gifts and first and second tithes and other such useless information that can only reinforce our hope that the Temple will never be restored in our lifetime, indeed, strengthen our prayers that the Third Temple may never be built. The classes would be held exclusively on a will-call basis—only on those days when there was a hot page relevant to our mission here at Camp Jeffrey Epstein, pertaining to gender and the uses and abuses of human sexuality, et cetera, et cetera, as Gershon had so sagely suggested. By a stroke of good luck, a really exciting page was coming up very soon, in just two days, she advised Gershon, this Sunday, February twenty-third—Berakhot, page 51. She'd provide a handout, he didn't need to bring anything. Attendance is optional, but she was positive he'd find the page fascinating, one of the rare cameo appearances in the Talmud of a woman who is actually mentioned by name—Yalta, the highborn daughter of the Babylonian exilarch, the fiery wife of the sage Rabbi Nakhman, a female force field who refused to simply lie down and just take it.

6.

Hedy's idea was to make the Talmud classes lighthearted, fun, extracurricular, a sorely needed break from the heavy-duty daily work of deep internal dredging and reconstructive therapy, from the demoralizing reruns of human disintegration. Not only would she schedule the sessions for days when the spicier, and therefore more accessible, Talmud pages came up in the daf yomi cycle, but she also had the brainstorm to hold each meeting in a different location on the property, ideally in a spot with some thematic connection to the page under discussion. Though the good Jeffrey Epstein was now, of course, the proud owner of the entire former Lokshin complex, for his highly selective Camp Jeffrey Epstein rehabilitation program, he had thus far renovated only the main building, including the grand lobby, the rooms and suites, the dining hall, the tearoom, and so on, as well as nostalgically updating what became the mental-health-design-award-winning Jeffrey Epstein Social Hall. Still scattered everywhere over the grounds were the monumental ruins of the golden age of this shining Catskill Borscht Belt resort, a city in itself—the Swiss chalets, the log cabin shopping plaza, the ice skating rink, the roller skating rink, the natatorium, outdoor swimming pools, ski lodge, artificial ski slope, twenty-lane bowling alley, miniature golf course and rolling championship golf greens, the synagogue modeled on the Great Temple in Jerusalem, the Bridge of Sighs with its quaint shops spanning the Neversink River and gondolas gliding underneath powered by singing gondoliers—all of these landmarks picked through by scavengers and sentimentalists but still so evocative of lost time.

For the Yalta daf yomi page, since the heart of the drama pivoted on wine, Hedy identified as a perfect site the ruin of the old Lokshin Bar and Grill, known by insiders in the old days as Shell Shock, a prophetic corruption of Shel's Shack, named for the owner's son, Sheldon Lokshin. As confirmed by Hedy in a quick inspection tour beforehand, the scene there was truly capable of triggering the onset of post-cataclysmic shell shock—walls pocked with mold and disease, plaster flaking in cracked sheets, vintage tin ceiling tiles leaking rust, mirrors and glass-paned cupboards violently smashed as by an invasion of barbarians, oak floors gouged out, clumped with heaps of vintage sawdust, desiccated human and animal waste plugging the holes. There was no heat, but this was not a concern, Hedy decided, as the February weather continued portentously hot, breaking all known records. To her surprise and relief, though, the electricity still functioned—three yellow bulbs suspended from wires attached to exposed ceiling studs, dangling scrolls of flypaper specked with the black dust of bugs and moths and other winged creatures that had gotten stuck and perished there nearly half a century earlier.

Nothing beside remained. Every movable object was gone, sold or stolen, or, with maudlin greed, appropriated as souvenirs. Left standing was only a row of high green barstools with cast-iron bases bolted forever to the earth's core, immovable objects, the bar, which once must have stretched out in front of them laden with drink and disappointment, long uprooted. All of this Gershon Gordon absorbed in an instant as he rolled into the space inexcusably late, following an internal struggle with regard to his own participation in this entire sentimental project with such inferior learning partners, overcoming his procrastination at last by telling himself he would show up only for this Yalta session and to no other, it was his duty as the father of the heroine. He gazed up at the barstools and took in the presence of those four losers, Fritz Rosenberg, Father Clarence, Wesley Wu, and Max Horn, all in a row, clutching their printouts of the double-sided page, Hebrew script with English translation, Berakhot 51. Horn remarked, "You're late, bro, we almost started services without you." Next in the row came Hedy Nussbaum, patting the seat of the empty barstool between the four men and the one she was perched upon. "We saved this one for you. Dr. Rosenberg and Mr. Horn have volunteered to help you up," was her greeting to Gershon.

"No way those rapists are laying their filthy hands on me, I'm staying right down here in my own personal tenth circle."

Accordingly, Hedy slid off her stool, handed him a printout, and proceeded to settle herself a short distance away from him, cross-legged on the ravaged floor, the seat of her black Michelin Man down-filled coat whitening with dust, positioning herself even lower than Gershon so that she was forced to look up at him, to twist her neck even more unnaturally to also take in the others, obliging the four men on their stools to lower their heads insincerely as a lesson in humility and cast down their eyes.

Hedy began. "So let's set the scene. It's somewhere between the third and fourth centuries of our common era. We're in Babylon."

"Ha, that's a good one, the whore of Babylon—is that this Yalta chick you've been so shamelessly hustling, Doc?"

"Watch it, Horn, that's my daughter's name you're blaspheming," Gershon snapped without even condescending to glance up in his direction. Instead, he looked down at Hedy there at his feet on the floor, the thicket of coarse curls crowning her head, and inquired, "How come I don't see my buddy Arnie Glick here tonight, Hedda? Don't think we haven't noticed that ever since his harmless little juvenile striptease in the dining room the other day, the poor guy's been missing in action, getting the full chemical castration treatment in Smiley's torture chamber up on the hill. So how long does it take to flatten a skinny guy's testosterone level by shooting Lupron into his butt for over forty-eight hours straight? Bring me back my Glick, Hedda, he's my only joy in my exile by the rivers of Babylon."

Hedy lowered her head into her hands, rocking forward and back as if she were praying again as she had prayed by the waters of Lake Ethel, as if her strength were seeping out of her body and at any moment she might simply give up the fight, simply quit pushing herself forever. How could anyone who knew her and all that she stood for ever possibly believe she would remain silent and allow sterilizations to be carried out without even a full-disclosure consent form?

"Yes, lady, we're in castration city here, believe it," Chef Wu corroborated in weary expertise tones. "All the food in this joint? Spiked with saltpeter, potassium nitrate, fertilizer. I can smell the stuff a mile away, I can taste it, it's my trained palate. My first job was cooking in a male-only prison, we poured in the saltpeter like water, it kills all your urges, you just don't feel like doing it anymore, no way, and besides, what's the point? You can't get it up anyway. My second job? That was in a Chinese hole-in-the-wall on Mott Street, everything on the menu we drowned in MSG—you know, Ac'cent. Now tell me, lady—didn't your old Yiddishe mama dump Ac'cent into your chicken soup every Shabbes to make it so tasty? Remember the headaches, and how you used to get so dizzy you almost fainted, and how you felt like vomiting? Doesn't turn you into a eunuch though, MSG, just gives you seizures, heart attacks, strokes. But up here at Camp Jeff, saltpeter's the number-one seasoning, they're dumping it in by the bucketful, believe me, and now our poor joker Glick's cocktail is being topped off with Lupron, which luckily only gives you hot flashes, breaks your bones, you grow little titties, and then you get breast cancer."

There was a long silence in which to absorb this new reality, which Father Clarence sundered at last by inquiring so plaintively, "Where can I get some, Wes—this Lupron stuff? The saltpeter's not working for me. My brain's in overdrive, I can't stop thinking about all those pretty boys in that kitchen dungeon right this minute, I'm like an addict. Every day I get down on my knees and pray to Jesus Christ—castrate me, Lord, I implore You, You're the only one for me, I only want to be addicted to You."

Gershon was thinking that he also wouldn't mind getting hold of some of that Lupron stuff for himself too, he would order Hedda to slip him some privately, she would obey, the Zoya wet dreams were killing him, he almost drowned in the lake the other night trying to clean himself up after his nap. The simple truth was that he needed to get his brain castrated, the sooner the better, the brain is the primary sex organ. This brilliant insight regarding the brain, as applied also to Jeffrey Epstein, was a major theme he was now unraveling in his book, which he was banging out with two fingers on his old electric Smith Corona portable in his room every night.

He would have liked to demand that Hedy fetch some Lupron for him right that minute and then he would have made his exit, he wanted to get back to his room, back to work, he couldn't take any more of this Talmud farce even for his Yalta's sake, but Hedy was distracted, she had picked herself up off the filthy floor, she was pacing, she was focused on reading the page, he could not get her to concentrate on him, she was struggling to read the page over Rosenberg's booming voice. They could all hear Rosenberg promising Father Clarence that as soon as he got his medical license reinstated he would write him a prescription for DES. "That's the drug they forced Turing to take, you know, the big Enigma genius, it's a female hormone, it will do the trick every time for guys with your problem," Rosenberg roared, which launched Gershon in his chair directly in front of Rosenberg's stool. "You do know that Turing killed himself not long after going on that stuff, Herr Doktor?" he screamed up into Rosenberg's face, its cold eyes sizing Gershon up as if diagnostically. "Just another case of life unworthy of life, as they used to say in the Fatherland," was the response Gershon heard, popping the blood vessels on his enflamed face, provoking him to gather all the saliva in his mouth and aim it up at this Nazi, though, as it happened, on account of the laws of gravity or for some other scientific reason that Turing could have explained, only a few dribbles hit Rosenberg's gleaming black jackboot, which he never even felt or noticed, while the bulk of the gob landed like pigeon droppings right on top of Gershon's black velvet yarmulke rakishly set over his bristling nest of white hair, much to Rosenberg's amusement.

"So relevant, guys, everything you're talking about now is just so relevant to our page," Hedy was shouting. "It's unbelievable, it's so on point. Really, guys, see for yourself, just take a look at the daf!" But, in fact, she no longer was reading from the page, she had given up. She was riffing now, even reducing herself to calling them "guys" in contravention of all her professional scruples and formalities, adlibbing desperately, fighting to at least get the main plotline cast before everything fell hopelessly apart.

"So we're in Babylon, like I said, in the home of Rabbi Nakhman and Yalta. They're reclining around the table, dinner is coming to an end. There's a guest at the table, Ulla, he's this itinerant rabbi who comes and goes between Babylon and the west—that's Israel, Judea, Palestine, the Zionist Entity, call it what you like—bringing the latest legal rulings hammered out by the sages, the stricter the better, as far as Ulla is concerned. Rav Nakhman now honors Ulla with the cup of blessing and they recite the Grace after the Meal. Then Ulla passes the wine cup to Rav Nakhman for the blessing, but Rav Nakhman says, 'No, give it to Yalta, my wife.' Ulla says, 'She doesn't need the blessing, the fruit of a woman's belly is blessed only from the fruit of the man's belly,' as the verse says—the fruit of your belly, bit'ni'kha, in the masculine form. Ulla speaks as if Yalta is not present, but she's reclining right there and she's thinking, Who is this Ulla anyway? Nothing but a little peddler with meaningless words dropping from his mouth and lice crawling in his rags. She gets up from the table, she marches down to the cellar, she picks up an axe, and she smashes open four hundred barrels of wine. Nobody puts Yalta in a corner," Hedy concluded there in the midst of the ruins of the former Lokshin Hotel and Country Club in the Catskill Mountains, betraying her poor little romantic heart pumping so bravely under strata of ancient books crumbling to dust.

"Spoiled brat, bitch," Rosenberg observed, unmoved.

"Who're you calling a bitch, Herr Doktor? Yalta happens to be my daughter, dickhead."

Father Clarence was now actually raising his hand. "Ms. Nussbaum, excuse me, Ms. Nussbaum, you said that the story was relevant to what we were talking about—you know, like our situation in this warehouse and why we're here in the first place. I'm sorry, but I just don't see how it's relevant. Wes, do you see the relevance?"

Chef Wu was shaking his head. "Nope, not relevant, completely off topic as far as I can tell. Max?"

Horn also shook his head, and for emphasis, rolled his eyes. "Sorry, Doc, I just can't relate to it, even though I happen to be a member of the tribe, which is beside the point and also irrel-evant. This story about some rabbi dudes and a rich bitch is a complete waste of time, it has nothing to do with me."

"Of course it's relevant," Hedy cried. "It's all about vessels—wine cups, wine barrels, men, women. We are all vessels—don't you see? Yalta is giving us a holy teaching. We are all vessels that can be filled with blessings, babies, insight. We are therefore of utmost value, because if the vessels are shattered, physically, emotionally, spiritually, everything inside is lost, wasted. What can be more relevant?"

From below in his wheelchair Gershon spoke, as if from on high. "Face it, Hedda, you screwed up. My fellow sex offenders are correct—none of this is relevant to us, if that matters, though it seems from how you've been carrying on that relevance is all. We were not talking about vessels—we unhappy few, we band of outcasts. We were not talking about blessings, or babies, or holy insight, or other such heartwarming pap. We were talking about the thing that is destroying us all. Desire. Sex. Lust. But I guess you don't have a PhD in lust. Maybe you should go back to Yale and get one."

The daf yomi kickoff was not a success, even Hedy had to concede that reality. Nevertheless, she decided to risk offering another session six days later, due to the auspicious confluence of leap year, always so ephemeral and unreal to her mind, and dreams, the topic riffed on by the rabbis on the designated page (Bera-khot 57) that fell on the upcoming quadrennial twenty-ninth of February: He who dreams of having sexual intercourse with his mother can look forward to attaining understanding; he who dreams of intercourse with a betrothed woman can anticipate Torah; dreams of intercourse with your sister, expect wisdom; dreams of intercourse with someone else's wife, count on the world to come—each interpretation backed up by a nonnegotiable verse from the unassailable texts.

Even Gershon Gordon would be forced to admit that this depraved material was relevant to the mission of Camp Jeffrey Epstein, Hedy figured. But lest he mortify her again with accusations of sophomoric over-interpretation related, in this case, to the performative power of dreams as a reflection of subconscious libido, she would undercut him by highlighting yet another dream on that very same page: He who sees a goose in his dream will attain wisdom, and if he has sexual intercourse with the goose, he will become the head of a yeshiva—validated in this instance not only by an authoritative textual citation but also by the great Rav Ashi himself who confirmed that he had had such a dream, he had seen a goose in his dream and had acquired wisdom, he had had intercourse with the goose and had duly ascended to greatness as the head of a major Babylonian center of learning. In normal times, Hedy would most likely have gone on to demonstrate how such a dream reflected a person's underlying sense of fraudulence, his imposter syndrome, not to mention his misogyny as well as his disrespect for fowls and poultry and other feathered creatures, but rather than belabor it in a way that would inevitably trigger Gershon Gordon's scorn, she decided instead to focus on its ridiculousness—the ridiculous dream of a ridiculous rabbi. Yes, she would highlight the absurdity of this goose dream and so many other dreams along with the ludicrous meanings attributed to them—that was Rav Ashi's point after all, she hoped—and she would do so by convening the daf yomi session in the Zuzi Epstein Playhouse, the thematically related theater space of the Jeffrey Epstein Social Hall, formerly the Murray Lokshin Casino and Lounge, where once in another life so many legendary comedians with big dreams had cut their teeth—Jerry, Joan, Jackie, the *J* for the you-know-what conspiracy. She, little Hedy Nussbaum, with her bushy, kinky head of ethnic hair, which, in multiple moments of self-loathing, she likened to the electrified wig of a clown, would run the session from the stage as if it were a stand-up comedy act. Too bad Arnie Glick was still in no shape to help her out, she prayed she could pull it off. Once again, after so many years cloistered in the academies of enlightenment instructed by eminences who fucked geese, she found herself praying.

But as Hedy was soon advised when she was summoned by Dr. Zoya Roy to an urgent private meeting, the recast theater space of the Jeffrey Epstein Social Hall known as the Zuzi Epstein Playhouse would not be available for one of her Talmudic séances that leap year evening. Furthermore, the event now scheduled to take place there on that night, the night of the upcoming February twenty-ninth, was one that everyone was required to attend, regardless of ideological stance, or physical or mental state of decay. Hedy should send out flyers at once canceling her little scripture club, preferably forever.

Zoya also felt obliged to add that she was extremely disappointed in Hedy's performance so far, her failure to recruit and deliver any of our campers' sexual harassment and abuse survivors willing to undergo Zoyaroyan Psychoempathy therapy up here at Camp Jeffrey Epstein, especially with all the incentives that were being dangled—the place had been turned into a goddamn spa to lure them up, Zoya declared. True, these were hard times, Zoya recognized that, what with word of a deadly virus spreading out of China, the number-one mass producer nowadays of anything and everything you can imagine in your worst nightmare, the virus already reaching our shores, moving relentlessly eastward from California—maybe people were not so willing to travel in such perilous times, Zoya speculated. But with some hundreds of victims at a minimum attributed just to their first cohort of ten campers at Camp Jeffrey Epstein, you would have thought that Hedy could have at least produced one traumatized soul who would be willing to make the trip up here to take the cure and simultaneously administer it to her abuser, even if only to get away from all that urban congestion as the grip of the epidemic tightened. Zoya had been ready to tear out her silken black tresses due to Hedy's failure of initiative, her lack of progress, her very bad hair, she felt so desperate, she felt as if her entire career was going down the tubes.

"Then out of the blue," Zoya went on, "I get this email from some nonprofit called JEV, Justice for Epstein Victims. Actually, the email was probably from an enterprising junior staff member or possibly even an intern there named Corona, some poor kid doing required volunteer community service or maybe a college dropout whose mom and dad were stoned out of their gourds when they chose that name for their neonate. Anyway, in this email, they— Corona's preferred pronoun is *they*," Zoya forewarned Hedy, "they informed me that they're handling a lecture tour for one of the premier Epstein survivors, who chooses to go by the name V—V for, well, never mind, you know for what, I don't have to spell it out—it's just a glimpse of how low her self-esteem has sunk, it is what she has been reduced to as a female, the organ distilled. For our purposes though, Zoya said, since our program also targets male survivors, it would be preferable to think of it as V for Victim, even if, as a general rule, we try to avoid that word with all of its negativity and hopelessness. Anyhow, bottom line, Zoya told Hedy, what they—that is, Corona—wants to know is whether we might be interested in having V come up to Camp Jeff to give a talk, maybe make a PowerPoint presentation of some sort, do a reading from her forthcoming book, a Q and A, whatever."

That "whatever" was the switch that had caused Zoya to pause just as she was about to press "delete" and eliminate the pitch. "Suddenly it occurred to me," Zoya recounted, her eyes crinkling wickedly, "that until our ineffectual little Hedy Nussbaum with her signature head of hair can get her act together and produce a proper survivor of one of our campers' abuse for a true, miraculously healing, epiphanic Zoyaroyan Psychoempathy therapy session, maybe we should do a kind of preview, like a trailer, a coming attraction, the professional debut of my treatment protocol, a teaser, so to speak—get this V up here with her handler, Corona, sit her down in a chair facing some kind of Jeffrey Epstein surrogate, and let her have a go at him in front of a full house. It even crossed my mind to ask our benefactor, the good Jeffrey Epstein, if he'd be willing to play the role of the bad guy, like Dr. Jekyll and Mr. Hyde, sort of like an understudy in the theater when the star gets sick or suddenly drops dead, it could be a blast, he might even get a kick out of it," Zoya said. She had actually flown this idea by her bestie, the other Zoya, the good Jeffrey's wife, as the two of them were lying naked on their stomachs with plush towels draped over the perfect domes of their rear ends, side by side on twin massage tables in her private bedroom suite in the Epstein Fifth Avenue penthouse. "Nyet," the stunning Zoya Epstein said, lifting her head and waggling a long, perfectly manicured finger side to side, then exploding into such a fit of hysterics, her whole body shaking, Dr. Zoya Roy reported to Hedy, that her masseuse could do nothing with her for the rest of the session.

Afterward, though, Mrs. Zoya Epstein pulled herself together like the true professional that she was, made a few quick calls with her characteristic efficiency, and now a life-sized effigy of the bad Jeffrey Epstein in his signature Harvard sweatshirt complete with an exact replica of his organ based on victim reports tucked into his sweatpants, perfectly reproduced in every detail, will be delivered on Saturday morning, February twenty-ninth, leap year day. V for Victim has very graciously agreed to the arrangement and will be arriving with her trafficker, Corona, later that morning. The show will go on that evening at seven p.m. promptly on the stage of the Zuzi Epstein Playhouse in the Jeffrey Epstein Social Hall to a full house of patients, staff, and very likely the good Mr. and Mrs. Jeffrey Epstein themselves in the front-row seats of honor. If Hedy aspires to tenure at Camp Jeffrey Epstein, Zoya added in a manner that Hedy experienced as deeply patronizing, not to mention menacing, she had better make sure that everything runs smoothly, without a single glitch or hitch. "This is a test," Zoya said. "Only a test. Not a real emergency. Only a dry run of violation and plague."

7.

No one who attended the event that February twenty-ninth in the Zuzi Epstein Playhouse could ever have imagined that this would be the last time into the indefinite future that they would be sitting in an auditorium shoulder to shoulder with other mortals capable of transmitting impurity. Not a single one of the plush seats in the hall was empty that night, a packed house of coughers, sneezers, snifflers, swallowers, lozenge suckers, throat clearers, belchers and burpers, nose blowers, nose pickers, gas passers, heavy breathers, heart beaters, death rattlers.

The patron who had endowed this dazzling facility and proudly flashed his name on its figurative marquee, the good Jeffrey Epstein, accompanied by his flamboyantly glamorous first lady, claimed their reserved places in the first row, their two IDF-trained bodyguards in black leaning against the wall chewing gum, mighty arms folded over major pecs. All ten campers were present and accounted for, Arnie Glick among them, curled up under a hospital blanket with his tongue dangling out of the side of his open mouth like the tail of the letter Q, seemingly comatose in a wheelchair pushed into the theater by Ms. Smiley and positioned at the end of the first row alongside Gershon Gordon's chair, prime parking spaces reserved for the handicapped and disabled, the consolation prize. Every employee connected to the operation was there—the dining room and kitchen staff, not excluding the sprung jailbirds, front desk, grounds, house-keeping and concierge, business office, maintenance and repairs, and so on. On top of that, thanks to Hedy's creative thinking, an open invitation had been extended to officials and residents of the surrounding towns in order to calm their steadily mounting fears concerning the presence in their midst of a facility bearing such a universally reviled name and, what's more, sheltering known sex offenders, including, most alarmingly, certified pedophiles. The displeasure of the locals had by now been vociferously made known in the media, online, and in person by screaming protesters waving placards, marching back and forth in front of the main gate in a spreadsheet rotation schedule seven days a week. Hedy had said to Zoya, "This is an opportunity, we can invite them to this public event so they can see for themselves that we're responsible actors." The invitation that accordingly was extended to the agitators was received with genuine distaste, though in the end the decision was made to hold their noses and dispatch a small fact-finding delegation to the event. Less public-spirited citizens, on the other hand, arrived in their multitudes, pouring in, swarming with curiosity and excitement, filling all the remaining seats, spilling into the aisles, packing the rear of the Zuzi Epstein Playhouse, leaking into the dedicated therapeutic spaces of the Jeffrey Epstein Social Hall. It was standing-room only, a crowd-control event that, within a few weeks, would be labeled a super spreader. Hedy would cringe with horror when she recalled the full-frontal display of her denseness, her tempting of the gods.

As the theater filled up, she rushed around on the stage, putting the finishing touches on the arrangements based on her conception of what a serious colloquium should look like, drawn from all her years in academia, and from her annual subscription to cultural events at the Ninety-Second Street Y on Lexington Avenue in New York City. Three armchairs had been set out, the one for Zoya in the center, facing the audience, the other two on either side angled slightly forward downstage, facing each other. A decision was made not to include a central table of any height in the interest specifically of achieving full exposure of the body language of the offender and the survivor. Instead, a low side table was set next to each chair with a pitcher of water and a glass on top, even alongside the chair reserved for the inanimate Jeffrey Epstein surrogate, in a nod to verisimilitude and inclusion. The names of the three panelists were beamed in lights behind them, positioned above, relative to their chairs—a classy touch, in the opinion of all, courtesy of the benefactress, Mrs. Zoya Epstein.

V for Victim, no longer nubile but more emphatically golden haired than ever, entered first accompanied by Corona, who with utmost solicitude helped to settle her in the chair to Zoya's left, planting her bulging handbag securely alongside her feet, pouring out a glass of water for her in anticipation of her need, and placing on her table within easy reach a jumbo box of Kleenex along with a receptacle for the inevitable moist and linty residue following heavy usage. Next, Dr. Zoya Roy strode confidently onto the stage in a bespoke burgundy pantsuit of the finest wool impeccably tailored for a licensed professional, paired with matching stilettos, her gleaming black hair gathered in a nonfrivolous coil at the nape of her neck, diamonds flashing in her ears to blink discreetly at the proud ethnic identity stud tucked in the cleft of her nostril, the earrings pressed on her for the occasion by Mrs. Zoya Epstein, at whom she smiled, waved, and even, at the risk of stepping out of her official role and popping the illusion, puckered a discreet kiss dispatched with one fingertip as she took her designated seat. A technician approached and affixed a mic to Zoya's lapel while she surveyed the audience, then rested her trained, piercing gaze on V, whom the technician was now miking, closely overseen by Corona.

Only after feeling fully satisfied that V was comfortable and at ease did Corona withdraw, grabbing a handful of tissues for her own needs as she retreated. She took up her position at the entrance at stage left from which to monitor V's status, like a private nurse at her station, a spot visible to Gershon in his wheelchair across the hall almost directly opposite, alongside the nonresponsive Arnie Glick, who by then had receded entirely underneath his hospital blanket in his own wheelchair, in the aisle at the end of the first row. Corona's head was shaved, their menswear button-down white shirt, tie, belt, and cuffed trousers concealed a bulked-up, though discordantly busty and full-hipped torso, the tattoo on the side of their neck that Gershon could not quite make out from that distance seemed to evoke in part the miserably familiar EKG skyline of #MeToo. Yet there was something in Corona's stance, gestures, the almost ladylike hand clutching tissue over mouth to suppress the rude noise of a bodily function such as a sneeze, no doubt as instructed by her mother, the total gestalt, that revived for Gershon the ghost of Yalta, his daughter, whom he had not seen in at least three years, ever since he had been nearly garroted by the hashtag and his whole world had crashed to pieces.

He watched in astonishment as, from that same corner where the haunting Corona was standing guard, little Hedy Nussbaum now emerged, lugging what looked like a huge duffel bag, or maybe it was a floppy mattress slung over her head and shoulders and hanging down below her waist on either side. She crossed the stage as if in a mobile tomb, Birnam wood come to Dunsinane, until she arrived at the chair under the Jeffrey Epstein sign flashing overhead and set her prop down. Zealously screening its mystery as she fussed over it, she seemed to finally have arranged it to her satisfaction. Ta-da—Hedy unveiled it to the crowd, which gasped in chorus as she flitted away toward the mysterious innards of backstage not far from where Corona had taken up her position, lingering at the exit there with a direct view of her two high-maintenance patients in their wheelchairs, Ms. Smiley erect at her station behind them.

The face on the figure that Hedy had revealed when she glided away so deftly was a masterful rendering of the dark prince of offenders—long, swarthy, Semitic, perpetually amused rays at the corners of the eyes, that smug, superior smile, the roguish boyishness belied by the silver hair, the look of something between a mugshot and a death mask, instantly identifiable.

"Jesus Christ, it's a Jeffigy," Gershon cried.

Like Bruno Schulz's tailors' dummies, Gershon's thoughts linked instantly—a Jeffery Epstein dummy, imprisoned in a joke, a parody, howling in the night, banging his fists against his prison walls.

From her lofty position of power on the stage Dr. Zoya Roy lanced Gershon with a forbidding look, then dismissed him completely in favor of bonding with an audience of commoners as together they went about the business of testing her amplification. "Can everybody hear me?" she inquired, casting her eye to the farthest reaches of the chamber, and instantly was rewarded with the approval and thumbs-up of a chorus of accomplices. She smiled, suctioning them all up into her radiance, and said, "Can *Anybody* hear me? This is our question for the evening."

To Be Heard, that is the goal of Zoyaroyan Psychoempathy therapy, she elaborated—for the survivor, complete purging and release through being heard, truly heard—for the offender, genuine empathy, vicarious understanding and compassion achieved through finally listening, truly hearing, taking it in, becoming in effect the other, the survivor, followed by a life sentence of remorse and restitution. She, Dr. Zoya Roy, was there only to facilitate the process, her verbal interventions would consequently be kept to the barest minimum. "Hopefully, the only voice you will hear will be that of our survivor." Zoya nodded and gestured warmly to her left. "Our speaker chooses at this time to go by the unhappy name of V, for Victim, but the hope is, after fully offloading onto her offender she will move on to V for Voice, V for Victory."

V for Vagina, V for Vulva—the litany rose up from various points in the pit—V for Viper, V for Venom, V for Virus! But as quickly and as crudely as the chant ascended and contaminated the airspace, so it faded away. The troublemakers, whoever they were, could not be nailed down. The bouncers in black who had been instantly dispatched by the ultra-alert Mrs. Zoya Epstein retreated to their watch post emptyhanded as Gershon Gordon, properly subdued, leaned on the armrest of his comrade Arnie Glick's wheelchair, resting his head on the blanket under which his friend lay curled up like a fetus.

Dr. Zoya Roy moved on as if the preceding disruption had been merely the crepitation of a perverse imagination. "Seated opposite V, ladies and gentlemen, we have our stand-in—or more to the point, slouch-in—for V's offender, the infamous Jeffrey Epstein, who is unable to be here with us in person this evening, because, as the whole world knows, he's dead. As his final, and, I might add, most cowardly act, he took his own life in his jail cell rather than face the consequences for his actions."

"Ma'am?" It was Dr. Fritz Rosenberg's raised voice. "Just so you know—no way Epstein did himself in, he was offed by the Elders of Zion."

"Shut up, psycho," Gershon spat out. He thrust his upper body forward in his chair as if he were about to lunge, but Ms. Smiley, positioned behind Glick's wheelchair, grabbed hold of the collar of Gershon's black sports jacket with one hand to rein him in, while with the other hand she slapped a mask across his mouth to muffle him, securing it with elastics around his ears, inconsiderately tipping his black velvet yarmulke to a drunken angle in the process.

Distracted, Dr. Zoya Roy followed this entire interlude as if mesmerized, then caught herself, stepped over to the dummy and sealed its mouth with a mask as well before returning center stage and segueing back to her opening remarks. "I hope you can all see the mask I've just placed across the mouth of our Jeffrey Epstein effigy up here, ladies and gentlemen." She pointed to the stuffed imposter. From all sides, audience members rubbernecked to get a good look. Yes, it was a fact, the mannequin was wearing a mask, one of the first to seize their attention in a long line of masks that in the succeeding months would become so commonplace, riveting one to the reality of the poisonous life breath of the other.

Dr. Zoya Roy continued, "In addition to choosing to represent the offender with a dummy, who, as the name suggests, is unable to speak, the placement of a mask across its mouth is our way of visually keeping your mental focus on the essential fact that in the psychoempathy encounter, the rule is, the offender must remain absolutely silent. Friends, we cannot and do not want to place masks across your mouths as well, but as this confrontation gets underway, we must insist on absolute silence from members of the audience too—no applause, no hisses, no whistles, no catcalls, no boos, no cheers, no hecklings, you get the idea. You must think of this space as a kind of operating theater in which the most delicate cutting-edge brain or heart surgery is being performed—a single unexpected sound, the knife slips . . . But no, we will not go there, we will not allow such negative thoughts, we will not countenance such a disaster scenario under our watch, we will follow procedures exactly for the sake of restoring health and, yes, justice."

She paused to appreciate her own rhetoric—like basking in her own body odor, Gershon thought, which only the one who emits it can enjoy.

"So then," she went on with a sly grin as if she had read his mind, "it is my duty to forewarn you to turn yourselves off completely, all of your audible bodily functions along, of course, with your cell phone appendages, anyone who breaks these rules will be automatically ejected, that's the protocol, no exceptions, nothing personal. In this ultimate showdown, only our survivor V may speak, addressing the offender directly in the second person—You! You!—doing her very best to sling into his face his very worst."

Zoya waited to allow the exquisite symmetry of her clause to sink in. To Gershon's eyes she seemed drained, he would have liked to comfort her, a foot massage maybe, he was her slave, never mind her intellectual limitations, her cockamamie theories, her adorable pretensions at gravitas.

"One more thing, ladies and gentlemen." She was wrapping it up. "Before I turn it over to our survivor, I would just like to take a moment to express our gratitude to our benefactor, Mr. Jeffrey Epstein, the good Jeffrey Epstein, the creator of our institute and for whom it is so rightfully named. You know, friends, Shakespeare famously asked, What's in a name? Infinite possibilities, infinite responsibilities, that is my answer, especially when one so good just happens to share a name with one so evil. Instead of allowing that coincidence to eliminate him from the game, lead him to give up—instead of getting a nose job, so to speak, and changing his name as so many others in his position might have done—our noble Jeffrey Epstein has come out swinging, boldly, proudly, generously, aiming to cleanse the name, to purify it, launder it, as it were—and, well, you know, whatever, the rest is history."

Abruptly, she halted, as if struggling to figure something out, something about this weird project of the good Jeffrey Epstein, something to explain his obsession, his futile effort to sever his connection to the bad Jeffrey Epstein, whose extreme debauchery and lasciviousness seemed to confirm the world's darkest convictions about the nature of the Jewish race. For the first time, as she was grappling with this idea, there seemed to be a lapse of confidence in the majestic countenance of Dr. Zoya Roy. Gershon observed this from over the mask, with which he had been gagged against his will as he rested his cheek on the blanketed chest cavity containing the beating heart of his poor Yorick. He found Zoya's obvious distraction to be almost touching, she seemed to have gotten lost in her words. He was a word man, he would have liked to help her out, to rescue her, disentangle her strand by strand, but before he could reach out to her, her well-toned survival instinct kicked in. She lowered her regal head and gestured in the direction of her patron, the good Jeffrey Epstein, who, unfortunately, seemed to be missing in action. During the entire time she had been so lavishly praising him he had not heard a single word she had said, she had not earned a single point, he had been gone, a call of nature no doubt. But his trophy partner, thank goodness, was faithfully in her assigned seat listening to every word, gorgeously filling in for her man. On cue, Mrs. Zoya Epstein levitated three-quarters from her chair, executed a three-quarters swivel toward the crowd, and simulating a notion of humility, moved her hand from side to side metronomically in a bobbly wave like her majesty the queen, acknowledging the applause.

"V? The floor is now yours," Dr. Zoya Roy declared, gesturing only the necessary amount to figuratively pass the baton, obviously depleted, poor thing, Gershon felt for her, yes, he empathized, already she was leaning back in her chair and deflating.

"You go get him, girl," Zoya whispered hoarsely, "and good luck to you." And good riddance, it rang to Gershon's ears.

V stood up, grabbed her bulbous handbag from the floor rather than leaving it there unprotected, and simultaneously she drew a bountiful mass of tissues from the dispenser, balling them in her fist. Equipped with these essentials, she lumbered like the bottle blonde matron she now was across the no-man's-land dividing her territory from that of her offender, and planted herself in front of his life-sized image. She plunged in, as Dr. Zoya Roy had instructed. "You! You destroyed my life. I was only fourteen years old, I still had braces on my teeth!" She raised her purse and swung it across the dummy's face—whack! "You said you were hiring me to give you massages, you had this thing for massages"—she lashed the bag again across its face in the opposite direction—whack! "You ordered me to take off my shorts and my halter. You forced me to take off my panties"—whack! "You told me I was beautiful. Thanks to you, I've felt ugly ever since"—whack! "I've never been able to accept a compliment again, you creep!"

"Gee, that's awful, I'm so sorry, that was really mean of me."

The dummy Jeffrey Epstein was actually talking from its designated chair on the stage. You couldn't see its lips moving, because of the mask, but there was no doubt that words were coming out of its mouth like a vocalized cartoon bubble, never mind that his speaking was a flagrant breach of the rules as set down by Dr. Zoya Roy. The men in black instantly stiffened in alertness, visually raking the territory to expose the source of this insult, searching in vain, returning to their mistress empty-handed and ashamed.

"You raped me, again and again"—V whipped him with the bag, this way and that.

"Hey, that really hurts. Can we talk?" The dummy was pleading.

"You groomed me to be a teenage whore. You passed me around to your power pals, like a plaything. You showed me your little black book with all their bold-face names. You showed me your command control center with cameras all over the place, in every nook and cranny, even in the toilets." Her pocketbook was slapping back and forth across the perfect facsimile of his face.

At the edge of the front row, Gershon appeared to be sleeping, his head on the curled-up form of Arnie Glick, his grizzled cheek under the mask that had been thrust upon him resting by the wet spot on Arnie's hospital blanket over Arnie's mouth, relaxing to the vibration and buzz of Arnie's larynx underneath, the soothing rise and fall of Arnie's diaphragm, absorbing the living exhalation, the internal groan of his voice thrown out to seek its fortune like a bird from its nest. From Hedy Nussbaum's concealed vantage point in an almost direct line, it was a rare, sweet sight, such tenderness between the afflicted, her two difficult patients as innocent as babes joined in repose. She wondered where Ms. Smiley was, probably the ladies' room, though it was definitely a dereliction of duty. She was asleep at the wheelchair.

V threw her sodden Kleenex ball at the dummy, and began rummaging furiously in her purse. "You sent me out to the high schools and the shopping malls and all the McDonalds to pimp fresh girls for you." She hurled her keys at the dummy. "You manipulated me with your money and your power and your connections." Her hairbrush slammed against its forehead. "You raped my little sister." She cluster bombed it with a burst of tampons. "You said I was fat." She smacked it with a bag of Jelly Bellys.

"Gee, you brought me your little sister." The dummy was talking again. "That was so nice of you."

Dr. Zoya Roy was standing up now with her hands in the air like a cop controlling traffic to forestall any possible attempt at interference in V's necessary post-traumatic catharsis by some heckler, some joker, some disruptive type in the audience, or by an obsessive staff member clinging to the original script mandating total silence from the offender, or maybe also by the over-protective Corona toward whom, in a designated patrol position just offstage, she glanced reassuringly, though from where Gershon was now resting his head on Arnie's chest, listening and marveling, the zealous guardian no longer was visible. Zoya was reframing the plot in her mind, for herself and also for her public, as if this outcome unfolding in front of them had been her therapeutic intention all along—to enable the survivor to get it out of her system in whatever way worked best for her, emptying herself out completely along with the contents of her bag on the journey to health.

V's handbag slumped to the floor, she was waving a pair of scissors triumphantly in the air. This was probably what she had been foraging for all along. She slashed the dummy's Harvard sweatshirt right down the middle, bisecting the V at the fork, on a roll as she hacked her way downward through the elastic of its sweatpants straight to the crotch. "You had this weird little egg-shaped penis with this itty-bitty stem—like a toadstool," she spitefully broadcast for public consumption.

A circumcised penis, that's what she's describing so flatteringly, a textbook case of implicit antisemitism, Gershon noted clinically as he observed her from so up close taking it all out on the Jeffrey ragdoll. Once long ago, in her beauty's prime, she probably had not yet run into a pecker like that, none of Jeffrey's little blondes had. "Yeah, a little shit-colored mushroom," she pushed on with her tour, "really teeny-weeny, can't even find it anymore, I guess it just got lost in all this stuffing." She was tossing what looked like volumes of shredded paper all over the floor of the stage, it was flying into the audience, snagging in the nest of Gershon's white hair like confetti at a parade, piling up on the blanketed hump of Arnie Glick, falling like flower petals into the lap of Mrs. Zoya Epstein front-row center who had paid for this custom-made filling and was now checking to see whether it consisted of the remains of books and articles about the evil Epstein, as she had requested, the perfect hostess's discreet, understated touch. She had also paid for a faithful replica of the bad Jeffrey Epstein's organ, now apparently missing and unaccounted for, she intended to demand a refund, she was born a poor girl in Saratov, USSR, in the bad old days of communism, she still understood the value of money.

V now seized the dummy's deflated shell with her two hands, clawing each shoulder, shaking it savagely. "You know what's the worst thing you ever did to me? It was when you went and killed yourself, you coward. You cheated me of my day in court. I'm not only demanding a big fat chunk of your filthy lucre, monster. I'm demanding justice."

Dr. Zoya Roy glided closer with exemplary diffidence, tapped V's trembling shoulder, and enfolded her in her arms as the poor woman sobbed pitifully, shaking and hacking out her wails. Still locked in the hug, the doctor-in-chief's face was turned away from the full unhygienic force of this gale of tears and looked toward the audience, which was already going about the business of rustling up its personal effects, releasing polluted batteries of suppressed coughs as during a break between musical movements at a concert, packing up and escaping. The evening has been a stunning success, Dr. Zoya Roy seemed to be mouthing, it has been a true catharsis for the survivor, the therapy session has run without a hitch, exactly as planned.

"Ma'am?" Dr. Fritz Rosenberg, standing at the foot of the stage, was calling up to V, intruding on her quality time with Zoya. "Ma'am, just so you know—no way your guy did himself in. It was the Mossad, they neutralized him due to the fact that they figured he'd rat on them to get a lighter sentence, they made it look like suicide. He was working for the Zionists, just for your information, trafficking underage blondes like you to service the top dogs, and passing all the dirt to the Israelis for blackmail purposes. And by the way, he only trafficked shiksas. Need I say more? Hope that helps."

He would have liked to say more, there was so much to add,

but just as he was opening his mouth to elaborate, he was flattened against the rising platform wall of the stage by a moving object navigated at top speed by Gershon Gordon who ripped off his mask, yelling, "Antisemite scum, Nazi pervert," propelling his wheelchair straight into the wrong turn in human evolution that was Fritz Rosenberg. Luckily, at that very moment, Ms. Smiley returned to the hall—at the same moment, as a matter of fact, as the good Jeffrey Epstein. Each entered through a separate door, one marked for Blacks and one marked for Jews. Thus, Ms. Smiley was well positioned to instantly slip into her role as first responder, to execute crisis intervention, to load Dr. Fritz Rosenberg, who, thank goodness, was not bleeding or discharging any other bodily fluids, into her Mercedes and spirit him away to her infirmary up on the hill in order to check him out for internal damages and to administer other necessary emergency services.

Gershon Gordon, meanwhile, remained stalled in place at the foot of the stage, dazed, as Hedy Nussbaum knelt at its edge looking down, as if she had crawled there, her hair electrified by fright. "You okay?" she whispered, leaning over. By way of answer, he spun his head toward his left shoulder, pointing with his chin to Arnie Glick abandoned there in his wheelchair. "She forgot the baby," Gershon stated simply. He waited to let the deeper implications of his words sink in. "No big deal, he's okay anyway," he added. As evidence, he pulled a rancid sock out of his pocket, punctuating the airwaves with its aged toe-cheese stink as he passed it to her. "All the pills she made him take to mess with his head are in there, you can count them. I'm trusting you, he gave it to me for safekeeping just a few minutes ago."

Hedy accepted the sock with two pincered fingers and nose averted, she looked as if she were undergoing a trial by ordeal, if her belly swelled and her thighs rotted, she was guilty. Then she closed her fist over the sock as if to claim it, to take possession of it, and Gershon nodded. She had passed, she had affirmed her loyalties, she was on his side—in the ceremony of the passing of the sock, she had declared her commitment by receiving the sock. Gershon assigned her first mission—to take care of Arnie Glick, convey him to his room, do whatever it takes to put him to bed. "He's a growing boy, he needs his rest after such a hard night's work," Gershon said, "it was a brilliant performance, five stars. For myself, I desire nothing more now than to be left alone—I need some 'alone time,' as you mental-health types like to say in your insidious, tyrannical kindergarten talk—you know, like 'thank you for sharing.' Well, sister, I don't know if you've heard the news yet, but our sharing days are over. The planet is being consumed by plague, and I must return to my cave, alone."

Exiting the theater via the handicap ramp under the sanctified new moon, Gershon Gordon in his wheelchair followed the paved pathway leading to the main building. The winter night was still eerily warm with that faintly unhealthy, unseasonal edge, and the days remained unnaturally hot in temperature and full of foreboding. He approached the grand entrance, but instead of proceeding straight ahead, he turned sharply to his right onto a dirt pathway that brought him around the great Gothic pile that had once been the Lokshin Hotel and Country Club and was now Camp Jeffrey Epstein, to the battered rear service entry and directly into the long bleak kitchen. He pushed against the door. As usual, it was unlocked, they always left it open for him though it exposed them to easy discovery and shrank their warning margin. He really should consider upping his group tip to a buck by way of gratitude.

Five bailed-out menials, former inmates, were lounging on some jumbo-sized garbage bags spread out across the eternally wet, lethally slippery floor, leaning against the wall alongside the industrial-sized freezer, illuminated only by the low-voltage lighting of the large appliances and the intense red glow of the tip of the circulating joint. Now and then one of them would thrust his upper body forward to stab a spoon or ladle inside the big slop bucket into which they had dumped all the leftovers from every guest's plate, and he would scoop out a mouthful or lean back to finish off the remaining beer or wine from a guest's clouded glass or uncorked bottle. By guest they mean people like me, Gershon kept in mind, asses we called them in our day, referencing the eaters by the body part warming a chair around the table, the body part through which the food being stuffed into wet mouths was destined to be evacuated. Now he, Gershon, had risen in status from server to ass, claiming a seat at the table, partaking of its bounty, a Camp Jeff privileged harasser, abuser, predator—alleged rapist even, like these five outcasts, these ex-cons. They were sprawled out on the plastic, each isolated in his own music delivered through his own personal lifesaving catheter, eyes closed, body rippling, head swaying. Looming above them, Gershon in his wheelchair rubbed the side of his nose up and down. Some blow would do him good now, some nice schmeck, he deserved it after all he had gone through tonight, but instead one of the guys passed him the roach, it looked like they were out of the real stuff. Gershon nodded and took a drag. It always bothered him that on account of his wheelchair they were forced to stretch their arms upward from the floor to pass him the junk, he was elevated as if enthroned. But they showed no signs of resentment, they gave off acceptance, pure resignation.

The food-sharing days, the joint-passing days—were they aware that all of these were about to come to an end? What deadly gifts had they brought to him from distant stricken lands, what unclean parts of their bodies had they fondled while cooking his food, with whom had they rutted? On a cloud of cannabis, Gershon summoned up from the orgone box of the abyss his ex-friend, Jeffrey Epidemic. No one loved him, nobody mourned him, other than the legions of women and girls whom he had used and discarded, who cursed him for dying and desired only to bring him back to life, to dredge him back up from Gehinnom so that they could crucify him, suck him dry, and then kill him all over again. This was an idea he intended to elaborate on in the book he was writing at the Camp Jeff artists' retreat, as he preferred to think of it. He had finally unblocked, thank God, he was going strong, already he had pounded out more than sixty pages on his electric Smith Corona portable complete with carbon copies. It was taking shape as a kind of journal of his Jeffrey Epstein days, for him a rare personal narrative, the story of two restless, ambitious Jewish boys from the same Brooklyn pale of settlement who set out into the wide world to seek their fortunes, each encountering obstacles and trials along the way, one sinking into the sloughs of evil, the other ultimately achieving enlightenment. Put this way, maybe it sounded a little self-serving, Gershon conceded, he wasn't recalling it properly, he had smoked a lot of weed. But as they used to say in his formative years in yeshiva, there was a khiddush here, a novel twist. The entire narrative was elevated and exalted from mundane memoir through creative fusing with the mysticism of the second century of the common era along with medieval kabbalistic texts, the teachings of Rabbi Shimon bar Yokhai of Meron and of Rabbi Isaac Luria, the Ari of Safed, touching on good and evil—the sefirot, the Divine attributes of the godhead on the side of the good, versus the sitra ahra, the other side, the emanation on the left, third air, the requirement to achieve purification by fire, to descend to the lowest depths of sin and transgression, like the angels descending the ladder in Jacob's dream—descent for the sake of ascending.

Gershon had no idea what time it was—coming up on two

or three hours before sunrise maybe, time for morning prayers. Without bidding farewell to his companions of the night, he left the kitchen, instinctively slowing as he maneuvered his wheelchair down the subtle slope of the kitchen floor and around the drop of the embedded drain along which so many waiters and busboys had slipped and trays had crashed, the topography had carved itself into his neurons, then out through the double doors that led into the vast dining hall, seeking his way out of the darkness through a labyrinth of tables with chairs turned over upside down on top blocking his passage, into the grand lobby, so much easier to traverse thanks to the iridescent lights sparkling in the spumes of water shooting up from the fabulous centerpiece fountain, and from there easily locating his handicapped-accessible room on the ground floor.

Everything seemed in order when he entered, the strong metallic smell of his typewriter whetted his creative appetite, raised his hopes for a productive next day. He headed straight for the bathroom, flipped the light switch affixed low on the wall for easy reach from a wheelchair, hoisted himself up by the two railings on either side of the toilet, unzipped and commenced his business without thinking too hard about the matter. But soon it registered that his stream was producing an unusual sound upon landing, causing him to cast his eyes down and gaze into the bowl at last. The formerly white porcelain had turned bluish-purple in color due to the carbon paper, the bowl itself was now stuffed with the viciously macerated pages of his manuscript plus two carbon copies per page, nearly two hundred pulped sheets of Jeffrey Epstein matter filling the bowl almost to the rim, as such pulp had filled his poor friend's sad effigy, all of this personalized on top with a fecal-deposit signature, a message from one sniffing dog to another. Unwittingly, he had been urinating on his work in progress, which was, of course, a sacrilege as it contained the name of God, including the tetragrammaton, due to the kabbalistic references. These were sacred texts, and this was an act of antisemitism, like Kristallnacht, but the genocidal destruction there before his eyes also explained the strange muffled sound of his stream upon contact, the still small voice. And what about the pipes and plumbing now stuffed with his output? The kindred spirit of Bruno Schulz, his soulmate murdered in the Shoah, gripped Gershon again, the uncle whose illness had turned him into the rubber tubing of an enema—Could anything be sadder? the author asks. Possibly a human turned into a dummy stuffed with the record of his own disgrace, Gershon thought. The source of the intense typewriter smell was then in short order also explained by the black ribbon ruthlessly unwound and soaked, dangling from the showerhead in the form of a noose—this was a lynching on top of a pogrom. The remains of his beloved typewriter were laid out for viewing like a corpse on the transfer bench for the aged and disabled under the dripping water, furiously flattened and destroyed.

Who could have committed such a vicious act against him, who could have hated him so much—he, the adored son of a mother, a Holocaust survivor, who had given birth to him in pain and who had loved him more than her own life? How had it happened that he, Gershon Gordon, the light unto the nations, had ended up in a sleepaway camp for superannuated, racist sex delinquents? And why of all campers had he been singled out to be stripped of the status of offender, to be so personally defiled and thereby downgraded to survivor, to victim? Why had he been targeted as the object of this barbaric camp tradition, this philistine raid—this unbearably intimate violation?

8.

Later, Gershon would resurrect the Talmudic dictum pounded into his head during a brief and disastrous youthful stint as a foot soldier in the Brooklyn division of Rabbi Meir Kahane's militant Jewish Defense League: If someone comes to kill you, rise up early and kill him first. Self-defense. Never again. The lessons of the Holocaust. But during those surrealistic predawn hours of that Kristallnacht when he had discovered the raid, he was not in any shape to channel what had been inflicted upon him in this way. It was only later that he recognized that it had been at that moment, when he had been confronted with the carnage and desecration of all his labors, when he had faced the pogrom directed so personally against his very essence and being—it was at that very moment, he later realized, that he had resolved to cease collaborating in his own destruction. His task had become far weightier than to expose the inane therapeutic system along with its practitioners in this two-bit sanatorium under the sign of the hourglass. It surpassed by far the perverse madness that had gripped the known world, private intimidation, public shaming, accusation followed not by trial or due process but by instant excommunication and erasure—the consensus that you no longer existed, civil death. It was then that his mission truly became nothing less than to rise up early and lead the battle against the ancient hatred that had detonated all of these latter-day atrocities, for it was clear to anyone with eyes to see that in every flare up, he and his people were singled out for blame and censure, for degradation and extermination in savagely disproportionate numbers. He, Gershon Gordon, had been called to action by the latest vicious spasms of Jew hatred that had also struck him most intimately, calling to him as if from the blue core of the burning bush that is never consumed to raise the flag and lead the battle. All of this Gershon recognized and understood—later.

But in those early morning hours when he had returned to his room and discovered that he had been the victim of so personal a violation, he in no way felt himself to be of the divine elect. He felt doomed, as if caught in some infernal replay of the moment when the hash-trap had first dropped over him and snapped shut, leaving him stunned, clawing at its metal grid like a rat. The difference this time was that it was not the intangibles of name and reputation and career that had been wiped out, it was his personal material culture, his private trove, his sacred texts, which he had tended so meticulously and over which he had taken such pains, the intellectual fruit of his loom, that had been pawed by strangers and trashed. As much as it embarrassed him to find himself thinking in clichés, he felt as if he had been raped. The irony was that he of all people had been thrust against his will into a state of psychoempathy. If that slut Zoya Roy wanted to squeeze empathy out of some poor schmuck, a raid that ravages his very being was the way to go, forget about your compulsory, coerced public psycho shows. Instinctively he had been transformed into the classic rape victim who desires only to crawl under a bush and disappear, who refuses to report the crime to the officials. There's your empathy, baby.

Having absorbed how radically he had been defiled, his most

urgent need, as he went on sitting there in that rising stench for he knew not how long, pondering his revised circumstances post traumatically, was to keep the whole matter absolutely confidential, top secret. No recollection remained to him of depositing himself back in his wheelchair after viewing the wreckage in the sterile bathroom space designed for unfortunates like himself, he reflected bitterly, with all of that flat square footage for maneuverability, all of those gleaming silver grab bars for support, under those pitiless glaring lights. But back now in his chair, his upper body tensed forward like Rodin's *Thinker*, elbow on knee and right hand propping his chin, he had a direct line of sight into the toilet bowl stuffed with his incredibly disrespected manuscript, and, in that ultimate statement, topped with the exclamation point of a turd. It was imperative that no one on the inside know what had been done to him, that was his uppermost concern at this time, such a disclosure would render his carefully honed persona terminally enfeebled, it would nail his vulnerability. This maliciously personal act of trespass and vandalism must remain one hundred percent confidential, and, most crucially, its decimating effect upon him must be hidden, especially from the perpetrators—naturally, he had some idea who these lowlife antisemites might be, but for now, all of that seemed beside the point. Above all, those cretins must not be allowed to derive satisfaction from having caused him distress on any level. He must, by burying the whole matter, engineer it so that they come to doubt that they had even committed this outrage, the vision of themselves ransacking his most intimate possessions in this targeted attack must be made to seem to them like a hallucination, let them come to feel they are losing their grip on reality, losing their minds. To push them over the mental-health edge by acting as if nothing had happened seemed to Gershon a vengeance far sweeter than whatever any public quest for justice might yield.

On the downside, this secrecy requirement also meant he would not be able to inform the management of the drastically unhygienic state of his private facilities, he realized. In the most immediate sense, this translated to refraining from summoning the janitorial staff to deal with the looming waste overload emergency. He did not require much, but functioning plumbing was a top priority. Would he be forced to do the job himself? The problem required a solution—meaning, a menial of no account to do the dirty work, an essential frontline worker in whose honor all rise and applaud at the end of the day, he, too, would stand up if only he could stand. Bottom line, though, for the foreseeable future, no one with any links to persons of interest must enter his room, even to empty his chamber pot.

Nor, for the foreseeable future, did he intend to leave his room; it was, for now, his sanctuary city, his prison cell. Considering all he had just gone through, how ruthlessly he had been invaded to his very anima, as it were, he simply could not imagine himself carrying on with the daily drill of this cuckoo's nest perched on top of its magic mountain—the three heavy meals, the therapy sessions in all their mindless permutations, the Teutonic schedule of forced exercise and socializing and medication and rest, the whole despotic deal. He deserved a break, a leave of absence, but it was essential that he arrange one for himself in such a way that those who had sinned so unforgivably against his essential personhood not get the satisfaction of assuming he had been critically wounded, or wounded at all, that they not take credit for having forced him to withdraw from the stage in order to recover from the staggering blow they had dealt him.

The solution came effortlessly, he was already implementing it even before he fully realized he had arrived at it. He did not own a cell phone, in accordance with his personal creed, but there on his nightstand was your basic hotel landline, a relic from the previous incarnation of this establishment, and taped to the wall was a list of emergency contacts, topped by Dr. Zoya Roy, number one on the hit parade. It was maybe four or five in the morning when he called, she fumbled connecting, her voice was gravelly from sleep, he could almost smell her humid bed warmth, from the same intimate airspace as her sleep-swollen body he could also hear a Slavic-accented female voice—could she actually be in bed with her predecessor and prototype, Dr. Zoya Rubinchuk? There was no time, however, for small talk. Ramming ahead, Gershon reminded her of all the coughers and fatal fluid sprayers in the audience at the Camp Jeffrey Epstein psychoempathy show last night—did she remember, or was she just in denial? Well, Gershon went on, he had checked, he had looked into the matter, and for Zoya's information, one of these hackers was now attached to a ventilator, having been rushed directly from the event to the ICU at the Liberty, New York, hospital right here in Sullivan County. This alarming news, Gershon went on, led him to consult his own family practitioner, as well as his personal attorney, Mr. S. Fink, Esquire, senior partner in the world-famous firm of Abercrombie and Fink, both of whom strongly counseled him to self-isolate for a period of fourteen days in accordance with the most up-to-date guidelines of the Centers for Disease Control following contact with a likely—in this case, a confirmed—novel coronavirus pestilence carrier. He was calling her as a courtesy to let her know that he was entering full quarantine mode as of now and would not be available for any form of therapy, however cutting edge and restorative, for the next two weeks at a minimum. He further strongly recommended that everyone who had been present at the event be apprised of the situation and be required to quarantine as well, the entire place must go into total lockdown, following the professional scientific guidelines of the CDC. That means, all of his fellow patients must remove themselves from all variations of human and animal intercourse, the clean and the unclean, staff and administration, as well as visitors and guests, including the Jeffrey Epstein dummy—"And #YouToo, Zoya Roy," he said, "you may be a Hindu brahmin princess, but you are not immune."

To Gershon's surprise, it was still dark when he hung up, it seemed to him that he had gone through an entire life-changing cycle of personal and ethnic trauma, yet the sun had still not risen. He drew out from the side pocket of his wheelchair the mask that Smiley had gagged him with so offensively only that evening. With the black laundry marker provided by the management he branded it indelibly with a Star of David to foreground his ostracism, then drew the mask across the lower portion of his face, concealing his big Jewish nose and big Jewish mouth, like an avenger preparing to set out at night to mow down all who had ever insulted and injured him, knowingly or unknowingly. He may have just scored a triumph over Zoya Roy, but the pathetic reality was that he needed to take care of the urgent matter of his nonfunctioning toilet before shutting down and isolating inexorably. He left his room, possibly for the last time in two weeks minimum, it struck him, provided he wasn't already fatally infected and carried out earlier on a bier to his final destination.

Like a film running in reverse, looking neither to his right nor to his left, he maneuvered his chair back through the long corridors and the grand lobby and the vast dining hall up the subtle incline seeded in his bones of the eternally darkened kitchen. There he encountered only one of his comrades of just an hour or so earlier, a larger-than-average specimen thanks to the Teutonic DNA of his pillaging ancestors who had settled in the Yucatán two centuries earlier. It was his strikingly full, wiry black beard, however, that had inspired Gershon to call him Fidel, though the name on his official documents, as Gershon later learned, was Raul—Raul Wagner—close, but no cigar, unless, of course, you count the discarded stub of the after-dinner cigar left by one of the hotel guests on which Fidel was puffing as he was relaxing post-coitally on the floor against the wall alongside a blonde teenager in shorts and halter suitable to this freakish tropical winter climate. Gershon had noticed her in the audience hunched over her mobile compulsively taking selfies at the disastrous psychodrama that evening—could it really have been just a few hours ago? She was exactly the type who in multiple mirror images had once been a central feature of the décor at the late Jeffrey Epstein hospitality centers, but Fidel now blocked her out, riveting all his attention on Gershon, who breathlessly dredged up his primitive Spanish, the errors would be blamed on the muffling of the mask. Por favor, Fidel. Mi dormitorio. Mi bano. Mucho mucho basura. Mierda. Vamos. Si, si, dinero.

Fidel nodded, unfolded, and the cigar still plugged between his lips, rose with enviable suppleness. He gathered up the heavy-duty garbage bags on which they had all been lounging, grabbed some rags and aerosols, and dismissing the existence of the minor female, probably some rebel from a local family enmeshed in the campaign to get rid of Camp Jeff, stationed himself behind the wheelchair. Deftly he steered it out of the kitchen, skillfully compensating for the unexpected descent, then onward through the dining room and the fabulous lobby, guided along the route by Gershon's agitated grunts and gestures delivered through the mask with eyes shut tight. Once inside his room, Gershon halted beyond the open door to the bathroom, and without any preliminaries pointed to the pogrom within. Fidel strode inside, pausing under the blazing institutional light and shaking his head, then turned to look over his shoulder at Gershon, the heat of whose eyes he could feel cupping his back, and he transmitted a thumbs up accented with a reassuring wink.

With no sign of squeamishness, Fidel went over to the toilet, plunged his hand into the grossness of its bowl and set to work drawing out the shreds of manuscript, wrapping the top layers moistened with Gershon's still warm, still foamy yellowish bubbles around the hideous piece of excrement, stuffing it all into a trash bag, repeating the maneuver, snaking deeper and deeper past his elbow into the pipes, gingerly testing the flushing mechanism as he evacuated more and more of the system, until he determined that all the sewage had been fully extracted, the network was clear, running smoothly, at which point he sprayed one of the magic chemicals inside and out, wiped it all down with a rag, and restored it to its original hospital sanitary whiteness. Next he turned his attention to the shower, disentangling the typewriter ribbon bleeding black ink and dark racial memories, ripping it off the pipes and the showerhead, and adding it to the bag. Solemnly, as if for a ceremonial post-mortem public viewing, he raised the corpse of the typewriter from the very transfer bench upon which Gershon would sit under the streaming water, deposited the remains in the body bag, and made the sign of the cross over it all. For good measure he also passed his rag over the sink, the mirrors, the white tiled walls, and all the other institutional fixtures, including his own hands and forearms, before nailing the coffin and emerging from the scene of the crime.

All of this Fidel accomplished in less than half an hour out of the goodness of his heart with the cigar still clamped between his teeth, Gershon noted, and the sun had still not risen—how could he ever thank this alien enough? He rummaged inside his wheelchair pockets for some coins but could not find any, so yielding to the special nature of this occasion, he pulled out from somewhere a soiled dollar bill and handed it to the good man. Fidel held it up by its limp corner between thumb and forefinger with far greater disgust than he had ever displayed during the distasteful act of scooping and scraping out the toilet bowl, then dropped it back into Gershon's lap as if this after all was the obscenity that had clogged up the works. Without a word, perhaps due to the cigar corking his mouth, Fidel slung the trash bag over his shoulder and headed out the door.

"Mi bolsa, mi bolsa," Gershon cried into the mask, wetting its black star, causing it to streak.

He had to have that bag back, it was his, because despite all that had happened, and the myriad ways in which he had been humiliated, somewhere within his being he still held fast to the conviction that the day would come when every one of his words, no matter how smeared and debased physically and theoretically, would be preserved and immortalized in a monumental archive housed in some stupendously endowed illustrious institution. He zipped down the hallway, long and wide, in pursuit of Fidel, who was strolling ahead of him with the bag over the shoulder. Five times Gershon on his wheels caught up with Fidel, and each time he held out to him a twenty. No big deal, Gershon told himself, visions of the ATM machines he had finally mastered impishly sticking out their green cash tongues at him—twenty is the new one. Each time Fidel neatly pocketed the proffered bill, but still he continued to move on without surrendering the precious bag. By the fifth twenty, they had reached the sumptuous centerpiece in the grand lobby. Fidel seized the bill from Gershon's hand, jumped onto the extravagantly sculpted marble ledge of the fountain, and with the cigar still jutting out from between his lips, he executed a triumphant salsa move, shoulder, torso, hips, feet, one arm extended out of Gershon's reach, twirling the bills so sensually, like a sultry dance partner now his alone. Then he let the bag drop into the chair onto Gershon's lap, where it landed on what remained of the poor sufferer's pride with a painful thud on account of the smashed typewriter.

What a stinker, Gershon was thinking as he raced back to his room—Keep this up, man, and they'll ship you back to the old country before you can even say, Hasta la vista, baby. Incredibly, it was still dark, he observed when he entered, maybe the sun had quit at last—nobody and nothing likes being forever taken for granted. Gershon opened the door to his closet and dumped the bag on the floor, pushing it toward the back with the foot-rest of his chair, out of sight with all its painful personal and racial memories of the human rights atrocity that had been committed against him. He pulled up to his desk, so thoughtfully engineered for wheelchair accessibility, yes, they had thought of everything, everything—except my soul, except my soul. There was just one more task he needed to complete before latching the door to his room from the inside and delivering himself over to sleep—the creation of a sign to post on his door. Wielding the black laundry marker, he once again inscribed a Star of David, and then under that, in bold letters, like the carving on a tomb-stone—Warning. Coronavirus Quarantine Zone. Danger. Keep Out. Turn Back. Lord Have Mercy On Us.

Was it the howling of the coyotes in this wilderness that had awakened him, or was it the blasted screeching of the telephone so close to his ear? Outside it was still a black hole when he opened his eyes, all the misery he had descended into sleep to escape now came churning back up from the sinkhole of his consciousness along with the shattering realization that the sun had still not risen, he could not have slept for much more than an hour or so—how would he ever function in the morning, assuming there would be a morning? He groped along the sur-face of his nightstand, first for his big black velvet yarmulke and then for the telephone, and, as if still snarled in a dream, his ear was assailed by the self-effacing voice of little Hedda Nuss-baum—"Thank God, you're alive!"

"What time is it?" He meant this as a chastisement, for crashing into his sleep at such a restricted, off-limits hour, but it was also information he needed to have in order to orient himself if morning ever came again.

"It's eleven o'clock at night," she told him. "The whole place is in quarantine for two full weeks. Check outside your door. There are three trays, untouched—breakfast, lunch, and dinner, you have shown no signs of life for a full day. Now go back to sleep, Gershon—now is the universal sleep time. I have to run and stop them before they call the fire department and break down your door."

"But how can I get back to sleep with the wolves howling outside?"

"It's not wolves, Gershon, it's Zlata Schick. She's been wailing day and night for all the daughters she has devoured, and she won't be comforted. Everyone thinks she's simulating in order to plead insanity and avoid prison, but we know better—right, Gershon?"

He at least knew better, the parts were coming together, the ancient story was swirling into shape. He lay there in his bed unable to recapture the sleep she had so rudely snatched from him, gripped by the urgency to formulate the insights that were bombarding him, clarifying everything, but thoughts of a midnight snack were interceding, churning from his gut upward and dominating, he decided to check outside his door for the three laden trays she had in such superior tones vouched to be still rotting there. Not surprisingly, they were gone, the three trays with all their bounty, maybe the Fidels had snatched them away to add to their troughs before the roaches and rats laid claim. The plague warning he had posted on his door was still in place, however, he was gratified to note in passing. The wide carpeted hallways unfolding the way through the labyrinth of Camp Jeffrey Epstein were dimmed by night lights, stretching into the distance on either side of him, emptied for now of disease spreaders. He was safe from contagion at this hour, he began to move down these corridors, turning corners, taking in door after door behind which sinners and sinned against were sunk in their troubled sleep, noting the stains and the nail holes and indentations left on every doorpost by the gouged-out mezuzahs from the proud Lokshin Hotel and Country Club days, unable to bring himself back to his own door with its own ghost mezuzah, into the fetid air of the prison cell of his own room, which had been so desecrated, his rancid bed, until well past the midnight hour.

She punctured his sleep again the next morning, this time in the flesh as a footnote to the towering Ms. Smiley striding forward blowing her whistle from under her mask, little Hedy scurrying behind steering the cart uploaded with his breakfast. Not condescending to knock, Ms. Smiley had inserted her master key into the lock, pushed the door open with no sign of exertion, oblivious to having popped a link in the chain latch, thereby gaining no resistance, a seamless entry. With Hedy functioning as supply train bringing up the rear, Ms. Smiley halted at the foot of the bed upon which Gershon was stretched out, yes, like a patient blah blah on a table, clutching with his two hands his blanket drawn up to his neck in the soap opera manner of a woman caught in flagrante, the black velvet yarmulke, which he had neglected to remove after Hedy's intrusion the night before, hanging askew from a clip in the weeds of his white hair. He gazed at his two providers stationed there before him—one so tall and stately, the other small and inconsequential, one the daughter of the gods, the other the runt of eternally persecuted humanoids—both surgically decked out in anemic blue protective medical gear from head to toe, gowns, gloves, goggles, caps, masks, Ms. Smiley, as high priestess, set apart and sanctified by a transparent face shield fashioned out of clear plastic descending from a headband inscribed with the awesome legend, Holy Unto Jehovah. "Are you planning to operate on me now—a lobotomy maybe?" Gershon inquired. Such an infantile question, moronic—he couldn't stop himself from asking simply to assert his personality.

"Where's the mask I slapped on your face the other night, buster? No mask, no mama. Get that mask on this minute."

Releasing only his right hand from under the blanket, he extended his bare arm out to the night table, grabbed the star-smeared mask and managed, with one hand and the flex of his shoulders, to loop the elastic around both ears, his grin underneath stretching the mask's coverage even wider in anticipation of accosting her with his identity politics. Ms. Smiley took one look and remarked, "Quite in your face today, aren't we, buster?" She moved over to the side of the bed and, with one whiplash snap, got rid of the mask along with its offensive ethnic graffiti, replacing it with the expert's current top choice in protective face-aperture coverings, which resembled a brassiere cup molded from foam and wired to retain its seamless memory uplift shape, which he noted out loud before being silenced by it forever, it was a bra like those he had observed proliferating during a turn through a high-end lingerie boutique the last time he had treated himself to this harmless personal indulgence before his castration by hashtag. Female undergarments had always been one of Gershon's minor areas of expertise—a hobby, ladies, only a benign little hobby, nothing to get excited about.

The head nurse dug this falsie into his face, masking him with it as punishment for exercising his right to free expression as a proud Jew who had learned the lessons of the Holocaust and as a Zionist, and for all the sins he had committed with unclean thoughts and lewdness, sealing his nose and mouth, squeezing, pinching, digging grooves into his flesh, which had become noticeably more copious over his sojourn thus far at Camp Jeff in consequence of the forced feedings, she pulled its straps pitilessly through the hard-wired web of his hair, flattening his black velvet yarmulke stippled with dandruff, and tightened the knot, torturing him mercilessly, his face went crimson, blue vessels swelling, he could hardly breathe. From her pocket she drew out a cold, impersonal instrument and pressed it flat over his cyclopic third eye in the center of his forehead, its infrared light flashing disease directly into his brain. "Normal," Nurse Smiley announced, "despite appearances to the contrary." That was when Gershon noticed that Hedy Nussbaum had taken over his desk, it had become occupied territory, he had an unobstructed view of the back of her head, covered, but with uncontrollable frizzy spirals of hair poking out in which all sorts of creatures must have dwelt, as she typed in his temperature and recorded other data as dictated by Ms. Smiley into some barbaric electronic device, the modern-day replacement for the humane, dignified medical chart, he reflected, stricken with terminal nostalgia—paper clamped to a clipboard, writing instrument in the hand, two mortals, face to face, healer and sufferer. Whose side was Hedda on anyway?

Gershon closed his eyes, surrendering to this inhuman reality, when Ms. Smiley unexpectedly forgave him his filthy, juvenile sin that she, too, had already experienced firsthand—his sick obsession with ladies' underwear. She loosened the brassiere mask gripping his face like a vise, lowering it so that it now rested only over his mouth—muting him, it's true, which was in everyone's interest this time, he appreciated that, possibly even including his own. This unexpected reprieve, this act of loving-kindness inspired him to open his eyes again to transmit a flicker of gratitude—for this relief much thanks, ma'am—when there, a few steps behind Ms. Smiley and partially concealed by her statuesque form, he spotted mousey little Hedda Nussbaum standing in readiness, holding out a rack containing a test tube half filled with a murky liquid. From a secret pocket in her body armor, Ms. Smiley drew out a long stick topped with a cotton swab, mustardy in color, it seemed to Gershon, which instantly triggered warm memories of his formative years in Brooklyn, the family bathroom with its earwax-coated Q-tips lined up in their box to be reused as often as possible by his frugal parents, survivors of the Shoah who had endured such extreme deprivation and expected a recurrence every hour of every day. He wanted to cry out, Mama, Mama, where are you now when I need you so bad? But Mama, like so many Holocaust survivors sooner or later, was no longer with us.

Ms. Smiley aimed this extra-long Q-tip at Gershon's face like an arrow, inserting it first into one defenseless nostril for what felt like an eternity, and then into the other, driving it up higher and higher, twisting and rotating it, pressing it against the interior sides of the nasal cavity and then, like a nightmare needle, straight up into his brain. So he was being lobotomized after all—she was suctioning out the gray matter from his brainpan, piercing and deflating his lobes, severing his wires. Gershon thought he would pass out. He was coughing violently, tears were streaming from his eyes, pooling around the base of the bust mask. Were it not for that padded mask over his mouth he would have wept out loud from pain, he would have heaved up the lining of his gut into the mask cup, which he estimated to be a double B or maybe a C, he had not eaten for more than thirty-six hours straight, during which he had been raped twice, first the raid, and now this, the second time, he was drowning in psychoempathy. Suddenly, his torturer pulled out, just in time, he did not know if he could hold it all in much longer, she had had her fun, she had done her damage.

"Shame on you, you're just one big slobbering baby," Ms. Smiley remarked. "That was your standard Covid-19 PCR test, you'll be getting them regularly from now on, like everyone else here at Camp Jeffrey Epstein, you're no exception, you're not a privileged character." She inserted her lethal spike into the test tube held out in its rack by Hedy, cotton-swab end first, stained with his brain scrapings. Then she snatched the rack with the evidence from Hedy's hands, drew her whistle up under her face shield and let out a blast as a kind of marching order, and made for the door, pausing there for a moment to consider Gershon again and once again disapprove. "Nobody in this nuthouse kicked up such a fuss when I did the test on them like you did just now," she observed in her parting words. "Not even your little buddy, the flasher."

Hedy, left behind, stood there bereft in her comical space suit, kinky hair coils springing out from under her pumped-up protective surgical shower bonnet.

"That was a serious malpractice violation of Arnie's right to patient confidentiality, not to mention human dignity," Gershon observed with exemplary detachment. "Highly unethical. Someone ought to report her to #AtLeastDoNoHarm, if such a vice squad exists, which I doubt. I hope you videoed her farewell speech just now with one of your high-tech gizmos. We need to get her out of circulation for everyone's sake, she's a real menace."

Hedy responded first with a defeated little shrug, and then, figuratively blowing her own whistle, she added, "The really weird thing is that what Smiley said just now does not even happen to be the truth, it's actually a pretty brazen lie. I guess she's counting on me to keep my mouth shut like any other underling—executive privilege, you know—but the real story is that whatever fuss you kicked up just now was like nothing compared to Arnie. We had to chase him all around his room, he was stark naked, not even a mask, dripping corona all over the place, over and under the bed, we had to schlep him out of the closet, he was crouching in there like from the Cossacks in a pogrom, amazing how he zipped around when only a few days ago he was as limp as a noodle. In the end we practically broke down the bathroom door and did the job right there on the wet tile floor with me sprawled on top of him pinning him down—nothing but skin and bones, his eyes popping out like a frog on the dissection table. Smiley was royally pissed that I forgot to bring the straitjacket, she broke maybe ten swab sticks trying to shove them up his nose, with him screaming and yelling the whole time that she's planting a microchip in his brain with a barcode to track him for life, that she was messing with his head big-time. I'm telling you, Gershon, you might not be too pleased to hear this, I know you like to be number one in all things regardless, but compared to Glick you were one very tame, very well-behaved little pussycat, a lambkin, believe me, a perfectly cooperative sheiffe'le."

He listened to all this, still lying there in bed, but his grip on his blanket had relaxed, it had now slipped down to his waist, the bulletproof vest he had been desperate to conceal now exposed—his tzitzit with knotted fringes and azure-dyed strings at the corners, like a string around the finger to remind him to love God even in the face of all the unexplainable cruelty and suffering in this world, to obey all God's commandments however irrational, but above all a personalized message to him, Gershon Gordon, to never again stray after the lustful urgings of his eyes and his heart.

Hedy took all of this in, his struggle, his pride, overcome by an unexpected weight of pity and tenderness that seemed to be pressing her into the ground. From her bag she drew out a laptop and held it up for him to see. "This is the only high-tech gizmo I have with me," she said. "I was delegated to deliver this one to you. Because from now on, everything here at Camp Jeff is going to be virtual, remote—the group sessions, private therapy, and so on, at least through the lockdown, maybe even beyond." She raised her eyes to gauge his response, but he was missing in action, he had gone underground, his entire body now, including his skull-capped head, buried under the covers.

"So I take it you don't want the computer—right? That's okay. We'll figure something out, conference calls, maybe, whatever. I thought you'd refuse anyway, but I decided to risk asking just in case you might have wanted it for word processing, it could make things a lot easier when you're working on your book project. I didn't see your typewriter on the desk, maybe it's in the closet for safekeeping."

"Ha, safekeeping," Hedy thought she heard him say, echoing her from under the covers, but the connection was lost, he was gone, out of sight, far away.

Still, she had been charged with passing on to him some momentous information, she had no choice but to address his absence. "I guess you're looking forward to the coming two weeks of compulsory self-isolation to really focus intensely on your book project and get a whole lot done," she pressed on, "so I need to forewarn you that there might be a disturbance in the field, a bit of a racket in the hallway outside your door over the next few days or so, first the cops and law enforcement and other authorities, and then the repair guys and cleanup crews, I apologize in advance for any inconvenience, thank you for your understanding. You're obviously not aware of what's been going on, because you've been stuck inside here the whole time, but just for your information, some seriously disturbing acts of vandalism have been carried out on the premises, acts that might even qualify as hate crimes, they could have very severe repercussions for all of us and for our reha-bilitation program. It seems that some joker has been skulking up and down these hallways late last night, defacing select doors with red spray paint, like blood on the lintels during the plague of the firstborn in ancient Egypt, targeting the sleeping victims inside the rooms by naming them on their doors with his red paint in a manner that could only be described as rabidly biased and racist, and, of course—surprise, surprise—antisemitic. On your door, Gershon, I'm sorry to say, this hooligan sprayed his poison right above that very thoughtful personal message you hung up there before going into deep quarantine, smearing you as 'Lord George Gordon, King Mob, Poisoner of Wells, Super Spreader.' On Wesley Wu's door he sprayed 'Chef Wesley Wuhan, a.k.a. China Virus Bat Man, Eat at Your Own Risk.' On Father Clarence's door, 'Black Cat, Black Hole, Black Death.' On Max Horn's door, 'MaxVax, International Jewish Conspiracy.' On Tzadik Kutsher's door, 'Trump City, Mask Free Zone, Kutsh My Ass.' And best of all—you'll really appreciate this, Gershon—on Fritz Rosenberg's door he sprayed 'Jew.Flu Rosenberg, Blood Matzah Child Killer.' I guess our guy took it for granted that Rosenberg was a Jew—what do you expect with a name like Rosenberg? Which leads one to conclude that he is some kind of outside operative, right? Though judging from the evidence, he managed to match each door to its correct room occupant with one hundred percent accuracy, and even the personalized insults and racist tropes sort of loosely fit in some weird way in each case, don't you think?"

Did he think? Super spreader? King Mob? Well poisoner? Lord George Gordon? Was that really him, his backup security name for the inevitable hour of another Holocaust? Had he really become such a prime-time mover and shaker as all of that implied, or was it just his pretensions that were being broadcast? Still playing dead under his covers, Gershon felt validated by the unchecked spread of the raid virus, sprayed Raid this time, like the insecticide, the zapping of Jewish vermin and parasites along with some collateral damage to any non-Semite unlucky enough to share our airspace but without doubt deserving of elimination anyway. It was not something he could discuss, though. The exclusive raid that had singled him out, targeted him alone, was still too raw and risky to talk about, especially to Hedda, who, he was beginning to fear, seemed gradually and systematically to be attaching herself to him like a ball and chain. Jesus Christ, wasn't he already handicapped enough? Hedy, for her part, having failed to draw him out of himself even with her stunning current-events updates, merely sighed in conclusion and began her fade out. "So that's the latest news from Lake Oy-Begone," she quipped, paraphrasing a fellow hashtag victim. She set forth plodding her way toward the defiled door, pausing there for a moment before turning to execute her final leave-taking, and adding, "I'll send someone to fix this chain, to protect your right to privacy. Well, shalom khaver, don't hesitate to call if you need anything, anything at all."

"Two things," Gershon's voice suddenly shot up crisply and in command from under the blanket, as from a dark cloud rising, "I need two things, two things in rapid response. Number one, I need a mezuzah on my doorpost within the next twenty-four hours, it's my constitutional right according to the First Amendment, to practice my religion openly and freely even in prison, as a Jew I cannot continue living in this cell without a mezuzah. For God's sake, Hedda, even the baronial door to Jeffrey Epstein's den of iniquity between Fifth and Madison had a mezuzah—how much more so ought the door of his sinless avatar? I want the mezuzah to be set inside the raw indentation on the doorpost still visible from the days when this place was an openly unashamed, proud Jewish resort. I want a kosher mezuzah containing a kosher klaf written by a kosher sofer so that everyone will know that herein, in this cabinet of curiosities, a kosher Jew is living, a living Jew still living, a real live Jew, we're still here, that's number one. Number two, I want you to let it be known that any Jew—and this applies specifically to fellow members of the tribe and not to Teutons and Huns who happen to be impersonating us with names like Schickel or Gruber or Rosenberg—any Jew by blood or by one hundred percent kosher conversion who wishes to enter my private space and meet with me one on one and in person must be a strictly practicing Jew, a Jew who observes all of the six hundred and thirteen commandments, the thou-shalts and the thou-shalt-nots for the males, and an abridged version, the nots only, as for a Canaanite slave, for the females—the neqevas, the perforated ones, the ones with a hole in their heads for not opting out long ago, considering all the naked misogyny directed at them. So tukhes on the table, what I'm saying to you, Hedda Nussbaum, since for better or worse you are a certified member without a member, as my dear, brave Arnie Glick was wont to say, is that you must come out of the closet and stride proudly into the open Jewish forcefield, you must change your ways forever, you must get your act together with regard to your abbreviated mitzvah performance requirement points if you ever want to come into my orbit again in this life."

9.

Upon the departure of Hedy Nussbaum from his isolation cell that Monday morning, the sixth day of Adar, five thousand seven hundred and eighty years from the creation of the world according to the Hebrew calendar, in the time of the corona plague, Gershon Gordon took upon himself the vow of a Nazir, consecrating himself to the Lord simply by conjuring up before his eyes the image of Bob Marley with his magnificent crown of Rastafarian dreadlocks, his hair the glory of a born Nazir, and then saying out loud the words, "Me Too—I will be like him, I will let my hair grow free and be beautiful too." From the dark ages of his Talmud force-feeding he dredged up the memory that taking the vow could be as simple as that—Me Too, easy peasy. No one owned a copyright on those two words. Now he had reclaimed them, repurposed them on his own terms by becoming a member of the elite Nazir fellowship of holy men. Through the simple utterance of his rebranded Me Too, he undertook the Nazir vow for the minimum of thirty days. And since there no longer is a Temple in Jerusalem with an altar upon which, at the end of the thirty days, a Nazir could burn his shorn hair along with the three requisite sacrifices, the vow he took by speaking out the words Me Too would become a life sentence from which he could never be released.

Three sacrifices—a burnt offering, a peace offering, a sin offering—for the three abstinence requirements of a Nazir that would lift him up and separate him from the masses to whom, in any event, he had always felt superior, and sanctify him to the Lord. Consulting his personal Old Testament in both Hebrew and English, Gershon reviewed the three Nazir renunciation requirements as outlined in the Book of Numbers and concluded that, overall, it seemed like a pretty good deal. Number one, No contamination through contact with the dead—check. Not a problem, his mother and father, like almost all Holocaust survivors sooner or later, were no longer with us, he had already processed their ultimate degree of ritual impurity. He had no brother or sister to pollute him someday. Yalta, his only child, was gone, lost to him, still he prayed for her long life, he prayed for her return, for her he would wait every day. And as for any fellow campers who might succumb to the plague and thereby impart the ritual impurity of the dead, they were not in his tent, not in his airspace, not in his air corridor—they were not his department. Number two, No haircuts—check. Indeed, this was more of a bonus incentive than a deprivation, his mass of brilliant white hair, once his flash and glory, was now unfortunately showing signs of depletion and reverse migration due to more than three score years of suffering, unlike the hair of brother Bob Marley, who at Gershon's age was already dead for twenty-five years, the captive set free. But now, as a Nazir, Gershon could let whatever still remained of his hair burst forth unrestrained, he could grow out his beard too, he would make his comeback appearance on the world stage when all of this madness came to an end, bearded and wild haired, immortal like Elijah the prophet, sage, and holy man. Number three, No wine—check. Granted, this might be an abstinence potentially more challenging, but he welcomed it joyously for setting him apart as a Jew even more emphatically, keeping him from mixing and mingling, keeping him separate and solitary—and, as always, despised. He would give Hedda Nussbaum orders immediately to alert the kitchen to his newly emergent allergy to the fruit of the vine in any shape or form, the sight of it alone could blow his consecration in an instant.

But the good news was there were no restrictions with regard to sex, no required abstinence in that department for either men or women—for shockingly, as he now read, women were permitted to take on the Nazir vow too, he had forgotten that detail or simply had not believed it and consequently had never taken it seriously. He now fully intended to convince Hedda Nussbaum to take the vow as well, it would be extremely therapeutic for her, it would do her seriously compromised self-esteem a world of good, she could consider it her true terminal degree, she could declare her education over and done with at last, thank the Lord, she will have finally found her true calling and vocation, the closest thing to the nun ideal that the Jewish faith had to offer a woman. Could it be possible that the omission of sexual renunciation as one of the Nazir requirements was inadvertent, an error, a textual glitch that the divine fact checker had failed to catch? Yet the most famous Nazir in recorded history was Samson, and Samson strode unconstrained, free and easy, harassing and behaving inappropriately up and down the Holy Land from Zorah to Timna to Gaza in a permanent state of extreme full-blown, fully charged perpetual sexual arousal and animal heat, radically enhanced erotically thanks to his magnificent hair, the source of his legendary male strength and power, in no way handicapped due to the absence of wine as a lubricant, fornicating and killing wherever he went, leaving a trail of corpses and body parts, no doubt the beneficiary of a special dispensation with regard to a Nazir's intercourse with the impurity of the dead. For the Nazir slayer Samson, the mighty one, as for the sweet singer Bob Marley with his thirteen known offspring by seven mothers, as well as for himself, the living reincarnation of the convert Lord George Gordon, the guiding light of King Mob, it was all about hair—two fluffy muffs of white hair naturally falling over his ears now reprocessed as the mandatory sidelocks, and, most strikingly, his venerable, wizard-like, triangular beard, like the singular beard of Lord George Gordon, white, streaked with the rust of age and wisdom, streaming down his chest, narrowing like the tip of an arrow as it advanced southward to below his waist, like a cautionary pointer to the source of all the troubles of this world.

Having now officially taken on the luminous aura of a Nazir simply by pronouncing the words Me Too, Gershon found his old blue velvet bag embroidered with his name in Hebrew in golden thread, and drew out from it the tefillin presented to him by his proud parents, the Holocaust survivors, when he became a bar mitzvah more than half a century earlier—he, their brilliant son Gershon, their continuity, their personal triumph over Hitler. Hoisting himself up from his wheelchair, propping himself against his desk, he recited the blessing and wrapped the black leather straps around his left arm, with the leather box containing the holy parchment pointed toward his heart. He donned the head strap, settling the black box with its scrolls on the soft spot of his head that his mother, the Holocaust survivor, had guarded so fiercely, on the fontanel that once had pulsed so tenderly like the breast of a newly hatched chick, resting it on this space now once again conveniently exposed thanks to follicle recession, positioning it like a sentry block to guard his precious brain—heart and brain, therein we find the Jew. Behind the box, the full glory of his Nazir hair dedicated to the Lord was now officially liberated and blessed to burst forth in wild splendor. He draped his boyhood tallis over his shoulders and, still standing, opened on the desktop his miniature siddur, the inside of its green fake-leather cover inscribed by Rabbi Fishel Rosenberg, head of his lower yeshiva, with a testimonial to young Gershon Gordon's exemplary tikkun olam visits all around Brooklyn to condemned old-age homes reeking of urine, packed with Holocaust survivors whose anguish he soothed in his sweet treble voice with songs recalling their beloved little shtetl, Belz, or musings on what could have happened to their promised seven good years that had sadly never materialized. Finding his place in this precious legacy siddur, Gershon began reciting the morning prayers with intense fervor, animated by a burning desire to achieve the highest spiritual level of full kavanah.

Yet in spite of all his sincere efforts to focus on the sacred text without distraction, two alien thoughts succeeded in creeping into his head. The first and less impious occurred during the blessing thanking God for not having created him a woman. It was at that point that he spontaneously resolved to wear his tallit and tefillin throughout the entire day, six days a week, excluding the Sabbath, he would be God's slave, it would be a personal commitment to a higher, more rigorous, stricter form of spiritual devotion that had been undertaken by select circles of righteous sages in ancient times, an extra-credit ascetic discipline that he, Gershon Gordon, took on in the throes of his prayers that morning, marred only by a subversive concern for how, thus bound up in sanctified leather, he would be able to manage bathroom business when the need arose, as well as the urge to pass gas. The second distraction happened during the silent Amidah, the Eighteen Benedictions, at the verse imploring God to wipe out all heretics, slanderers, and informers, when his mind wandered again, and he found himself suddenly adding on a personal request to the Lord to come to his aid in resurrecting from the septic tank of the marauder the Jeffrey Epstein book he had committed himself to write, he implored God to restore those pages so vital to his being, despite his acknowledgment of their intrinsic profanity, saturated with immorality and depravity and sin, at troubling odds with the vows he had just taken and his newly acquired elevated state of purity.

Accordingly, upon completing his prayers, on the leash of his tefillin, Gershon drew his wheelchair up to the desk, took out from the drawer a pen and one of his stacks of index cards and stared down at their sickening blankness. His plan was to retrieve by hand, while the memory was still as fresh as it ever would be, the typed words on the pages of his manuscript that the barbarian raider had so sadistically decimated. The opening sentences that he had labored so long in shaping now kept eluding him in their intricate, allusive brilliance. All he could remember was that they had something to do with two boys, strangers to one another, standing each one alone and apart on the pavement of a Brooklyn playground, slouching against the chain-link fence, watching the young black sons of the gods as they loped up and down the basketball court, both of these solitary watchers identifiable members of the chosen people, albeit never themselves chosen for any team. As Gershon recalled, the scene then jumped cinematically fast forward four decades or so to an island in the Caribbean, both boys now grown men, one of them, Gershon himself, a world-renowned public intellectual and moral force, a kind of hip grand rabbi self-ordained, universally recognized for the dazzling brilliance and erudition of his discourse in arenas both secular and sacred, watching as the other, the king of the island, the Emperor Jeff, stood beside the famous relative by marriage of Rabbi Tzadik Kutsher, recognizable from the back by his greased orange hair slicked together from either side to replicate a duck's ass, a coiffure known as a "DA" throughout the five boroughs of New York City and beyond. In a manner similar to the way that Gershon was watching Jeffrey Epstein and Tzadik Kutsher's famous distant relative by marriage, these two power players were also engaged in watching—grinning, pointing, adjusting the jewels in their trousers, kibbitzing, commenting—watching like buyers at a cattle market as a dozen or more nymphets, all of them supple and tender, with long silken golden tresses, none of them older than sixteen, pranced and frolicked and squealed in the Olympic-sized swimming pool wearing nothing but a thong with the strap beguilingly tucked deep between their rosy rump cheeks.

The variety of watching experiences—that had been the theme of his opening paragraphs, and now as he was struggling to recapture it, it all seemed to Gershon to be hopelessly puerile and inane. Maybe he could salvage it somehow by pulling it all together in the pandemic present under the sign of the corona at Camp Jeffrey Epstein. Rabbi Tzadik Kutsher, the pervert wrestler of smooth-skinned young yeshiva boys, could carry on blissfully monitoring on the screen his famous distant relative by marriage hollering from his bully pulpit that it's all a hoax, this China virus, just stay calm, it will all go away. As for himself, Gershon Gordon, now resembling some kind of bondage freak in his black tefillin straps, which disturbingly also summoned up the profane vision of the thongs of those lovely pale-skinned slave girls, he could remain caught forever in self-isolation in the hashtag, crying out in vain at the injustice of it all. It was all a tragic mess, a disaster. Gershon pressed his face down on his desk, tried and failed to soak his mound of index cards with real tears, and fell asleep.

What startled him into wakefulness were cries that resounded like a strangulation taking place in his vicinity, which, when he was fully restored to the dull present, translated into the shrill ringing of the house telephone. He opened his eyes and saw that outside it was dark again, he could justifiably return to his sleep cave, but the shrieking of the phone would not stop, it was like a baby wailing in the night, nothing would quiet it except an exertion by him. Giving up, he conveyed his burdensome body in its wheelchair to the flashing light on the nightstand beside his bed and picked up the receiver. "Thank God," Hedy Nussbaum exhaled, "I was about to call security to check if you're still alive and kicking. Naughty boy, your lunch and dinner trays are still in the hallway outside your door, decomposing in this weird March climate. I hope and pray that you at least ate some of the breakfast I brought you this morning."

Who did this woman think she was—his Jewish mother? This time she was truly crossing a line—so annoying, as his lost child, Yalta, used to say. How alone he was, the only connection remaining to him in the world now was this insignificant woman at the other end of the line, Hedda Nussbaum, the last person standing who showed any sign of caring. He had no choice now but to submit to a conversation of sorts with her. It was necessary to alert her to his revised dietary requirements, since, as a Nazir, he could touch absolutely nothing on the Camp Jeff tray until he received an ironclad guarantee that it would not contain anything grapey, from pip to seed to pulp to skin to the color purple to the four hundred barrels of wine smashed by the magnificent Princess Yalta, daughter of the Exile King. He had taken the vow, he told Hedy, he had become a Nazir.

"A Nazir? Wow, that is so exciting, Gershon. Mazel tov! What a coincidence, I'm a Nazir too—well, a Nazira—I just started my twenty-first year, like the famous convert Queen Helena of Adiabene. I don't know about you, Gershon, but for myself I've always felt that I took on the burdens of Nezirut to atone for some soul sin, a blemish I felt that had always existed deep down inside me, that's my personal take on the words of the venerable Eleazar HaKappar in Nedarim who described the Nazir as sinning against the soul. Anyway, never mind, the good news is, bottom line, you don't need to worry about the food situation— not a problem. I know all the dietary restrictions backward and forward, and the kitchen staff also already knows the drill, they still have to feed me even though I'm only a woman. Welcome to the cult, friend. Just relax and finish everything on your plate. Rest assured, all food and drink sent your way will be Nazir friendly."

So that explains her hair, Gershon thought gloomily, her big frizzy lusterless mop, apparently not every Nazir ends up looking like Bob Marley—a realization that, so early in his spiritual journey, raised painful questions in his heart about ever personally achieving enlightenment through renunciation, like a sannyasi, much less a state of radiant transcendence through his vow of abstinence. She sounded so uncharacteristically self-confident and superior as she babbled on, Gershon noted morosely, taking such pains to reinforce him in his decision, which for some reason that eluded him she obviously considered exactly the right choice for him, the ideal step forward toward personal growth, but at the same time, she couldn't stop herself from letting him know that she had been there before him, she, too, deserved some recognition for all the points she had already racked up as a veteran modern-day Guinness Book of Records Nazira. He could barely suppress the urge to deflate her for her own good, it was all so painfully ironic. Here he had been planning to put some gentle pressure on her to go Nazir for her own personal mental and emotional health, ready even to sacrifice some of his own precious writing time to take her by the hand and serve as her guide, and now she tells him that she has already been down that rabbit hole for over two decades. Who would have guessed? Who would ever have chalked up her pathological selflessness to an arcane vow? He could not even begin to picture what she must have been like before she took the Nazir cure. He found himself struggling to keep from sinking into a state of end-stage depression.

Gershon held the receiver away from his ear but still he could hear her voice streaming nonstop, sounding abnormally self-assured and excited, something about a brilliant idea she had just had. Instead of your standard therapy session during their required daily phone call, they could study the Talmud tractate Nazir, she proposed—yes, she would drop off a printout outside his door that very night. "It's the tractate right before Sotah, you know the one I mean, about a woman suspected of adultery and the really bizarre ordeal they put her through. It's all part of the order Nashim, don't ask me why they stuck Nazir in there, maybe as an atypical rabbinic nod to the female practitioners. *Nashim* means women," Hedy added gratuitously.

Gershon felt the sting. Of course he knew that *nashim* meant women, he was Jewishly educated, Jewishly literate, he had routinely been praised extravagantly for his Hebrew, delivered with such aplomb, it was unforgivably condescending on her part to translate that word for him. He was about to smash down the receiver, but then that truly sad thought gripped him again— Shit, she's my only link to the outside world. He sank into a silence so punishing that at the other end Hedy Nussbaum felt it acutely, and recognized instantly that she was to blame. "Sorry Gershon, really, really sorry, that was unforgivable of me, of course you know that *nashim* means women. I only meant to highlight it because the issue of women and all that is what in the end landed you here at Camp Jeffrey Epstein, so working on tractate Nashim could be considered relevant in a way for our daily sessions, it would fulfill the requirement. But it came out all wrong, so patronizing, I'm so sorry, I hope you can forgive me, Gershon. Let's forget I ever said it, let's forget I ever suggested we study Nazir, it was a really dumb idea, really stupid of me. I hope you'll pick up the phone when I call, we really need to be in touch, I need to know if you're okay, I need to let you know what's going on, please, please give me a second chance, give me a sign that you forgive me, Gershon."

She chose to believe that Gershon was still there at the other end of the line, there had been no reverberation of a receiver crashing down to lead her to conclude otherwise, no dial tone or busy signal or recorded message filled the void, she thought she could hear his breathing at the other end, his heart beating. She went on talking, explaining that the main reason she had called was not only to inquire about how he was holding up in these strange out-of-body times, of course, but also to let him know that a fellow member of his Camp Jeffrey Epstein cohort with whom she knew he had been in close physical contact had developed extreme breathing difficulties and a very high fever, and was now intubated at the hospital in Liberty, New York, in critical condition, the situation looked very dire.

It's Rosenberg, Gershon was thinking at his end of the line—Hallelujah!

Hedda had witnessed Gershon crash his wheelchair into that rabid Nazi at the end of the great psychoempathy extravaganza the other night, she would definitely classify that as close physical contact, a near-death experience. What a creep he was, Rosenberg. He must have known that he was personally infected, he was a medical doctor after all, even if his full-time specialty was the stealth impregnation of racially correct females who trustingly climbed up onto his examining table and spread their legs, propagating his superior seed—a variation on Jeffrey Epstein's cherished super-species genetic-engineering scheme, come to think of it, it now occurred to Gershon, which would make Rosenberg the all-around camper at Camp Jeff, in the image of the founding father, he gets the trophy. One thing was certain though. A rat like Rosenberg knew he was dying, so he figured, I'll just piss off the Jew before I abandon ship, force him to mix it up with me, goad him to expose himself to my fatal toxin, then drag him along with me straight to hell.

But still Gershon remained silent, he held back as Hedy went on in her irritating pedantic mode that she could never shake off, no matter how hard she tried, no matter how palpable the discomfort of her audience desperately seeking an escape hatch, informing him that she had actually been born in that Liberty, New York, hospital where everyone was now dying. In those days it was called Maimonides—Maimonides Hospital, she went on—isn't that a weird coincidence? Maybe that's why she ended up at Camp Jeff—because she was destined to die at that hospital too, coming full circle, another one of God's sick jokes. But yes, it was a sad fact, it was in that very same hospital that she had entered this vale of tears, a terrible shock from which she has not recovered to this day, Hedy said. Her father was the rabbi of the nearby town of Woodridge, New York, at the time. In those golden days there were small, civilized communities of Jews living full-time in Sullivan County, not just chugging up to the bungalow colonies and monster hotels in the summer to escape the city heat—well-behaved Jews who tried not to call attention to themselves, tried to fit in, who needed the services of a respectable rabbi once in a while for life-cycle events, Hedy added pathetically. "But nowadays, as you probably know," she persisted, "the place is flooded with Hassidim in their blacks and whites, their precious Borsalinos covered with plastic kosher market bags as they rush around in the rain from bank to bank making deposits and withdrawals, eating their knishes in the streets, tossing their garbage out of their car windows, crashing their bumper cars into each other in the fun house, their side-locks flying, their eyes shooting total indifference to you or your opinion. From Monticello to South Fallsburg to Woodbourne, the Hassidim rule, you don't want to mess with these Jews," Hedy said, taking in Gershon's articulated disinterest, searching for a self-respecting way to segue from the former name of the hospital back to the great man himself. "Was Gershon aware that the peerless medieval philosopher and physician Maimonides— the Rambam, as he was known, Rabbi Moshe ben Maimon, well, of course you know that," she quickly caught herself, paying due deference this time to Gershon's Jewish immersion no matter its quality, "yes, the Rambam was also an expert on plague as on so many other topics. For epidemics, the Rambam prescribed lockdown, quarantine, masks, hand washing, social distancing, and waiting a few years while the old and infirm die out and the population reboots. Which shows how way ahead of his time the Rambam was," Hedy said forlornly into the mouthpiece, nearly defeated.

But then, to nail his focus at last, she asked Gershon if he happened to know the name of Arnie Glick's mother—Arnie, son of Mrs. Glick or whatever. She needed to know because since both she and Gershon prayed three times a day in their respective corners, maybe they could each recite a misheberakh for Arnie during their prayers, plead with God to have mercy on Arnie, son of Mama Glick or whatever, now lying gravely ill in his hospital bed in the former Maimonides hospital in Liberty, New York. It is a well-known fact that God is much more inclined to take pity on a sick person for the sake of his mother, maybe even to go so far as to reverse the decree. Lord, bring this mother's son a complete recovery, a healing of spirit and a healing of body— El na, refah na lo, Cure him now, Lord, Please, I'm begging You.

Gershon let out a grinding sob, which was how Hedy now knew for sure that he was still there at the end of the line.

Hedy called every night at around nine o'clock, as promised, saving Gershon for last on the principle of the very last, the most dear, which she applied to Gershon no matter how unrestrainedly he humiliated and abused her verbally. Now, the moment he picked up and heard her voice, he started crying as if a switch had been turned on, unable to stop himself, crying inconsolably like a baby at the realization of the disaster that had befallen him in having been born, weeping and wailing until he was utterly drained, then panting spasmodically in a state of depletion. "It's all right to cry, go ahead, give yourself permission," Hedy said the first time this happened, at what she deemed to be the right moment, as the waves of his desolation were gradually subsiding, leaving longer and longer stretches between frayed breaths. Seeking to comfort him on a higher level, to which she believed he would be more likely to respond, she dredged up once again the sublime Rambam for his teaching that in times of trouble, one must blast the trumpets and cry out to the heavens to take pity on us all. "So go ahead, Gershon," she told him, "blast your trumpet, get it all out of your system"—which did in fact cause him to cry even harder, but in a different register this time, with a sound more like the twisted groan of a trapped animal trying to escape, which raised in Hedy a concern that he might actually be in pain, most likely intestinal, maybe a side effect of his new Nazir diet. On subsequent nights, therefore, as his sobs finally seemed to be easing up and drying out, as they were pumped out at greater and greater intervals, she allowed the great Rambam to rest in peace, and staying strictly on message, said, "It's okay, Gershon, he's still fighting. Pray for him—Arnie, son of Mama Glick. Good night, Gershon. I'll call you tomorrow. Our regular appointment, same time same place."

So irritatingly selfless, Gershon reflected miserably, the way she allows him to dump on her like that, holding out to him a poisoned cocktail made up of guilt and catharsis, yet the reality was, all of that histrionic display, his daily pathetic meltdown, it was all basically a form of exploitation, it was nothing if not insulting to her, and as for himself, Gershon, it was more wrenching than relief. Naturally he was pained by the unfairness of it all, the sorrow, the pity, the horror, the horror. Why did the virus have to pick on sweet little Arnie, his own dear Yorick? If there were any justice in the world, it would have swooped down on the in-house Mengele, Dr. Fritz Rosenberg, chewed him up and spit him out onto the dung heap. But the truth was it wasn't for Arnie, son of Mama Glick, that he was crying, Gershon recognized this very starkly. It was for himself, publicly shamed son of Holocaust survivors no longer with us. And it wasn't even really an act that could strictly be characterized as crying. What it most resembled was the tantrum of a brat, disturbingly regressive. Crying was the only form of expression he was capable of by the time poor, deluded Hedda Nussbaum telephoned at the end of his soul-crushing day spent tethered to his desk struggling to resurrect the pages that had been so savagely and humiliatingly despoiled. It seemed to Gershon that he no longer could remember how the act of writing was performed. He was like an athlete freezing in the clutch, hopelessly panicking. All day long he sat facing his cards, squeezing out word after word like a terminally constipated worm creeping along the line getting nowhere, leaving behind only a trail of slime to be ripped to pieces and hurled furiously into the bin.

So that when a few days later the phone rang in late morning rather than at its usual scheduled hour at night, Gershon instantly sensed the vibrations of the news about to be delivered to him, and the overwhelming emotion that engulfed him at that moment was a joyous feeling of liberation from his writer's shackles, at least for the rest of that day. "I'm so sorry, Gershon," Hedy said, "I know you loved him, it's really so unfair. He was all alone when he passed, no family surrounding him, no loved ones, attended by strangers. He didn't deserve this, such a pure soul deep down. Feel free to grieve, Gershon, let yourself go, privilege yourself, you've earned the right."

But instead of the harsh sounds of wholesome weeping and lamentation that she had come to expect from him at the other end of the line and that would at this time have been so appropriate and normative, the term she had taken to using instead of just plain normal, there was only a black silence, like a long dark tunnel gradually fusing to a point in the distance and sealing, which was to Hedy far more disturbing than ever his crying could have been. She called his name helplessly, again and again, her voice growing more and more high pitched and frantic, a sense of dread tightening in her chest, rising in her throat, while, at the same time, she was anxiously struggling to work out in her head a plan, a list of the steps she needed to take immediately in order to save him from a possible act of self-inflicted, irreparable foolishness.

"Hedda," he suddenly called out of that pit into which he had descended, rattling her profoundly by speaking when she was least expecting it. Her relief was so enormous, it extinguished any thought of correcting him for so pointedly articulating that despised corruption of her name. In a voice calm and business-like, showing no sign of being on the verge of weeping again nor any signs of having embarked on the early stages of mourning or of contemplating an act dangerous to himself or others, he inquired if progress had been made toward finding the culprit who had vandalized the Camp Jeffrey Epstein doors with those antisemitic slurs.

"I don't think we'll ever find anything out now," was Hedy's too-swift response, instantly alerting Gershon, putting him on his guard. It seemed obvious to him that she had been armed and ready with that answer should the question arise. It was too automatic, robotic, too cautiously formulated and rehearsed, it flashed a warning signal, almost a threat, so strikingly different from her usual mode of communication with him, as if to advise him as plainly as possible to cease and desist from asking any questions about the doors incident for his own good—Do not go there, Gershon Gordon, the case is now officially closed. He felt all this at once, keenly and bitterly. Had a consensus been reached among the higher-ups to consider that juvenile graffiti spree a single, isolated act of mischief perpetrated by the late nutcase Arnie Glick, now no longer able to defend himself? That would have been a classic move on the part of those two alien shiksas, those Lilithian witches, those two plotting, conspiring Zoyas, Zoya Roy and Zoya Epstein, to blame the acts of antisemitism on a dead Jew, give him all the credit, and thereby save the good name of the institution.

The good name of the institution—Camp Jeffrey Epstein?

Addressing Hedy across the wires, barely able to suppress his disgust, Gershon advised her that yes, he understood, he got it, he was not at all paranoid, as she very well knew, but yes, her message and its subtext had all come through loud and clear, and in his humble opinion she ought to feel ashamed of herself for colluding in smearing by innuendo the late comic genius Arnold Glick, when she knew very well that no way in hell could the door action have been Arnie's work, it was not Arnie's style at all, he would at the very least have marked up his own door along with all the others to avoid suspicion, he was not so stupid. And by the way, Gershon pushed on, the doors are only one small part of the story so far, for Hedda's information, already there has been more, far more destructive and deadly acts, he, Gershon, had already personally been at the receiving end of that more, he had been that more's target and, yes, victim. "And let me just give you a head's up, Hedda, there is more to come, take my word for it," Gershon advised her. Swearing her to secrecy by the bonds of her mental-health-practitioner ethics oath, threatening to have her defrocked if she ever leaked a word of what he was now about to reveal, he proceeded to unburden to her across the airwaves—how he had suffered the violation of his most personal assets in a vicious raid that took place basically within the same time frame in which the doors had been defaced, how his manuscript had been ripped to shreds along with its carbon copies and dumped into the toilet bowl and crapped upon in what amounted to a pogrom, how his typewriter had been mauled and tortured in the shower in what was effectively a lynching, how he now as a result of this violation was condemned to sit all day long chained to his desk like a zek chained to his wheelbarrow in a Siberian gulag, condemned to sit in his isolation cell here at Camp Jeffrey Epstein with pen and index cards from morning to night struggling to resurrect his art from the ashes, like a crippled phoenix, how he felt paralyzed in mind as he was in body, hollowed out and wasted, no longer able to see the point of going on.

A long silence followed from Hedy's end. When finally she spoke, her voice shook so hard that Gershon felt as if he had to strain to hear each word, like catching teeth being knocked out one by one. "I'm so sorry this happened to you," Hedy said, attempting to reassert her professional persona. "I want to help you, Gershon, but I don't know how I can ethically keep your secret when at the same time you display such classic suicidal ideation with your talk about not being able to see the point in going on any longer."

"Help me? How can someone like you ever help me?" Gershon shot back so spitefully. "With one of your patented daf yomi, one-a-day Talmud multi-culti vitamin pills maybe?"

It was like a slap in the face, bringing her to her senses. He was in good fighting form, bursting with aggression, testosterone, no way did he sound like a guy about to throw in the towel any time soon. In recounting to her all that had happened to him and how he had been invaded and then blocked and then despairing, he had simply been riding the crest of his rhetoric to its designated shore. She knew his rhythms. Guys like Gershon do not kill themselves, just everyone around them.

Her bright little laugh of relief at this thought bounced toward him along the wires, taking him aback. "What's so funny?" he demanded.

"I was just thinking," Hedy replied. "The daf yomi daily

Talmud pages we've been reading these days—check them out for yourself, Gershon, like Berakhot 62? You won't believe this, but they're actually amazingly relevant in a way to what you went through—as it happens, they're all about bathrooms. The sages considered bathrooms to be very dangerous places, crawling with snakes and scorpions and demons, the *beis kiseh* they called them, house of the seat, like a throne room—but you don't need any of my translations. They were referring to outhouses in those times, of course," Hedy went on, "but the main lesson they were teaching us is Beware, take the necessary precautions, really horrific things can happen around the vulnerability of bathrooms—a lesson you, too, have unfortunately now learned the hard way at such personal cost to yourself, Gershon, I'm so sorry to hear."

He was stunned into a kind of silence of disbelief that he was even listening to her spouting this stuff as she went on describing to him how in the relevant Talmud pages of the cycle that just coincidentally happened to come up for study on these very days—isn't that amazing?—it is recounted that the woman who was like a mother to the orphaned sage Abaye had also raised a lamb to accompany her darling boy to the toilet, maybe a goat would have been better protection than a lamb from fiends lurking in there, but goats themselves, as everybody knows, were possessed by the demonic, Abaye's mama surrogate thought of everything. And as for Abaye's Talmudic sparring partner, Rava, before he became head of the yeshiva, his wife would rattle some nuts in a copper pot to fend off the demons while he sat defecating in the outhouse, and then, after he got the top job, she kept her hand on his head through a window for extra protection the entire time he sat there doing his business in the beis kiseh.

Rava and Abaye, Abbott and Costello, Mutt and Jeff. Gershon was coming out of his trance. "So what's your point, Hedda?" he wanted to know. "Are you planning to get me a therapy dog to hang out with me in the toilet from now on in case I have a PTSD attack? Do you want to hold my hand every time I have to go take a crap to get me through the flashbacks about how I have been figuratively raped there? Can you do me a big favor and make an effort to cease and desist from acting like such a saint? It's so unattractive. Nobody likes a saint. Everyone hopes to see them martyred, the more sadistically the better. I'm telling you this for your own good, Hedda."

At her end Hedy absorbed it all, taking it like a man. "I want to help you, Gershon, if you'll only let me," she ventured after partially recovering.

Arming herself against his predictable mockery, she proceeded to tell him that she had an idea that might actually work to unblock him—"I'm not talking about bathroom blockages this time, you know what I mean, I'm referring to your book-project blockage," she hastened to clarify, holding on to what remained of her self-respect. Her idea was for Gershon to get back in touch with his natural creativity, so unconscionably violated in that horrendous raid, by writing down on a sheet of paper or, better yet, on one of his index cards, the Nabokovian method, and Gershon's as well, of course, or even scribbling on a piece of toilet paper if that's when the inspiration grabs him, any random thought that pops into his head in connection with his book project—words, phrases, bullet points, fragments, observations, and so forth. He would then place that index card containing his jottings under his door, poking out into the hallway just enough to be visible to someone looking for it. She would make a point of passing through his hallway several times a day. If she noticed something sticking out under his door, she would take it back to her room, type it into her computer mechanically without actually reading it—she took pains to assure him that this was quite possible, it was a proven speed typist's skill, transcription by word capture and decoding—then slip the printout back under his door as the seed from which to grow his book project. Some text on the page, like pieces of a puzzle to fool around with, these could be incredibly helpful in unclogging the pipes, jogging the system back into working order, so to speak, Hedy said. Not that it matters, but it was a strategy she herself had used during her own writing saturation period—her research papers, her dissertation, that novel long ago rightly forgotten, whatever. At the same time, in her professional capacity, she would continue to call him every night, as required, to check in and to chat. He could rest assured that during those officially scheduled telephone sessions she would never bring up the parallel creative writing track or comment on her minor role in aiding and abetting it, it would be as if all of that were unfolding in a separate, alternate universe. "Think about it, Gershon," Hedy said. "I'll pass by now and then over the next few days to check if you've left something for me, some words on the page or, more to the point, on an index card, to jumpstart your book project."

"Thanks very much for your concern, Hedda," Gershon muttered at last following an extended pause, "but if you don't mind, I'd really appreciate it if you stopped calling my book a project." And he slammed down the phone.

"No problem, it's a deal, if you stop calling me Hedda," she whispered into the dead air.

10.

Like a mummy unwinding, the March days unfolded ominously toward spring, but nothing appeared under Gershon's door. On the eleventh of March, the World Health Organization declared a global crisis—pandemic. Two days later, Friday the thirteenth, Rabbi Tzadik Kutsher's distant relative by marriage, the president of the United States of America—just another oddment among all the oddments squeezing the breathable air out of the planet—had the bad luck to be forced, against his instincts, to declare a nationwide emergency based on rumors of a fake virus on the loose. On Saturday, the fourteenth, all the armadas of the great cruise ships on the seven seas sailed into port, flying black flags, screaming, Beware, Beware, as they disgorged their sick and dying aging revelers in walkers and wheelchairs and stretchers. The next day, the Ides of March, upon which, more than two millennia ago, great Caesar was et-tu'ed and felled, exposing his mortality for all to take note, little Hedy Nussbaum at last retrieved from under Gershon Gordon's door an index card containing some scrawls.

It was a fact, with these index cards Gershon had gone Nabokovian, Hedy reflected, which would make her his Vera, to whom would be dedicated every golden word in order to keep her forever chained to her Royal portable. Nevertheless, the index-card method suited Gershon's episodic output, Hedy decided, she chose not to regard it as grandiose or pretentious. Every day thereafter the cards appeared, sometimes several times a day, sometimes several cards at a time secured by a paperclip and once, a thicker pile, by a young girl's ponytail band with a dangling pink plastic heart-shaped charm, the writing growing more and more dense and urgent. She transferred the content to her computer, printed it out, and delivered the fair copy back to Gershon, same-day service—one-hour service, more often than not—delivered it to him as it had been delivered to her, like bad news, like a bill from the exterminator, like an eviction notice, like a death threat slipped under the door.

In offering herself up as Gershon's girl Friday, and in carrying out the task as she had described it to him, Hedy saw herself as a kind of human processing machine. Her job as she envisioned it was to transfer his content exactly as it had been passed on to her, without enhancement or refinement, to move it intact and unaltered from the perishable card upon which it was subject to all the scourges of fire and water and, above all, human malice, and to dispatch it to the great cloud above, from where it could always be retrieved, where it would exist for eternity and could never again be liquidated. To the degree that she could perform this task like an automaton without engaging in a true act of reading, she scrupulously made an effort to do so.

But then it happened that certain word clots leaped out at her by virtue of their repetition, most alarmingly, the coupled pair, Jeffrey plus Epstein. She was instantly gripped by the possibility that she might unwittingly be engaged in the act of aiding and abetting Gershon in the writing of an insider account of life at Camp Jeff, perhaps only barely disguised as a work of fiction, a lurid exposé, including confidential details about patients and staff that would inevitably be traced back to her, tanking her career and her livelihood and whatever remained of her future, for surely she had more lived life behind her than ahead of her, as God had reassured Rabbi Eleazar ben Pedat in the Talmud when he was faced with deciding whether or not to go on suffering on this earth. Even more appalling to Hedy's mind was the chance that Gershon might also be writing explicitly about her, Hedy Nussbaum, however uninteresting he found her to be, a shameless betrayal that tormented Hedy mercilessly but that she recognized as a real possibility, having once long ago been a novelist herself. All of this justified in her mind the reciprocal breaching of the high principles of confidentiality, abandoning the technique of capturing and decoding that she had promised Gershon in favor of scrupulously sounding out and evaluating every syllable in her head. The possibility of such an act of bad faith on Gershon's part gave her permission to focus, with all her faculties operating at peak lucidity and comprehension, on the relevant cards for the sake of being forewarned, of saving her life.

Her first thought when she started reading his strained output was that this was a segment of some postmodern work of fiction written in the first person, in which the narrator shares the author's name, Gershon Gordon, and other players, living or dead, also have recognizable names from the rogues gallery, most notoriously, the character Jeffrey Epstein. The setting seemed to be a resort of some kind, but in no way did it resemble the dowdy former Lokshin Hotel and Country Club in all of its emblematic and endearing bad taste, recently given a superficial facelift as Camp Jeffrey Epstein in the New York Catskill Mountains. This obvious difference between the two places was a source of instant relief and comfort to Hedy, enabling her to continue her illicit close reading with greater concentration as the pulsing in her throat subsided and the pounding of her heart quieted down. In fact, the resort evoked by Gershon was not even a resort, or a hotel, or a country club. It was a private island in the Caribbean of the highest standards of flaunted wealth, owned by the super mysterious oligarch Jeffrey Epstein. The centerpiece of the prose on the index cards that Gershon had managed to squeeze out was a fabulous swimming pool in which naked young female blonde beauties splashed, as mighty men from the boldest-faced list lounged around and watched them at play, absently taking drinks and delicacies off trays held out to them by invisible black natives in white uniforms—like negatives, as Gershon rather insensitively metaphorized, though Hedy, of course, had not been hired to strike with her red pencil. Jeffrey Epstein himself was not present in the flesh on these pages. Instead, his chief procurement officer who went by the name CPO, her job-related monogram (like V for Victim, who also lost her good name), was on duty in his place, the only female in the vicinity clothed and dry and above seventeen years of age, stretched out in a lounge chair alongside Gershon Gordon comparing notes like old buddies, like landsleit.

Hedy was feeling much calmer as she went on with her conscious old-fashioned reading while typing into her computer, at relative ease now thanks to having convinced herself that neither she nor the traumatized and fragile souls under her care at Camp Jeff were in imminent danger of exposure. By right she should now turn off the deep reading function and resume her robotic persona as she went on transcribing, she recognized that, there no longer was any justification for her prying. On the other hand, Gershon was her designated mental-health client. Much useful information might be gleaned about his issues and obsessions and hangups and so on, even, or especially, from a work of fiction, as Hedy knew so well from her own ventures in those treacherous fields, insights that she could then apply in leading him to true healing, a healing of soul and a healing of body. Then again, maybe this wasn't fiction at all, it suddenly hit her. Maybe it was creative nonfiction or some other mongrel genre like that, a memoir of sorts—Jeffrey Epstein and Me, that kind of cheap breakout thing. After all, it was not unreasonable to assume that Gershon had known and consorted with Epstein in the outside world. Gershon Gordon had been a player, a recognized public intellectual, never mind the compromises and sellouts such a role entailed, his presence and his palaver had once been widely sought after. It was not improbable that Gershon at some point might have operated as Jeffrey Epstein's trophy intellectual performing in exchange for the perks, as Arnie Glick, may his memory be for a blessing, had performed, in his fashion, with respect to Gershon himself, Hedy reflected, and so on down the food chain.

What excuse did she have then to go on violating her pledge to Gershon by persevering in her snooping? Clearly, the answer was the unexpected introduction of CPO into these particular cards that Gershon had dropped for her to fetch like a dog off the floor under his door. Only the night before, at a staff meeting that Zoya Roy had conducted by Zoom from the good Jeffrey Epstein's waterfront estate in Palm Beach, Florida, to which she had decamped to wait out the black death, not too far down the prime-real-estate row from one of the late bad Jeffrey Epstein's main sex-traffic-control headquarters, Zoya had informed them that Lady CPO, as Zoya chose to refer to her, the bad Jeffrey Epstein's chief procurement officer, would be arriving in the coming days to Camp Jeff to take shelter there from the plague and from her victim avengers and from her law-enforcement pursuers in a luxury suite of rooms now being readied for her on the topmost floor—"Hiding in plain sight," Zoya had commented snidely, "where those types would never think to look for her." Lady CPO, Zoya went on most unprofessionally—criminally, in Hedy's opinion—would be recovering at Camp Jeff from a lifetime of abuse that began on the day she was born. She is perhaps the greatest victim of us all, the archetypal female victim, said Dr. Zoya Roy, brandishing her professional authority, adding that she had decided to share with them the extremely exciting top-secret news that Lady CPO was now considering participating in a public psychoempathy session at Camp Jeff as a survivor opposite her offender, to be impersonated by a two-faced dummy, one face, her father's, the other face, the bad Jeffrey Epstein's. "Keep your fingers crossed," Zoya told them. In the meantime, it was of the utmost importance that Lady CPO's privacy be secured and protected, her presence on the reservation was not to be disclosed to anyone, Zoya was counting on their discretion, any violation would bring down upon the head of the guilty party the most severe consequences.

That sounded like a threat aimed directly at her—a threat that Hedy duly registered. For the sake of her personal survival, she had no choice but to arm herself. She now had a legitimate need to know. Circumstances now compelled her to proactively take on the ethically distasteful task of closely examining Gershon's latest product. Only in that way could she be prepared and protected, only by facing this danger head on and taking the necessary actions would she ever have the moral luxury of returning someday to business as usual, including her secretarial duties for Gershon in full robotic mode.

Based on the index cards left on the floor for Hedy to collect, which she now was duly transferring word for word onto her computer, Gershon had broken the ice poolside by announcing to CPO that they both were official members of the Second Generation club, offspring of Holocaust survivors, and therefore honorary Holocaust survivors themselves, which made them relatives of a sort, kin, as in "All Israel are brothers"—and sisters, Gershon amended, in a polite nod to gender inclusivity. This launched them at once into a delightfully flirtatious back-and-forth, showing off their respective Second Generation post-traumatic-stress-disorder credentials, material Hedy was now reading and typing with even closer attention as a trained mental-health practitioner. Number-one Second Generation symptom? Hereditary paranoia, driven by the unshakable conviction of the imminence of another Holocaust recurrence at any moment, a morbid case of insecurity that demanded a state of constant vigilance and preparedness. Both CPO and Gershon heartily concurred on this point. But on a day-to-day basis, the most chronic and debilitating Second Generation symptom, hands down, was a desperate need to satisfy in every way imaginable a wounded parent's impossible expectations, to make up for all that papa and/or mama had suffered and lost—and never once succeeding, no, not one bloody time could we ever fully satisfy them, damn it, they both agreed. This shared confession of mutual failure launched them into spasms of hilarity, Gershon recalled in the section that Hedy was now transcribing, two damaged children of the tribe, laughing achingly until the tears were streaming down their cheeks, as Gershon described it. So how long had she known Jeffrey? Gershon inquired now with all the insider privileges of family. All her life, it seemed, CPO replied wickedly, Jeffrey was her father's protégé, his clone. And then she added something suspiciously odd, far too personal after so brief an acquaintance, in Hedy's opinion, especially coming from one as sophisticated and self-disciplined as CPO was reputed to be. "All his life I was my father's slave, and now I'm Jeffrey's slave," CPO supposedly had said, according to Gershon, and once again she was seized by a fit of hysterics, Gershon recalled. When she regained her composure at last, she added, "Daddy was a good Jew, you know, they love him in Israel to this day, they miss his great big appetite for everything, his great big booming voice, and Jeffrey is a good Jew too in his way, only instead of prayer three times a day, it's massages three times a day, plus three orgasms." Here Gershon inserted a note to himself on a separate card to fill in details on the uncanny similarities between these two alpha Jewish males, CPO's Jewish father and Jeffrey ("Yidel") Epstein—their legendary sexual voraciousness, their secretive dealings in the worlds of high finance with a specialization in shell companies and offshore banking, their flamboyant penetration into the most elite circles of society, their Jewish stigmata and top-secret Israel entanglements, their mysterious death, CPO's father by suicide, or maybe it was homicide, or maybe an accident, falling one night off the side of his luxury yacht while urinating naked into the wine-dark sea as was his wont, and more than a quarter of a century later, Epstein's death in a cockroach- and rat-infested New York jail cell by suicide or by murder, which even Gershon could not have prophesied during his first meeting with Lady CPO in the Virgin Islands, but which loomed heavily now as he was exhuming the two men on his index cards.

The segment that Hedy had been transcribing ended abruptly right about here. CPO no doubt felt that she had been letting herself speak too loosely, Hedy speculated, that she had been too carried away as a consequence of the intoxicating, unexpected proximity of newly discovered family connection. "Oh dear, look at the two Bills," CPO said, by way of distraction, as Gershon reported it, firmly putting the kibosh on their conversation and directing her dark-shaded gaze toward the opposite end of the pool where every exposed centimeter of the alarmingly boiled red flesh of Bill Clinton and Bill Gates was at that moment being anointed and soothed with sun-blocking cream and aloe vera lotion, expertly applied and rubbed in by a bevy of naked nymphets.

The Two Bills. The Two Bobs. For Hedy, the association clicked instantly. The Two Bobs were also celebrities, granted of a lesser order than an ex-president of the most powerful nation on earth and one of the earth's richest men, it's true, but even so they had been major stars in the media firmament, their faces and voices on the screen penetrating the stale, fetid corners of nearly every cave in America. They, too, no doubt had been sought after by the bad Jeffrey Epstein, they, too, must have had social intercourse with the omnivorous Epstein in their former lives, and very likely they, too, had sampled Epstein's poisoned largesse, like Gershon and so many other vain, weak souls, Hedy now grasped. It was as if she were getting a crash course in how the world really operated beneath the surface, in the realm of the rich and powerful, as if she were being slapped awake from a dream of innocence into the brutish reality.

"They're no longer with us, the Two Bobs," Hedy had informed Gershon during their regularly scheduled phone call a few days earlier. "Not, God forbid, like Arnie Glick, a'lav ha'shalom, not sucked up by the great Covid global vacuum cleaner," she hastened to clarify upon realizing how somberly she had broken the news. "They just split, they're gone, they didn't even bother to say goodbye. A black limousine pulled up one day in front of the main building and whisked them away. Looks like it's the end of your Gang of Four—with Arnie, may he rest in peace, also eliminated," Hedy added rather passive-aggressively, she felt to her shame, augmenting her chronic state of guilt and regret.

The Two Bobs were heading north toward the hook of Cape Cod, to Massachusetts, or so Hedy had heard. A breathtaking house perched high atop a collapsing dune overlooking the Atlantic Ocean was said to be awaiting them there, offered for their use for the duration of the pandemic by a reclusive fan of exemplary loyalty who preferred to remain anonymous. Their plan was to create their own bubble there—or Bobble, as they called it—in which to isolate together, lying in bed facing the great wall of glass, watching the sun rise every morning over the silver-blue iridescent waters ruled by the kingdom of great white sharks. Here they would continue to produce the videos they had been churning out at Camp Jeff, as the sand beneath them inexorably ran down into the sea and all the material culture that ever had been desired and coveted by humankind was washed away. Could it be that Gershon truly had no clue at all that the Two Bobs had been making these videos? Actually, it was Wesley Wu who handled the videoing, he was now their official tech guy. Wes had also absconded with the Two Bobs in the limo to carry on as their videographer, plus, as a side job, to take charge of the cooking in the state-of-the-art kitchen and to oversee other domestic maintenance, as far as Hedy knew. Where had Gershon been? Was he not even aware that one of these videos had already gone seriously viral—viral in the time of virus—stirring up the zeitgeist?

In the viral video, Bob Bloom and Bob Blatt, fully decked out in matching media-ready suits and ties, are sitting side by side at a desk in one of their rooms at Camp Jeff, assuming the instantly authoritative, familiar posture of seasoned co-anchors. Good evening, Bob began. We're reporting to you today from Camp Jeffrey Epstein New York, the other Bob chimed in. No, not that Jeffrey Epstein, not that sicko sex maniac goombah, interjected the first Bob. Right, Bob, a different Jeffrey Epstein, another rich guy with the same common Semitic-sounding first and last name, unfortunately for him, who set up this camp here to sanitize his name and reputation by rehabilitating so-called harassers and predators like you and me, crazy but true. That's right, Bob, like a mikvah. Folks, do you know what a mikvah is? It's a kind of pool, not a fun pool like a jacuzzi—it's a religious artifact, a ritual bath, something like a Jewish baptismal font, full immersion, no fooling around. You go down naked in the mikvah, you dunk over your head, then bingo, you're pure again, you can come up for air and return to the tents of meeting. The good Jeffrey Epstein dunks in the Camp Jeff mikvah, and his good name is restored. We get dunked in the Camp Jeff mikvah, and we can venture back to the fringes of civilized society—maybe. That's right, Bob. So, as you've probably guessed by now, we're two Jewish goys, excuse me, guys, like those two loaded Jeffrey Epsteins, the bad Jepstein and the good Jepstein, only we're not really what you would call seriously rich Jews, we're poor Jews by those standards, if you can believe such an entity as a poor Jew exists, we're here at Camp Jeff because we've been #MeTooed even though we're just minor, small-time harassers, Bob said. Exactly, the other Bob said, but to our credit, we're equal-opportunity affirmative-action harassers, we don't harass shiksas only, like most normal Jewish males when they're let loose, we believe in diversity, equity, and inclusion. That's correct, Bob, and we don't harass by pinning women against the wall or throwing them down on the floor or trapping them like bunny rabbits, which is the modus operandi of one of our fellow campers here, who shall forever remain nameless, a major-league harasser who unfortunately also happens to be a member of the tribe, which is very bad for the Jews. This aforementioned sleaze, he rips off women's bodices and knickers, but we never do that. We never wank off in front of the ladies. Or surprise French kiss them. Or grab a body part, and squeeze for all it's worth, or smack a passing derriere. No, no, that's not our style at all, the Two Bobs agreed in the viral video, that's not how we were brought up. So what kind of so-called harassing did we do that was so bad that it got us #MeTooed and kicked out of the known world and we ended up in this joint as if we're already dead and stuffed for public viewing? the Two Bobs asked each other so plaintively. Back rubs. Playful hugs. A surprise dry kiss now and then, a peck really. Harmless little jokes. Raising the ladies' culture levels with great works of art, like *L'Origine du monde* by Gustave Courbet. Appreciating a nice-fitting skirt, a tasteful sweater, lips, legs. Reminiscing over drinks about the performances of former girlfriends and wives, hot and cool. The ladies seemed to like it, Bob said. I thought they liked me, Bob, said Bob. I thought they liked me too, Bob, Bob said. Nobody complained, the Two Bobs said in chorus. But now they tell us they were extremely offended, they hated every minute, they say, they felt violated, they were traumatized, tormented, they struggle every day to get out of bed with their PTSD symptoms and other assorted negative aftermaths, or so they say. How were we supposed to know that they really hated it? Bob wondered out loud in this viral video. They seemed to be having a good time, but now they tell us that they were only pretending, they say they had no choice, they say they were forced to submit and act like they wanted it, because we Bobs of the world, we have all the power. Hey, do we look like guys who have all the power—do we look powerful? The Two Bobs turned as to a mirror to inspect each other's face and shook their heads solemnly. You know what I think, Bob? What, Bob? I think we look Jewish. I think powerful is code for Jewish. Here's my question: How powerful do you think we Jews looked in the ghettos and the pogroms and the death camps? Hey, let's show them what allegedly powerful Jews really look like. Let's grovel, let's crawl, let's toady, let's suck up to the ladies like two big-nosed fawning little Yids. Gifted and talented ladies, please, we implore you, look at us, we are pounding our chests, we are beating our breasts right over our hearts with the knuckles of our bare fists. For the offenses we committed against you, knowingly and unknowingly, we're sorry, sorry, so, so sorry. Will you forgive us, mama? Can we come home now?

Hedy played this video for Gershon during one of their daily calls. "What? What? What?" Gershon kept yelling. The volume was at peak level, but to his frustration, every other word kept sluicing away from him, dropping out of his range. "Type that damn thing up and shove it under my door in the next fifteen minutes," he yelled, and slammed the session to its end. Something in the video, which for Gershon at his end, due to his persistent refusal to join the wired masses, could only be relayed as an audio over the telephone, seemed exceedingly urgent, seemed to touch a painfully responsive chord in his psyche. This is what Hedy understood during the less than thirty seconds that she took to consider whether or not to comply with his command, so crudely transmitted. What Gershon was experiencing, Hedy decided, was a sensation far deeper than unfiltered fury at the Two Bobs, once so deferential to him, practically obsequious, two stereotypical truckling Yids, exactly as they had described themselves. It was their outright flat desertion at their eureka moment of realization and clarity that rankled Gershon, Hedy understood, the way they had so publicly, and yes, so virally, identified and named the ancient enemy who rises up against us now in our time to destroy us, and in every generation has risen up to destroy us, they drop that bombshell that explains everything, yes, everything—why we are here at Camp Jeffrey Epstein, why of all sinners we have been selected for special opprobrium and condemnation, singled out as oppressors just as the State of Israel has been singled out, a mere lambkin among the wolf nations on the planet, why everything that had befallen us befell—and then they just take off to the beach and leave him there to face the eternal enemy alone. Gershon's abandonment, even by God Himself, was now painfully on view in his moment of bitter enlightenment. As his provider, Hedy had no choice but to stick with him and provide. She produced the script, she conveyed it to his door barred to her for so long, she kowtowed to the floor, banged her forehead, and slipped it into his lair within the allotted quarter-hour.

11.

Over the next few days, Hedy faithfully paced up and down Gershon's hallway, but no index card leached through under his sealed door for her to claim and transcribe. Their scheduled sessions continued by telephone every night as required, on the basis of which she concluded that he was still in this world, she believed it was to him she was speaking, though he hardly reacted or responded with anything more than his rasping exhalations. The one topic she thought might rouse him from his despondency was his great work in progress, but it was not for her to be the first to violate their pact to keep that territory strictly off limits during their official sessions. Had he given up his book project? This was a question of deep concern for Hedy. The consequences of such an abdication as it played out in terms of his mental health could be calamitous, in her professional opinion. By nature Gershon Gordon was something of a gossip, like so many intellectuals Hedy had known. There had been a time when she had been able to entertain him with the latest dirt on Jeffrey Epstein, the one who counted himself among the good, the two Zoya furies, Smiley's daily rounds in the trendiest hazmat outfit blowing her whistle, sticking Say-Ah tongue depressors into open mouths poking through the prison bars.

But now all of these juicy bits seemed to leave Gershon cold, he seemed to have lost his appetite for this kind of stimulus. Out of her rising concern for his state of mind, Hedy even recklessly endangered her own future by betraying to him the highly classified news that CPO was now in residence in the penthouse at Camp Jeff, the madwoman in the attic, rebranded as the prototypical female survivor and victim, but even that exceptionally juicy shocker produced no tropism from Gershon.

The latest Camp Jeff bulletin that Hedy dredged up to shake Gershon out of his troubling withdrawal was the news that Father Clarence and Rabbi Tzadik Kutsher had been rushed by ambulance in extreme physical distress to the former Maimonides Hospital in Liberty, New York, and though Gershon's attention seemed in no way piqued by this update, as far as Hedy could determine, she persevered in unpacking the story, as she put it. Quite independently, Hedy recounted, possibly due to the loneliness wrought by their respective isolations, the rabbi and the priest had gotten into the habit of slipping out of their rooms after midnight in their pajamas and slippers and matching masks stamped with the Camp Jeff logo, and making their way through the fabulous lobby of the former Lokshin Hotel and Country Club, past the fountain with its brilliant undulating rainbow spumes in the direction opposite to the institutional dining room, to the world-famous tearoom lavishly decorated in the rococo chinoiserie style, which Rabbi Tzadik Kutsher regarded as truly appropriate in this age of the China Virus, as his distant relative by marriage had so eloquently dubbed the plague. Here in this tearoom the two men sat theologically distanced from one another at opposite ends of the huge aquarium that stretched across an entire wall, brightly illuminated in psychedelic colors, celestial blues, scarlets, golds. So much comfort was to be drawn just from sitting there, watching the alien creatures in their silent underwater universe swimming unperturbed back and forth, indifferent to the coming end of the world, which, from their aspect, might already have taken place. Without exchanging a single word, each man felt the presence of the other and was comforted by it, Hedy believed, two clergymen past their prime with a forbidden shared weakness for pretty boys.

Nobody knew exactly what happened next, but it seemed that one of them, most likely Rabbi Tzadik Kutsher, must have been idly reading the label on a sack that was lying around containing a product meant for cleaning out fish tanks, prominently featuring the ingredient chloroquine phosphate, a drug recently extolled at a news briefing by Kutsher's distant relative by marriage, the president of the United States for our sins, who riffed on its proven efficacy in preventing and treating malaria. He had a really good feeling that this stuff could do the trick and zap the China Virus too, Kutsher's distant relative by marriage had declared, he was a guy who went with his gut, he had great instincts, a terrific track record for being right on the money on just about everything, he had a genius IQ, he was actually a pretty smart cookie if he had to say so himself. All we know at this point, Hedy said, is that when the paramedics arrived to wheel the two clergymen away, they tagged as exhibit A the dregs at the bottom of two celadon bone china teacups painted with wraparound dragons which, upon subsequent laboratory analysis, were shown to be laced with an alarming dose of the tank-cleaning chemical, enough to flush a prophet out of the belly of a great fish.

"So where are they now, our two sinner men of God?" Gershon spoke up loud and clear, to Hedy's surprise and relief. She had not expected him to react at all to this news update, much less so remarkably in character. Was he about to rejoin the game, was he still playing?

"Father Clarence? He's still at Maimonides, on life support, unfortunately, he's in a coma, doesn't say a word, you know, just like the Supreme Court justice with the same name. Kutsher's back in his room at Camp Jeff, strong as an ox, biting his toenails and fressing away as usual. As we all know, there's nothing he won't put into his mouth, so long as it's either kosher or circumcised."

Did she really say that? There was a prolonged pause, as if Gershon had retreated underground for an intake of breath and to reconsider his assumptions about mousy little Hedda, or so she took some paltry satisfaction in imagining, before he emerged again to give her his orders. "Listen to me, Hedda Nussbaum. Ever since you played for me that seminal video by the Two Bobs and then typed it up so that I could review it painstakingly, I have not been able to rest or to sleep. Quite by accident, in spite of their lack of depth and their intellectual limitations, those Bobbsey twins have hit upon the truth that I have always known. I have no illusions that they themselves possess any real understanding of what they have unearthed, but the message to me is clear: the time has come for me to stand up, figuratively speaking of course, and to act. What has happened to the Bobs and to me and to such a disproportionate number of us here inside and outside of Camp Jeffrey Epstein is an old story tangled up like a poisoned vine in the timeline of history—hook nosed, lecherous Jews, world-controlling, powerful, superhuman and subhuman at one and the same time, bringers of plague since time immemorial but also its cures, the designated objects of the oldest and longest-running hatred in the history of the world, for which we get no pass, no credit at all. Tell me, Hedda," and here Gershon's tone shifted, eliding to the almost solicitous, "you must have a Hebrew name—or is it just Hedda in Hebrew too, or Hoda, or Hodaya, or maybe something painfully ordinary, like Hedyota?"

"Hulda," she replied, wondering what he could be wanting from her now.

"Ah, beautiful, like the prophetess from the age of the great Jeremiah, one of the seven female prophetesses of Israel. I suppose you know what the word *hulda* means in Hebrew?

She nodded, though of course he couldn't see her. "Weasel," she mumbled.

Gershon let out something that resembled a laugh, she had never heard such a sound come from him before. "Maybe I'll call you my little weasel from now on—affectionately, of course," he said.

"So, my little weasel," he tried it out as Hedy noted that he had hit the session time limit, she waited for the familiar bang of the receiver, like the pounding of the gavel closing the case. "For extra credit, my little weasel," Gershon surprised her now by holding on for a coda, "I want you to come by tomorrow morning, early. There will be a little surprise waiting for you under my door."

When obediently she arrived at his door early the next morning, she found three index cards poking out onto the hallway carpet. It looked like a statement of some sort, one block of prose per card, each card numbered, tightly written in Gershon's cramped hand that she had come to know so well, pressing down hard, scoring the surface with the black ink of his pen. Attached on a yellow Post-it was an order to transcribe what he called his manifesto onto the computer, and then to print out a minimum of one hundred copies and guard them with her life as she awaited further instructions.

The text was as follows:

1. I, Gershon Gordon, hereby declare that I am the reincarnation, the gilgul, of Lord George Gordon, as anticipated in the name George Gordon inscribed by my Holocaust-survivor parents, no longer with us, on my birth certificate, as was the practice among refugees for the inevitable hour when the Jew-hating monster rears its head

again. In my previous life, I was a British aristocrat born in the year 1751, a member of Parliament, and, most infamously, the Protestant leader of the Gordon Riots against the Catholics. But more importantly, indeed most gloriously, in my former life as Lord George Gordon, I became a Ger Zedek, a righteous convert to Judaism, taking the name Yisrael bar Avraham Avinu. I lived my final years as a proud circumcised Jew, bearded and sidecurled, in skullcap and kaftan, studying Torah and observing as many of the six hundred and thirteen mitzvot as was possible in the exile of Newgate Prison in the city of London, where I was unjustly incarcerated, and where I died of the typhus plague at age forty-two with my tefillin box between my eyes while singing Adon Olam.

2. Over the more than two and one half centuries since my passing my soul did not cease to cringe with shame at the memory of my false ardor in the so-called Gordon Riots. What are Protestants or Catholics to me or I to them, other than their universal, age-old shared hate object, the purported killer of their false messiah, the stubborn rejecter of their god? I am a Jew, I cry, as I am forced to kneel on the ground and bare my stiff neck again and again through the millennia to the hooded executioner eternally brandishing his blade. It matters not at all what we Jews do or do not do, we have been chosen as the one-size-fits-all repository for every misfortune, for every variety of evil, however contradictory or deranged, that lubricates the wet dreams and conspiratorial fantasies of the antisemite darkening the sky over our heads, we are the vampires forever rising from the dead spreading disease, sucking the lifeblood out of the world.

3. Now at last, in the pandemic year twenty-twenty, five thousand seven hundred and eighty years by the Hebrew calendar since the Holy One Blessed Be He created heaven and earth out of unimaginable emptiness, finding myself once again imprisoned in my dying days as I was in my prior life, this time at the Camp Jeffrey Epstein correctional institution in the idol-worshipping State of New York, everything has been clarified. I now know who I am, I know who the enemy is, I know what must be done. I am here in this place because I am a Jew. The enemy is the antisemite who has targeted us above all others as sexual predators. My mission now is to reenact the Gordon Riots: Part Two, the Sequel—Color War!— the climactic end-of-time, end-of-season camp activity, with me, the gilgul of Lord George Gordon, serving as the general of the Blue Team of the Holy Tekhelet Fringe, fighting alongside my own people, my true people this time, against the White Team Hooded Spreaders of Jew-Hating Poison. May the Holy One Blessed Be He give our team the power to confuse and crush the enemy with strategic direct actions and targeted raids in the wilderness of Sin on the road to Zion. Mi LaShem Ai'lai, Whosoever Is with the Lord, Follow Me—Reb Yisrael bar Avraham Avinu, Lord George Gordon!

Hedy took this document to her room, sat down at her computer, and processed it as commanded, dazed by its content, which struck her as a form of divine apocalyptical madness possessing a searing element of truth possibly dangerous to self and others, concerning which she, as the mental-health-practitioner in attendance, might be ethically bound to take prophylactic action. Nevertheless, she continued typing and reading, automatically going on to press print times one hundred, no, make that two hundred, bypassing the minimum, when her cell phone, resting on her desk face up to her left, came alive. It was a text message from her boss, Dr. Zoya Roy, MD: "Hedy, despite repeated warnings from me, you have continued to fail to produce a single survivor for the psychoempathy sessions. On top of that, your serial betrayals of our agenda and your flagrant disloyalty to me and our joint enterprise are public knowledge. I therefore regret to inform you that your services at Camp Jeffrey Epstein are no longer needed. Corona (they, them), V for Victim's escort to our wildly successful gala debut opening-night psychoempathy event, has already been hired to replace you. They will arrive at Camp Jeffrey Epstein tomorrow morning with approximately forty survivors, members of their organization, JEV (Justice for Epstein Victims, in case it slipped your mind). They will isolate here from the pandemic for an unlimited period of time, as long as they require, free of charge, full room and board plus all healing and recreational amenities, thanks to the generosity of our benefactor, the good Jeffrey Epstein, reparations for the crimes of the bad Jeffrey Epstein. The entire third floor of the main building has been reserved for the Epstein survivors. Corona, however, as a staff member and your replacement, will require your living quarters and your office space ASAP. I am therefore requesting that you clear out all your junk and vacate no later than tomorrow a.m. and exit the premises. Have a good day. As ever, Zoya R."

Instinctively, like a pilot crash landing to avoid a black hole, Hedy tapped the only name listed in her mobile favorites— Gershon Gordon. It was midmorning, hours until their nightly therapy session. "Who died this time—Father Clarence? Any words from him at last?" was Gershon's greeting upon picking up.

Hedy read to him Zoya's text message. "Bitch!" said Gershon. She elected to interpret this outburst as an expression of support for herself even as Gershon plunged into a clinical disquisition, pointing out what you get if you just double the V in JEV, the proprietary name of that Epstein survivor sorority. "Wiktim! Need I say more?" Gershon added meaningfully. As if to answer his own question, he went on to observe that they better make sure these loony JEVs never find out that CPO is squatting there right over their heads, they will tear that Jewess to pieces without mercy like a bunch of harpies, it would be a regular pogrom.

Shaking her head in the solitary confinement of her end of the line, Hedy gathered the necessary strength to push on. "I have nowhere to go, Gershon," she informed him, in her desperation so uncharacteristically foregrounding her own crisis. "I gave up my apartment and almost everything I owned except for my most basic necessities before starting this job at Camp Jeff. With regard to whatever life remained to me, I expected to finish up here. I'm an orphan, I'm an only child, I have no family to take me in, no friends, no children, no one who loves me, I'm forty-nine years old, I'm all alone, I have nothing, no one."

She was crying, yet the words kept coming out of her mouth, carrying her along to an uncharted place.

"Can I squat in your room?"

She heard her own voice as if detached from her body, as if projected in a cartoon speech balloon over her head making this request even before she knew to which spheres those words were transporting her or where she truly wanted to go.

The word balloons were dropping her a rescue line now to grab onto and soar above it all to survive. Her word balloons informed Gershon that she would leave Camp Jeff the next morning with her backpack, her computer, her printer, including the two hundred copies of his manifesto. Tomorrow morning, she would say goodbye to everyone in sight, she would wave bye-bye to the quarantined inmates staring through the bars of their cells, they would all register that she was leaving and spread the news, they would cross her off their lists, forget she had ever existed. She would walk some distance beyond the main gate. Thanks to the plague, the area no longer teemed with citizen marchers screaming about pedophiles in their midst. At a certain point, she would circle around back to Lake Ethel—"You remember Lake Ethel, Gershon, how I once saved your life there?" There she would wait out the day crouching in the bushes until deep night, catching up on her daf yomi pages, listening on her cell phone to the teachings of the Talmudic princes of the higher-learning academy in Lakewood, New Jersey, as long as her battery lasted as she wept by the shores of Lake Ethel. When darkness descended she would return to the main building by a back route, avoiding the guard tower surrounded by electrified barbed wire, where Smiley kept watch for intruders through her telescope between humping sessions with the good Jeffrey Epstein, whenever he ventured up from the Sunshine State to take care of business. She would enter through the dangerous kitchen and make her way in the night to his door.

"You will let me in, won't you Gershon?"

Impossible. He was a pious Jew, she a strange woman, with all varieties of first-degree ritually impure emissions, including what comes out of her mouth.

She would make a nest for herself inside the closet with its garbage bag weighed down by his pancaked typewriter and his pulped manuscript, his dried-out souvenir turd, his chamber pot, his spray paints, and all his other junk. Within this space she would pray and study. She would observe all the negative mitzvot incumbent on a female, all the thou-shalt-nots, and she would even keep the time-bound thou-shalt positive commandments from which as a female she was excused. She would clean the room, since housekeeping responders no longer entered in times of contagion, she would scrub the bathroom, nothing would disgust her. She would handle his laundry. She would type for him and print for him and distribute the flyers for him while the whole camp slept, expanding his influence and reach, she would devote herself to him, she would be his muse and inspiration and slave, Vera to his Vlad. She would be steadfast at his side as he, Gershon Gordon, the gilgul of Lord George Gordon, rallied the King Mob in the new Gordon Riots: The Sequel—as he led the Blue Team of the Holy Tekhelet Fringe to victory in the final battle of the season. She would fight like a tigress alongside him against all those Jew haters who hashtag us as both creeping vermin and world-control wannabees, as the trodden dust of the earth, the lofty stars in the sky, as God Himself likened us in number and power, the lowest of the low, the highest of the high, looked down upon with revulsion, looked up at with murderous envy, either way we lose. "I can be a big help to you, Gershon, in your new project," she said. "Your cause will be my cause. I won't be a useless eater. I will pay rent for my daled amos, full price, no bargain rates, no special deals for me in my four cubits of personal space. I will not burst your bubble, I will wear a mask twenty-four hours a day. I care about you, Gershon, and I will take care of you. Your silence now I liken to consent. Expect me tomorrow in the dead of night. Tape the door key to the dark side of your newly restored mezuzah, invisible to raiders and other antisemites, but within easy reach of an invalid Jew and an insignificant Jewess. I will not disturb you. I will enter silently, like a mouse. Like a passing shadow, I will let myself in."

12.

She's really here, Gershon took in as he lay on his side under the covers in bed the next morning hardly breathing, watching under heavy lids as Hedy in a faded Yale T-shirt and stale sweatpants, an ungrateful excuse for the small favor of ladies intimate wear, some nylon negligee maybe, or a cheap babydoll nightie that even on her would have so cheered him, made her way hugging the wall from the closet, where she must have slept in strict compliance with her pledge, to the bathroom, taking utmost pains to give no offense. Yes, there she was in the flesh, attending to her bodily needs, emitting her female animal smells, breathing through the orifices of her face pumping a pleated disposable mask, bloodless blue. All her efforts to erase her physical existence were for naught, she was palpably present, violating his solitude. It was not a tenable situation, Gershon now felt his qualms to be fully justified. It was not only his creativity that was at risk, but also the purity of his religious practice, he was countenancing a state of seclusion with a female to whom he was not lawfully bound in marriage. "I knew I was right," he said out loud, referencing his misgivings, his scruples, his plain revulsion when she had first proposed, pleaded for, this living arrangement. The words so sharply enunciated burst suddenly out of his mouth, startling her, causing her to drop her toiletries with a clatter, her sad little toothbrush, her lumpy bar of soap in which a coiled black hair was embedded like a fossil, her steel Afro hair pick, it was all intolerable.

Gershon was a literary man. The articulated formulation that had sprung from his mouth echoed the title of his favorite Trollope novel. The declaration was applicable on several levels, but the mundane truth was that the triggering association had been far from literary. Rather, it had tracked from the unsavory image of Rabbi Tzadik Kutsher that had flashed through Gershon's brainpan, to Kutsher's alleged distant relative by marriage sporting his orange-sherbet DA, to the distant relative's virtuous vice president with his perfect helmet of snow-white hair, who had announced to the hilarity of the entire enlightened world that his Christian faith precluded him from lunching or in any way allowing himself to be secluded behind closed doors with a woman not his wife even for reasons involving the gravest matters of state. Mike Pence, you're my rebbe, Gershon concluded.

This insight brought him full circle back to the clerical authority of Rabbi Tzadik Kutsher, as it became clear that to enable his isolation with Hedda Nussbaum, his sole option in these grave times was to marry her in accordance with the faith of Moses and Israel, adhering to as many of the ritual requirements as was possible, though, of course, under present circumstances involving perilous sickness and secrecy, it would necessarily be a bare-bones transaction, most likely not even featuring a cleric, even one as sullied as Kutsher. The fact was, Hedda Nussbaum was essential to Gershon's mission, he recognized that, he could not afford to lose her at this time, he needed to be alone with her and her worldwide web to get the job done. As Gershon saw it, he was in a position now to offer her only your basic marriage package, which, as she knew very well from her Talmud deep dive, consisted of a two-part deal that could also be expedited without the benefit of clergy, a do-it-yourself job involving, first, sanctification, the euphemism for the acquisition of the female via an object valued at no less than a penny, a brown penny, while uttering the magic words "Behold you are consecrated to me" and so on, followed wham-bam by part two, consummation, looping himself in the loops of her too-Jewish hair. Once his mission was accomplished and her services no longer were needed, he could simply throw the bill of divorce within her four amot, into her personal space as she stepped out of the shower, she need simply bend down and without losing her grip on her towel coverup, pick it up off the floor to be released from their marriage bond. His venerable models were those Talmudic superstars long ago in the good old days, before his almost-namesake Rabbenu Gershom the Light of the Exile banned polygamy, arriving in a strange town in Babylon on a lecture tour and marrying for the duration of their stopover a warm, soft female body, then afterward, when it was time to hit the road again, it's thank you, ma'am, don't forget to get your get on your way out, goodbye and good luck.

Gershon lay in bed listening to Hedy as she carried out her morning ablutions. His eyes followed her as she emerged from the steaming bathroom with one towel babushking her coarse hair and another draped around her torso, secured with both hands pressing her toiletries case and discarded night rags against the toga tuck of the body wrap concealing her mainland from armpits to knees. He made a mental note to himself to fill out the form requesting extra towels and linens and blankets from housekeeping, also he would ask for more food, including maybe a few Nazir noshes to share, on the house, in accordance with his marital obligation to provide for her and sustain her, and also to grant her her conjugal rights, whether he felt like it or not. He would chat up the maids through the door, joke that there was nothing to do during the lockdown except eat and sleep and play with oneself, it was critical that they not suspect he might be sheltering an extra mouth within these walls, most especially the mouth of timid little Hedda Nussbaum, it would not reflect well on his personal desirability.

"I have some good news for you," he said to her from his bed across the room, just as she reached the closet and freed one hand to place it upon the doorknob, preparing to reenter her cave. She turned her head, facing him with an inquiring look. "You only have to stay in there for one day, today—until it gets dark," he announced, indicating the closet. "When it's dark, you can come out, go down to the lake and dunk in the water, full body, like a bride before her wedding. I'm taking for granted that it's been seven clean days since your last cycle, or maybe seven years, just kidding—because, guess what? We're getting married tonight, right after you come back from the Lake Ethel mikvah, nothing fancy, just your basic no-frills wedding plan, not even a rabbi officiating. It's the only way we can be alone together halakhically in a closed space, only as a married couple with all the rights and privileges of sharing a single cell, cellmates—this room will be like our bunker, our underground command control center to strategize for the struggle ahead. Don't worry, when it's all over and we have triumphed, I'll give you a get and release you, no problem, just like those rabbis in the Talmud with their mini marriages when they were on the road. My buddy Shepsie Fink and me, when we were still in yeshiva, we used to tear through the Soncino English translation of the Gemara looking for the dirty parts, we were that desperate, bored out of our minds."

"Yes, Yevamot 37," Hedy said wearily as she was retreating into the closet. "Rav when he would arrive at Dardeshir, and Rabbi Nakhman when he came to Shakhnetziv, each of them would make a public announcement, Who will be my wife for a day? It's a classic bit of Talmud trivia." Then turning again, Hedy gazed for a few seconds at Gershon in his bed now propped up against a bolster of cushions, and said, "So I take it that was a proposal? Fine by me, I'll be your wife for a day or whatever, but meanwhile, would you mind if I keep the closet door open for now? It gets pretty stuffy in there."

It had not escaped Gershon's notice that, without asking permission, she already kept the closet door slightly ajar to allow the wire that powered her devices to snake along the baseboard to the outlet, partway to the john. She was recharging, yes, Gershon accepted the necessity of this annoyance, she needed to recharge good and hard for him after all, for the sake of their common cause, the battle before them. But this open-door policy she had just requested could easily turn into a slippery slope, in his opinion, the overhead light in that closet with its switch so thoughtfully situated at wheelchair disabled level was industrially glaring even during the daytime hours, it was shooting its beam directly at him, blinding him in his bed, where he, too, had planned to recharge on this day, to take it easy, to recover from all that he had endured in this winter season of his discontent here at Camp Jeffrey Epstein, the lashings of #MeToo and corona and antisemitism, the triple-stranded plague, like a braided whip—he, too, needed to rest, to strengthen himself for the epic struggle that lay before them.

"Okay, you can keep the door open just a bit for some air," Gershon relented at last, "but if you don't mind, I'd appreciate it if you'd shut the overhead light, it's stabbing me like a galactic sword directly into my eyeballs, you can work by the underground rays of your electronics, like in a bomb shelter. It's going to be another freakishly warm day," Gershon the bad news weatherman went on to report, "almost eighty degrees Fahrenheit, the first day of spring. Like the Arab Spring, the Beijing Spring, the Prague Spring, sliding inevitably into failure and disappointment, the high hopes of spring ferrying you directly into the tragic blistering inferno of summer. Think about it, Hedda

Nussbaum," Gershon said, "two world wars last century, both bursting out in the dog days of summer." He observed her as she continued standing there, on the verge of fading out into her closet. How unnatural it was for two Homo sapiens of antagonistic genders to be forced to dwell domestically together in one cave full-time with no relief, he mused. "The good news," he now said to her, "is that the heat of the day will warm the water and ease your ritual immersion in the lake tonight when darkness descends. When you return from the Lake Ethel mikvah," he told her, "we'll dispose of the two stages of the marriage requirements chic-choc—you know, the kiddushin-acquisition business followed immediately by the bi'ah-consummation obligation, no need to elaborate. We'll get all of that out of the way tonight so that tomorrow morning we can wake up refreshed bright and early, and get right down to work face to face, fully licensed to cohabitate in a single enclosed space together in accordance with the law handed down from the hill by the holy Rabbi Mike Pence, finalizing our war plans against the eternal enemy bent on destroying us, coming at us yet again from the right and the left, from above and below."

She waited in the closet through the day for the darkness outside to assert itself definitively, then wrapped herself in the black insulation tubing of her space-age coat, with its hidden black hood drawn over her head, a stiff black yarmulke of a mask covering the pestilential vents of the human nose and mouth. Watching from his bed as she made her exit into the night, Gershon speculated to himself, in a manner completely detached, whether or not she might be naked underneath all of that synthetic packaging. How efficient that would be. She could simply slip off that coat in the water, it would hover nearby like an inflated raft as she immersed herself, she could hang on to it and let it float her back to shore when her ritual was completed. But no, no such luck. Under that body bag she was no doubt still shrouded in her dorm-room leisure wear from thirty years ago, the glimpse of which had already ruined his morning. There was nothing about Hedda Nussbaum to feed his fantasies, she was not his type. In better times, he could perhaps have wrangled a special dispensation from some progressive rabbi, allowing him to be secluded with her since there was no attraction, at least from his side, laboring alone together without any extreme commitment in order to carry on their noble work for the sake of the survival of the Jewish people. But now, unfortunately for him, with antisemitism metastasizing perniciously in these terrible times of trouble, sweeping him up along with so many others of our congregation, singled out for elimination, #MeTooing us, deleting us from the history of the world, he had no choice but to marry her for the sake of the cause the minute she returned from her dip in the holy waters.

As she made her way in the darkness along the dirt road to the lake, Hedy felt as if she were being guided by an internal roadmap, the circuit seemingly imprinted in her memory. Yet her passage through this landscape now was so radically different from that night when she had stumbled back to the main house from Lake Ethel with no sense of where she was in the world, her body painfully arced and contorted, pushing Gershon, a furious, sodden mass in his wheelchair, whose life she truly believed she had saved. He, for his part, considered himself to owe her nothing, she was delusional, he told her, he had not been sinking when she found him, he wasn't drowning, he was not offing himself, he had merely been reenacting his evolution from the primal waters, she had interfered with his ontogeny. But in her heart she still silently continued to take credit for saving the life of this Jew, which, as the Talmud teaches in tractate Sanhedrin 37, is tantamount to saving the entire world, she reminded herself. Heartwarming words, driven by maudlin repetition to a dead end—banal, clichéd, false. Where had all those words, those almost two million words of the entire Talmud, gotten her? To Camp Jeffrey Epstein, on the road to Lake Ethel.

Above, her passage was illuminated by a waning moon, the planets Jupiter, Mars, Saturn visible in the night sky, a ruthless beam from Smiley's guard tower scanning overhead, delineating the primeval craters and ruts and rocks underfoot as she made her way onward to the lake, following orders. Why was she doing this, why had she agreed to this mikvah folly, to marrying this narcissist, this zealot, even with the built-in divorce guarantee, marrying him for the sake of a delusional, hopeless cause and such shabby shelter, so grudgingly given? She had been married once before in her life, soon after her novel had come out, she could scarcely pull up before her mind's eye now an image of the face of this certified husband. It had lasted less than a year, that marriage, ending definitively one winter's night, when finally she practically hurled herself down the four flights of stairs from their railroad walkup on One Hundred and Thirteenth Street, corner Broadway, into the freezing cold and slush, barefoot, the rats foraging, wearing nothing but a slip, one strap torn, stained with blood, blood pouring from her mouth and nose, the nose broken, smashed, both eyes blackened—what did the #MeToo Nazis know about harassment? Hedy now asked herself as she recalled that night, and all the punishing nights preceding. A young girl passing by had stopped that night, she recalled, carrying a cello case—Was she okay? Did she need some help? the touching query of a female not yet disabused—only to be wised up in the ways of the world by two city cops in blue, drawing near with pistols dangling under their big bellies, Don't get mixed up in this, girlie, it's just one of your lovers' spats.

Nobody wore slips anymore, almost nobody even owned one, it was no longer an essential article of apparel in a woman's wardrobe, it occurred to Hedy as she continued along the path. Only she, Hedy Nussbaum, she still wore slips, groomed in the genteel parlor of her melancholic mother reclining on her velvet chaise longue with a forearm bent over her eyes, dreaming of her Hedy in a white slip on a hot tin roof. I'm wearing a slip now, Mommy, under my coat, for you, it's my wedding night. Are you happy, Mommy? I slipped on the slip at the last minute, it's white with lace trim, I thought this would be the perfect little number to slip off and then slip on again when the time came for me to enter the water, full fathom five. No wonder it's called a slip, k'shmoh ken hu, Hedy now mused, as we are apprised in the book of Samuel in connection with an even more than usual unsavory husband—his name suited him. At that moment, for some reason, the image of her former patient Max Horn, burdened with such an unfortunate name given his context, levitated before her eyes. Horn, Hedda, Hulda—she was a believer in the power of the name to shape the reality.

She could tell that the lake was nearby now, she could hear the rushes moving in the airwaves, liquid sounds, the hum and murmur of living creatures, she could smell the sludge and decay. Somewhere along the way she must have mistakenly taken a wrong turn, she was coming upon the lake from an unfamiliar angle. A fox vaulted out of the thickets to her right and ran across the path directly in front of her to the brush on the other side. There it stopped and turned its small, pointy face, set apart from other foxes by a shocking white streak amid its dark fur, like Susan Sontag in her new incarnation as it stood there gazing at Hedy with slanted, condescending eyes. The vixen turned, dismissing her, confirming that Hedy was a person of no consequence, no threat at all, not worth the trouble, it lowered its head and vanished into the woods. What could this fox emanation mean? Hedy tortured herself. How did it signify?

The hum of the lake was beckoning, she moved ahead looking

neither to her left nor to her right, maintaining a steady and controlled pace, in case the fox with its highbrow, cerebral white streak might still be watching from among the uprooted, tangled limbs, and grow aroused by the scent of her terror. She sank to mid-calf in mud as she approached a high bank of reeds, it concealed her up to her eyes, her mass of hair blending with the shrubbery, camouflaging her entirely. Just beyond the reeds, leaning against them, she could see the overturned ancient row-boat she had glimpsed from across the lake the night she had saved Gershon's life.

A couple was sitting side by side, pressing against each other on the upended bottom of the rowboat, giving off a postcoital aura, it seemed to Hedy, though she could see only their backs, stirring up memories of summer camp nights, the activity they used to call a social raid stealthily carried out deep into the post-midnight hours, well past curfew, breaking the rules, cou-ples fumbling desperately with each other's body parts, making out to save their lives on the banks of Nookie Beach. They were conversing intensely, this pair on the rotting boat by the shore of Lake Ethel, her head resting on his shoulder, her shoulders gal-lantly draped for warmth in an elegant oversized jacket, which must have been his, which explained why he was clad only in his designer pink shirt on this night as it cooled relentlessly. Hedy recognized the man instantly, even from behind. Max Horn. She must have heard his voice in the distance when she had been summoning up examples of unfortunate but all-too-fitting names, the buzz of his voice must have prompted the associa-tion, Hedy now realized. The woman's head was mostly hidden by the high turned-up collar of the jacket. Hedy could not iden-tify her, but given Horn's well-known preferences, she figured it was probably someone like Smiley, maybe even Smiley herself, cheating on the good Jeffrey Epstein, bestower of luxury sedans and other hard-earned bonuses.

Hedy from her side of the reed bank could now hear every word Horn was saying with such focused intensity to the woman beside him warmed by his jacket. He was, of all things, urging this woman to go to Israel at once, immediately, he was citing the Law of Return, one Jewish grandparent will do the job, get thee to Zion, do not tarry, make the ascent without a moment's delay, he would escort her there himself, it was an offer she could not afford to refuse, he counseled her, he was personally very close to a Russian oligarch who shall go nameless for now, with a fabulous estate in the Herzliya area, right on the blue Mediterranean, Horn said, the guy is hardly ever there, most of the time he's in his superyacht on the high seas, or docked in the port of some fascist state, or in one of his Londongrad properties, or wherever. He, Max Horn, could arrange for her to stay in that empty castle by the sea, no problem, the Israeli government is very tolerant of oligarchs, oligarchs get the best protectia, the Israelis don't ask questions, they don't interfere, and besides it's an entrenched mitzvah of our faith to redeem Jewish captives, there's no chance in hell that they'd ever turn her over to the goyim, they'd never extradite her back to the States, she could count on it, Horn assured the woman.

Who would have thought—Smiley, a member of the tribe, maybe an Igbo from Biafra aspiring to official Jewish certification, and on the most-wanted list too? For some minutes Hedy coddled this insane idea in her head and then it popped, with the deflating sound of a wrong answer on a TV quiz show. Once again Hedy got it wrong, she was wrong so often, about so many things, she believed she made the right synapses, but now as before, she was off, mistaken. Hedy knew Smiley, and the woman now responding to Max Horn was no Smiley, she was an aristocrat, the real thing except for the taint of her Jewish blood, a posh Oxbridge accent, from another planet entirely. Hedy should have connected the dots. It was CPO, of course.

Hedy knew she was in residence. How could I be so dense? Hedy lashed herself.

She listened now as CPO was pounding into Horn's thick skull how daft he was, he was mad, mad, the Israeli government would never let her into the Promised Land, the Law of Return would not be applied in her case. And if by some chance she managed through some dodgy oligarch connections or the like to penetrate the borders, the officials would find her and post her collect right back to the US in a flash, forget about all your bloody little prisoner redemptions and other idjit mitzvahs. Feelers had in fact been put out on her behalf, CPO disclosed to Horn, outright requests, petitions, pleas, cris de coeur, to the very top poobahs of the Holy Land, from that madwoman Sara Netanyahu on down. The rejection had been unequivocal. No way would Israel publicly get mixed up in anything or anyone having to do with Jeffrey Epstein, he is that toxic, CPO said to Max Horn, they would not touch anything that smacked of Jeffrey with a ten-foot pole, even though, and this is entre nous, they owed Jeffrey plenty—plenty! Same with Daddy. Not even for the favorite daughter of her charming and brilliant Daddy, never mind how central Daddy had been to the creation and founding of their provincial little Statelet, never mind what they owed him, they would not extend any form of sanctuary to his equally charming beloved daughter, it was a nonstarter. Forget about it, Max, Hedy heard CPO tell Horn, it's a lost cause. She, her Daddy's little princess, had been transformed into the female Jonathan Pollard, that was the most degrading part of it all, CPO added, despite her service to the cause as selfless companion to two of its unsung heroes, to be rejected like that low-class religious fanatic settler spy. "It's not pretty, Max," she said, "but there it is, the facts on the ground—Israel is not an option for this Jewess, nobody wants me, I have nowhere to go, nothing." The very words Hedy had uttered when pleading with Gershon for refuge. Lady CPO, so high class, practically royalty, herself also now seeking asylum, Hedy reflected, and exactly like her inconsequential self then, CPO was weeping now too.

But Horn would not be deterred by the female ploy of her tears, this was an emergency situation, it was tough-love time, it was absolutely essential that CPO get her ass out of Camp Jeffrey Epstein—not tomorrow—yesterday! Horn pronounced. If not Israel, then some hideout in America, Montana maybe, the Unabomber's abandoned shack, the ruins of the Waco cult compound in Texas, the remains of the Rubashkin kosher meat-processing slaughterhouse in Postville, Iowa, the New Square ghetto in Rockland County, New York, ruled by its grand rabbi, she could put on a wig and a housecoat like that pedophile lesbian Zlata Schick and push a shopping cart around the Super Glatt with all the other pious matrons. She could go wherever, Max Horn said, but she had to go somewhere, anywhere but here.

"Do you see that creature swimming over there?" Horn directed CPO's gaze across Lake Ethel where a molded human female form encased in a full-body black latex swimsuit and coordinating black bathing cap was silently cutting through the water. Like a dart, like an arrow, Hedy marveled as she, too, stretched her neck to get a glimpse from behind her bank of reeds. Did CPO happen to know who that water creature was? Horn inquired severely. Well, for CPO's information, that big fish is Corona—yup, it's her nom de guerre, like the virus, like the crown of the penis. She likes to keep in shape by swimming laps in the polluted Lake Ethel, from one end to the other, back and forth, so that she can lead by example her Jeffrey Epstein Victims when she gives them the good news that you, the madam herself, the procuress and groomer, the mistress of the house of the rising sun, are now conveniently ensconced at Camp Jeff only one flight up, a non-moving target nailed to the floor awaiting torture and evisceration. "You will be chopped up into little pieces, chewed up and spat out by the Jeffrey victims. Dr. Zoya Roy, the psychoempathy doyenne and impresario, no matter how sweetly she shines her luminous blue face upon you now and grants you sanctuary, will add your head to her Kali necklace of skulls," Max Horn said to CPO, helping her up from her perch on the decomposing underside of the sinking boat. As CPO rose, Hedy observed that her legs below Horn's jacket were completely bare, naked, poor lady, and winter, such as it was, still howling.

CPO was leaning against Max Horn, he supporting her like a survivor of a disaster, as if pulling her out from under a collapsed tower. As they made their slow ascent toward the path back to Camp Jeffrey Epstein, Hedy strained to catch his words as he outlined his plan. The Mountain Dale dairy truck will be delivering at Camp Jeff at five the next morning as per usual, Horn was instructing her. He had already arranged for the two of them to hitch a ride incognito in the cooler among the milk cans and sour creams and cottage cheeses. They would be dropped off at the ruins of the old Homowack Lodge in Spring Glen, New York, where Max's people, disguised as cult members of the extreme Jewish sect now squatting there, would be waiting to convey her to a faraway place he had secured, where no one would ever find her again. This was the fallback option that he had set up for her in case she committed the fatal sin of rejecting Zion, forgetting Jerusalem, her right hand forgetting its cunning, his tongue cleaving to the roof of his mouth, his voice in Hedy's ears fading away as he maneuvered the defeated, humbled woman into the darkness.

Forsaken there behind her screen of reeds, Hedy contemplated what awaited her, she needed to think fast, it was a matter of survival. Corona, her successor, her replacement, her rival, was moving over the face of the water. There was no doubt that Corona would recognize Hedy from the night of the great psychoempathy fiasco—the worried little woman lumbering across the stage weighed down by the Jeffrey Epstein dummy slung over her head. A ruthless competitor like Corona would not hesitate to report Hedy's continued presence to Zoya Roy and her goons, Hedy had been seen trespassing illegally on the property, Corona would let it be known. The authorities would be summoned, she would be carted away, hurled off the cliff to the wilderness of Azazel and burned in the sacrificial fires. The inevitable conclusion for Hedy was that a full bridal immersion as per Gershon's orders was too hazardous to carry out now under the circumstances, it would draw Corona's attention like a shark to prey. Standing there concealed by the reeds, bundled in her inflated coat, she made the decision to simply bow her head into the murky waters of Lake Ethel as if praying, wetting her hair thoroughly, then make her way back to Camp Jeff past the sneering fox, back to Gershon's headquarters, and report to him that she had fulfilled her prenuptial immersion strictly in accordance with the laws of Moses and Israel. The sages in Yevamot 65 teach that God Himself had been known to depart from the strict truth in order to keep the peace, to which Hedy, authorized by her PhD license in Talmud, now added the leniency of lying for the sake of peace in the household, which she knew from past experience translated as survival.

Bent over with her face suspended over the deep, spreading the corkscrewed tangled strands of her hair in the lake to wet them so thoroughly they would remain damp evidence for the man when she voluntarily returned to the punishment of his den, she suddenly felt a great weight pressing down on her head, submerging her fully in the water. She thought, Yes, it's okay, I accept. But the weight lifted just as her breath was failing her,

her head was released, automatically it seemed to spring up out of the water, while the creature who had pushed it down was now darting around her like a sea serpent, loosening the binding of Hedy's coat and setting it afloat. They were standing now face to face, she in her soaked white slip, the sea monster in a clinging full-body black rubber suit accentuating a breathtaking womanly fullness, contemplating Hedy and remarking, "The last time I saw a slip was when I was a little girl maybe ten, fifteen years ago, stuffed in the back of the drawer of Daddy's nightstand. It was from Victoria's Secret, I think Daddy got it from his buddy Jeffrey Epstein, who was screwing the owner, literally and figuratively." Without further explanation, the creature tore the slip off Hedy's body, balled it up, and dropped it to find its place among the other flotsam and jetsam at the bottom of the lake, then smoothed Hedy's hair and caressed her breasts, singing, "How beautiful you are, Mommy, your hair like a flock of goats streaming down from Gilead, your breasts like two fawns, grazing among the lilies." Carrying Hedy like a rescuer, a lover, deeper into the water of Lake Ethel as if crossing a threshold, the creature sang out, "Let's do this right, Mommy, like a bride," and they immersed together thoroughly, floating underwater, their arms wrapped around each other. As they rose, the creature kissed Hedy on the mouth, and with the parting words "Don't be afraid, Mommy, I will never betray you, I will come to you in the night, don't forget to open up for me, my sister, my bride," dove into the black waters, emerging once more in the distance to call out, "Say hi to sugar daddy for me," and disappeared again back into the deep.

It all unfolded as if in a dream, yet here she was, slogging naked through the muck of Lake Ethel to the shore, once again on course, obeying the man's orders, wondering how in this state she could make her way back to Camp Jeffrey Epstein without even a fig leaf to cover her, how so pitilessly exposed, in this alarming state of nakedness, public nakedness, as in a nightmare, she would ever get past Susan Sontag lurking in the woods, Smiley's searchlight, the Fidels horny and hungering in the kitchen dungeon, back to Gershon's unforgiving lair, when, climbing up the banks of Lake Ethel she saw before her, hanging neatly from a tree branch as from a hook, as if picked up from the ground and placed there by the loving hand of the great mother, tenderly offering itself to her now for cover and warmth, her black coat, drying by moonlight.

13.

"Get me my wallet, Weasel!" Gershon called out the minute Hedy cracked the door open and set one mud-caked foot in the room, back from Lake Ethel. To the untrained ear it would have sounded imperious, annoyed, but for Hedy it was a matter of exegesis, and she could sense that on this occasion he meant it to some degree welcomingly, even semi-affectionately. This was good enough for her, though it was also true that he could possibly have blown her cover by neglecting to confirm that it was she, the illicit squatter and fugitive who had invaded the room, having failed to take the simple precaution of looking up from his bed in which he was still planted as she had left him, naked amidst his soiled linens, his clumped tissues, the remains of his meals and Nazir snacks, plus his index cards, pads of paper and leaking pens, and of course the books—Camus' *La Peste*, Sartre's *Réflexions sur la question juive*, and *Mémoires de Jacques Casanova*. Hedy had procured these three basic texts for him at his behest just before her termination, in the original French, by no means an easy assignment, she had charged them to her Camp Jeffrey Epstein employee expense account, in accordance with his instructions, inserting a note in his chart that the books were absolutely critical to his rehabilitation, an essential element in his therapy. They were acquired for a "piece" he had been drafting and dictating to her intermittently during their telephone sessions, when, seized by a blast of inspiration, he had hatched the idea to mine the central themes of these three texts to inform a brilliant, original insight he had had, exquisitely and painfully relevant to our troubled historical hour, he had asserted to Hedy. It was also the case, though, that often he would despair, as Hedy could not but note, and when at those dark times during their phone sessions she would attempt to raise his spirits by suggesting that they do some work on the "piece," he would mutter despondently, "Yeah, right, the piece—the piece of shit." But then, as unpredictably, his state of mind would flip, hope would shoot up like a weed flowering in the ruins—maybe he was afflicted with some sort of officially recognized DSM mood disorder, Hedy speculated not for the first time. During those brighter phases he would declare that once the piece was completed to his standards, which were almost inhumanly high, as he reminded her ominously, and then when the piece appeared in some major, unassailably influential publication to which she, Hedy Nussbaum, will have sold it, the intersectionality of these three major strands—plague, antisemitism, sex—plus a few others that might get braided in along the way, would clarify all our travails and woes, humankind would be able to move on, enlightened and optimistic once again, on the path to healing and health.

Dutifully, still wrapped only in the black pneumatic tubing of her coat now sticking to her bare skin, Hedy plodded across the room to his wheelchair and rummaged in its inner and outer pockets, in all of its sunken areas, its racks and recesses, beneath and between its cushions and padding and its metal frame, pasty with dust and lint and dead insects, where she knew his wallet was usually stashed or somehow materialized on its own. She had hoped to have a few minutes upon returning to wash away the environmental contamination of Lake Ethel, to soften and rein in her hair, to freshen up, change into something more comfortable, as they used to say so meaningfully in the great movies of old, but as always, she, little Hedy Nussbaum, never got a break, no, not even on her wedding night. The wallet revealed itself at last on the floor of the closet, her erstwhile room of her own, she could not help but wonder how it had gotten there. Had he been scrounging through her personal effects for some reason while she was dunking at his behest in that polluted premarital ritual pool? And if she floated to him the coordinates of where she had finally located his wallet, would he, for his part, assume she had stolen it?

One of the first things they needed to work on when they were married was building mutual trust, Hedy resolved as she stood now by his bedside holding out the wallet to him. Without even extending an arm to claim it, still without turning his head to acknowledge her physical presence, he asked her to check whether there was a penny in the change compartment. Accordingly, she unzipped the pouch and listed each item as she extracted it: rusted key, lint-coated cough drop, twisted paperclip, condom, free sample ibuprofen packet, mini school photo, worn, faded, hard to make out, the face of a little girl, maybe seven years old, the age at which a female is at the peak of her beauty, according to the sages, after which it's all downhill, and yes, a few coins—"I don't see a penny, though, but here's a nickel."

"No, no nickel, that's way overpriced, the value has to be no less than a prutah, but also no more as far as I'm concerned, the lowest denomination coin of the realm, which in our day and age is still your penny, even if no one will even deign to bend down to pick one up—right? This is not about money, Hedda Nussbaum, it's about the cause," Gershon added severely. "Go check my wheelchair again. Check all my jacket pockets and my pants pockets, you have my permission, there's always a lone penny stuck in some crease or crevice somewhere that the pinchers forgot."

"I'll give you a penny, it's no big deal, then you can just hand it back to me to complete the transaction," she offered.

"God help us, Hedda Nussbaum, whatever happened to your self-esteem?" Simulating a state of shock, he turned his head and waggled a finger at her as at a naughty girl—this is what it took to get him to look at her at last. "Acquire you with your own prutah? It's a sin, woman, it's against halakha, it's like marrying yourself, it's like onanism—what can you be thinking? The prutah I acquire you with has to be mine, one hundred percent. Go. Find it."

What she found was herself back in the closet again, as if sent to her room for misbehaving, the air suffocating with the metallic smell of Gershon's smashed typewriter mixing with a faint fecal odor and the musty waves of his unlaundered garments lined up on the rack, black, black, everything black, and now, on top of all that, the rot of Lake Ethel. Standing there taking all of this in, not knowing where to start, she felt her mother clinging to her back like a monkey, Mommy's monkey legs clamping her waist, Mommy's long monkey arms draped over her shoulders, noosing her neck, Mommy's fat monkey lips wetting her ear whispering, "Sweetie, just go ahead and give him one of your own pennies and get it over with, he'll never know the difference, they never do, what a cheapskate, you're worth a quarter at least, make up some bubbameiseh about how you found the darn penny in his loafer, his penny loafer—get it? You're almost fifty years old, sweetie, but you still don't know how to manage a man. You know why the word manage has man in it? That's why!"

Mommy Monkey leapt off Hedy's back to the closet floor, crouching on all fours, tilting her head and staring up at her terminally disappointing daughter with large round mournful eyes, deeply pained. "Sweetie, get rid of that awful puffy black sad clown outfit you're wearing, it really doesn't flatter you, it makes you look fat, like a blimp, please, do it for my sake, sweetie, looking at you just makes me want to cry. You still have such a nice little figure, why are you hiding it, why don't you show it off?"

Hedy unzipped her sodden, deflated coat, peeled it off, and let it flop to the floor where it spread like a murky accident puddling out toward the hairy legs of Mommy Monkey, releasing the smell of underground swamp and sewage still clinging to her skin. "Now put on something nice, sweetie, it's your happily-ever-after night," said Mommy Monkey, as slowly, gradually she faded away in the closet gloom even as Hedy was crying out, "But Mommy, I don't have anything nice." She could hear her mother's voice receding in the distance, "I would give you my last shirt off my back, you know that for a fact, sweetie," but she was gone, vanished, useless, Hedy had lost her again.

Fatalistically, she took the only nightgown she owned out of her suitcase and drew it on over her head, covering her silt-marinated nakedness. At least it was white, mostly white, passably bridal white—white flannel, printed all over with little pink roses, white cotton frill around the high neck, at the wrists of the long sleeves, circling the floor-length hem. Now, if she just made things easy for herself for a change by using one of her own coins in this scenario after all, as Mommy Monkey had so subversively proposed, based on her long-held principle that what a man doesn't know won't hurt him, she will have engineered an illegitimate marriage with the built-in long-range benefit of not even having to petition Gershon to grant her a divorce when the entire bizarre, unkosher arrangement fell apart, as she never doubted it inevitably would.

Accordingly, ruling halakhically on the authority of her PhD in Rabbinics, drawing from the concept of preemptive writs of divorce, she dug out an old penny from the gritty depths of her signature overstuffed backpack, underneath the bottommost stratum of her hoard. Clutching it in her fist, she took up her post once again by the side of the master's bed and said, "Here's your prutah, Gershon. I found it in the lining of one your jackets, there was a hole in the pocket, it must have fallen through, I'll mend it later." He stretched out his hand for the coin, turning at the same moment to look at her. "You've got to be kidding," he said as his gaze traveled slowly over her, downward from top to bottom of her granny nightgown, neck ruffle to foot ruffle, then east to west from ruffled wrist to ruffled wrist, as if nailing her to a cross. Hedy said, "Just so you know, in business dealings, the sages of the Talmud offer an 'Item Not As Expected' option, which also applies to a transaction such as acquiring a wife. All you have to do is click on Mekakh Ta'ut—that's 'Mistaken Purchase.' I can print out the prepaid return postage label for you, and you can ship me back to the country of the Amazons."

Gershon stared hard at her as he scooted up against the headboard of the bed with an agility that was totally unexpected. Could this sophomoric display of erudition be her way of flirting, her pathetic stab at seductiveness? he wondered. Rejecting the idea as preposterous, he said, "Would you mind cutting it out already with your Talmud kitsch? It would actually help a lot, since we're stuck here together for the foreseeable future. It's not like you didn't know from our therapy sessions that I happen to get turned on by sexy lingerie. I could have used any help I could get in this situation, the least you could have done was to make just a small effort, especially since you have nowhere else to go. I'm doing you a pretty big favor by letting you stay here, you know, including undergoing this marriage of convenience since, morally, according to all the religious experts, including Reb Pence, it's the only way I can be secluded with you. So is this how you thank me? Never mind, let's just get this over with already for the sake of the cause—okay?"

Head bowed, nodding throughout this tongue lashing, she seemed chastened. Without any fanfare, he handed her the penny, expertly reciting at the same time the sanctification phrase, Harei aht mekudeshet li, deftly replacing taba'at with prutah, ke'dat Moshe v'Yisrael. Yes, mekudeshet, she was thinking, set apart, sanctified, like hekdesh, like some lamb or goat designated for sacrifice, bound on the altar, though she buried her references lest he chide her again for her Talmudical strutting. Even so, she was struck by how smoothly the formulation tripped off his tongue, probably due to his serial marriages, albeit not necessarily to members of the faith, she reminded herself. As it happened, though, he had known these lines by heart since the age of nine years and one day, upon the emergence of two pubic hairs, when marking the momentousness of these signs of maturity as they had been taught in starter Gemara class, he and Shepsie Fink would run around the Brooklyn lot known as Kitzel Park, where the wild Jewish rebels mixed and mingled, sneaking up on girls in all stages of longing, shoving metal rings from soda cans on their fingers or pennies into their nail-bitten fists, reciting the magic words, Harei aht, then yelling, "Harriet, mazel tov, we're married. If you change your mind and decide to marry someone else, you have to beg me for a divorce first. Maybe I'll give you one, maybe I won't, so you better be nice to me."

"Check," Gershon announced, as if ticking off from a list. "Okay, I just purchased you with my money, that takes care of Part One, the ownership clause. Onward to Part Two, consummating the deal." He slid back down on the bed, to a supine position, as onto a rack, submitting to the injunction to fulfill his marital duty at the designated time.

"Right, bi'ah, or bi'i'lah," Hedy confirmed, slapping her palm over her mouth in mock realization of her reversion to Talmudish despite his chastisement. She had a right, she fortified herself, she had earned it, she had worked damn hard for that PhD.

Gershon pushed on, ignoring her. "I was thinking that tonight for a special treat I would go on top, the traditional way for a guy, to show who's boss—you know? I can do it, I can perform, but then I took one look at you in that sack, with your hair all frizzed out like a crazy bird's nest, full of dining needles and dragonflies from fake Lake Ethel, so naturally I decided, no way I'm knocking myself out for someone who doesn't even care enough to make the smallest effort. I'm really sorry, but it looks like you'll have to do all the work this time."

Theatrically, he swished off the blanket, like a matador's cape, exposing the raw hairy skin of the unholy animal lower half of his body. There it stood, the one-eyed monster. As if on automatic, Hedy raised her flannel nightgown over her head, let it drop to the floor, and impaled herself. In less than thirty seconds, he let out a deep moan, shuddered, and it was over. As she detached, he surprised her by moving his large body a few centimeters to grant her some space on the bed. It was an act of kindness that she had not anticipated, she tried not to cry. There they lay for a long time, side by side in silence, their two Jewish proboscises broken by life pointing in vain to the heavens.

They were a couple, this was a fact that was now beginning to sink in for Hedy. But as she lay there next to him on that bed, her cheek brushing his triangular Lord George Gordon gilgul beard, now already midway down his chest thanks to its enhanced Nazir growth, narrowing to a point, it remained almost unimaginable that simple domestic perks commonly recognized to be part of the marriage package, such as pillow talk, for example, could ever be possible for her with this man. Above all, there was the insurmountable fact that until her sudden termination by that mediocrity, that climber Zoya Roy, he had been her patient, which had placed him firmly in the center ring of their circus. She had been his dedicated social worker, the vessel into which he had been rightfully entitled to deposit all his junk—which, come to think of it, it now struck her, could easily translate as wife. In these revised circumstances of wedlock, therefore, would it be ethical now and then to turn the conversation to herself? She could feel the woman's voice inside her rising, demanding to be released, struggling to break out of her control, agitating for its proper share, she could hardly restrain it, it was riding the sound waves, selectively testing its boundaries, she was barely able to hold back all that had happened to her that night, at the lake, though that would have been too incendiary, too provocative, too much about him ultimately—he would claim it, take it over. Instead she offered what had happened to her here in this room, in the closet, the momentous fact that she had felt the presence of her mother on this night of all nights, her mother so long gone, who had taken herself away too soon on an overdose of antidepressants—"And all I could think of saying to her was, Mommy, I'm sorry, I'm sorry, forgive me, Mommy," Hedy found herself telling Gershon. "The only thing she ever wanted was to be a good mom, that was her whole ambition in life, she really tried in her way. Then she read my book and realized she had failed at that too. Writing fiction—it's like committing murder, literally."

Gershon eyed her coldly. "You give yourself too much credit," he said. "What was it called anyway, your book thing?"

"*Mommy Monkey*, it was a novel, fiction."

"Whatever. Never heard of it, probably never even crossed my desk for possible review, relax, nobody read it. It's curious, though," he went on, homing back to the main topic, "tonight I was also thinking about my mother—actually, about the two of them, my mother and my father—my parents, the Holocaust survivors. I don't believe it's a coincidence. It has nothing to do with this Potemkin marriage. I believe they were trying to say something to me, and for sure it wasn't mazel tov."

Not questioning for a moment that she was once again required to assume her position at his service even in this bed, that she must forever set aside her own stuff and focus professionally on his every expression, he went on to reveal to her something about himself that, to her stupefaction, she had never heard before, not even once. It was the prequel to his legendary summer as busboy and then waiter, the summer that featured most memorably his life-changing erotic hazing by Dr. Zoya Rubinchuk in the days when Camp Jeffrey Epstein had been known as the Lokshin Hotel and Country Club, a biographical highpoint that had been molded into lore, and that he had readily recounted to Hedy on multiple occasions, each time with an added creative fillip. It had, in fact, been his mother and father, the Holocaust survivors, who had gotten him that busboy job, he now informed Hedy, he was not even quite eighteen years old at the time, below the minimum age to be considered sufficiently qualified to wipe up the slop from the tables, but this was an emergency situation. The founder Lokshins—Murray and Ethel—were exceptionally loyal, longtime customers of his parents' dry-cleaning business. As a special favor, the good Lokshins ordered Adolf, the maître d' of their hotel dining room, to make an exception in this case and take Gershon on as a busboy.

As soon as his parents, the Holocaust survivors, let him know that it had all been arranged, he hitched a ride directly to the Lokshin Hotel and Country Club from Spring Glen, New York, two towns over, from the former bungalow colony once known as Mrs. Cohen's Cozy Cottages, now converted into the Jewish Defense League military training camp, known locally as Kamp Kahane (or KaKa, as his father, the Holocaust survivor, insisted on calling it in disgust), with a yellow-starred clenched fist as its emblem, borrowed from the enviably sexier Black Power movement. Against the wishes of his terrified parents, the Holocaust survivors, shouting "Never Again, Ma, Never Again, Pa," he had run off to Kamp Kahane immediately after high school graduation to shed his Jewish nebbish skin and morph into a mighty fur-pelted Jewish warrior, like Jacob disguised as Esau stealing the blessing, until the day, some weeks into his initiation, when he found himself sobbing in a payphone booth outside a Hebrew National deli in Ellenville, New York, stuffing nickels and dimes and quarters into the slots as his mother hollered, "Call us back already, Gershe'le—collect!" He was struggling to explain to his parents, the Holocaust survivors, that he was sure he had been recognized during a camp training exercise involving emptying sacks of blood over the heads of suspected Nazi war criminals swinging their tankards in a beer cellar in Woodbourne, New York, while bellowing, "Ja, ja, ja, ja." One of the Nazis was the father of a kid he knew from the nationwide high school tournament of champions debating team, a very strict dad who attended every meet with a gun stashed on his person, the bulge not unintentionally visible. Top law enforcement was definitely on the way to Kamp Kahane to arrest Gershon and lock him up for life in the maximum-security correctional facility in Woodbourne, New York, where these Nazis no doubt were employed as prison guards and torturers, given their elite Teutonic prior experience. His college acceptance would be rescinded, he was ruined. There were even cries of ritual murder circulating in the ether, your old reliable blood libel, Gershon now recalled—that we had murdered some Christian boy to drain his blood for matzah, but since Pesakh had already passed over, we used it instead for our commando blood dump on the heads of the Nazis ja-ja'ing in the Woodbourne beerhall just beyond the sinister high stone prison walls. "Ma, Pa, just so you know,"

Gershon had tried to calm his parents, the Holocaust survivors, "we got the blood at a discount rate from the super glatt kosher meat-processing plant in South Fallsburg, New York, they actually charged us for that blood, mostly from beef for cholent and from chickens for matzah ball soup, I have the receipt." Even then Gershon had been stunned by how easily that primitive blood-libel canard could rear its head and grow fangs again, he told Hedy, even in our super enlightened age of artificial intelligence and space travel.

Thus had Gershon's short career as a foot soldier in Rabbi Meir Kahane's Jewish Defense League come to an abrupt and humiliating end, as he recounted it in their nuptial bed to his bride, Hedy Nussbaum. Jewish pride, Jewish power—for a brief, innocent, youthful moment he had been swept up by Kahane's manipulation of the vulnerabilities of first- and second-generation Shoah-traumatized Jews. Kahane's militancy was the only way to stand up against the antisemites who despise us as weaklings, parasites, sheep marked for slaughter, eternal victims, soap—"Sabon," as Gershon had declaimed to his parents, the Holocaust survivors. "In the intervals between murdering us," Gershon went on, passionately spouting his master's teachings, "our continued existence is suffered even here in the land of the free and the home of the brave, so long as we keep our heads down, our mouths shut, and behave ourselves like good Irvings," as the Rabbi used to put it so wittily, he explicated for Hedy's sake. Meir Kahane—he would have done a lot better if he had become a stand-up comic getting his chops at the Murray Lokshin Casino and Lounge, he was a clown, a joker, a lapsed clergyman like Jackie Mason, angry, intense, stoned, like Lenny Bruce, a lecher and schlemiel like Woody Allen, Gershon said, he might even have been alive today, a very senior citizen by now, drooling in his wheelchair in a trailer in a settlement outpost on the lunatic fringe of Samaria.

In the wake of the beerhall putsch and his flight to Lokshin from Kamp Kahane, Gershon had renounced his understandable and really rather touching youthful infatuation with the thrilling boldness of Kahane and Kahanism, he made this clear to Hedy. Kahane was a fanatic, a zealot, but bottom line, Kahane was a very sick guy with very serious mental and emotional problems, Gershon said. Later on, in Israel, Kahane came out as a certified racist, a sicarii with a hidden dagger in his fly, but in the American goldene medina, Kahane was a false prophet, never in history had the Jews had it so good as they had it in America in those days, that was a fact, incontrovertible. Among the youth who flocked to Kahane in his native Brooklyn, the true idealists like himself who could get the girls quickly peeled off, only the losers stuck with this madman—and he, Gershon, most definitely was not put on this earth to be counted in the camp of the losers, he stated emphatically.

"So here's the thing," Gershon now posed to his newly anointed bride lying there naked alongside him in his bed, lowering his voice almost to a whisper on their shared pillow. "I start out in Kamp Kahane and end up in Camp Jeffrey Epstein. How do you explain that? What does that tell you about me and the story of my life?

"This is what it tells you," Gershon answered his own question following a long pause, as had clearly been his intention from the start. "The explanation of my life story is nothing less than antisemitism. It starts with antisemitism and it ends with antisemitism. Between the inevitable cyclical eruptions, this oldest hatred in the world that never dies goes underground to the lowest depths to recharge, and we carry on as if it had never ever existed, as if nothing had ever happened, like normal human beings at home in this world. Then, for one unfathomable reason or another, it suddenly rears its venomous head again—this time landing me along with a suspiciously disproportionate number of my faith mates here at Camp Jeffrey Epstein. Enough already, I say. From this foul place I have now been called to come forth with all my powers as the gilgul of Lord George Gordon, to arm myself as the reincarnated Reb Yisrael bar Avraham Avinu and lead the King Mob in the final color war against all those who in every generation rise up to destroy us—with you at my side, Dr. Hedda Nussbaum, my sister, my bride."

He hooked his arm over Hedy's shoulder, drawing her closer, as if to concretely illustrate the concept of his "side," a gesture of tenderness so rarely bestowed upon her that it suppressed, not for the first time, any rising thoughts of his possible madness. He began stroking her hair, lovingly, she almost dared to think, when suddenly, grinning proprietorially, he was raking his fingernails along her scalp through the tangles, almost drawing blood, trying in vain to straighten out the strands, as if her distinctive bush were their shared private domestic concern, its incorrigible unruliness requiring constant discipline. "Did that hurt, Hedda Nussbaum? So cry then, Hedda, cry. Because I want you at my side weeping, weeping openly and mightily for the suffering of our people, like Mother Rachel weeping for her children and refusing to be comforted. Or, better yet, poaching from another faith with which I was once so famously at war long ago, when I was Lord George Gordon, before my life-altering epiphany that turned me into Reb Yisrael bar Avraham Avinu, I want you weeping at my side like Dame Margery Kempe, the Catholic so-called mystic, a traveling reality show more than half a millennium ago, her full-time wailing in public drove everyone so crazy they were ready to give her something to really cry about instead of the erotic Jesus visions that usually turned her on and set her off. Can you cry for me, Hedda Nussbaum, can you cry like Margery Kempe, ravished by Jesus? Such crying could be our secret weapon. Are you capable of crying in the public domain to stir up the mixed mob over the persecution of our people? Can you do this spontaneously, or will I secretly be obliged to slap you around or do something else even more drastic to get you going?" By way of illustration, he grabbed a hank of her hair and yanked it down, snapping her head back, exposing her neck as to the knife of the priest. Then he quickly let go, and gently, began to stroke her cheek. She pressed her face into the side of his fleshy body, in the shelter under his arm, surrendering, sobbing in great loud bursts as he crooned, "Yes, cry, Hedda Nussbaum, go on, cry, cry your heart out, it's good for the system, like bleeding the pipes, cry like that creature Margery Kempe, let the world see what they have done to us."

She tried to get some words out, she longed to thank him for taking pains to avoid tearing her hair, which would have compromised her record-setting Nazira vow, but her words were snarled in the sobs that were shaking her whole body, she felt as if she might explode out of the depths of her loneliness from this bit of closeness now being granted to her, her gratitude was stirred up to a point that was almost unbearable. How could she thank him? What did she have to give him in return other than her pathetic Talmudic riffs? Nothing, nothing really, short of sacrificing herself for him—self-sacrifice, yes, that was her specialty, she would have made a good mother, a great mother, a ferocious, self-sacrificing mother.

"Do you know who I saw at the lake tonight?" she suddenly offered, her weeping done for now as she placed her korban toda gratitude sacrifice for him on the altar to be consumed by the flames. Gershon turned to look at her, alert, on guard. "CPO—with Max Horn. I think they might be an item. I saw them together, but they didn't see me. I could hear every word they were saying though. Horn—he was putting a lot of pressure on her to get out of Camp Jeff as fast as possible, because of the Jeffrey Epstein victims streaming in, they would claw her to pieces if they ever found out that she's there, Horn kept telling her. She's leaving tomorrow morning, very, very early, escaping. I thought you might be interested to know."

"You waited until now to tell me this?" Gershon hissed.

He withdrew his arm like a whiplash, like sandpaper his arm grated her skin that for so long had not been touched by a man, he pushed her away so hard, she slid halfway off the bed, desperately dragging the blanket along for modesty's sake as she descended. "I wonder what else you might be holding back from me, what other secrets. CPO—I need to see her right away, before she is disappeared forever."

She wrapped herself in the blanket to cover her nakedness, crouching now on the floor in the corner by her closet door, reclaiming her patch, homeless, an untouchable, like a street sleeper curling up on the pavement in Kolkata, trying to make herself as small as possible, invisible. With lowered head, from under her brow, she watched Gershon as if in a dream, unable to pinpoint the exact reason for the strangeness of it all. He was moving about, drawing on underwear, socks, black tight-fitting trousers, too tight, smoothing his white silk shirt. Only when he pulled up his gleaming black boots of the most buttery leather did it strike her that this time he was actually walking in those boots, standing up with both feet on the ground, setting one boot in front of the other, moving on, leaving her behind, she was no longer needed. She observed him as he strode in those fine black leather boots to the large rectangular hotel mirror over the fruit wood veneer hotel dresser left over from the Lokshin period. He gazed at himself in the mirror as he removed his black velvet yarmulke and deftly folded it into the pocket of his black brocade waistcoat, the white frill of his jabot almost completely hidden by the copious fall of his emerging triangular beard. How did he acquire all of this Lord George Gordon finery? Hedy was wondering. Entranced by the novelty of himself reflected in that mirror in an upright position, he slowly drew a hairbrush through his Nazir cloud of luminous white hair and fluffed his sidelocks, then moved the brush downward to tend to his emerging beard in long, sensuous strokes, as if he were alone in the room and unobserved, since she was nobody. He could topple over any minute, Hedy told herself. Her throat constricted with alarm. He's a cripple, after all, he could break his neck, God forbid.

Risking everything, she rose from her punishment corner, struggling to clutch her blanket with one hand like a veil over her bridal body. With the other hand she was pushing his wheelchair forward, positioning it directly behind him so that he would be able simply to lower himself into it when he was fully satisfied with his grooming. In the mirror he could see her behind his chair. Without taking his eyes off the fine points of his toilette, he lifted one foot in its black leather boot and delivered a powerful backward push to the footrest, sending the wheelchair rolling away farther back from him at launch momentum, pushing Hedy along with it in its trajectory as if she were some discard it had snagged on the way, her blanket dragged down, caught in the wheels, until its advance was halted by impact with the bed against which she was flattened and onto which she then pulled herself up, hopelessly exposed.

She sat on a sliver of the bed's edge, all the space she deserved, stripped of everything. "But I thought you were disabled," she said.

"Who among us is not disabled?" Gershon asked her through the looking glass. "For what I need to do tonight, I don't require the added optic of my wheelchair to be recognized as disabled in order to get all the fringe benefits. For tonight, my Jewishness is disability enough."

He turned around, shameless in his vanity. "Beard good?"

Without lingering for her preapproval, he grinned naughtily, then drew on his best black jacket, long and fitted, like a frockcoat, lifted his beard and tucked it inside. "My Nazir beard, it will be my signature feature, like the great Bob Marley, his dreadlocks, but I'd definitely risk being noticed if I let it all hang out—unless of course the shock of me ambulating on my own two feet would lead a bystander to wonder if it's really Gershon Gordon, or maybe some crazy Gordon impersonator. Better to play it safe—don't you agree, Weasel?"

At the door, he adjusted the extra-wide brim of his luxurious black fedora, shadowing his red-rimmed eyes dragged down by heavy white bags, and drew a black mask against the plague over his tribal nose and lustful Semitic lips. Hedy watched in mortal fascination as a helpless circle of wetness gradually spread on his mask over his pumping mouth when he formally spoke his parting orders to her before setting out to seek his fortune in the fearsomely dangerous world. "Color war is breaking out tonight at Camp Jeffrey Epstein," he briefed her through his mask, the circle of living moisture growing wider and wider. "As general of the Blue Team of the Holy Tekhelet Fringe leading our troops into battle against the White Team Hooded Spreaders of Jew-Hating Poison, I am deploying you as my stealth weapon to move from cell to cell in this fortress tonight at post zero hundred hours and to infiltrate under every door our manifesto, which I composed in a burst of divine inspiration, as you no doubt recall, while you performed the clerical follow-up. Your orders now are to deliver the payload—tonight. Take care not to pass over a single door, Petty Officer Nussbaum. Return to base before reveille. Go Blue Team!"

14.

The sleeve of his black frockcoat drawn down over his fist raised in midair, Gershon had not quite made prophylactic contact with the leprous door of the penthouse to plant a knock when it opened as if of itself. A squat, rotund creature leapt into his arms knocking his dashing black hat off his head, nearly toppling him over backward, crying, "Gersh, old buddy, friend of my youth—how ya doin', bro?"

"You trying to kill me, Fink? Where's your goddamn mask, asshole?"

With his black mitted fists, Gershon squeamishly divested himself of Shepsie Fink's doggie slobber—this oldest friend, this virus incarnate. "What are you doing here anyhow? Don't tell me you've been #MeTooed too. They're really scraping the bottom of the barrel, no way as selective as they used to be." But Fink was too stricken to counter. Gershon watched as this most faithful defender and ally across the decades retreated to pat himself down, searching his person everywhere for some rag of a mask, coming up in his desperation with a pathetic improvisation at last—the reconfiguration of the blue velvet yarmulke stamped on its lining with the legend, Bar Mitzvah of Gordon Fink, Shepsie's son, now Rabbi Gidel Fink of Dharamshala,

India, presiding from a replica of 770 Eastern Parkway, the holy multistoried red brick Chabad headquarters in Brooklyn, New York, bizarrely recreated and tucked into the foothills of the Himalayas like some alien virtual reality, like a colonizing interloper, like a pagan temple. This yarmulke, this shabby party favor—Shepsie carried it around in his pocket at all times not only out of longing for his boy, so far away among the lamas and other assorted idolaters, but also for security, lest he happen to run into a relative or teacher or rabbi from the dark ages poised to disapprove of his brazenly uncovered head and dismiss him as a lost cause from this life and the next. Now Shepsie cupped this yarmulke, this cheap ethnic souvenir, over the polluting vents of his nose and mouth, looping around his ears some strands of detached silver tinsel trim that curled along its edge, doubly securing it with two metal clips pinching his ears painfully. Yes, he deserved to suffer for so thoughtlessly endangering the health of his dearest friend, Gershon Gordon, the world's longest-running prodigy.

Gershon meanwhile had picked up his elegant black hat, brushed it off demonstratively, then handed it to Fink as to a butler, having already replaced it reflexively with the black velvet yarmulke drawn out of the pocket of his brocade waistcoat. The bounty of his well-brushed, brilliant white hair was now released, liberated, he shook his head and ran his fingers through the richness of his locks, fluffing them like a trailing cloud of glory to show them off in all their Nazir splendor, then proudly he stroked his remarkable Lord George Gordon triangular beard while looking around this opulently appointed salon in spectacular bad taste to see whether CPO had emerged from her bower to celebrate the arrival of her noble champion. Instead, striding toward him with all the authority of the master of the house was that suck-up rapist Max Horn, looking fit and in charge, wearing a handsome black mask, obviously costly, obviously bespoke, inscribed with the legend "MaxVax, International Jewish Conspiracy." That struck a chord with Gershon, it resonated, though for a moment he blanked, he could not quite place it, all he could think of saying was, "Nice mask, Horn."

"I've been expecting you," Horn replied. "I saw your little mole at the lake tonight, spying on us, so I was sure you'd show up here, sooner or later. Very pleased you like my mask, I'm wearing it in your honor, I had my personal tailor make up a whole set, each one stamped with the customized graffito you painted on his door. Here, I brought you yours—present." Gershon was shaking his head—in denial? refusal?—as Horn extended the mask to him while turning to Fink and remarking in an aside, "See, didn't I tell you he'd show up tonight, wasn't I right?"

It was as if Horn were taking in Fink's living reality for the first time, perhaps due to that sad rigged-up excuse for a mask by which this singularly unthreatening being was now muzzled. Accordingly, Horn retracted from Gershon his outstretched gift-bearing hand, and proposed that since he, Gershon, was already outfitted with a perfectly respectable, functional mask, would he mind terribly if this little fellow here, Gershon's oldest friend in the world as well as his trusted legal counsel, according to all reports—Would it be too much of an imposition to allow Mr. Fink, Esquire, to borrow your personalized mask for the evening? Without bothering to wait for the expected obligatory acquiescence, Horn instantly handed the mask with Gershon's name on it to Fink, who donned it at once. In a flash, Shepsie Fink grew six inches, bulked out, his hair grew back, black and rich and shining, he was transformed by the power of Gershon's mask, stretched even more across his now chiseled, square-jawed face by the wide, teeth-baring grin underneath boldfacing its legend—"Lord George Gordon, King Mob, Poisoner of Wells, Super Spreader."

Observing all this, Gershon was overcome with a terrible sadness bordering on despair, as if the vital energy that now imbued Shepsie Fink had been pumped out of him, like a full body-fluid transfusion, rendering him unable to even recall what urgent mission had brought him up to this place. Gershon had not spared himself on this day. Just getting married would have been more than enough to wipe out most normal men, especially a marriage as delicately strategic as his to such a damaged specimen, but on top of that, he had also fired the opening shots of all-out war against the antisemites, he had blasted the shofar to bring down the walls, he had stood up on his own two feet after such long paralysis, emotional, mental, physical, he had even loped up the stairs to this penthouse instead of taking the elevator, so empowered and energized had he felt, and now he had to deal with this—this degenerate, Horn. He practically staggered toward one of the two plump gold satin sofas on either side of the rococo white marble fireplace, loveseats as they were known ironically, cooing at each other—and calling out for some water, he sank in.

"Get him a glass of wine," he heard Horn command some underling, possibly Fink.

Instantly, Gershon pulled himself together, summoning up his hereditary second-generation-survivor skills to cope with whatever outrages were about to be lobbed in his direction. "For God's sake, no wine, I'm a Nazir," he cried. "Can't you tell from my hair? I've taken the vow. No wine, no fruit of the grape, nothing the color purple, no Johnnie Alice Walker, that cheap antisemitic poison—you want to kill this Jew? So where's CPO, Horn? Have you murdered her already? A Nazir's not allowed to be in the same tent with a dead body, so I need to know. Tell me what you've done with her, I wouldn't put anything past you, you creep. Only a person with a sick mind like yours would ever accuse a cripple like me of schmearing those idiotic graffities—

so not my style at all, so juvenile, so unoriginal and illiterate, like the quotes next to the pictures of those poor doomed kids in high school yearbooks. It was a raid, a graffiti raid, Horn, I was one of its victims too, and just for your information, I've been the victim of other raids far more invasive and crushing. When I first heard about this sad little scribble raid, I said to myself, It's the work of either Horn or Rosenberg. To tell you the truth, I was leaning toward Rosenberg, the usual suspect, but now I'm sure it was you, Horn. You want to know why? Not only because you're a self-hating Jew, no, and not because you're a self-loving Jew either, who wants to stir up right-thinking citizens against the menace of antisemitism, no. It's because you're a self-loving jerkoff Jew who thinks he's so clever, fondling your own limp words so tenderly that you go and make these luxury masks out of them, like for the carnival of the merchant of Venice. And now that mask you so thoughtfully commissioned for me is saturated with Fink's sickness unto death. If I ever wanted to wear it, I'd have to sterilize it first or bury it in the dirt for a year, I'd have to soak it for a week before putting it through the heavy-duty cycle in the industrial-strength washing machine, I'd have to take it to the mikvah to purify it, breaking my back dunking it forty times."

As if on cue, though Gershon did not quite synapse the coincidence right away—but at that selfsame moment, in strode Lady CPO from the wings, from what must have been one of the bedchambers of this penthouse suite. She was barefoot, wrapped in an opulent black satin Chinese robe embroidered down the front with a golden dragon, and masked in another of Horn's special-order creations, the one meant for Father Clarence, which oddly seemed to work for her as well—"Black Cat, Black Hole, Black Death." Her dyed black hair, freshly washed, no doubt, to look her best for the grand escape at dawn, was piled in a turbaned plush white towel embroidered in gold with the looping Lokshin Hotel and Country Club insignia. A few paces behind her, a thickset older man with a full gray beard shuffled in through the same door, wearing on his head a high red fez with a black silk tassel, no doubt to conceal his baldness, Gershon figured, giving him the look of something like a spice seller from Smyrna or maybe a false messiah, in Gershon's opinion, were it not for his bright orange prison-pajamas jumpsuit and the mask on loan, "Jew Flu Rosenberg, Blood Matzah Child Killer." That reminded Gershon—Passover was coming soon, the holiday of liberation, the entire free world would be sitting down to the first seder in a few weeks or so. How did one celebrate the festival of freedom in the spiritual confinement of Camp Jeffrey Epstein in the middle of a plague and a war? Where could he ever find the handmade round shmurah matzahs he required, his Jewish madeleines, delicately singed along the edge, guarded and watched every second lest they become contaminated by leaven from the planting of the seed to the selling to the faithful at over one hundred dollars a pound, eight great big matzah cracker frisbees?

Gershon remained tucked in the cleft of the golden loveseat, the only sitting figure in the room. The others were standing, CPO alongside the bearded guy in the fez and the orange prison jumpsuit and the mask meant for Rosenberg, with their backs to the fireplace, not at all socially distanced from each other at any decent, community-minded level. Whatever mortal disease this false messiah had contracted in his prison cell had no doubt already been passed to CPO, and from CPO to Horn, and from Horn to Fink, and from Fink to him. Khad Gadya.

From the window where Fink was still standing, still absorbing the Gershon superpowers through the mask that bound him, looking as if at any minute he might take off into the night sky to defend truth, justice, and the American way, he summoned his oldest friend back into the deepest past. "Hey Gersh, don't tell me you don't recognize Fallick—Hymie Fallick, from heder, from pre-pre-K? I just got him released from prison today, early medical discharge due to the coronavirus pandemic. I did the job pro bono, it's a major mitzvah, pidyon shvuyim, just in time for Pesakh. 'Redemption Song' time, Gersh—remember how crazy we used to be for the holy Rebbe Bob Marley? 'Exodus, Movement of Jah People'—oh yeah! Maybe you two guys, you and Fallick, can finally get it on together to do some daf yomi, now that you're both stuck in the same facility, Nashim maybe, everything you ever wanted to know about managing the opposite gender—sound good? What do you think, Gersh? CPO has very kindly arranged for Hymie to move into this penthouse full-time when she checks out tomorrow a.m., his family has disowned him, he has nowhere else to go. She was just showing him around."

Right, showing him around—Fallick, the mikvah weirdo, the peeping Hymie, it had definitely occurred to Gershon that the guy looked familiar. He set down the glass of water, now even more half empty, on the plush wall-to-wall carpeting, green and gold brocade, staring at its swirling topography unseeing with an elbow on each knee and his head sunk in his hands. Who had brought him this glass of water? He hadn't even looked up to acknowledge that human being. But maybe it wasn't a human being at all, maybe it was a dog, one of those service dogs trained for the disabled, in which case by right it should have been assigned to him down below as he was the reigning star of the Camp Jeff handicapped basket-case team. Or maybe it was one of the brown-skinned, bailed-out, ex-con kitchen slaves, detailed to the penthouse to help transition Fallick in case he was feeling insecure on the loose, missing his chain gang. It seemed to Gershon to be radically unfair that the penthouse was equipped with servants in addition to all of its other perks and amenities, and that this sicko voyeur Hymie Fallick, fresh out of the slammer, should be handed this entire vulgar spread on a silver platter as sole occupant except for an occasional hooker when he might be in the mood, while he, Gershon Gordon, was stuck down below in such tight quarters, furnished in your basic laminate motel décor, which, to make matters worse, he was now sharing, albeit clandestinely, with a passive-aggressive PhD clamoring not to be noticed.

Feeling another sinking body close by, Gershon looked up. There was CPO in her Father Clarence mask settling in at the other end of his loveseat. Directly opposite from her, on the matching sofa, Fallick was straining to relax in his Fritz Rosenberg blood matzah mask and absurd false-messiah fez, offering Gershon a full-frontal view of how grotesquely he had aged—his steel-wool-gray beard, the corner of his mouth turned down on the left side as if he were nursing an obscene cigar, his eyes darting in every direction like a cornered animal behind his thick lenses. Far better to twist his neck a bit for a better view of Lady CPO in her black-satin Chinese dragon robe, Gershon decided, beneath which he pictured a sensuous, costly matching silk bra and panties set of the sort he always appreciated and preferred even more than nothing at all, your assembly-line nudity, he had been so deprived. She was parked there forlorn, muffled in her Father Clarence mask with all of its dark references that so suited her, bringing out her vulnerable underlying sadness. Gershon was wondering if the two of them, CPO and Fallick, had known each other from before, or had they just met—and suddenly, without quite realizing it was happening, he found himself asking.

"Oh dear, no, I've known Hymie for ages," CPO laughed. "He's the guy who converted me—you know, the rabbi, before he was defrocked."

What could she be talking about? Gershon wondered. Converted her? Who had more right to call herself a Jew than this daughter of the preeminent Holocaust survivor boasting more than three hundred murdered in his own extended family, Hero of the State of Israel in its birthing hour, operating full blast in the mid-twentieth century with all guns blazing, at the absolute peak of unfolding Jewish history?

CPO instantly got it, obviously this was not the first time she had unrolled this story. "Mummy was French Huguenot aristocracy," she gaily proceeded to clarify. "She wasn't Jewish at all, and to her credit, she never converted, it was the one and only thing she never gave in on to big bad Daddy. She insisted that she's more effective in her Holocaust memory work as a Christian, that was her official excuse for declining to join the flock—'No thank you!' Mummy said."

She then went on to disclose to Gershon the interesting fact that early in her relationship with Jeffrey Epstein, when for a brief period of time he was diddling with the idea of marrying her, it was a major problem for him that she was not halakhically Jewish, which, as Gershon no doubt knew, is determined by the double-X, through the matrilineal line—we can always know for sure who the mummy is, right? "Not surprisingly, true to his nature, Jeffrey was obsessive about the strict observance of the very few selective points of religion he chose to practice," CPO glossed, "just as he was obsessive about perfecting the minutest details in the execution of his sexual preferences. Daddy, on the other hand, parlayed Mummy's refusal to convert to his own personal glory by gallantly, publicly hailing her as the keeper of his Jewish soul. In the end, Mummy was Jewish enough for him, just as we, his mixed-race mongrel kids, were Jewish enough for Hitler, as he liked to remind us again and again when we were naughty. In that brief window of time, when Jeffrey was toying with the idea of marrying me, unlike my brave Mummy, I did not dare refuse to go through the conversion ordeal—everyone thought I was Jewish anyway, I had already experienced the negative side effects from birth, in London, at Oxford, and so on, I had nothing to lose. So, Jeffrey being Jeffrey, naturally he asked around for recommendations from his friends—who's the number-one, top, super-kosher, strictly Orthodox conversion guy? Money was not an object. Jeffrey's friends could afford the best, nothing but the best was good enough for Jeffrey Epstein. And that's how I met Hymie Fallick," CPO said.

Fallick, sitting there on the loveseat opposite them, was nodding his head in its red fez, the black tassel swinging like a pendulum. This would be his fate for the rest of his life—to endure such public degradation and scorn in silence, to be forced to just sit there and take it. "Luckily, Hymie never had to go to the trouble of secretly videoing me dunking in the mikvah, since I walked around just in my knickers all the time anyway, and often in nothing at all, it was part of my job description," CPO went on. "And had Mummy changed her mind and decided to convert, he would never have videoed her either, she was too old, too matronly, if you know what I mean, she was Daddy's Holocaust replacement machine, she gave birth to nine children, nine babies she carried in her body, I was the youngest, the last, and yes, the least."

Here, CPO paused to cry.

When she was done, she looked up at Gershon, grinning slyly. "Do you care to know how Jeffrey paid Hymie for the conversion job?" she inquired. "By subsidizing and overseeing the wiring of every nook and cranny of Hymie's mikvah, all the cameras and other gizmos, so that the good rabbi could spy on the pious naked matrons and the naked Jewess wannabes and wank off from the privacy and comfort of his home or wherever. Nothing but the best, of course, the latest spyware and surveillance technology, top of the line, Jeffrey paid for it all and oversaw the installation, which was done by the same Rolls Royce outfit that had wired every one of Jeffrey's properties down to the bottoms of the toilet bowls and up to the kazoo—Russians, I think they were, or maybe former East German Stasi, the best. Hilarious—don't you think?"

She was shaking with laughter now, laughing too hard, rocking the entire loveseat including Gershon at the other end. Her whole body seemed convulsed, the laugh sounds coming out of her growing more and more shrill, piercing, until they turned into something like animal wails, like keening. As she keened, she waved her arms wildly in front of her face streaked with her tears, struggling to get out the words—"It's okay, Don't worry, I'm fine"—addressing these words not to Gershon, and not to Fallick either, who seemed to have disappeared as from the scene of the crime, but to Max Horn at the other end of the room, looking up to check on her from his huddle near the door with Shepsie Fink, their heads lowered over what was probably some kind of contact-free pizza-delivery flyer, deciding what to order.

"I don't know what comes over me, it's as if I'm out of control, which is so not my style," CPO said to Gershon, when finally she seized hold of herself, calming down to her usual level of low-grade despair. "It has been happening more and more often lately, ever since Jeffrey escaped, presumed suicide or whatever, like Daddy, turning me into his evil surrogate, leaving those furies with just me to pour their wrath into and tear to shreds—oh yes, they mean to destroy me and confiscate all the assets. I have become a fugitive, running, running, always running, that's my life now. At dawn I'm being secreted out of here in a moving fridge packed with sliced American cheese and bottles of prune juice for the old folks, carted to another hideout, God knows where. I'm being hunted like a rabbit. It's history repeating itself all over again. I hate to say this, I know it sounds terribly provincial and, at the same time, well, self-serving, grandiose, but I've really been feeling the weight of my Jewishness in these awful times, yes, I feel like I'm stuck in the contemporary version of an ancient nightmare, der ewige Jude pursued forever by the eternal Nazis."

By now Gershon was sitting very close to her, having shimmied on his haunches along the golden loveseat. He was holding both of her hands by the wrists on his lap, looking eloquently into her eyes and nodding his head fervently. CPO said softly, "Yes, I'm feeling too Jewish, as if I have a Jewish smell that the bloodhounds are picking up. I feel as if the intensity of the hatred against Jeffrey, now transferred to me, is too extreme, too categorical, too absolute—there's not one dissenting voice, it's unanimous. I feel as if all of that has something to do with our being Jewish, and our Jewishness explains it, makes it acceptable. Others have sinned far worse, but about us there seems to be universal agreement—we are not quite human, we are beyond redemption, it's permissible to hate us, it's okay to destroy us, no one disagrees, no one will object, can't quite explain it."

"Don't hold back," Gershon cried, clutching her wrists, "speak it out, call it by its name—antisemitism, nothing less. Do not fool yourself, they're out to kill you."

Barely able to suppress his fervor, he went on to relate to her, talking very fast as if at any moment he might be silenced by the inquisitor, his voice box plucked by the gestapo out of his throat—pouring out to her with a desperate urgency how the news of her pending flight had lifted him out of the spiritual and physical paralysis into which he had been plunged from the moment he had been so unjustly canceled from the living world, it was as if he had risen from the dead, like a vampire, because the Jew is the antisemite's mythic vampire who never dies, the avenging predator monster who sustains himself on the blood of the white-throated shiksa. Suddenly restored to his former strength and mobility, he had practically flown up here to this decaying penthouse to bring her the good news, and to plead with her, yes, to get down on his knees—here Gershon dropped onto the moldy green and gold brocade carpet, prostrating himself fully like a supplicant and seizing her ankles—to implore her to join him in the great struggle against the Jew haters, to fight, yes, to fight and not to run away in a milk-of-magnesia truck like a common deserter. He had identified the enemy, he told her, already the opening shots had been fired, the battle has begun. You must not desert us, you must stay and fight, you must come down with me at once to my headquarters, my war room, my bunker. Another combatant, a fellow traveler, is already there, a low-maintenance refugee who doesn't really count, doesn't take up a lot of space, it might be a bit tight, but we will survive, yes, we will more than survive, we shall overcome, we shall prevail, Gershon heartened her, as Max Horn, drawing ever nearer, bent down over him splayed there like a great prehistoric black moth pinned to the floor, and shoved in front of his face the manifesto that had been slipped under the door.

"Lord George Gordon, a.k.a. Reb Yisrael bar Avraham Avinu, I presume?" Horn vocalized so patronizingly.

Before Gershon could raise his voice to protest, before he could summon the force to resist, he was silenced by the poisoned mask that took his name in vain, willingly handed over by that traitor, Shepsie Fink, and stuffed into his mouth by Fidel, the ingrate, the turncoat, the collaborator. It was Fidel who had brought him the water from the poisoned well, Gershon now understood, it was this hustler, this bootlicker, this storm trooper, who now was hoisting him up like a sack of twitching rabbits after the hunt, slinging him backward over his shoulder, encircling his dangling legs in front and gripping them tightly, jamming Gershon's face in back against the crest of his high, muscular rump—an utterly mortifying position, the classic schlock-art position of a too-ample naked woman being carried off by a barbarian from the north to be raped.

In this way Fidel transported Gershon Gordon out of the

penthouse, backward and blinded, writhing and moaning, his face smashed against his abductor's adamantine back to muffle the screams. At the elevator they rendezvoused with Ms. Smiley, who, without preliminaries, deftly exposed his buttocks so conveniently locked in place by the faithless Fidel, positioned to moon her head-on, and jabbed in the syringe, unloading a mighty dose of tranquilizer. They boarded the elevator for the ride down to the main floor, where Ms. Smiley took her leave without a word, her part of the mission accomplished for now. By the time Fidel, the delivery boy, lugged his freight through the lobby past the grand fountain to the handicapped-accessible room, Gershon had ceased to protest. Fidel deposited his package alongside the door, banging on it hard with his fist as if with full knowledge that there was a variety of life form inside that room. The heart-stopping presentiment that it might be Gershon in some kind of Gershon mess gripped Hedy with such alarm that she ventured at last to open the door a crack, the chain still hooked, of course. Fidel pointed meaningfully first to the heaving mass on the floor that he personally had hauled, then extended his cupped palm through the narrow opening for a tip, rapidly rubbing his thumb across two fingers in a stale parody of ethnic greed before dancing away.

15.

Not even an hour had passed since Hedy had returned to the room after dutifully fulfilling her assigned task of sliding the manifestos under every door throughout that great fake gothic pile when she was confronted with this pulsing special delivery, the fallout of Gershon's first outing as an evolved two-legged primate since his ensnarement in the hashtag. Her immediate thought was that she would now need to compose and distribute, ASAP, an urgent follow-up announcement of a temporary cease-fire in the seminal color war—the fighting to be resumed at the earliest possible date, stay tuned, at which point she would then need to repeat the entire clerical and distribution exercise yet again, informing the public of the restart. She was still frozen at the door inside the room, peering out over the hooked chain, when she was weighed down by this doleful thought—she hated how her mind inevitably took refuge in such mundane house-keeping and maintenance details at life-altering intersections. Fidel had long faded from the scene, yet she did not venture out immediately, remaining within to process the shock of his insult, craning her neck now and then to glance to her right and to her left up and down the long, wide hallway, blessedly untra-versed at this post-midnight hour as far as she could see, her eyes invariably coming to rest on the black heap that allegedly was Gershon Gordon, her mythic husband of not even one night, obviously knocked out cold, though she had no idea how deeply or for how long. That information would have been extremely helpful in figuring out how to convey him back into the room, overwhelmingly the priority of the moment.

With no other options remaining to her, she bowed, as always, to her duty, steering Gershon's empty wheelchair out of the room into the hallway, taking pains to minimize its chronic rumbles and screeches, bringing it to a halt alongside the subject. As far as she could tell he was heavily sedated, a dead weight, she was hopelessly aware that she did not possess the physical strength to lift him up and position him in the chair. Yet it turned out that he still retained enough animal instinct to latch himself like a slug to the footrest of the wheelchair and to hold fast as she pulled it back into the room, dragging him along, wiping the floor with him until they drew up alongside the bed. Next came the challenge of getting him up onto the bed, she almost despaired, already she was considering bringing the bed down to him, setting him up on the floor for an indeterminate period of time and tending to him there. To her profound relief, his second-generation-survivor instincts kicked in again, and working together instinctively as a kind of frantically bumbling team, they succeeded in stages—upper body, lower body, limb by limb, head crammed with such awesome brain matter requiring the most delicate handling—and the transfer was complete. There he lay, stretched out as for a public viewing, her job now as far as she understood it was to ready him for an extended intermission.

The front of his garments, so carefully chosen, were sensationally filthy, burred with needles of synthetic carpeting and clumps of dirt due to the unfortunate circumstance of his having been hauled so ignobly and then dragged belly down into the room. Hedy regretted immensely having to deal with him in this undignified way, but she had no choice, really and truly, it hurt her more than it hurt him. As she was removing his elegant black boots of the finest leather, her cell phone pinged with a text message, which she was too busy to view just then but which nevertheless, to her annoyance, distracted her from fully recapturing, in all of its splendor, the moment only a few hours earlier when he had so commandingly walked in those boots again for the first time after so protracted a period of stasis. The black stockings and black breeches came off with comparative ease. Somewhat more complicated, requiring strategic shifting of his heavy corpus, was the removal of his black frockcoat and black brocade waistcoat. But the greatest hurdle of all was his full-sleeved white shirt with the jabot attached, such a lovely accessory, in Hedy's opinion, she tried so hard not to damage it. In the end, though, she had no choice but to cut the whole top off him, it was a pity. The only tool she could find in the room was a package opener, and this is what she used. The trajectory of the blade as she sliced through the cloth just a centimeter or less above his throat, his vital vessels, his beating heart, the veins at his wrists, terrified her, constricting her loins, forcing her to steady her right hand by propping it up with her left until the pieces of cloth fell away in shredded rags of varied sizes, like white petals scattered down the aisle by a flower girl, revealing, against the background of his black V-neck undershirt and his black Jockey underpants, his fringed garment, luminous in its whiteness, rendered even more sacred by the celestial strings of tekhelet azure turquoise accenting the white tassels at its four corners.

She washed his face and was slowly brushing his radiant white hair, taking in the wifely moment, when Mommy Monkey jumped on her back, her long arms encircling her neck, and hissed in her ear, "Sweetie, you can't leave him like that in just his gatchkes. What if somebody comes to visit?" So Hedy dutifully searched for and found his great moth-eaten white woolen prayer shawl with the wide licorice-black stripes and the silk neckband atarah richly embroidered in threads of silver and gold, and propping him up even higher against the cushions, she draped it over his shoulders. Then she bound the leather straps of his tefillin around his left arm with the parchment-filled box turned inward toward his heart, and set the other black box on his head, directly in front of his black velvet yarmulke, upon his fontanel still oddly soft and faintly pulsing, she noted with maternal tenderness, accomplishing all of this swiftly and with impressive ease thanks to the decade or so that she had devoted herself to the study of Talmud, when she, too, had donned tefillin every morning at prayer, like the brilliant and tragic and, yes, let's face it, sorely abused Bruriah, wife of the great Rabbi Meir. If I am a Bruriah wannabe, then it follows that Gershon is my Rabbi Meir surrogate, Hedy thought, though more likely he's my Akher, Meir's teacher, the heretic and apostate Elisha ben Avuyah, excommunicated and ostracized, the Other about whom a voice from behind the curtain was heard to call out, Return all my rebellious children—all except Akher.

"He looks like a holy sage, like the Gaon of Vilna on all those rebbe cards that the Haredi kids used to flip and trade—don't you think, Mommy?" she commented to Mommy Monkey, revising her rabbinic model as she stood at the foot of the bed assessing her handiwork, staring at Gershon, decked out in his hallowed uniform. Hunched over, regressing to all fours, Mommy Monkey was now perched on the floor at her side, stretching her neck, looking up, evaluating the product too. "You're so right, sweetie, he looks like a real genius," Mommy Monkey said. "I knew you could do it—didn't I say so? Take a picture, sweetie, for your personal-memories album." Obeying, Hedy aimed her cell phone, but then, as if she had just thought of something unbearably horrifying, she turned and cried, "But Mommy, what about all those yucky parts that I might have to take care of now for God alone knows how long—you know, like number one and number two and all of that gross bathroom stuff, how do I handle it?" At that moment, ping, another text message coming in, and, predictably, Mommy Monkey was gone again, just when she needed her most.

The text message looked alarming, like an end-of-time warning from command control central, its bold capital letters zigzagging like lightning about to strike. It was graphic aggression, she recognized that at once, a visual reflection of Smiley's annoyance at not having gotten an instant response to her first text, most likely, the text Hedy had put off dealing with while tending to Gershon, caught up as she was in circumstances beyond her control. Smiley's main purpose in writing was clear from the very first sentence, bookended by apocalyptic emojis: "I know you're squatting there illegally, but if you rub my whistle the right way, the psychoemp bitch never has to find out. The client you are now tending has received a megadose of long-acting Haloperidol, which should keep him minding his manners without any supplementary boosters or refreshers for three to four weeks. Mainly he will sleep, now and then waking up to carry out some bodily functions, but don't count on it. Fidel will drop off a case of adult diapers, a bedpan, some extra sheets, outside your door. Don't worry if he's not eating much, consider him to be in a state of hibernation like a great white bear in this wintertime of his life, the main thing is to keep him hydrated. In an emergency, call 911, above all, do not call me, my med line connects you directly to the earbuds of the Hindu Zoya, frolicking in Palm Beach on pink satin sheets with the Slavic Zoya, her co–evil twin, ungrateful cheating spouse of the too-good-for-his-own-good good Jeffrey Epstein."

Another ping, leaving her no space to absorb and process these instructions. Ominously, at the same time, the door creaked open to the full length of the extended, taut chain, which still held fast, thank God. Wide-eyed, Hedy took in the message that flared up on the screen in front of her: "Didn't you see my text a while ago to unhook the chain for me, Mommy? I told you at the lake that I would come tonight. I will come every night. I have a master key to all the rooms in this dump in case one of my victims slits her wrists in the tub, but their doors have no chains. You have a chain, I need you to release your chain. Open up for me, Mommy, my head is wet with dew, my hair is drenched from the night."

Hedy unhooked the chain and let Corona into the room with exemplary deference, taking their hand and leading them to her closet nest, but they rejected that path. "No more closet sleeping for you, Mommy, it stinks from stale ink, from all the wrong words," Corona said. "There's enough room in the bed for all three of us. It's a king-size bed, we're a co-sleeping family, Daddy, Mommy, and me—I'm baby Corona again, with you in this bed I'm once again the little girl I used to be, I'm not they/them here, for you I'm she/her, I give you permission, I empower you, Mommy," Corona said, stating her terms, sublimely dispelling Hedy's panic with regard to wrong and right words, going on to mention that, by the way, she had chosen the name Corona herself, "In honor of Daddy's favorite typewriter of blessed memory on which he banged his brains out," she said. The special word privileges and other sweet favors granted by Corona had the effect of drawing Hedy among all women into a level of closeness that she had long ago concluded would never be her portion in this life. The novel way Corona provided for Hedy of visualizing Gershon on the bed, as a self-contained unit, packaged and bound like a mummy, in his prayer shawl and phylacteries, defanged, confined to his side as in a crypt, sleeping in his vault, rendered him no longer dangerous, at least for now. The effect was to liberate the two women to claim their place on the other side of the bed, naked and entwined, a serpent around a fig tree, taking up the space of no more than one sleeper, mama sniffing the fragrant fuzz on the top of baby girl's shaved head, baby girl suckling at mama's breast through what remained of the night before detaching and disentangling in the early morning hours to rise and go forth to lead her victims in the daily healing program.

She was gone all day enforcing her program, returning close to midnight, strictly maintaining this regimen seven days a week throughout the period of Gershon's long sleep. Hedy never inquired how Corona had spent her day, she never asked about any of the patients, nor was any information ever offered or advice sought as a colleague and fellow professional. Corona was, after all, Hedy's successor, her replacement, perhaps she even surpassed Hedy in job performance, but Hedy was not capable of envy in this instance, such envy would have been unseemly, not to mention abnormal based on the teaching of Rabbi Yossi bar Honi in Sanhedrin 105 that while it is natural for a person to be jealous of others, to envy just about everyone else, one can never be jealous of one's own child or one's student. Corona sucked at her breast through the night, Corona was her child. Therefore, Hedy could only take pride and delight in Corona's success, Corona's superior therapeutic gifts, Corona's leadership skills, elements of which, as it happened, were on display through the window directly from their warm bed not long after Corona slipped out every morning.

"Such nakhas, my heart, it's bursting from pride and joy," Mommy Monkey kvelled, having for her part immediately slipped in under the toasty covers to watch alongside Hedy as Corona rallied her more than three dozen masked Jeffrey Epstein victims in all shades of blonde, five or six per row, like the points of a star radiating from a flagpole that until now Hedy had not known existed, she had never noticed that flagpole planted right there on the lawn outside the window. One of the victims came forward to raise the American flag to half-staff in tribute to all the elderly and immunocompromised, fellow victims in the pantheon of victims, who had perished so tragically and so alone in the plague. This was followed by a group recitation of the Pledge of Allegiance to the flag of the United States of America, each victim with her right hand pressed over her wounded heart beating under the Camp Jeffrey Epstein logo of her hoodie sweatshirt, followed by the singing of the national anthem, O Say, Can You See, their treble female voices coming forth somewhat muffled from behind their masks, which were also etched with the Camp Jeff stigmata. Nevertheless, despite the flawed acoustics, Mommy Monkey enjoyed it all thoroughly, pledging allegiance and singing along, snuggling up against Hedy and exclaiming, "So beautiful, like a Broadway show, you know, like the singing nuns."

When next the victims launched into their morning calisthenics routine to the rhythmic beat of Corona's gleaming black whistle like a chunk of obsidian hanging from her neck on a silver chain, the defining feature of her work uniform, Mommy Monkey stood up on the bed and worked out right along with them—jumping jacks, pushups, squats, trunk twists, sit-ups, touching toes, and so on—as Gershon slept on peacefully, undisturbed, occasionally growling in his sleep, incomprehensibly, unthreateningly. Blowing her whistle, Corona walked up and down the rows of straining victims ranging in age from midteens to mid-fifties, in all shapes and permutations of female possibility and decline from nymphet to nymphet grotesque, in all shades of blonde, from yellow gold to white gold to the palest platinum almost dropping off the spectrum, taking in each exercising victim as she moved along the rows, adjusting a limb here, finetuning a stance there, encouraging, motivating. "That baldie, she's a real professional, mind and body, not just your brainy type like some people I know," Mommy Monkey commented with a sly smile like the Cheshire cat, fading away entirely as Hedy absorbed the blow and doggedly went on watching alone.

Corona was now blowing her whistle in a rousing march rhythm, leading her victims single file to the entrance of the main building, where Ms. Smiley and Dr. Fritz Rosenberg awaited them on either side of the door. All of this was still clearly in Hedy's line of sight from her bed without too much straining or adjustment, all still within shooting range. One by one, each victim stepped forward in front of Rosenberg and, upon command, opened her mouth wide. With one bare hand Rosenberg grasped her tongue in his fist and twisted it to the side, while with the other he held up a flashlight, peering deep into the orifice of the victim's mouth past the obscenely swinging uvula, searching within for a disturbing length of time. Now and then he would also stretch out the band of a victim's sweatpants in front, lower his head, and point the flashlight downward, taking a long, serious diagnostic look inside. Most of the victims, their masks back in place, were then passed along assembly-line fashion to Ms. Smiley, who pressed the disc of an infrared thermometer on their foreheads, then, nodding, directed them into the dining hall for what must have been a socially distanced breakfast, Hedy figured. On several occasions, though, during the three weeks or so that Hedy viewed this spectacle each morning from the comfort and warmth and coronal fragrance of the bed, one or two victims, generally from among those the contents of whose pants Rosenberg had inspected so assiduously, were shunted to the side. As far as Hedy could tell, those singled out in this way did not enter the dining room, at least not through the front door, and due to the fact that all the victims resembled each other so remarkably, a reflection of the bad Jeffrey Epstein's articulated and meticulously serviced preferences, Hedy could never really say whether they ever rejoined the group.

This singling out of particular girls was naturally very disturbing for Hedy to witness, evoking a whole haunted house of racial memories of past selections for experimentation and other murderous ends, never mind your basic sexual prurience and violation, but even so, she continued watching day after day, transfixed. She was so proud of Corona's professionalism, she took comfort in her untroubled demeanor—Corona standing there like the shepherd on judgment day, under whose staff the flock passes, counted and tended and sorted to find their place in the world, who to live, who to die, who by fire, who by water, who to rest, and who to wander. Did that make Hedy a guilty bystander? Of course not, she told herself, she believed in Corona, she had faith in her, Corona was devoted to her victims, Corona would never allow them to come to harm, Corona was showing them the way to tranquil acceptance and to health. When Corona came back to the room at night there were no signs that she was troubled in any way, she was calm, at peace with herself, fulfilled. And it was also the case that in the depths of her being, Hedy knew that these were by far the sweetest days and nights that she had passed in memory, her honeymoon days, she was loved by a woman who knew her as she knew herself, it would be tragic to darken with petty suspicions and probings what she recognized to be, for her, so rare, so precious, and likely, so short-lived an interlude. Her days were restful, free of tension and stress and anxiety, only mildly interrupted by her duties tending to Gershon's physical needs, which very soon became routine, almost mechanical in execution, far from evoking the revulsion she had dreaded, while the nights entwined with her baby Corona at her breast were marked by a tenderness that had never been granted her until now, she had never imagined that such closeness would find her in this life.

Gershon remained locked in his deep sleep as the April days flipped by, even as the Passover holiday drew near. He would sleep right through it, Hedy felt certain—good, let him sleep, she thought, he needs his rest, and so do we all. And she, too, for the first time in her life, serenely did nothing in anticipation, forgoing all preparations, letting the festival creep up, slide by, liberating herself from the burden of that liberation, when our forefathers traded one form of enslavement for another, as she told herself. It came as a surprise, then, when on the night of the seder, Corona returned from her workday bearing the basic elements of the ancient ritual in her backpack. Hedy had not even known for sure whether the girl was Jewish, though she definitely fit the body type, but here she was, pulling out of her bag the three essentials, shank bone, matzah, and bitter herb, without which a person has not fulfilled her obligation, according to Rabbi Gamliel, plus two Gender and Sexuality Social Justice Haggadot, so appropriate at Camp Jeffrey Epstein, and a bottle of pomegranate juice for the four cups instead of wine, out of consideration of Hedy's unexpressed ambition, which Corona must nevertheless have intuited, to set a world record as the longest-running female Nazir, a gesture so thoughtful on Corona's part that it almost brought Hedy to tears.

Stretched out, truly reclining like free people on their side of the bed, Hedy and Corona enacted an improvised seder picnic with Corona as the youngest in this family constellation reciting what she called the One Question—"Because it's really just one question with four examples, that's what I always used to say at the seder when I was a kid." (There, Hedy knew she looked Jewish!) "Everyone thought I was so clever," Corona recalled, "it became a ritual at our family seder table for me to say this—like, I have one question for you, Daddy, just one question—bitter herbs, strange fruit, saltwater tears, broken backs, why, why, why, why," she demanded in the direction of the stupefied Gershon.

Hedy offered a teaching drawn from her Talmud immersion. In the days of the Holy Temple, Hedy taught, a system was created whereby groups of people registered to partake in the obligatory Passover sacrifice by buying shares in a lamb or kid. It was a great annual meat market, a holy barbecue, feet sinking into rivers of blood. Every Jew had to pay to be registered for a piece of a Paschal lamb or a kid, every Jew was obligated to eat at least an olive-sized portion of a Passover sacrifice in the Temple, women and men, the animal was sanctified but still it was for sale, registering was big business, everyone was registered, everyone—you could register your prostitute—imagine, your personal sex worker—for her share of the sacrifice as payment for her services, Rabbi Oshaya said. "Let's not unpack Oshaya's comment too critically in the spirit of the holiday," Hedy said. "Let's just privilege it as a really heartwarming example of inclusivity and diversity before anyone ever even heard of inclusivity and diversity or considered them good things."

Corona said, "Mommy, just please do not ask me as the baby of the family to open the door for Elijah the Prophet and demand that he get God to wipe out all the nations of the earth that had ever messed with us Jews, because I'm telling you right now, I'm not doing it, I've always refused, that's my tradition, I'm not into that kind of revenge trip, I always said, No way I'm buying into that Pour-Out-Your-Wrath shit—right, Daddy?" And once again her eyes rested on the stagnating corpus rolled up there on the other side of the bed, which now seemed to be in some sort of state of agitation, churning, stirring like a golem painfully shedding its clay mold, struggling to tear off its bindings. The two females clutched each other as they watched his wrappings fall away, as he rose up and stood erect on the bed in his adult diaper, his prayer shawl and phylacteries and yarmulke clipped to his wild white mane almost grazing the ceiling, his Lord George

Gordon, a.k.a. Reb Yisrael bar Avraham Avinu, long triangular beard unfurling like a proclamation. Standing there on the bed, still apparently deep in sleep, insensate, eyes closed, he declaimed in a booming voice in the holy tongue as if from the heart of the flames shooting out of Sinai, "Sheh-lo ekhad bil-vad amad aleinu le-khalosenu…elah sheb-khal dor va dor, omdim aleinu le-khalosenu." He paused weightily, then added, "And if you think for one minute that you are the exception in your generation not marked for annihilation by the eternal Amalekite haters of the children of Israel, you are just another useless Jewish idiot, and you will learn the hard way." Having brutally communicated this fact, ignoring the built-in divine deliverance palliative extolled in the Passover Haggadah, which was, after all, the point of their celebration, he accordioned his large body back onto the bed with eyes still shut, burrowed his way again into his cave under the covers, and resumed his long sleep as if it had never been disturbed, never been invaded by the revelations of the night.

He went on sleeping through much of the month of April, mostly uneventfully—"Such a good sleeper," Mommy Monkey clucked—though toward the end he slept for shorter and shorter stretches and more fitfully, waking up at last on Thursday, the twenty-third of April, the day on which William Shakespeare was born, and also, it is said, the day on which he died, separated by fifty-two years, having completed the perfect circle of his life's mission. Moses, too, it is said, was born and died on the same day, the seventh day of Adar, one hundred and twenty years apart, the optimal number of years for a lifetime, perfectly rounded out in holiness and service, you could not wish for anything more.

On that same Thursday that Gershon Gordon woke up definitively, the twenty-third day of April in the year of the coronavirus, two thousand and twenty of the common era, the twenty-ninth day of the month of Nissan, five thousand seven hundred and eighty years from the creation of the world, Rabbi Tzadik Kutsher plunged into the orifice of the rear end of his body, the place where his brain was housed, a large-volume enema filled with close to one liter of heavy-duty bleach. He took this action out of loyalty to that great friend of the State of Israel, his relative by marriage, the president of the United States, who had extolled during a primetime news briefing that very day the curative power of bleach, a really terrific cleansing agent, which, as he asserted with full executive authority, knocks out the virus in a minute, in just one beautiful minute, it does a really big number on it—a really fabulous, original, cheap, creative solution, if he had to say so himself.

Escorted by Mrs. Zlata Schick, Rabbi Tzadik Kutsher was immediately carted by ambulance to the former Maimonides hospital in Liberty, New York, where he was placed in the same room with Father Clarence—two flawed clerics of weak character, the old and new testaments, no longer able to breathe on their own, lying intubated and ventilated and muted side by side, cut off forever from the trembling delights of silken young boys, from all illicit temptation. Both were now attended by Mrs. Zlata Schick who would not leave them, she would stay put at the hospital to the end. She would join the exalted ranks of frontline workers hypocritically lauded and cheered to keep them on the job, expendables, stuck forever in the lowest of minimum-wage slots, consigned forever to doing the world's dirty work—this would be her penance, her road to redemption. She would attach herself permanently to the rabbi and the priest who came into a hospital, like a bad joke, she would expose herself fully to their pestilence and contamination, their sullied bodies and their dirty minds, she would not spare her woman's body under her seven shawls, she would contract their fatal disease and succumb to it, she would be carried in a procession from the hospital wards to her resting place past lawns sprouting signs and posters like weeds, Thank You, Thank You, Mrs. Zlata Schick, You Are So Essential.

Gershon, of course, did not consciously note the connection between the day on which Rabbi Tzadik Kutsher took the bleach cure and the day on which he, Gershon, finally opened his eyes fully reborn as Lord George Gordon, like a caterpillar transformed into a butterfly—the twenty-third day of April. He believed at first that he was experiencing an ordinary awakening after an unremarkable night's sleep, he had no idea that he had been out of the time zone for almost four weeks under the spell of the soporific Catskill Mountains, like Rip Van Winkle—or like Honi the Circle Maker, who slept for seventy years, the length of the Babylonian exile, it was as if we were dreaming. This Talmudic morsel was conveyed to Gershon, in the form of a morning mini lesson, by the dried-up little female now occupying a good portion of his bed in a disturbingly proprietary way. He blinked and recognized her as his recently acquired wife of necessity playing the coquette again with her Talmud come-ons. He had caught her propped up against a bank of pillows, naked, clutching a bag of chocolate babies, stuffing one chocolate baby into her mouth after another, brown saliva dribbling down her chin, chewing audibly, visibly, while gazing out the window at what he concluded to be an early-morning yoga class being held on the lawn, all of the ladies frozen in the obscene downward-dog position. The entire frivolous scene disgusted him. These were times of trouble, this was not the time to be lounging around snacking on bonbons plucked from the Talmudic carob tree. Ruthlessly, he disrupted her cozy morning routine. "For God's sake, Hedda Nussbaum, what are you doing watching that porn? Get your ass out of my bed this minute."

Wielding one calloused foot, he kicked—mercilessly, he kicked her out. "Was that good, Hedda Nussbaum? Did you like it? Want more?" he drilled cruelly. "What on earth were you thinking stuffing your face with those little idols, those get-schkes, those obscene little stolen t'rafim? This is an emergency situation. This is war, color war has broken out. Move it, Weasel, get lost, I need my space, there's important work to be done."

16.

There she was again, crouching naked on the floor, folded in on herself to nestle her wounds and protect the glass face of her cell phone, which she had been clutching with both hands to save her life when she was catapulted out of the bed. Doubled over, she staggered toward the wall opposite, sliding her back down along it as she gingerly lowered herself to the floor. From this position she had a direct view, when she dared to raise her eyes, of the calloused soles of his feet, those yellow, cracked, scaly hooves that for so long had not touched the ground, had lost the power to propel his body forward, and now, thank God, see what they could do. They could kick, and with such force, one could only marvel, it was nothing short of a miracle. She knew that a deep bluish-purple bruise would soon flare out, like a Rorschach telling its own personal tale, spreading and blackening over her skin along the side of her body where he had struck, he might even have broken some ribs, damaged some internal organs, but no matter. The physical insult, the pain and the nausea that now were engulfing her, however acute, were as nothing in comparison with her spiritual joy at his restoration. She had uncovered his feet as it were, enabled them, as the righteous convert Ruth the Moabite had uncovered the feet of the landowner Boaz asleep in the field after the long day of reaping as recounted in that sweet pastoral we chant on the holiday of Shavuot, the time of the giving of our Torah. What is meant by uncovering the feet in this instance? Hedy posed this exegetical question to herself. Nothing less than exposing the organ that the convert Ruth desperately needed in order to nail her place as the preordained link that would lead four generations down the noble line to David the king, alive and everlasting, and ultimately to the true messiah himself, may it be soon and in our time.

But why am I thinking of Ruth at this moment, and of good, obedient Ruth's special day still almost five weeks away? she asked herself. It was because from the palanquin of his bed, Reb Yisrael bar Avraham Avinu, as Gershon Gordon would for the foreseeable future be known, had just asked her for the date on the calendar of the gentiles when Lag B'Omer would fall in this year of the coronavirus. For some reason beyond her understanding or her depth, he was focusing on Lag B'Omer, the thirty-third of the forty-nine days of the Omer count between Passover and Pentecost—Shavuot, the festival of weeks, seven in all. Perhaps it was because Lag B'Omer was a day of rejoicing, the day marking, it is said, the end of the plague that had wiped out the twenty-four thousand students of the great Rabbi Akiva for the sin of baseless hatred—that must have been one brutally competitive academy to get into, Hedy thought. May the plague ravaging our people in our own time for the atrocities we have committed against each other and against the earth upon which we dwell also soon be brought to an end, she prayed.

He was talking down to her from the heights of the bed, stretched out along its center as if to stake his claim to both sides, occupy all of his territory, and reassert ownership, lying almost flat with his nose pointed to the ceiling, in communion with the One Above, mouth to mouth they would speak. Across from him, Hedy, a wounded supplicant on the floor, lowered her head even more abjectly when he asked his question—erasing herself out of modesty, yes, but also, as was likely, out of shame for her sins of carnality committed night after night right beside his swaddled comatose body in his own bed, in the immediate aura of his physical presence and his mental absence, for this alone she deserved forty lashes, as if in violation of her Nazirite vows. But now, at this moment, she bowed her head in order to consult her cell phone for the answer to his question. "It starts on May the eleventh, Lag B'Omer, a Monday night this year, that's almost three weeks from now," she confirmed despondently as she took note of the deep crack that had materialized on the glass face of the phone running from right to left, resembling the Hebrew letter zayin. "Today is the twenty-third of April," she ventured to add in order to tactfully orient him even as despair engulfed her. Why had he not even asked what day it was when he had awakened, why had he not inquired at all about what had befallen him, why did he fail to show any interest whatsoever in how long he had been lying there in a nappy, stupefied and inert? Why was he so proud, so ungrateful?

"So that's two and a half weeks from now, just about the perfect length of time for a honeymoon—right?" said Reb Yisrael bar Avraham Avinu, causing Hedy's head to jerk up as if shocked by an electric current.

"Just so you know, I intend to go on our honeymoon alone—unaccompanied," he said.

Go was not exactly the right word, he proceeded to clarify, at least with respect to himself. He planned to stay right there in his room, in solitary confinement as it were—to reclaim his personal space, he added bitingly, foregrounding her stale mental-health jargon—bottom line, he wasn't going anywhere for now, at least not physically. He would use the honeymoon to lay out the strategy for the decisive battle of the color war that will be fought right here at Camp Jeffrey Epstein on the eve of Lag B'Omer, the eleventh of May.

She, on the other hand, must go. She must set forth alone on their seven-blessings honeymoon at once, ideally within the hour, to recruit the warriors for that seminal battle. No worthy heroes remained here within this defiled Camp Jeff fortress to fight alongside their Blue Team of the Holy Tekhelet Fringe in the apocalyptic war against the ancient, hard-core, unshakable Jew hatred that has hashtagged our people to ashes and in so many other unforgivable ways sought to solve the problem of us, to render us extinct. All of our coconspirators and cellmates are dead or dying or have ingloriously deserted. Alas, the flesh of my poor Arnie Glick has by now already rotted off his frail slender white bones, decomposition and decay, they set in so shockingly fast. The clerical delegation, Kutsher and Clarence, along with their devoted handmaid, Sister Zlata Schick, are wasting away inexorably in the isolation wards, they, too, would soon be given over to the maggots and worms, to the microbes bursting from the gut. The Two Bobs, pampered by the pliant Chef Wu, and that mewling lecher Horn, all of them in the grip of the fantasy of escape, have made their way along the twisting road over the dark chasm opening beneath their feet to suck them in and swallow them up. Only the Nazi Rosenberg and I remain for the interim, to face off at high noon, he said. There no longer was any point in such niceties as slipping manifestos under doors to reach the remaining underground partisans, he declared. We must draw our troops from outside our domain—God's mercenaries, the Gordon Group.

Toward that end, he went on, she was to depart for their honeymoon at once, instantly, within the hour, making her way alone, either by foot, like a pilgrim fleeing the plague, or harnessed to a wagon, or on the back of a camel, by whatever conveyance she could rustle up. She must drag her beaten, undesirable body from village to village, from town to town in Sullivan County and beyond, seeking out the multitude of proud

Hassidim who have settled here in the Catskills and whom she had so fulsomely extolled for their contemptuous disregard of what anyone else thinks, for their total dismissal of anyone else's existence except that of the members of their own tribe, for their stiff-necked assurance that they alone were possessed of the truth, their inborn conviction of being above the law of the land, of having been chosen by God among all the nations, by Him most beloved and most desired. She must find them wherever they gather, these holy Jewish superheroes, their kosher markets and kosher pizza joints, their synagogue hangouts and stifling study halls. She must go walking and weeping nonstop like that creature Margery Kempe, prophesying like her namesake Hulda, kin of the prophet Jeremiah, champion deliverer of bad news, prophet and prophetess cousins descended from the union of Moses's protégé Joshua the conquistador and Rahab the harlot of Jericho, about whom it was said that simply by glancing at her a man was brought to instant orgasm.

In the manner of that minor prophet Hulda, and that weeping sex- and Jesus-obsessed creature Margery, those two female preachers, she must make her way through the Catskills from Swan Lake to Loch Sheldrake to South Fallsburg to Monticello to Woodridge to Liberty, New York, and onward, deeper and deeper, bringing the good news to these fierce Jews wherever they congregated. She must reveal to them that the spirit of the sublime mystic, the reputed author of the Zohar, defier of the Roman tyrants, none other than the incomparable cave man, Rabbi Shimon bar Yokhai himself, will be making a special guest appearance right here in the Borscht Belt on the eve of Lag B'Omer, the day almost two millennia ago on which his soul was lifted out of his body to soar to the spiritual heights, and therefore with his last breath he commanded us not to mourn—Do not grieve for me but honor my life by rejoicing, by grasping for ecstasy every year on the day of my Hillula, my Yahrzeit, Lag

B'Omer. Her mission was to draw the stiff-necked Hassidim of Sullivan County and beyond away from their blintzes and to deliver them on the eve of Lag B'Omer in their hundreds, if not in their thousands, to the war zone in the field behind the kitchen of the old Lokshin Hotel and Country Club, now downgraded to the lunatic asylum known as Camp Jeffrey Epstein for society's #MeToo outcasts, a suspiciously disproportionate number of them floating belly up in the Jewish gene pool. Let our Catskill Hasidim come armed with whatever they can find, baseball bats stored in the trunks of their cars for collecting rents in the slums and cudgeling the antisemites, slingshots and stones from the valley of Elah for braining the roaring Jew-hating giants, whatever they can muster, a combat-ready army of the faithful inspired by the spirit of Bar Yokhai, united in resolve, ready to do battle with the latter-day Romans on the eve of Lag B'Omer, after sunset, in the field behind the Camp Jeffrey Epstein kitchen as darkness descends and the fires are lit.

"But what in the world are you going to wear on your honeymoon trip?" Mommy Monkey demanded. "I'm dying to know." She was constricting her with those spidery skeletal arms and legs of hers, squeezing every elevated thought out of the sponge of her brain. "Pantsuit, or fun fur? Is it more business trippy or honeymoonish, you think? Pantsuit, yes—that's it, your all-purpose professional gender-bender solution, there you go. No, wait, scratch that, no pants for you if you want to get anything out of those fanatics. Long skirt, loose top, long sleeves, thick stockings, rubber soles, total head covering like a nun, you should excuse the comparison, the official uniform, everything black. No, scratch that, not black—white, everything white, like an angel, a vision, the Sabbath queen, like the heavenly shekhina, white has always been your color, you've always looked fabulous in white." But Hedy was not responding, not reacting, she was sinking ever deeper into the floor, burying her face in the pungent pit between her crossed legs, where her cell phone lay with its shattered face. Elbows angling out sharply on either side, she was struggling to work the keyboard with both thumbs, a farewell text to her beloved, but Mommy Monkey was interfering, Mommy Monkey would not be still, she would not let her go on. "Listen up, sweetie, I've been meaning to tell you, I read your book—well, actually, not the whole thing, just the parts about me," Mommy Monkey was saying, digging in mercilessly. "Yes, yes, I know, it's not really about me, it's fiction, one hundred percent fiction, but I forgive you anyway, I don't want you to blame yourself for what I did in the end, God forbid, it's not your fault. Still, I have to admit it, it hurt my feelings, what you wrote about me, I tried so hard to be a good mom, I did my best—and this is how you repay me? All I can say is I hope that one day, when your daughter grows up, she pulls a stunt like that on you too, gives you a taste of your own medicine—then you'll know how it feels."

Her daughter? Had Mommy Monkey been hovering in the heat above her bed on her Corona nights? Hedy was feeling more and more defeated, but Mommy Monkey was riding a streak, shouting triumphantly. "What's wrong with you, sweetie? Do you realize how much pain it gives me to see you sitting there on the floor naked as if somebody just died, punishing yourself? Why do you want to torture me like that? What ever happened to my brilliant little girl with the beautiful black curls and the big black eyes and that bright, hopeful smile? How did that little doll turn into such a downer? Look up, sweetie, the sky has not fallen, the sun is still shining," Mommy Monkey boomed as Hedy dared to look up and, nearly blinded, saw Mommy Monkey take flight, flapping her bat wings against the perfect circle of the sun.

"Come back, Mommy," she cried, "I need you to lay out my clothing for my honeymoon trip, I need you to make me ash-ishim cakes from red lentils with sesame seeds fried in olive oil and dipped in honey, I need you to comfort me, Mommy, I'm sick, Mommy, sick with love, I need you to take care of me," but Mommy Monkey was gone, she had disappeared, she had dived into a cloud. Abandoned again, with no one to turn to who loved her, Hedy sank back into the surpassingly urgent business at hand. With her thumbs she pounded out the message beneath the cracked glass: He Woke Up. I'm Gone. On Assignment. I Am Not Here. Do Not, I Repeat, Do Not Come in the Night.

That night, she let herself into the room with her key at the end of her day's work with the victims and lay down on her back on the bed. "Come closer, daughter," he said, "I've been waiting for you." She drew nearer and he pulled her in. "Closer still," he said. "I've just risen from the house of the dead, daughter, let me give you a blessing." He placed both of his hands flat on top of her shaved head, awaiting the words. They leapt out of his mouth before he could snatch them back: For Your Salvation I Was Hoping, Lord. Where did that dire vision come from? Had he seen something, something horrifying? He parenthesized his hands on both sides of her cranium, moving them downward over her ears, finding his way within their labyrinths, with his fingers pressing the eye-lids, outlining the arc of the eyebrows, the animal teeth, the noble Jewish nose, the stubble and bristles on the crown of her head, the dread shape of the skull underneath.

"Why did you shave off your woman's glory, why did you do this to yourself?" he asked. "Illness? Head lice? Feminist statement?"

"Shame," she said. "For consorting with the enemy."

Noiselessly she left the bed in the early morning. Even so, he woke up, having felt the loss of her body's warmth. He propped himself up against a bolster of pillows and watched through the window as she lined up her Jeffrey Epstein victim charges single file at the flagpole, all of them masked and socially distanced, forty or so victims in all, give or take. With a large metal bucket slung over her wrist, the handle topped with a fluffed pink bow, she strode along the ranks, inspecting hands and fingernails held out by each victim, inquiring whether each victim had had a bowel movement that morning, then inviting the victim to fish from the bucket a pink plastic razor blade and a gold tube of red lipstick, compliments of Zuzi Epstein & Sons, Ltd. She made her way from the head of the line to its tail bestowing these goodies, and when she was done and the bucket was empty she set it down on the ground, took her place at the end of the line behind the last victim, and blew her gleaming black whistle to focus their attention.

With all eyes now upon her, she demonstrated a shaving maneuver using her own pink razor blade along the head of this last victim in the line standing directly in front of her, coupled by a spoken command that he could neither hear nor read her lips to decipher, and she commenced the shearing. At this signal, each victim in the line accordingly lifted her personal pink razor blade and set to shaving the head of the victim in front of her. By the time she brought this punishing tonsuring orgy to a halt by blowing her crystalline black whistle again, then raising her hand and slicing through the air with a cinematic cut gesture, some of the heads were fully shaved, others only partially and savagely, still others were left with just half a head of hair like the half beards lopped off by Hanun, son of Nakhash the snake, to humiliate the messengers of David, the Israelite king. The ground was littered with mounds of hair in all grades of texture and thickness, straight and curly, in every shade of yellow.

She held up her pink blade once again and when all eyes were upon her, she slit the back of the garment of the victim in front of her from the collar to the buttocks, exposing the flesh. Uncapping her tube of red lipstick, she marked the naked back before her with the letter *V*, its crotch rising from the top of the victim's natal cleft, its two tips grazing the victim's jutting shoulder blades. Accordingly, each victim in the line slit the back of the garment of her sister victim positioned in front of her and branded the bared skin with the *V* in flaming red lipstick, its raised arms outstretched, as if crying for help. From the bed he watched as she strode purposefully over to the mounds of freshly shaved yellow hair, struck a match, and set the hair on fire, releasing a stench like burnt chicken feathers rising from the sulfurous depths and seeping into his room through the cracks in the masonry.

How deliberate and confident her movements were, he was swelling with pride. His eyes followed her as she made her way to the head of the line of victims, the heel of her palm rhythmically beating the bottom of her bucket, which she had flipped over like a drum, beating between blasts of her polished black whistle clenched between her teeth. Bang blow, bang blow—proudly she led her victims in a long straight line across the lawn from the flagpole to the grand façade of the former Lokshin Hotel and Country Club, now Camp Jeffrey Epstein for the rehabilitation of sex deviants and predators, pausing neither for the invasive morning ministrations and violations of Dr. Fritz Rosenberg nor for the heat monitoring interventions of Ms. Smiley, cutting defiantly right through them straight into the viscera of the vulgar rockpile.

From that point on he could no longer see them, but late that night as she lay beside him for the last time, she recounted how ferociously Rosenberg had raged, spewing saliva at having been bypassed, at having been blocked from performing the mandatory morning checkups on the girls, as he put it. His arms were flailing, his face was as red as the ass of a female baboon in heat, she reported. She therefore had had no choice but to tackle him, hold him down on that dining hall floor, and, with her pink Zuzi Epstein razorblade, she cut off the thumbs on both of his hands and the big toes on both of his feet, after which she shoved him under one of the round tables, behind the floor-length overhang of the tablecloth, where he would not be visible and no one would be offended or lose her appetite from the sight of him. There he remained captive throughout their leisurely breakfast, howling so annoyingly, quieting down only to snatch up the bits of bagel and croissant, poached egg and omelet, pancakes, quiche, granola, smashed-avocado toast, and so on through the menu that the socially distanced victims seated around that table would toss down at him just to shut him up for a few seconds while they were dining, forcing him to fetch with his mouth, . lick the scraps off the floor, like a dog.

By the end of the meal he was a suppurating mess, she continued, bloody from the punishment she had exacted and stained with food droppings and the layers of filth and scum accumulation ever present under the tables in the spaces not visible to guests. In that foul state, there was absolutely no way that Smiley would allow him to be transported up to the infirmary in her pristine Mercedes. The kitchen ex-cons were consequently rounded up to manually convey him in a wheelbarrow, bleating like a wounded, trapped animal, all the way up the hill under the command of Fidel, who then set out to alert the Aryan knights of the templar, as well as all the other patriotic citizens, of the likelihood of an imminent attack by Jewish fanatics and zealots, possessed by the unshakable conviction that everywhere, in every corner of the globe and in every generation since the beginning of time, the antisemites were lying in wait.

"I am so done with the romance of victimhood," she said to Gershon. "If it ever comes to a faceoff between Rosenberg and you, the good news is, at least I've evened the playing field. Now you're both handicapped."

17.

Within the hour, Hedy was standing outside the grand wrought-iron scrolled gate of the former Lokshin Hotel and Country Club following orders, sobbing loudly and sloppily, by no means marvelously like that creature, the Christian ecstatic Margery Kempe, turned on by the agony of the passion. Hedy's regard for the wisdom of Reb Yisrael bar Avraham Avinu was genuine, but she also knew that a Margery Kempe weeping extravaganza would get her nowhere with her targeted audience. The Hassidim she had been charged with enticing to the gladiator arena in the field behind the Camp Jeffrey Epstein kitchen would instantly suspect her of coming into their midst as a missionary for the sinister purpose of proselytizing, to seduce their children and other fragile souls in the congregation of Israel away from the faith, she would be branded as an abomination. With no nod to due process, they would drive her out of town at once, out of the county, screaming, "Shiksa, shiksa," whipping her with their palm fronds, blinding her with the deadly pointed spears.

Nor was she crying out like that lesser prophet Hulda, that little weasel, that obscene little karkushta in the Aramaic of the Talmud that Hedy had wasted so much of her life poring over, the backup prophet the elders consulted only in an emergency when the main guy, Jeremiah, was out of town, the lady prophet who had the nerve to refer to good king Josiah as "that man," to demand that if they wanted her prophecy, they come to her, a woman, not she to them. The Hassidim of Sullivan County whom Hedy had been tasked with drawing to the burning field behind the Camp Jeff kitchen on the eve of Lag B'Omer, would automatically dismiss her Hulda gig as the ravings of a mad-woman or, conceivably, even a witch, a sorceress from Endor in the marketplace who somehow had managed to climb out of her foul pit, they would never heed a single word coming out of the mouth of such a freak, this so-called prophetess, whatever that means, like poetess or authoress, no way on this earth would they ever take her seriously.

Yet there she remained frozen outside the gate of Camp Jeffrey Epstein, crying bitterly and loudly, unable to restrain her-self. If, in the state she was in, she were compelled to name a model for such weeping, she, too, like the elders, would have turned to Jeremiah over Hulda, she admitted this to herself, even at the risk of betraying her own sex. Like Jeremiah she would have summoned up as her model the Jewish weeper, Mother Rachel, Rachel's voice heard in Ramah, as the prophet sang it out, weeping for her children who are no more—gone, gone. Hedy in the state she was in would have thrown herself at Jere-miah's feet for his words of consolation—Hold back your voice from weeping, your eyes from tears, there's a reward for your labors, there's hope for your future.

Future? What future? She was alone, cast out, beaten down, humiliated, ailing. She had been given an impossible task by her master, she had no idea how to carry it out, she did not know where to begin, in which direction to turn. She was stuck on the wrong side of the fence, locked out forever, she needed to move on—Don't just stand there blubbering, girl, pull yourself together, put on your walking shoes, do something! she admonished herself. One swollen foot shot out in front of the other as if of its own accord, and she found herself walking straight ahead into the galaxy. Her head lowered, her eyes fixed on the dirt path along the side of the road, Hedy went on walking and crying, visualizing herself as others would see her if they even bothered to notice her and turned to look, a weird old lady with tangled bushy hair and a worn pack on her back still dragging herself along. Why did she bother? What was the point of her existence? Who let her out of the house? With no sense of conscious forethought, she suddenly halted. Her right arm shot out, four fingers folded and thumb obscenely erect. Where was Mommy Monkey now, why wasn't she hanging from Hedy's neck by her spidery limbs, strangling her out of maternal love, warning ominously against the perils of hitchhiking—hadn't she told her a million times? Mommy Monkey was nowhere, Mommy Monkey was very far away, Mommy Monkey no longer cared, Mommy Monkey was finished with her. Hedy stood there waiting, her thumb beckoning grotesquely. The first car that stops for me and throws open its door, that is the one I will enter, and if I perish, I perish.

It was a beat-up silver Lexus from the last century with the twisted remnants of a side-view mirror and yellowed, cataracted front headlights that screeched to a halt right alongside her, far too close. The rear door swung open, almost knocking her over, but still she allowed herself to be sucked in, weeping violently. Where to? the driver asked—a woman's voice—but Hedy had no idea where in the world she was going, and in any event, she could not speak for her sobbing. The driver executed a quick turn of the head to get a look at her. "She's spritzing corona all over the place, slap a mask on her," she called out. It was only then that Hedy noticed the woman sitting right there beside her in the back seat, who instantly leaned over and muzzled her with a saffron-colored rag that smelled of fenugreek and looked like it had been torn from an old cotton sari. The driver then addressed someone in the passenger seat—so there were three of them in all, Hedy was beginning to pay attention, all women it seemed, their shaved heads ringed with golden halos, or so it appeared to Hedy through her veil of tears, all three dressed in white, the color that Mommy Monkey had so wickedly urged for this honeymoon mission, though she knew very well that Hedy possessed nothing white, not even a white rag for her miserable wedding, everything black, like a Roman matron climbing the worn stone steps, viewed from the rear, her whole story behind her. "She looks to me like she's been knocked up," the driver was saying to the rider occupying the passenger seat. "I guess we'll just take her back with us to the Homowack."

Hearing this, Hedy's crying, which had been showing signs of abating as she was taking in her situation, now burst out even more intensely, muffled only slightly by the bandana mask. No way had she been knocked up, it was physiologically impossible, chronologically, she was on the tail end of the slope, tapering off, and besides, the action always took place in the women's section, behind the partition, for God's sake, and as for the mandatory bi'ah to nail her sham marriage, that had been in violation of the laws of gravity, entirely perfunctory, loveless, nothing could come of it. They were kidnapping her, taking her against her will to the Homowack, of all places—The Homowack Lodge, a name almost as outrageous as Camp Jeffrey Epstein. She saw herself now back at Camp Jeff, standing in the murky water of Lake Ethel among the reeds, overhearing the postcoital escape plot laid out between CPO and Max Horn, every word spoken that night sealed forever in the folds of her brain. The ruins of the Homowack—that had been the designated rendezvous point with the coyotes, the Jewish cult gang squatting there that would smuggle CPO to her final hiding place. Hedy tore the rag off of her face and screamed, "Let me out of here, I can't go to the Homowack, I'm on a mission, he's depending on me, he'll kill me if I don't deliver." Her crying became terrible, alarming, broken only by her screams, "Oh God, Oh God, Let it be all right! Let it be all right!" as the three angels carried her out of the car, through the fire-and-brimstone-blackened shell of the ravaged Homowack Lodge, where a few righteous souls could still be found, down into the rusted-out remains of the indoor swimming pool, and deposited her on a pile of old mattresses in a cozy tent-like partition set up at the deep end, constructed out of madras cloths, softly lit with aromatic candles inside rainbow-colored paper lanterns—an obvious fire hazard was Hedy's last thought before diving into a dark tunnel and passing out.

She spiraled downward along the walls of the tunnel, growing smaller and smaller as it narrowed until she was no more than a black speck in its depths, she was fading out, the feeling was unexpectedly peaceful. But then against her will, her eyes opened, snapped open, and instantly a familiar sensation clutched her, like the throat-constricting panic she would experience in her student years, the doomed feeling of a vital task still unperformed, the weight of the dread consequences that inevitably would ensue. "Gotta go, gotta take care of it, gotta get it done," she was muttering to herself, but she was all tangled up in the blankets and sheets that had been spread over her, she was wearing nothing but her underpants, some stranger had undressed her when she had been unable to defend herself and done who knew what else to her, she was paralyzed.

In the shaded candlelight she could make out a human form sitting cross-legged on the floor on a piece of carpet, like a genie, smoke ribboning tranquilly upward from its magic lamp. "Relax, Mommy," the genie said, "everything is under control. The wild and crazy Hasidic squatters of the former Homowack Lodge have been joyously released from all of their burrows and holes," she told her. "They have already fanned out across Sullivan County and beyond, plastering onto every available wall and surface awesome signs and posters and pashkevilim in Hebrew, Yiddish, and Aramaic, announcing a major rally rumble uprising on Lag B'Omer eve against the deadly epidemic—we're talking here about the real epidemic, not your puny, meaningless epidemic with its ridiculous masks, as if every day is some kind of rocky horror Purim spiel. This is the Epidemic of Antisemitism we're talking about now, the real deal, the Oldest Hatred in the World, no Jew is immune, we cannot remain silent, and so on and so forth. Grab some sticks and stones, weaponize your household items, whatever you can lay your hands on, come with your flaming swords to light the bonfires of Jewish power. Special guest appearance by the holy Roman gladiator Rabbi Shimon bar Yokhai, and so on and so forth, plus such essential information as time and place, have no fear, Mommy, nothing has been forgotten, nothing neglected, nothing omitted. And Mommy—in case you're still worrying, these announcements will be refreshed and renewed in brilliant, eye-catching color every day except the Sabbath until an hour before erev Lag B'Omer, they will be blared out all day except for Shabbes from speakers mounted on the roofs of SUVs crawling up and down the streets and backroads of the county and beyond, the Catskill mountains will dance like rams to the sound, the hills like baby sheep. Busses have been ordered, carpools arranged, they'll be rolling in on all kinds of wheels and, worst-case scenario, on their own two feet, never fear, thousands will willingly show up at the umschlagplatz behind the gangplank of the Camp Jeffrey Epstein kitchen on Lag B'Omer eve, I promise you, a record-setting crowd, guaranteed, they will come thundering in from all over the county and beyond to fight the real plague of age-old systemic Jew hatred, not your pisher plague with its pathetic masks and useless social distancing and other such shtus and nonsense, all in violation of our constitutional right to practice our religion with the entire community of our extended family and the whole nation of Israel in our synagogues and our wedding halls and our cemeteries, it will be a super spreader to beat all super spreaders, because what will be spread is God's holy fury, a dynamite display of God's fierce love for his chosen people—and, needless to say, your boss will also be very pleased by the turnout, Good girl, Hedda, he will say, and he will give you a loving potch on the behind. So for God's sake, Mommy, stop stressing, stop aggravating yourself, it's bad for your health, you're in a very interesting, very delicate condition, we're here to take care of you, I and my band of angels."

She rose and came toward her bearing her lamp with both hands like a libation offering. Hedy could see it now for what it was: a chipped white enamelware pot with a black rim, black handles, a great burn scar, containing the remnants of a candle dying in its Yahrzeit glass. She set it down on the floor and stretched out alongside Hedy on the royal heap of mattresses. She wrapped her arms and legs around her as on those mystical nights while Gershon hibernated, and placed her mouth gently on her breast, already tender and fuller and moist, and in this way they rested for a while, recovering, until she drew back her shaved head, as if better to see her, and said, "So, Mommy, now you know where I go. This is my real passion. Camp Jeff is just my day job."

The child wanted to talk. Hedy had been trained to pick up such signals, automatically she assumed the listening position.

"Just so you know, Mommy, this postapocalyptic temple to the end of time—it hasn't been the Homowack Lodge for years already, she said. Its most recent incarnation was actually a girls' camp belonging to one of the strictest Hassidic sects, Camp B'nos, it was called, the daughters' camp, condemned as a fire trap and health hazard with an endless list of violations very bad for the Jews—brown water dripping over live wires, black mold creeping up the walls, burst pipes, broken glass and rusted metal all over the place, vermin and dead birds, foxes in the house of the Lord, the works—exactly as you find it now, we keep it as a shrine, everything the same except for the internet, installed by us. The super glatt owners ignored all the citations and warnings, dismissing them as if they had come from a lower life form. They categorically refused to close down Camp B'nos. It's good enough for the girls, they said— and they went on shipping their daughters to this disaster zone for ten weeks every summer. So to move things along, the day of our arrival, we burned down a major building on the property and sent those sages a message: This is just for starters, boychiks—that was the message. It did the trick, I'm proud to say, they shut down the camp immediately and evacuated the girls to God knows where. So thanks to the girls of Camp B'nos, we found our passion and our fortune—burning down old hotels in the Catskills at the strictly confidential, top-secret request of the owners—for the insurance. We take ninety percent of the payout. These Jews have fantastic insurance policies, that's because they believe with full faith in the coming catastrophe. Remind me to give you our card, Mommy, in case you're still in touch with someone at the old Lokshin place who might be interested in our services. We call our company B'nos, Inc. Our motto is: It's Good Enough for the Girls— which means, five stars, the best, nothing but the best for our daughters, Mommy, your daughter and mine."

All of this Corona unspooled while they were lying on their backs side by side, and this is how they remained when she was done, silent beside one another until Hedy blurted out, "I wouldn't want you to burn the whole thing down, because Gershon's still there, I still have feelings for him, you know, maybe just do the kitchen for now, it's a death trap anyway. You can leave a note blaming the arson on Zoya Roy, she's the evil witch who fired me, that would be like fighting fire with fire"—and she let out a feeble little laugh.

"You really don't get it, Mommy—do you?" Corona cried.

She leapt over her, off the mattress pile and onto the floor layered with strips of salvaged carpeting from the abandoned hotel rooms, landing on her feet, stuck like a gymnast. "I've been trying to tell you something about me, about our mission—about you, Mommy!—in all kinds of different ways, and you just laugh and make some lame joke. At least you're not crying anymore, I guess that's progress," she added as she stood up, holding in both hands the white metal pot from which she had removed the smoke-stained Yahrzeit glass with its blackened wick. "You see this pot? I want you to think of it as a kind of pish teppel—you know, like a bedpan, a chamber pot. Your bladder must really be full by now, I want you to pee in it for me, like the lady in the doctor's office says—"'for me.'"

She held it out, but Hedy, who by now was sitting up on the mattress pile with the blanket tucked under her chin to cover her nakedness, made no move to accept the votive. "Come on, Mommy, I won't look," Corona said. She deposited the pot in Hedy's lap and turned her back. "You'll hear," Hedy said. Corona stepped outside the tent of meeting, checking her cell phone while waiting for Hedy to do her business and then summon her back in. She went on checking as Hedy took one of the plastic sticks that Corona had set down beside the mattress pile on the twisted remains of a pool lounge chair, and following the instructions, dipped the stick into the rich, dark urine with which she had filled the pot. She watched as the red bar formed on the stick—positive. In the maw of diagnosis, positive means negative, she reflected. A deep, grating sound burst out of her, which launched Corona back inside thinking, Oh God, she's crying again. Hedy showed Corona the stick with its red gash. "Ridiculous," Hedy managed to get out—like Mother Sarah, struggling to hold back her laughter.

18.

Over the close to three weeks of their honeymoon Gershon had not heard a word from her. He had tried to contact her cell phone using the antiquated Lokshin bedside telephone as they had agreed, but there was no answer, only a recorded voice informing him that no space remained any longer for a message from him, followed by a hollow, infuriating silence at the other end. During that entire nearly three-week period he had not left his room, not once, he had not spoken a word to anyone, not a single word to a single soul, she had faded out as if she had never existed, never been real, and he, due to her incompetence and criminal neglect, had been condemned to solitary confinement, cruel and inhuman. How could she do this to him? Where were the warriors she had been mandated to deliver? What about the ultimate Gordon Riot, the heralded grand finale of the color war, the apocalyptic battle of the Blue Team of the Holy Tekhelet Fringe against the White Team Hooded Spreaders of Jew-Hating Poison, which illuminated so much about all that we have suffered over the millennia and in our own time? She had failed him, she was such a loser, he should never have put his trust in her, she disgusted him.

This he unloaded upon her and more when she finally called

that Monday, May the eleventh in the year twenty-twenty by the solar calendar of the nations of the world, late afternoon of Lag B'Omer eve, before the setting of the sun and the start of the holiday. I have not been well, Reb Yisrael bar Avraham Avinu, I've been sick, she had tried in vain to tell him, once even attempting to expel the exotic words *pregnant, expecting, with child*, but every inconsequential bleat coming out of her mouth was smothered by his rant. He had been cast by her into hopeless isolation for almost three whole weeks, cut off from all connection to the outside world, it had been torture, she was a disaster, he went on raging as if he were flushing out his pipes unused for so long, blasting her with the projectiles of all his accumulated waste matter as punishment for her abandonment, her treachery. Traitor, bitch, prtizka, slut, cunt, he fumed. It always comes down to that when a woman gives you a hard time, even a goddess or a queen—or a mother, she thought.

His outburst was followed by a long silence, an alarming void. Could he have hung up? She held on, she had vital information to pass on to him related to the evening activity program coming up. She believed she could hear labored breathing from his end as she waited, no doubt he had put on weight during these past two-plus weeks, she figured, eating for two, as the professionals recommend for women in her alleged interesting condition, gorging on her unappetizing Nazir portion as well as his own dropped at the door—what else was there for him to do but stuff himself in his confinement? "I'm sending my messenger to deliver your get, probably that traitor, Fink," he abruptly broke in. "He'll just throw it within your daled amos wherever the hell you are, wham, bam, thank you, ma'am. He throws like a girl, the schmuck, he always had lousy aim, but he'll manage somehow to get it into your personal airspace, maybe even hit you with it, whatever, you deserve to be smacked around anyway. And that will be that, we'll be officially divorced, in accordance with the laws of Moses and Israel, end of story—behold, you will be permitted to all men, assuming there's any man out there who would ever want you."

He was standing alongside the bed pressing the receiver against his ear, getting the talking out of his system after such prolonged abstinence, speech after long silence, gazing idly out the window as he rambled on so callously, scarcely taking in the movement in the dying light on the great Lokshin lawn, as busses, cars, taxis, and other assorted conveyances rolled over the fresh spring grass carpets that had only recently been laid out, flattening and shredding them, and disgorged the troops of Hassidim in their unmistakable uniforms, the black gaberdines and the black wide-brimmed hats, undefiled by masks. From where he stood spewing his fury into the phone as if on automatic, it took him a while to register what was happening before his eyes, it was all unfolding in the deceptive twilight hour, like a hallucination, it was unfolding in such a remarkably orderly fashion, so uncharacteristic of this population group. There appeared to be designated officers organizing the troops as they offloaded, directing them to the pathway to the left of the main building with its stone turrets and watchtowers, leading around it to the trenches in the great field of ashes behind the kitchen, the meeting point from where the final battle would be launched. Streams of men and boys seemed to be pouring out of the transports, lugging bulging sacks stuffed with potatoes and other domestic projectiles, armed with sticks, bats, shovels, umbrellas, brooms, canes, as well as a whole array of kitchen utensils and garden tools. Many were carrying on their shoulders little girls with long shiny hair who looked to be about three years old, carting them to this place to be married off, Gershon assumed, he had retained this minimum-age-limit trivia from his abbreviated back-to-the-Talmud phase centuries ago, or so it now seemed to him, just around the time he had voluntarily committed himself to the Camp Jeffrey Epstein loony bin. Then it dawned on him that these were not three-year-old girls after all, these were three-year-old boys being borne like lambs to the altar for their first shearing, as was the custom on this designated auspicious day—their upsherin, their second cutting to enter the faith, leaving them with long sidelocks, visibly, outwardly marked as a people set apart that dwelt alone.

He could hear the Hassidim singing as they made their way along the pathway to the campfire field behind the kitchen, it was the hymn to the holy sage, Rabbi Shimon bar Yokhai—All praise to you, Bar Yokhai, Bar Yokhai, ashrekha. To Gershon's ears it was transcribed as Bar Yokhai, Ayeka—Where are you, Bar Yokhai? Panicked, he yelled into the phone, "Where the hell is he, Bar Yokhai, is he going to show up or not for God's sake?"—taking for granted that no matter how hard he pummeled her and however long he suspended communication as if she did not exist, she would still remain steadfast in her place at the other end of the line ready to absorb whatever new missile he might hurl her way. But this time when she spoke, he paid attention, pausing his excoriations, it was critical that he know what was happening. "Listen to me, sinner man," she was saying, an unaccustomed ring of authority in her voice, "your answer to Ayeka is Hineini—Here I am. Tonight, you are Bar Yokhai. When the darkness fully descends, and the great bonfire has been lit, and the ground is covered with the silken curls of all the little boys, you will make your appearance, you will glide out of your cave in your wheelchair chariot, your heavenly Merkavah as in Ezekiel's vision of God's throne, the Merkavah battle tank of the mighty army of Israel. You will be robed all in white like a holy man who has hidden in a cave immersing himself in the mysteries for thirteen years, like a ghost rising from your tomb in your white kittel shroud and your white mask and your white tallit drawn forward over your head, you will come out to bless your warriors and lead them into the final battle of the color war."

Still flattening the receiver hard against his ear, he made his way closer to the window to get a better look at what was happening out there on the great Lokshin lawn as darkness overtook creation, dragging the cord to which he was tethered for his only connection to the living, unwinding and stretching it, crashing the telephone off of its bedside pedestal. He watched as the transports continued to arrive, the Hassidim in their blacks still streaming out with their bundles, making their way in so uncharacteristically subdued and docile a fashion along the path to the back of the main building singing out their longing for the immanence of the shining mystic Bar Yokhai. The outdoor lights switched on. At the flagpole, as in a dreamlike dusky haze, a large gathering of men seemed to be roiling about in horned helmets, animal pelts, fur hats, visored caps, and gleaming boots, but most by far in the hooded white robes of the White Team, belting out God Bless America as they raised a white flag emblazoned with a black swastika, or maybe it was a black skull with fangs and crossbones, the deepening darkness rendered it more and more difficult to decipher, most likely it was just your basic all-purpose black cross, which usually did the job. He turned away from this vision toward the main building, and watched as Corona with her gleaming shaved head was carried aloft as if to her coronation within a prancing circle of her skinhead victims, one of them on her phone waving her arms animatedly, perhaps to give advance notice of their leader's arrival, preparing the way for the anointment of their champion as they processed to the grand entry of the main house, cutting through loiterers hanging out in front waiting for the show to begin. He spotted the traitor Fidel posted outside, like a bouncer at a club standing guard against gate crashers and other uninvited guests, yet it had not been so long ago that he had sat with him and the lesser bailed-out kitchen boys in the soot of the kitchen dungeon partaking of their stash, accepting their gifts even from their blistered hands, their unclean mouths. He saw Smiley pushing Rosenberg in a wheelchair, his hands and feet engorged inside what looked like white socks padded with layers of dressing and gauze—could Smiley have taken out her little sewing kit, moistened the tip of the thread with her tongue, threaded her needle, and reattached his severed parts? He saw a high-priced female standing apart on her stiletto heels, lounging against the building in what seemed to be a pantsuit professional uniform, impeccably tailored and styled. He put his mouth against the receiver, fully expecting her to be there in abject attendance still, awaiting his next order. "Is that one of the Zoyas I see, shamelessly hustling out there right in front of the main house?" he yelled. Was there something else scheduled for tonight that he hadn't been notified about?

"This was what I've been trying to tell you all along," she said. "It's a Zoya Roy special, another public psychoempathy production—The Sequel."

He did not respond, he held back, waiting for her to unload the answers to the obvious questions. Did Reb Yisrael bar Avraham Avinu recall that she had told him, it now seems a lifetime ago, that one of his alleged victims had come forward and expressed her willingness to participate in a psychoempathy session? Well, it looks like she has finally shown up, though Hedy had heard that she was now having second thoughts, cold feet most likely, she was refusing to go on, and now since the whole thing had been arranged and the invitations had already gone out, Corona might have to step in to do her part—Corona, the universal understudy.

The invitations had gone out? Then why had he not received one? Was he no longer a certified member of the Camp Jeffrey Epstein ratpack? These were the obvious questions. Even more to the point, in this little drama scheduled for their evening entertainment he was the alleged perpetrator, or whatever they were calling it this week, he could have played himself. Did they think he had dropped dead in his Camp Jeffrey Epstein cell, and they were just too revolted by the prospect of digging him out, liquifying in his virus soup? Or, as was more likely, were they simply terrified by the possibility of a live opponent occupying the so-called offender chair, confronting the victim— excuse me, the survivor—refusing to remain silent? He held back from asking—what did it matter? He had a far more vital commitment on this night of nights, a sacred responsibility to his gathering troops, a holy mission, the justification of his life's work, it could not be deferred. Had they invited him, for the sake of heaven and the future of our people, he would have torn off his mask and spit in their eyes.

"So who's playing me?" he nevertheless inquired at last, with an affected air of disinterest.

"An empty wheelchair," she told him, "with a blowup of your face and a mask taped to it. The Zuzi Epstein Playhouse is much too small for regulation social distancing," she went on, "so that's why they're doing it in the dining room—it's a huge canyon, immense, the perfect venue under the aspect of plague and contagion. It will be a very exclusive audience of invited guests only, very widely spaced," she had been told, "everyone will be masked, everyone will have an assigned seat, the rules will be very strictly enforced."

She might have told him more, but just then he was cut off. Inside the grand dining hall, Dr. Zoya Roy had risen, casting repeated glances charged with perplexity in Hedy's direction as she tottered on her heels to her place in the circle marked out in the center of the dining room with the tables generously separated from each other all around it, the nightclub theme. There was something disturbingly familiar about that survivor slash victim with her shaved head talking so urgently into her cell phone, but at the present moment Zoya did not have the luxury to puzzle it out, she had far more important matters to attend to. Having reached her designated chair in the center of the circle, she grasped the microphone, turning away definitively from this irritating distraction and dismissing it. She stood there for a calculated number of seconds imprinting the force of her presence on the onlookers, like a ringmaster flicking his whip in the center of the arena. Then she turned and nodded approvingly to Corona, already in place in the survivor's chair, and she took note of the wheelchair with its garish masked photo standing in for the offender, like a wanted poster of the emblematic bad guy with half his face concealed by a bandana while holding up a stagecoach. At last, she condescended to turn her attention back to the audience, as if to grace them with her notice. Glaring hard over her own mask tailored from the same rich fabric to coordinate with her pantsuit, she warned the chosen invitees with chilling severity that all phones and other devices must be turned off at once before they could begin—and Gershon's connection was lost.

19.

The chopping off of her steel-wool shrub of too-Jewish hair by which she had come to be identified marked a wistful ending to Hedy's more than two decades as a Nazira, possibly a third millennial world record set by a female. As a Nazira forever, which was how she had long classified herself talmudically, she had regularly taken advantage of the special dispensation to lighten the burden of her ethnic hair by trimming it every thirty days or so, in rhythm with her cycle, a lunar shedding that, come to think of it, now also seemed to be defunct, fizzled out. Reflecting on all of this against the background static of Zoya Roy's unrolling of the oppressive ground rules governing the psychoempathy showdown, she was once again able to console herself with the truism of a great load lifted off her head. It was, without doubt, a physical as well as a spiritual relief to be rid of that weight of hair, she was firmly on the road to liberation, should the astonishing promise of the angels actually come to pass, she no longer would be able to indulge herself with the privileged separateness of a Nazir. The relief that swept over her at surrendering her Nazir state now combined with a sense of bittersweet triumph as she observed Zoya eyeing her repeatedly, her tormentor groping mentally in vain, racking her brain to place her, struggling to figure out who she was—she looks so familiar, Zoya doubtless was ruminating as she staggered across the vast dining room on her punishing stilettoes to the spotlight.

The ceremony of Hedy's ultimate shearing, which had transformed her so radically, her personal upsherin, had been enacted that very morning of Lag B'Omer eve at her own request, she had bestowed upon Corona the honor of performing the ritual. She lowered herself in a squatting position—"Squatting is good for pregnant women," the angels said—into the very center of an old mangled net that had been used in the Homowack days by the lifeguards to fish the detritus out of the swimming pool, the dead insects and small reptiles and other impure creepers and crawlers, the dried-out turds of all sizes and shapes left by the guests, marking territory like dogs. Corona had spread this net outside their little nest over the fractured concrete and remaining shards of tile at the deep end of the brutally gutted indoor pool, and then she had knelt down upon it beside Hedy frozen in her hygienic squat to perform the surgery. Great hunks of coarse black hair streaked with gray fell all around them onto the net, encircling them like a rim of ashes on an altar, sacred residue which cannot simply be discarded as ordinary rubbish but must be disposed of in the prescribed way, the sanctified remains of the ritual sacrifice marking the end of her Nazir vow. This was Hedy's mystical cutting, her orlah, her forbidden fruit of the first three years, her foreskin. Then Corona shaved Hedy bald with one of the Zuzi Epstein & Sons pink razors, and Hedy recited the blessings, thanking God for having created her a human and not an animal, a woman and not a man.

In the reconfigured dining hall, Hedy willingly took her place at one of the tables reserved for Corona's flock of victims—or rather, survivors, the preferred term. She didn't mind being labeled a survivor, it meant you made it, you came through, it identified you as one of the elect. Seated there in the company of these survivors with their shaved heads, she was barely distinguishable from the others except for the stippling of black instead of light roots on the taut skin of her newly exposed scalp outlining the contours of the skull underneath. As Zoya droned on, the freshly inducted survivor sister Hedy Nussbaum listened anxiously for the sounds coming from the field behind the kitchen. There was a tolerable-decibel-level buzz at first, suggesting controlled, supervised movement and activity, the steady hum of the business of the holiday eve being attended to and carried out—the lighting of the great bonfire and the other lesser fires all around, the cutting of the virgin hair of the three-year-old boys, the setting out of the food and drink, and overlaying all of it, nonstop, the steady background chanting of the hymn to Bar Yokhai, again and again, the exaltation of the holy sage Rabbi Shimon Bar Yokhai, superhumanly endowed with the ten heavenly attributes, the ten sefirot leading to the deepest secrets at the core of the divine mystery. Hedy knew this piyut well, she could recite the poem by heart, she could sing it on demand, and even now from this distance, through all the barriers and interference, she could make out some of the words—rocky cave, sword unsheathed, blazing light, holy of holies, secret teachings, divine radiance, all praise to you, Bar Yokhai, Bar Yokhai ashrekha.

Then unexpectedly, at the same moment that Zoya Roy gestured to Corona, the stand-in for this evening's featured survivor, to come forward to slit open her heart and pour out her bitterness like water onto the wheelchair, now serving time as the offender, a thunderous shout erupted from the ravaged field behind the kitchen, an ecstatic chorus penetrating the stone walls into this inner space of the dining room, rumbling like an avalanche, deafening like an explosion, rendering all levels of civilized communication impossible. "Bar Yokhai," they sang it out unrestrained, bellowing over and over at the top of their lungs like a mantra, their voices rising with exquisite longing, "Fortunate the one who bore you, Fortunate those who learn from you, Fortunate those who partake of your secrets!"

He has arrived, this is what Hedy now understood and accepted. He has come forth in his sacred white garb in his celestial chariot as she had directed him. He has fulfilled his promise, he has not disappointed. He has appeared, and now no hope remained for healing through words in this hall. War had been declared, the war cries were permeating the space, filling and swelling it, drowning out everything else, rendering everything else inaudible, trivial, and of no account.

Instantly, as if this contingency had been factored in, Fidel, until that moment picking his teeth above his lowered mask as he leaned casually against the rear wall of the dining room, swung into action. He unlocked the double doors to the kitchen, pushed his fellow galley slaves inside, then relocked the doors behind them in accordance with established protocol, to keep out the disturbance of kitchen staff when a public program was underway. He raced across the dining hall as if on a mission, zigzagging through the maze of widely spaced tables and the stunned captive audience, through the lobby and out the grand doors of the main building as his former cellmates stumbled along the strait of the darkened kitchen into the field in back, never to be seen or heard from again. People automatically assumed that they had either been torn to pieces by the frenzied dancers or that they had perished in the events that ensued and had gone unidentified, dumped into unmarked graves. But Hedy, for her part, knew that the moment they had appeared in that field behind the kitchen they had been swept up into the rapturous circle of men and boys, hoisted aloft on shoulders and whirled around so lovingly, in a manner so long and so painfully missing from their lives, they had been absorbed completely by the Hasidim in their Bar Yohai rapture. With the powers of her prophetess namesake Hulda, she could see the day in the future, in a good hour, when she would encounter them again on a street somewhere in the world in the hectic week before the marriage of her brilliant daughter to the miracle boy survivor of the last battle of the Camp Jeffrey Epstein color war, the miracle boy survivor who had lost all his faith, the miracle boy survivor who had become the brilliant apostate. The former galley slaves would appear before Hedy on that day in the future in their regulation Hassidic blacks, white shirts, no ties, fringes dangling, their black fedoras on their heads over their black velvet yarmulkes, they would stop her and ask, "Excuse me, are you Jewish?" And even though she had taken a Talmudic vow with, blessedly, no husband or father around empowered to annul it— Netula ani min ha-Yehudim, she had vowed, I am so done with the Jews—she knew she would nevertheless answer their question truthfully, she would bravely take the risk, she would not deny it. "Yes," she would say, "I am a Jew," the last words spoken before you are beheaded. As her reward, they would hand her the Sabbath candle kit designed especially for Jewish women to bring light into the world in atonement for the sin of the first woman from whom they were descended, Mother Eve, who brought us death and darkness direct from the Garden of Eden by tempting the first man to eat of the forbidden fruit of the Tree of Knowledge, good and evil.

In the middle of the center ring of that cavernous dining room, Dr. Zoya Roy now claimed her reserved seat, she stationed herself there as in a dentist's chair, that was how it looked to Hedy from her place among the survivors—Zoya's tortured feet crossed at the ankles, her fists clenched in her lap, her eyes half shut above her luxurious mask, which seemed to be pumping in and out from her suppressed coughs, a purplish blotchiness creeping relentlessly up her neck from her chest like an alien invader, as if to constrict her entirely. Still, Zoya sat there stoically and suffered it, observing the events as they unfolded. Everything was playing out exactly as expected, she told herself, she was preparing herself to make the case for the therapeutic effectiveness of this radical treatment mode even in extraordinary circumstances. There would be no words spoken out loud by the survivor tonight, everyone was masked, everyone was muted, in these dark times the survivor would go unheard above the clamor from the blighted field behind the kitchen, there would be body language instead, pantomime role-playing leading to catharsis. This was just another road to the psychoempathic climax, equally healing, she would argue. Backed by the support of the good Jeffrey Epstein and his faithful consort, now alas giving off signals of distancing herself, cutting ties, and drawing closer to her master protector in classic Slavic survival mode, Zoya Roy, the supreme survivor of them all, would push as hard as she could her conviction that the Camp Jeffrey Epstein program had run its course, it had come to its natural end, every one of its participants will have been discharged in one way or another, it had been a huge success, she did not doubt that the good Jeffrey Epstein would be awarded the Nobel Peace Prize for his service to humanity if only he changed his name.

To enact her role in this therapeutic dumb show, Corona now crossed the divide to the wheelchair of the offender, represented by the grotesquely enlarged black-and-white photograph of his face propped on the seat. From her pocket she drew out her golden tube of Zuzi Epstein & Sons lipstick, which she used to scrawl in great blood-red letters across his face the words *I Forgive You, Daddy.* Holding up this sign, she painstakingly made her way around the circumference of the center ring, circling slowly for all to see. When she had satisfied herself that the message had been delivered, she returned to the wheelchair, repositioned the photograph back on the seat, the writing across the face adjusted for full impact, then sat herself down there as if cradled in his lap, legs dangling over one side, her arms embracing him, her lips pressed against his image, as to an icon, in devout adoration.

"Judische schmutz," Dr. Fritz Rosenberg screamed, his shrill ejaculation reverberating in that great dining room even over the battle cries coming from the field beyond the kitchen, still rising, higher and higher. But before his minder, Ms. Smiley, could stop him, blowing her whistle to no avail in that din as long as her breath lasted, he zipped out of her custody across the floor intending to crash his wheelchair into the rival wheelchair of the abuser in which Corona had enfolded herself so obscenely. Fully alert, Corona pivoted and righted herself in an instant. With the open palm of one strong hand pressed firmly against Rosenberg's chest she halted his advance and with the other she wielded her Zuzi Epstein & Sons complimentary pink razor, calmly inquiring, "And what shall we cut off today? This ear or that ear? This nose?" With the naming of each protruding body part, she waved the blade menacingly in its airspace. "Or maybe this?" Corona went on, as she glided the blade downward to dangle over the soft little lump at the point where his skeletal legs forked—like a helicopter it hovered there, slowly, slowly descending for the crash landing.

It was at that moment that Hedy Nussbaum realized she had been hearing every word Corona was saying. An ominous silence had fallen upon the field behind the kitchen and seeped with all of its mournful weight into the dining hall. Reb Yisrael bar Avraham Avinu was giving his band of brothers their final instructions before the great battle, girding their loins as they stood in silent prayer sanctifying their spirit, like the high priest addressing the people—"Hear O Israel, you are about to go into battle with the enemy, do not lose heart, do not panic, do not be overcome with dread, the Lord is with you, marching to victory."

She could hear them moving toward the dining room through the long, narrow soot-blackened tunnel of the kitchen illuminated only by the light of the large appliances. She could hear the rumbling of the wheelchair of Reb Yisrael bar Avraham Avinu at the head, gaining speed as it made its way down the gradually sloping floor toward the embedded drain, the concrete ramp wet and slippery, propelled forward by the warriors, more and more of them rallying in from behind. Desperately, Hedy's eyes sought out Corona to come to her aid at once in throwing open the doors to the dining room that Fidel had so deliberately, so cynically relocked. That was when the White Team Hooded Spreaders of Jew-Hating Poison charged in from the lobby with Fidel at its head. They advanced across the enormous dining room at lightning speed, flattening everything in their path, and took up their position against those locked doors, blocking even more hopelessly all entry from the kitchen by the Blue Team of the Holy Tekhelet Fringe massing on the other side to surge through into the light. There they stood, the Whites, in a solid phalanx with their backs pressed against the doors, facing the audience in their horned helmets, their animal pelts, their fur hats, their visored caps and gleaming black boots, but most by far in hooded white sheets, their arms folded across their chests, waiting. "Did someone remember to turn on the gas?" one of them cracked to pass the time, and the laughter was general.

But very soon the pressure became intense, the time for idle chatter was over. The task now was to concentrate their energies on keeping out the Blues, wave after wave of Blues churning into the kitchen chamber, piling up against the barricaded entry to the dining room. They could hear them wailing pathetically from the other side of the doors, those lecherous elders of Zion, those leeches and ticks, spreaders of pestilence, pushing against the doors with all the force of their desperation, those eternal outsiders and outcasts, those aliens and undesirables, no one would ever let them in. From what could be fathomed they went on swarming into the kitchen from the field in back, blindly following Reb Yisrael bar Avraham Avinu into doomed battle, while others, having crossed the kitchen in the first waves and reached the sealed doors to the dining room, were flattened against this immovable barrier, struggling to turn around to save their lives, pushing against the incoming multitude to get back out along the very narrow bridge of the blackened kitchen to the burning field beyond, their hearts clamped with terror. A nightmare collision, a furious crush, stampede, bodies falling over, trampled, suffocated, mounds of bodies, raw panic unleashed all around, cries of I can't breathe, I can't breathe, cries of Sh'ma Yisrael, Sh'ma, Ma, Mama, Mama, everyone could hear—grown men crying Mama, the miracle child still whimpering Mama when they pulled him out hours later, head shaved raw, long golden sidelocks fused to pure baby skin.